Don't You Marry
the Mormon Boys

Don't You Marry
the Mormon Boys

JANET KAY JENSEN

Bonneville Books
Springville, Utah

The views expressed within this work are the sole responsibility of the author and do not necessarily reflect the position of Cedar Fort, Inc., or any other entity.

This is a work of fiction. The characters, names, incidents, places, and dialogue are products of the author's imagination, and are not to be construed as real.

ISBN 13: 978-1-59955-075-6

Published by Bonneville Books, an imprint of Cedar Fort, Inc., 2373 W. 700 S., Springville, UT, 84663
Distributed by Cedar Fort, Inc., www.cedarfort.com

LIBRARY OF CONGRESS CATALOGING-IN-PUBLICATION DATA

Jensen, Janet Kay.
  Don't you marry the Mormon boys / Janet Kay Jensen.
    p. cm.
  ISBN 978-1-59955-075-6 (acid-free paper)
  1. Polygamy—Fiction. 2. Mormons—Fiction. 3. Interpersonal relations—Religious aspects—Fiction. 4. Religious fiction. I. Title.

  PS3610.E566D66 2007
  813'.6—dc22

          2007026328

Cover design by Nicole Williams
Cover design © 2007 by Lyle Mortimer
Edited and typeset by Annaliese B. Cox

Printed in the United States of America

10 9 8 7 6 5 4 3 2 1

Printed on acid-free paper

Dedication

To my husband, my sons, their wives, and the next generation:
Miles, Kevin, Emily, Benjamin, Marica, Jeff, and Paige . . .

And to my mother, who married a Mormon boy.

Acknowledgments

Thanks to Charlene Hirschi, Sammie Justesen, Nadene Mattson Carter, Josi Kilpack, Carole Thayne, Arianne Cope, Rachel Ann Nunes, LaWana Kirby, and Myrna Humphreys, who provided edits, proofing, feedback, and continued support. Special thanks to Annaliese Cox of Cedar Fort, Inc., for her insightful and thorough editorial assistance. Appreciation to my neighborhood book club for introducing me to great books and for their unqualified encouragement. To my big sisters, Anne Cloward and Ellen Croft, love and special thanks for providing all the above and for always being on my team.

Chapter One

Gather round, girls, and listen to my noise,
Don't you marry the Mormon boys.
If you do your fortune it will be,
Johnnycake and babies is all you'll see.

Dr. Andy McBride hummed the old Mormon folk song as he consulted the crumpled map. If his Eagle Scout training and instinctive sense of direction hadn't failed him, this large log home with the friendly wraparound porch and wooden rocking chairs would be his for the next two years.

He had one basic impression of Kentucky as he drove across the state: it was green. In contrast to his native Utah, a mountain desert region dependent on irrigation and careful water management, Kentucky's lush meadows and gentle rounded hills might have been the Garden of Eden.

He glanced at the map again, stepped out of his new red Jeep Cherokee, and stretched his travel-weary body. Holding the door open and slipping his backpack over one shoulder, he said, "Come on, Eliza, let's check out our new place." The dog leaped out, tail wagging, and began to sniff the unfamiliar turf.

Andy climbed the three steps to the porch and fished a key

from his pocket. With one click the door opened. He was greeted by a collection of smells: fresh paint, varnish, lemon oil, beef soup or stew, and—another sniff—lilacs.

"Anybody home?" he called, feeling foolish as his voice bounced off empty walls.

A stone fireplace filled with logs and kindling dominated the living room, while empty bookcases lined the opposite wall. The broad-paneled pine floor was freshly oiled and scattered with braided rugs.

He dropped his backpack by the door and followed his nose to the kitchen, searching for what smelled like his mother's home-made soup. He lifted the lid of the slow cooker and smiled. Vegetable beef. A pan of fresh cornbread sat on the counter, still warm. The cupboards bulged with bottled preserves, and the refrigerator was well stocked. A vase of pungent lilacs sat on the kitchen table.

He walked down the hall, exploring. Five bedrooms. A sizeable family must have lived here. He pictured them eating dinner at the long oak table, the children doing their homework afterward, and popping corn over the embers of the fire when their homework was done. Patchwork quilts piled high on wrought iron bedsteads reminded him of his grandmother's handiwork. He inspected the bathroom, clean and functional, supplied with towels and homemade pear-scented soap.

Each window in the home offered its own view: the meadow and hills from the front, the gravel road and the woods beyond it from the side, and the barn, pump, and outhouse in the back. A ring of mountains called the Knots surrounded the valley, but they were hills in comparison to the Rockies where Andy had camped, hiked, and skied since boyhood.

Eliza padded over. He stroked her head. "Wonder how old this house is."

"About a hundred, near's we can figure," a deep voice boomed.

Eliza gave a sharp bark. Andy bent and grabbed her collar. "Eliza! Sit." He looked up at the imposing figure of a man who smiled as he stooped to enter the doorway.

The stranger appeared to be nearly seven feet tall and held a pie in his hands. "Blackberry," he said in a deep booming voice as he set it on the table. "Saw your Jeep in the driveway. We been watching for you. You'd be the new doc."

"I am. Andy McBride. And thank you for the pie. It smells wonderful." He extended his hand and almost winced at the strength of the man's grip.

"Too Tall Jones," the visitor gave a bashful grin. Andy wondered if he sang bass in the choir.

"Good to meet you, Mr. Jones."

The giant of a man grinned. "Heck, nobody calls me Mr. Jones. You can use my real name. Obadiah. Obadiah Too Tall Jones."

"Obadiah for short?"

"Short? Good one," the man chuckled. "Obadiah's from the Bible, of course."

"So is Andrew. But I was also named after my grandfather." Andy smiled back at the dark-haired visitor, clad in flannel shirt, threadbare denim overalls, and heavy work boots. He liked Obadiah already.

"I hear you're from Utah."

Andy nodded.

"Me and the missus, we listen to your Mormon Tabernacle Choir every Sunday morning. Fine music."

"Really? My mother sings with the choir."

"No kidding?"

"She loves it." A sudden image flashed in his mind: his mother standing with the other sopranos in a long blue dress, the stage lights catching the strands of silver in her hair, her eyes intent as she blended her voice with three hundred fifty others. It was a dream she'd had all her life, to sing with the choir.

"They call 'em America's Choir, don't they?" Obadiah said. "I have some of their albums. Well, now, that makes you kind of famous in my book."

Andy smiled. Eliza nudged his leg. "Oh, this is my dog, Eliza R. Snow. Eliza, show your manners and shake hands."

Obadiah squatted, his knees making sharp popping sounds,

and took the dog's paw, gently, Andy noticed. "She looks like a border collie."

Andy nodded.

"Well, she's a beauty. Now, that's right unusual for a dog to have a last name and a middle initial, too."

"I know. When I chose her from the litter, she just looked like an Eliza. Then, when her first winter came, and I'd throw her ball, she'd dive into the snow for it, no matter how deep. She'd shake her head back and forth, and use her nose to clear the snow away. There was a famous poet in Utah named Eliza R. Snow, and before I knew it, that's what I was calling my puppy. I hope her namesake doesn't mind," he said with an upward glance toward where he assumed heaven and Sister Snow might be.

"She's a lovely mutt." Eliza was on her back now, inviting a belly rub. "A real fierce one, I can see," Obadiah said. "What's the red coat for? She's not a seeing eye dog, is she?"

"No. She's a—a service dog. In training. She's . . . sort of a hobby."

"One of them helper dogs? I saw a program on TV about what they can do for people. Pretty amazing."

"Yeah." Andy jammed his hands in his back pockets and rocked back and forth on his heels. That innocuous question always caught him off guard, even though he had rehearsed a little speech just for occasions like this. "She's trained to antici-pate my seizures," he'd imagine himself saying in a casual voice, "to give me warning so I can find a safe place and some privacy when one's coming on. But I've been seizure-free for three years, and I've been off medication for eighteen months now, so I really don't need her anymore." He had yet to deliver that speech.

The red vest still allowed Eliza to accompany him nearly everywhere. She liked being on duty, Andy was convinced, and he was too attached to her to think of ever giving her up.

"She must be right smart then." Obadiah stroked the velvet-soft hair in front of Eliza's ears, "But then most collies are, so I've seen."

"Eliza, shall we show Mr. Jones a few things you can do?" Following a series of commands, Eliza demonstrated her ability to open cupboards and doors, turn lights on and off, walk backwards, give a gentle bark in her "inside voice," and to search for the cell phone in his pocket and place it in his hand. She sat at his feet and did not budge when he offered distractions such as dog biscuits, a tennis ball, a squeaky toy, and her favorite tug-of-war rope.

"All right, Eliza, you're off duty now," Andy said as he untied her vest. "Good girl."

"Well, I'll be durned," Obadiah said.

Andy nodded toward the dog biscuit on the floor and Eliza pounced on it, disposing of the treat in a few seconds. Then she trotted over to Andy's backpack, nosed in an outer compartment, and retrieved a worn yellow tennis ball. She returned to Obadiah, ball in mouth, an entreating look in her eyes. Obadiah laughed, opened the door, and tossed the ball outside. Her nails scrabbling on the wood floor, the dog was a flash of black and white as she dashed after her toy.

"She'll chase that ball for hours," Andy said.

"Just give me a holler and I'll send the kids over to play with her. They can work off some of their energy. Does she ever herd anything?"

"Oh, yeah," Andy smiled, thinking of the last McBride family reunion, when Eliza had been in her element among the younger cousins. "She'll round up kids and march them wherever she thinks they should go."

"My brood could use a bit of herding now and then. Well, glad you're here, Andy. Hope the place suits you."

"It's great. But it's much more than I need."

Obadiah cleared his throat and studied a nail in the floor. Then he looked up. "Well, we figured as you was a Mormon."

Question Number One.

Andy nodded.

Eliza dashed in with the ball and skidded to a stop in front of Obadiah, who tossed it outside again. "And we thought you might be bringing a wife with you." He coughed and gave a sideways glance at Andy. "Maybe two or three."

Question Number Two.

"*Ah!*" Andy smacked himself on the side of the head. "I *knew* I'd forgotten something! LaVera! LaRue! LaDawn! LaVon! How *could* I have left them behind?"

Obadiah blinked, open-mouthed.

Andy grinned. "Nope, I'm single, Obadiah, and there's been no polygamy in my family for over a hundred years."

"But don't some Mormons still—"

Andy shook his head. "No. Not for more than a century. There are some polygamist groups in the West and in other states, but they don't have any connection with the LDS Church." Andy felt a familiar pang. Louisa would be home in Gabriel's Landing by now, probably promised to a man twice her age, a man with half a dozen other wives and a house bursting with children.

"They're not real Mormons, you say?"

"No."

Obadiah appeared to digest that information for a moment. "Was you ever one of them missionaries in a white shirt and a tie, riding around on a bike?"

Question Number Three.

"I spent two years in Finland."

"Finland! Mighty cold there, isn't it?"

Andy nodded, remembering frostbitten knees after a long day on his bicycle, and the warmth of the people who had invited them into their homes.

"Well, now, Finland must've been pretty exciting. Far as I've ever been from home is Lexington."

"It's beautiful here," said Andy, happy to change the subject from polygamy and his own often-misunderstood religion. "Tell me about the Jones clan."

He learned that Obadiah Too Tall Jones was his nearest neighbor, and that the man's great-grandfather had built a dozen homes in Hawthorn Valley, including this one, and with his wife he had enjoyed the sunsets from the front porch for almost sixty-two years. Obadiah and his missus had six children, a couple of whom promised to be taller than their father, and "if they're smart they'll practice a lot of basketball."

Obadiah was a carpenter. He told Andy he'd spent a little time at the house to "freshen it up," but other neighbors had helped, too, by donating rugs, quilts, furniture, and food. Wanted to make him feel welcome; it had been two years since a regular doc had lived right here in Hawthorn Valley. "Even had the phone company come over and wire this place for the Inner Net. You got a computer?"

Andy nodded.

Obadiah's kids had been begging for a computer, he said; they'd learned to use them at school. For himself, he couldn't imagine why he'd ever need one.

For Andy it was a link to friends, family, news, and a reliable source for medical updates. He'd rather be without a television than a computer, though he was such a fan of the Utah Jazz that when he was away during his residencies his father would record their TV games for him.

Obadiah had come to offer a proper welcome, he said, and to bring a pie from the missus, and did Andy need anything lugged in from that handsome red Jeep?

Andy knew that accepting Obadiah's offer was the neighborly thing to do. As they unloaded boxes of clothes, dishes, and books, he explained he'd always planned to keep his perfectly sound six-year-old Honda Accord when he moved to Kentucky, but his grandfather had insisted on buying him the Cherokee "with all the extras," including a sophisticated sound system. He would sleep well at night, he said, knowing his namesake was driving a reliable vehicle, where he could "hunker down" if he was caught in bad weather. It drove, the Navy veteran said, "straight and sure."

Obadiah assured Andy that he would appreciate four-wheel-drive when bad weather and worse roads made driving an adventure. And he'd best keep the lantern and flashlights handy for storms, too, when the power was "more'n likely to go out." He told Andy the name of the enormous trees in the front yard with large locust-like leaves and deeply furrowed trunk. "Kentucky Coffee Trees. The early settlers used to roast the pods and seeds when they didn't have real coffee. Bitter stuff. Poisonous if you eat them raw. You'll want to make sure your dog don't chew on them. Most dogs won't because they taste nasty. You play this?" he gestured toward Andy's guitar case.

"Uh-huh."

"Do you sing?"

"Some."

Obadiah gave him a speculating look. "Tenor?"

Andy stretched to his full height of 5'7". "Yeah."

"Well, now, glad I got to you first. We need a singer and picker in our band. Had to retire our last one. I think his cheese has slid off his cracker. Old-Timer's Disease. Started to get real forgetful." Obadiah shrugged. "He's a Tuttle. Runs in the family."

"Oh."

"So are you interested?"

"Well . . ."

"Good. We practice tomorrow night at the high school gym."

"What do you play? Bluegrass?"

"Mostly. And old songs from the hills. They say the first hill people brought them here from Scotland and Ireland more'n two hundred years ago. Some of 'em are supposed to be more authentic than the versions the other folks sing today. I play bass. And I sing bass. You gotta meet Mel Daniels. He plays one mean banjo. And Harm Collins plays a fine fiddle. Bo Rawlins, he can play most anything you put in his hand—fiddle, hammered dulcimer, spoons, tin whistle."

"I like bluegrass. I like most kinds of music. I guess I could give it a try, and see if I can keep up with you guys."

"Fair enough. Mind if I try this out?" Obadiah ran a broad finger along the curve of the guitar case.

"Go ahead."

Obadiah took the instrument out of the case and quickly tuned the strings. His large hands flew over the guitar, nimble and skilled, and a familiar melody floated through the room.

Andy did a double take. "That's Bach."

"Yep." Obadiah continued to play. "Heard it on the radio. I play by ear."

Andy sat on a box and listened to the strains of "Jesu, Joy of Man's Desiring." Louisa would have loved this, all of it—Kentucky, this home, and the exquisite music Obadiah was coaxing from his guitar.

The last note hung in the air for a long moment. Obadiah gently set the guitar back in the case and flipped the latches closed with a soft click. "So you'll join the band?"

Andy blinked. "All right. But I don't play like that. I mean Bach."

"Neither do the others," Obadiah grinned. "You won't tell them, now?"

Andy shook his head. "No, but you'll play for me again sometime, won't you?"

"Sure. Now, tomorrow," Obadiah promised, "I'll show you around town." He left with another bruising handshake, ducking as he passed under the doorway.

Andy surveyed his new home. Boxes littered the floor. They could wait. Evening was approaching and he was too tired to unpack tonight. Despite this comfortable home, its beautiful surroundings, and the friendly welcome from his neighbor who played classical guitar by ear, a sudden wave of homesickness and uncertainty washed over him. Forgetting about the tempting soup and cornbread waiting in the kitchen, he plopped into a large armchair, sinking deep into the cushion. Elbows planted on his knees, chin in hands, he formed a slumped triangle as he thought of home and family and the life he'd left behind.

His mind wandered to an April day at the University of Utah campus, where the broad leaves of venerable old Horse-chestnut trees formed cool green umbrellas of shade. Trying to concentrate on organic chemistry and ignore the signs of spring around him, he heard rustling in the grass. He looked up and there she stood, two dripping ice cream cones in her hands.

Every encounter with Louisa Martin felt like seeing her for the first time. She was a vibrant, lovely woman with masses of waist-length auburn hair falling over her shoulders, her eyes hazel or green depending on her mood, the weather, or the color she wore, a few light freckles dusting her nose and cheeks.

"Mint chocolate chip," she said with a wry smile. "My treat."

He'd scored one point higher than Louisa on the last neurology exam. Their running bet assured several ice cream cones a week, but Andy usually had to buy them. Louisa wasn't easy to beat. Not that he needed to compete with her. He just wanted to study with her, share a laugh, or take her for a hike in the canyon. Eliza would come too, and when he took off her vest, she would take a swim in the creek, scramble to the bank, and spray them with a vigorous shake of her coat.

He wanted a life with Louisa Martin.

But graduation from med school put an end to hikes in the canyon, impromptu ski lessons, free concerts on campus, and conversations late into the night. Since graduation they'd had no contact at all. Residencies in other states had sent them in opposite directions for four years, and casual communications would have been too painful for both of them. After residency he had packed his truck and headed for Appalachia. He assumed Louisa had returned home to Gabriel's Landing, as promised.

Of course, now that their training was completed, nothing compelled them to stay apart. Nothing except the rigid traditions of Gabriel's Landing, a community founded on the practice of polygamy, a way of life Andy could not live and Louisa could not escape. It was as simple, as complicated, and as heartbreaking as that.

A moist prompt from Eliza's nose roused Andy from his memories. He gave her a vague pat, sighed, and gazed around at the boxes piled on the floor. The evening shadows were deepening and the hills loomed in the distance, dark, mystifying, filled with a compelling presence he could sense but could not name.

He had never felt so lonely in his life.

He glared at Eliza. "Whose idea was this, anyway?"

Chapter Two

Dr. Louisa Martin arrived in Gabriel's Landing in her ten-year-old Ford Taurus, followed by a cloud of fine red dust. Her sixteen siblings, their spouses, and children crowded around her, jostling for the first hugs. Exclaiming over each of them and admiring the new babies born since her last visit, she looked up and met the tired, smiling brown eyes of her father, Joshua Martin.

The old pain gripped her throat as she thought of her mother, Rachel, Joshua's head wife, who should have been standing beside him today. It was nearly five years now since a sudden cardiac arrest had abruptly ended her mother's life.

If I'd been there, Louisa thought, *I would have known what to do. I would have seen the signs in time. And I'd have rushed her to the hospital, even if it meant having outsiders treat her.* She read the same emotions in her father's eyes: sadness, loss, and a stabbing sense of blame for his wife's death. If he had only known it was so serious, he had told her afterward. That was one reason Louisa had returned to the little town of Gabriel's Landing. They needed a doctor they could trust, one of their own. The Council of Brothers had even voted to send several thousand dollars each year to help with her education.

"Father," she said, finding her way through the throng.

Joshua Martin took his daughter's face in his hands. "So like your mother," he murmured, and kissed her forehead. "Rachel would be so proud of you."

She closed her eyes and breathed in his familiar scent, a bit of starch in the old-fashioned, yoked cotton shirt, the high banded collar worn but still respectable, the smell of pungent homemade soap, and a whiff of clean sawdust. Pine. Father must be working on pine cabinets in his shop today. He took her hands in his own, rough and stained, with purple and black half-moons under two fingernails. She couldn't remember her father's fingernails when they hadn't borne the telltale marks of his carpentry trade. Joshua searched her eyes for a long moment and then he smiled, deep crinkles forming around the outer corners of his eyes.

A tap on the shoulder and a musical voice broke into the silent exchange with her father. "Louisa, dear, you haven't forgotten us, have you?"

"Aunt Sarah! Aunt Hannah!" Louisa turned and held out her arms to two older women. They were identical twins, her mother's cousins, her father's remaining wives. With a shock she realized that silver was overtaking black in the long braids that wound regally around their heads. She glanced back at her father over their shoulders and saw that his once dark wavy hair was now sprinkled with silver, too. When had that happened?

Dear Aunt Hannah and Aunt Sarah; how comforting it felt to be in their embrace. Gentle women, dignified and soft-spoken, they were also strong, practical, and capable of hard physical work. They were unwavering in their faith and devoted to their family as they efficiently managed their large household. If sharing a husband and home strained their relationship as sisters as well as sister wives, it was never evident to the children.

"Aunt" was a title of respect, for Hannah and Sarah were actually her stepmothers, and she was one of their many "adopted" children. As they were also her mother's first cousins, Louisa had another blood connection to Hannah and Sarah, and to their children, too, but she'd given up mapping her genealogy long ago.

Some things hadn't changed. Though the day was warm, the women all wore long sleeves, high collars, and ankle-length skirts, Hannah in her favorite shade of light blue and Sarah in a soft yellow calico print. Though Louisa's roommates had persuaded her to adopt jeans and sweatshirts as a student, now that she was home she had returned to the traditional long skirt, with her hair woven into a French braid that hung down her back.

"Come inside, dear. We've been cooking all morning," Aunt Sarah said, slipping her arm around Louisa's waist. Feeding the family was a never-ending occupation for the wives and daughters; growing children were always hungry, and the husband and sons had hearty appetites from laboring in the workshops and fields. Two more long makeshift tables had been added in the dining room today. Fourteen of Joshua Martin's seventeen children were married, most with children of their own, and they would all come to dinner today in Louisa's honor.

Amidst the happy dinner chatter punctuated by the babbling of babies and toddlers, Amy, the youngest of Joshua's children, piped up with the question Louisa knew lurked in everyone's minds: "When are *you* getting married, Louisa, so you can have your own babies?"

Conversations stopped in mid-word. Louisa shot a quick look at Aunt Sarah, who had given birth to Amy at forty-two, and nearly died of complications. Sarah was smiling fondly at her Amy, who always spoke her mind. "If she'd been a boy," Sarah always said, "we would have named her Frank Ernest Martin, because she's very frank and certainly earnest!"

Joshua answered for Louisa. "Your sister will be very busy for quite a while, Amy, getting everything in order at the clinic, and taking care of all of us here in Gabriel's Landing."

From the corner of her eye, Louisa saw Hannah direct a sharp look at Sarah, and then both women looked at Joshua, who was rearranging the mashed potatoes on his plate. Louisa knew their eyes held the same question, for the twins often read each other's thoughts and finished each other's sentences. They had an unusually close connection; when Sarah went into labor with Amy, Hannah had doubled over in pain. Louisa knew they had discussed the merits of her prospective suitors many times in anticipation of her homecoming. No doubt there was a short list already. With a slight shiver she turned back to her younger sister.

"Father's right," she said, though she was also surprised at her father's ambiguous reply. "I'll be very busy."

"But aren't you getting old? Samantha's only eighteen, and she's already married, and she's going to have a baby right away!"

"And I'll help her when it's time for the baby to be born. That's my job." Looking at the expectant faces around her, Louisa began to think that deliveries might be one of the easier aspects of moving back home to practice medicine, not that a delivery was ever easy.

Joshua met Louisa's eyes, and in his deep voice she heard the unquestioned tone of patriarchal authority.

"Marriage," he said, "will come in due time."

~

Samantha shifted in her chair, trying to ease the pressure on her back, one hand on her very pregnant abdomen. "Now that you're home, Louisa," she sighed, "the sooner this baby comes, the better. I can't find a position that's comfortable, not sitting or standing or lying down." Louisa read anxiety mixed with antici- pation in her sister's flushed face; Samantha had always longed to be a mother. As a child she had owned the biggest doll collection in the family.

Samantha was a rosy-cheeked little girl when Louisa went away to college, but marriage and impending motherhood had erased most of her youthful glow, leaving a quiet, thoughtful, tired young woman in its place. Samantha was Henry Taylor's fourth wife. Upon marriage she became a stepmother or "aunt" to his thirteen children, as well as "sister wife" to the three older women he had married, the first legally, the rest "spiritu- ally." Henry had come today to be with Samantha's family. His other wives were at home with their own youngsters. He was

· 14

a good-looking, strong man, not yet thirty. When he reached over and rubbed Samantha's back, she glowed under his touch. Louisa knew Samantha had been in love with Henry since she was twelve; there had never been anyone else in her heart, and both families had approved of the union.

After dinner, Louisa took Samantha aside and examined her swollen hands, feet, and face, noting her slightly elevated blood pressure. She instructed her sister to go home, head straight to bed, put her feet up, and drink plenty of fluids. "I'll check on her in a couple of hours," she promised Henry.

⁓

"Amos took your bags to your mother's room," Joshua told Louisa while the other women cleared the table and began to wash the dishes by hand, the girls drying and putting them away.

Joshua led the way up the narrow stairs. With a shock, Louisa noticed that her father used the banister as he climbed. First the gray hair, now the banister. At the top of the landing he opened the bedroom door. "I haven't . . . well, I guess I should have, but I haven't touched a thing of hers," he began, a catch in his voice. "Except last week, when we decided that Sarah and Hannah should pack her clothes away so you'd have a closet and a chest of drawers of your own. The boxes are stored in the attic, if you want anything in them, but there's plenty of time for that. Everything else is as she left it. Your aunts keep the room clean and dusted, and they put fresh linens on the bed for you. Of course, you can change anything you like."

Louisa stood at the threshold of the room that held so many memories—the lace curtains, soft faded quilts . . . the doily on the nightstand. It was made by Susannah Miller, an ancestor who had joined the Mormon Church in Ireland, immigrated to the United States on a treacherous voyage over the ocean, and then made the brutal trek west to Utah in a covered wagon. The small piece of handwork was a prized heirloom, a legacy attesting to the woman's strength. Rachel's worn scriptures rested on the nightstand, a faded ribbon marking the last verse she had read.

All was as Louisa remembered. Of course, she'd been home several times since her mother's death, but she had shared Samantha's room then; Samantha had been married less than a year. Louisa's visits then were short and filled with family parties, catching up with friends, and avoiding the reality of her mother's absence. Her throat tightened and tears stung in her eyes. She blinked them away.

Joshua reached for the knob to pull the door shut. "It's a big house. You can have another room."

Louisa shook her head and walked into the room. Her eyes rested on the sepia tones of her parents' wedding photograph, taking in the youth and confidence and joy in their faces. Rachel was the first wife, the wife of Joshua's youth, the mother of five of his living children, two boys and three girls. They had been monogamous for five years before Joshua took Hannah and then Sarah to wife. Louisa was the eldest surviving child of Rachel and Joshua's union. The grave of Rose, her older sister, who had died in infancy, lay in the nearby cemetery, marked by a small white stone engraved with the image of a lamb.

The room had a comforting presence. Rachel's presence.

Louisa inhaled. Roses. Dear Sarah had cut some of her precious roses and arranged them in the chipped Oriental vase on the nightstand, adding long stalks of wheat to make a unique bouquet. Brigham Young had prophesied that the desert would "blossom as a rose." Sarah's roses were a testament to his promise.

Each of her mothers had special gifts and talents. Sarah grew roses and other flowers in the unfriendly desert soil year after year, and they flourished under her care. In the winter she pursued fine needlework and quilting. She also tended a brood of the "most pampered chickens in the state of Utah," according to Joshua, and the hens rewarded her kindness with a bountiful supply of smooth brown eggs. Sarah's chickens never found their way to the dinner table; she couldn't bear to kill them. Instead, she traded pies for her neighbors' chickens, birds who weren't her personal acquaintances.

Hannah had her quilting and her piano, and she made the

best whole wheat bread in Gabriel's Landing, according to Joshua. She gloried in growing, preserving, and preparing food for the family. The sisters were skilled seamstresses and made most of the family's clothing.

An avid reader, Rachel had offered every child in the family a quarter for memorizing and reciting poems to her. They soon learned that indulging Rachel's love of literature was profitable. Louisa had a sudden memory of standing beside her mother's bed, proudly repeating the words of Lewis Carroll's nonsense poem:

> *"You are old, Father William," the young man said,*
> *"And your hair has become very white.*
> *And yet you incessantly stand on your head;*
> *Do you think, at your age, that is right?"*

It was years later before she learned what *incessantly* meant. Awash in memories, she turned to her father, who still hesitated at the threshold. "It's all right," Louisa reassured him, a gentle hand on his arm.

"I just thought . . ." his voice trailed off. He cleared his throat. "As her only daughter, I mean . . ."

"I know, Father. Zina's not coming home."

"Louisa, we—"

"I know. We do not speak her name."

Joshua shook his head, staring vaguely at something beyond Louisa's shoulder. Her gaze rested on a picture in a heart-shaped frame: Louisa and her sister Zina, two smiling girls no one would guess were full sisters. One favored the mother in coloring and the other the father; one had followed the rules and met the expectations of her family and community, while the other was lost . . .

Joshua's voice failed him and he cleared his throat. "It's my fault Zina left."

"Your fault?"

"She must have overheard me giving Cyrus Hamilton permission to court her." Courtship in Gabriel's Landing was more like an engagement; once the father agreed to courtship, marriage usually followed within a matter of months or even weeks.

"Cyrus Hamilton?"

"A fine man. But not—not for my Zina. She never told me in so many words, but now I believe the very idea of polygamy was repugnant to her. He was so much older . . ."

Louisa swallowed. She had always assumed that when the time came, though she had preferred not to think about it, she and Zina would both enter into polygamous marriages; it was expected of them. She had been away at college when Zina became of marriageable age. How desperate and alone her younger sister must have felt.

But she could have come to me. Why didn't she find her way to me in Salt Lake City? Louisa agonized.

"I believe she didn't feel she had any options. To contact you, or to ask you for help," Joshua said, understanding her unspoken question. "It would involve you in her disloyalty. It would have put you in an impossible situation. I am totally at fault. I believe the fear of disappointing me and your mother and her aunts was so great, she simply fled. Many a night I have turned this over in my head. Not a day goes by when I don't pray for her. It was my pride, my commitment to The Principle, that drove her away.

"Since then, I have made no promises of marriage regarding my children. We counsel together. Samantha has never cared for any man other than Henry, and he's a fine man, so that union had my blessing. I believe my children must desire the marriage for themselves rather than marrying to please their parents. The Brothers have called me to task over this, of course. That is part of my punishment for losing my Zina, and I accept it willingly. No sanctions they could impose would be as harsh as the ones I wrestle with every day."

Louisa searched for words but found none. Her father had never been this frank with her. Maybe, in his eyes, she was grown up now.

"There is a God-given precept we do not practice here, Louisa, in any significant way. It is agency, the privilege of making decisions of our own free will. You'll find it in the Bible, but I doubt Gabriel's Landing would exist if agency ran rampant among us."

His shoulders slumped and he ran his hand through his hair. "I get an occasional postcard from her, you know, without a return address. I don't even mention them to your aunts anymore. It distresses them. Our Zina's been quite the world traveler—the cards have been mailed from nearly every state and a number of foreign countries, too." He glanced out the window again and took a deep breath. "I have always felt a deep sense of pride in having an unusually harmonious family. I believe my children have had three loving mothers."

Louisa nodded. "We have, Father."

"Yet Zina's deep unhappiness went unnoticed. My illusion of harmony blinded me to the truth."

Louisa winced. *And I was away. She had no one else.*

"I sacrificed my daughter for The Principle."

"Father—"

"It's . . . good to finally talk to someone about Zina. It lies heavy on my conscience." He reached the door and turned, his hand on the doorknob. "I don't expect to see Zina again in this life. Perhaps she will forgive me in the next." His expression was so desolate, Louisa reached for him with a soft cry, but he turned and took a quick step to the window, cranking it open to the fresh, dry desert air. When he faced her again a few moments later, he was composed. "It's only right that you should have your mother's things," he repeated, and left her alone in her mother's room.

Louisa sat on the bed, fingering the seams of the hand-pieced Dresden Plate quilt, worn and soft. *Was it enough, Mother? Being married to Joshua, a good and honest man? Being the head wife, a sister wife to your cousins Sarah and Hannah, sharing your husband with them? Raising your children together? Filling the traditional, rigidly defined roles of mother and midwife? What dreams did you have, longings you never spoke of? What did you sacrifice for The Principle?*

I'm here now, fulfilling one of your dreams. You always wanted me to be a doctor, and care for my people . . . but I'm not so sure about the rest, Mother . . . you see, there's a boy, a man, I mean. His name is Andy . . . he has the most honest smile in the world, but there's some mischief in it too, and when he smiles you can see there's one tooth, the left upper incisor, it's a little crooked, and when he laughs, he's got crinkles around his eyes, they're so blue . . . he's not very tall, we're almost the same height, but he's very athletic; you should see him on skis and on the soccer field. He plays with all his heart, and he never holds back. His right eyebrow has a little scar where he ran into the soccer goalpost and knocked himself out one day . . . oh, he was so funny when he woke up, I mean, after we took him to the ER and they said it was just a concussion . . . until he had a seizure. From the head injury, they think. That was terrifying. But he's all right, at least he was; he takes medication . . . I think he still does. I even wrote down some of the silly things he said when he came to, but of course he doesn't remember anything about that day, not even the goal he scored in the first half, and that probably still makes him mad . . . he has an assistance dog to help him if he has a seizure, and she's named after Eliza R. Snow, your favorite poet . . . But I can't think about Andy now. I can't think about him, ever.

She bent to smell the roses. It had been a joyful homecoming, seeing everyone again, eating her aunts' delicious dinner, and now moving into this lovely bedroom filled with tender memories. She glanced in the mirror, squared her shoulders, and murmured, "Welcome home, Dr. Martin."

An hour later, before she had even unpacked, Louisa was summoned by Henry. Samantha's water had broken and she was having contractions. Louisa met them at the clinic, fumbling to find instruments and supplies in the unfamiliar office, as labor was progressing rapidly. By midnight her niece was born, Louisa's first delivery as Gabriel's Landing's official doctor. They named the six-pound girl Rachel Louisa. Samantha and her baby would be attended through the night by her sister wife Luella, who was also a midwife and had assisted capably with the birth.

Joshua met Louisa as she opened the heavy varnished front door, which still squeaked.

"I never got around to oiling that hinge. I could always tell when someone was sneaking home too late at night," he said with a sheepish smile.

Louisa returned his smile, weary from a long day and a longer night.

"Well," her father said, "that's a fine evening's work. A beautiful little granddaughter's been added to the family. Henry came by with the good news."

"I'm glad I got home when I did. She's precious."

"Will you sit down with me and talk for a few minutes? I won't take long. I know you're tired."

Louisa knew what was on his mind. "I'm exhausted." She rubbed her eyes. "Can't we talk in the morning?"

"Since Amy brought up the subject," Joshua said, "we should talk about marriage."

Louisa knew that look on her father's face and with a sigh she sat on the sofa, years of independence and self-reliance and her newly acquired status as an adult fading away.

"Louisa," her father said, "The Council of Brothers—"

"Am I an aunt or an uncle?" a sleepy little voice asked. Amy stood at the top of the stairs, her long cotton gown touching the tips of her bare toes, her waist-length brown braid over one shoulder.

"Where did *you* come from?" Joshua feigned surprise.

"My bed." Amy padded down the stairs.

"And what woke you, little one?"

"*I* woke me. I wanted to know about the baby."

"Well," Joshua smiled, hoisting her in his arms, "your sister had a lovely little girl this evening. Her name is Rachel Louisa. You can see her tomorrow."

"Can I hold her soon?"

"Of course," Louisa said.

Amy frowned. "Father, why did Louisa bring Samantha a little girl? Girls are the best, but I think Henry wanted a boy. Do you think he'll send the baby back?"

Joshua opened his mouth to reply, looking helplessly at Louisa, who could barely restrain a giggle. With some effort he regained his composure, his face serious as he said, "Ask your mother, little one. In the morning. Tell her *I* said to ask her. Now kiss your sister and scoot to bed."

"Can I sleep in your room tonight, Louisa? Just this once?"

Louisa wondered if she could ever deny this child anything. "Just this once," she agreed. "Only if you don't hog the bed."

"I promise, I'll sleep on the edge, and I'll be ever so good. I'll just get Agnes," for Amy couldn't sleep without her favorite doll, "and I'll scoot!"

"I believe," Joshua said, as Amy's white gown flitted down the hall like a small ghost, "we'll say good night on that note." He wiped a tear of laughter from his eye. "Where did we get that child?"

"Ask her mother. In the morning. Tell her *I* said to ask her. Good night, Father."

Chapter Three

*White chestnut tea can help people
who can't let go of a problem.*

—Miss Carolina's Remedies and Advice

Andy opened a box of books and stared at the heavy organic chemistry text. He had a sudden picture in his mind, of a day in May four years ago as Louisa packed her own organic chemistry text into a carton. It was the afternoon before their medical school graduation, and he was trying, one last time, to convince her they could plan a life together after their residencies.

"You'll meet someone," she said, shaking her head.

"Don't say it," Andy warned, teeth clenched.

"A good Mormon girl." In her suddenly steady voice he heard the clipped clinical tone she had acquired in med school. "Your family will be delighted." He almost expected her to whip out her prescription pad, scribble something on it, and end the conversation with a brisk, professional handshake. "Andy, we've always known this day would come. We'll graduate tomorrow. You're headed for the west coast for your residency, and I'm going to the east coast."

"But—"

"We could see each other during the holidays? You know that will only prolong the inevitable."

"Which is—"

She sighed.

"Say it, Louisa. I want to hear you say it."

"After my residency, four years from now, I'm going back to Gabriel's Landing, to my people, as I promised. And after your residency, you're going—wherever it is that you're going, wherever you decide to practice."

"So you're giving up on us?"

"There never was an 'us.' We knew that from the beginning."

She finally met his eyes, and he saw the familiar look of steely resolution and determination in them. *Never have a wishbone where a backbone should be,* she always said.

"And I think you should leave," she said quietly.

"Eliza," he finally said in a low voice. Eliza whimpered, breaking the spell. "It's all right," Andy lied to the dog, who looked from one to the other in confusion. He fumbled for Eliza's leash and red service vest as he searched Louisa's face once more for a trace of yielding, encouragement, or hope. But he found none. Through clenched teeth he muttered, "You heard what the lady said, Eliza. It's time to go." He turned, groped for the doorknob, nudged the dog onto the porch, and slammed the door behind them.

There were advantages to living alone. On the short walk home from Louisa's, Eliza had strained at the leash and whimpered. Then she barked in alarm. By the time they reached Andy's apartment she was frantic, pawing at the door as he fumbled with his keys. She raced inside to push his bedroom door open with her paw. With shaking hands, Andy yanked at his shirt collar and loosened the top buttons while Eliza circled him, throwing her weight against him as she herded him toward the bed. With a groan, he dropped to the floor in a full grand mal seizure.

"Ma-" followed "Mc-" at medical school graduation, so the next morning Andy McBride had found himself sitting next to Louisa Martin in the University of Utah's historic Kingsbury Hall, where they had attended so many lectures and concerts together. She gave him a brief nod, studied the program intently, and then sat with her hands folded in her lap and a composed look on her face, though he saw shadows under her eyes.

It should have been one of the most thrilling occasions in Andy's life. Instead, under his black graduation robe, his heart was breaking. When today's ceremonies were over, after their MD degrees were presented, he would not see Louisa again.

The dean adjusted the tassel that swung in front of his eyes and began his annual graduation speech, the same one he also delivered to each entering class. "The University of Utah School of Medicine has three major missions: education, research, and clinical service. The three missions are closely interrelated. Each supports and, in turn, benefits from the others. All are considered to be of equal importance."

The dean droned on, and Andy's thoughts strayed elsewhere, to days spent with Louisa: her smile; her laughter; the gleam in her hazel eyes when she tried, unsuccessfully, to contain a girlish giggle; her natural grace and melodious voice; the moods he couldn't quite understand; her cooking disasters; her stubborn competitive approach to her studies; her calm confidence under pressure; the way she had cared for him after he suffered a head injury in a soccer game (the resident had allowed her to suture the laceration on his forehead, which she had done with care and precision); the mute apology in her eyes when he winced as the local was injected . . . the loyalty and commitment to her family that kept her from ever sharing his life . . .

His thoughts returned to the present as he felt the slight pressure of Louisa's shoulder against his arm. He felt her warmth, comforting as always, and let his hand stray over to hers. She responded with a soft squeeze and a hint of a smile and kept his hand in hers, continuing to look straight ahead.

"Hey!" a classmate nudged Andy, who didn't want to let go

of Louisa's hand. "It's time to line up so we can hear everybody's real names when they hand out the diplomas. We've been waiting four years for this."

Louisa touched Andy's arm as they stood in line. "You look pale," she murmured. "Are you all right?"

He tried to shove his hands in his pockets but found himself fumbling with the side seams of the pocketless, voluminous black graduation robe. "I . . . had an . . . event . . . yesterday. After I left your place."

"A seizure?"

He shrugged.

"How bad?"

"Since I was alone except for Eliza, I can't be sure, but I don't think it was as severe as the last one." He glanced out over the audience, wondering where his family was sitting.

"What brought it on, do you think?"

"Sleep deprivation. Final exams. I should know better."

"You are still taking your Lorazepam, aren't you?"

He nodded. "I'm fine. Really. Eliza sensed it coming. She always does. We made it home in time."

"Andrew . . . Cole . . . McBride . . . Louisa . . . Rachel . . . Martin . . . Their names were pronounced in a dignified, measured cadence. Andy and Louisa shook hands with the dignitaries and received their long-awaited MD diplomas in embossed maroon leather folders. They returned to their seats, where they held hands once more, until Brad Aaron Zimmerman received his diploma.

The dean stood again, but instead of bringing the ceremonies to a close, he fumbled with his papers for a moment, evidently searching for something, and then cleared his throat. "There is one more item of business before we conclude today's graduation."

Andy looked up in surprise. The dean hadn't mentioned anything additional on today's agenda at yesterday's rehearsal. He looked at the student next to him, who shrugged and shook her head.

"The governing board of the School of Medicine is pleased to announce a new endowment which recognizes the achievements of students who have dealt with challenging and unusual circumstances to excel in their medical training. This endowment is named the Martha Hughes Cannon Fellowship—

Martha Hughes Cannon? The name was familiar. *I've heard of her. Wasn't she—?*

"—in honor of the first woman physician in the state of Utah."

Yes. Louisa told me all about her.

"I would like to tell you about the woman whose life inspired this award. Martha Hughes Cannon was truly a pioneer, a strong and determined woman who challenged many traditions and defied existing norms of society. She acquired her medical education with considerable struggle and personal sacrifice, and in addition to practicing medicine for many years, Dr. Cannon established a school of nursing and was responsible for Utah's first public health laws. This began with a simple measure—abolishing the single tin cup used at public drinking fountains in Salt Lake City, resulting in a significant decrease in communicable diseases.

"Not only did Martha Hughes Cannon pursue a long and distinguished career; she was a major contributor to state and national governments. She was also an outspoken and tireless suffragette. When Utah achieved statehood in 1896, thanks to the efforts of Dr. Cannon and others, women were also given the right to vote, making this state the third in the nation to do so. Dr. Cannon was then elected as Utah's first senator, defeating a slate of several other candidates, which also included her husband. Newspaper accounts the next morning pronounced her 'the better of the two men.' "

Andy smiled. No doubt the reporter had been correct.

"While serving in the Senate she authored several significant public health bills that passed both Houses and became law. In addition, she also embraced the traditional roles of wife and mother."

Didn't Louisa say . . . yes, she said Martha Hughes Cannon was the fourth wife of a polygamist. What a study in contrasts she must have been—suffragette, politician, physician, mother, plural wife . . .

Andy glanced at Louisa, who listened with interest, nodding as the dean described Dr. Cannon's life and achievements.

"A statue of Dr. Hughes graces the rotunda of our State Capitol Building. A petition is circulating at our legislature to have a statue of Dr. Cannon commissioned and placed in the rotunda of the Capitol Building in Washington, DC. A formal request has also been made to the U.S. Postal Service for the creation of a stamp in her honor."

He looked up from his notes. "This endowment provides a fifty thousand dollar stipend to support the recipient's postgraduate residencies."

There was a collective gasp from the newly graduated physicians, most of whom had significant student loans and all of whom faced four more grueling years of training.

"Today we are especially pleased to celebrate her life and her spirit by honoring a student selected unanimously by the faculty, a young woman who has excelled in classroom, laboratory, and clinical settings. She has made significant sacrifices and dealt with many personal challenges in order to obtain her education at the University of Utah. In her time here with us she has exemplified the warmth and compassion every physician should strive to develop."

Of course. It should go to a woman.

"We are pleased to present the first Dr. Martha Hughes Cannon Endowment to a member of today's graduating class, Dr. Louisa Martin."

Dr. Louisa Martin? My Louisa?

"Dr. Martin, will you please join us on the stage?"

Andy put his arm around Louisa, who had stiffened. "Louisa, look at me!" He knew by her pale face and wide eyes that she hadn't fully processed the dean's announcement. "Louisa! It's you! They're calling your name! You've won the award!"

"Me?" she whispered, still uncomprehending.

"Yes, you! I'm so proud of you! Go on, go up there!" He pulled her to her feet and gave her a gentle push toward the aisle. Her fellow students stood and applauded. As she made her way to the aisle there were hugs, handshakes, and good wishes. She looked at the imposing stage and then turned back, a look of uncertainty on her face. Andy grinned and waved her on. "Go!" he mouthed.

By the time Louisa reached the stage, everyone in Kingsbury Hall was standing and clapping. The dean shook her hand and the university president handed her a framed certificate and a check.

"Dr. Martin," he smiled, gesturing toward the lectern, "I know you're surprised, but please take a moment to gather your thoughts. We'd like to hear from you."

There was rustling and excited murmuring as everyone was seated again. Louisa gripped the lectern and took a deep breath, giving a slightly nearsighted gaze across the audience. After a moment a sudden bright smile lit up her face. She must have found her father.

"Actually . . ." she began. The microphone squealed. The dean stood and adjusted it. "Actually, I've known all about Martha Hughes Cannon . . . since I was a little girl. My father read about her. He told me I could become a physician, too, like she did. That's one reason I'm here today, because my family believed in me. I'm astonished and—and honored, and . . . very grateful. To the faculty and staff of the School of Medicine," her eyes roved over the black-robed faculty distinguished by their brilliant colored hoods from respective alma maters, "to my fellow students" . . . she met Andy's eyes for a moment . . . "to my friends, and most of all, to my parents, thank you with all my heart for . . ." she faltered, "for your trust in me." Andy knew by the tremor in her voice that she was close to tears, and so was he.

" 'Thank you' seems inadequate, but it's all I can say. Thank you so very much." The audience applauded and she turned to the dean. The microphone caught her whispered question, words that elicited a chuckle. "Was that all right?"

He stood and shook her hand again. "Perfect, Dr. Martin," he said with a broad smile.

Louisa returned to her seat, acknowledging more congratulations from her classmates, a cohesive group of a hundred students bonded throughout four years of rigorous classes, labs, clinical rotations, and endless hours in study groups.

When she finally sat down again, she covered her face with her hands for a long moment. Andy rested his hand on her shoulder, softly massaging it. She turned to him and gave him a radiant, teary smile.

He thought his heart would break.

After that, the graduation proceeded as every other graduation does, with the dean's final words: "This concludes our graduation exercises today. Congratulations to you all!" The orchestra played a triumphal march and happy pandemonium broke out as graduates and their families spilled out of the auditorium and scattered into the bright May sunshine. They gathered in clusters on the green lawn of the tree-shaded historic section of the campus. Cameras snapped, classmates embraced, and parents wiped away proud tears.

"Louisa!" called a fellow graduate some distance away. "Come and meet my parents!"

"Andy! Over here!" his father waved, standing in a crowd of friends and relatives, all smiling and armed with cameras. Andy searched the crowd, looking for a certain young woman with hazel eyes, a light sprinkling of freckles over the bridge of her nose, an infectious smile, and a thick, glossy auburn braid that reached her waist.

He had meant to say good-bye.

Chapter Four

Louisa prepared for a long day at the Gabriel's Landing medical clinic. She had a full schedule of appointments, and she was still training her two assistants, Georgia and Emma. She paused before the mirror, her fingers racing through her hair as she wove it into thick braids. She hadn't cut her hair for months. She paused and then smiled, thinking of her first real haircut, when she was a medical student.

She had walked into her apartment and dropped her backpack on the floor. "I'm all studied out," she told her roommates. "I don't think my mind can hold another fact."

Erin looked at Susan, who nodded. "We think," Erin said, "it's time for Project Louisa. It's just what you need."

"Project Louisa?"

"Listen, Lou. Med school is a new world for you, a new start, and we think you need a new look."

"A new look? Are you kidding? There *is* no new look. This is it, ladies." She posed with one hand behind her head and twirled, her long skirt circling her ankles.

"Haven't you ever wanted to look nor—I mean, like every-body else?" Erin challenged.

"Don't you trust us?" Susan asked.

Louisa's eyes narrowed. "No. Not tonight I don't."

Susan pulled out a chair. "Sit. This won't hurt a bit."

Sitting backward on a chair, Louisa covered her eyes with her hands. "I can't believe I'm *doing* this!" she wailed. "I can't believe I'm *letting* you do this."

Erin knelt in front of the chair and pried Louisa's hands from her face, giving them a gentle squeeze. "It's just a few inches. When you go back to Gabriel's Landing, twist it up in a bun again and no one will ever know."

"But *I'll* know."

"Louisa Martin, aren't you tired of being different? We've seen the glances and the whispers. People don't know what you're really like; they judge you by how you look. You're a beautiful girl. Why not let yourself be one?" Susan challenged, waving the scissors at her.

"You *know* why. It's *tradition*. It's the way we've always dressed and looked. After med school and residencies I'm going back home, where all the other women look just like this."

Erin raised her hands in the air, swaying from side to side, and sang "Tradition, tradition . . . tradition!" from *Fiddler on the Roof.*

"As a matter of fact, we have the album at home. My father says he can identify with Tevye, trying to marry off all his children to the right people, and keeping peace in the family . . . except, of course, Tevye only had one wife."

Erin smiled and pulled up a chair beside Louisa. "Here, in Salt Lake City, you can be somebody else for a while. Won't you give it a try? We're not talking about anything extreme."

"What do you mean?"

Erin fingered a lock of Louisa's hair. "Just a few inches, honest. When it's loose and flowing over your shoulders, before you braid it and pin it up in the morning, it's beautiful."

"But loose hair is—it makes men have impure thoughts,"

Louisa protested, scarlet blotches flaming on her cheeks.

"That's the idea," giggled Susan, and took the first snip.

Erin quickly swept up the locks of hair on the floor so Louisa wouldn't see them. "No, you can't look yet. We're going to wash it, work in a little mousse, and let it air-dry. With your natural curl, it'll be gorgeous. And while it's drying . . ."

An hour later, Louisa gasped at her image in the full-length mirror. She didn't know the young woman in jeans and sweater, a light touch of foundation, mascara and lipstick accenting her fair coloring. She looked in wonder at her oval-shaped fingernails, shining with a coat of clear polish. And her hair, freed from some of its weight, curled softly around her face, tumbling over her shoulders and back. She looked like somebody else. Like a typical student.

"Here." Erin handed her some running shoes and a denim jacket. "We're going out on the town."

"Out on the town" meant a milk shake at the mall food court. Louisa had never been to a mall until her roommates took her to the Crossroads Mall in downtown Salt Lake City. Since most of her clothes were homemade, she had been amazed at the stores and what they offered, and appalled at the prices. Few of them, she knew, would even carry any clothing that would pass muster in Gabriel's Landing.

"I feel so conspicuous sitting here, like I'm on display," Louisa said half an hour later, giving her milk shake a nervous stir. Two young men walked by, paused, smiled, and sat at a nearby table.

"They're checking you out, Louisa," Erin whispered.

"No, Erin, they're looking at *you*."

"Louisa?" It was Jim Christensen from her study group, looking down at her from his lofty 6'4" vantage point. He blinked. "Oh, I'm sorry; you look like someone I know."

Erin and Susan burst into laughter. Louisa blushed.

"Louisa, introduce us to your friend," Susan said, pulling out a chair for Jim.

"Well, I'll be!" was all Jim could manage.

An hour later Andy knocked at the door. Louisa answered.

"Hi, is Louisa home? Jim said she had some notes for me and—oh, my gosh! It's you!" He was speechless as he gazed at the new Louisa.

"He likes it," Erin grinned, giving Louisa's shoulders a quick squeeze. "Hey, Susan, I need help with my PowerPoint presentation for tomorrow." They disappeared, leaving Andy and Louisa alone in the living room.

"You've always been beautiful to me," he finally said.

Chapter Five

If a rooster crows at your threshold,
a visitor will soon appear.

—Miss Carolina's Remedies and Advice

His spirits revived by the soup and cornbread, Andy relaxed in an oversized wooden rocking chair on the front porch, already planning his first hike and deciding what speed of film to load in his camera.

A faint whinny interrupted his reverie. Andy stopped rocking. There it was again. *I wonder if a horse got loose*, he thought, *or if someone's riding on the road. Maybe I should go and check.* The whinny grew louder as he approached the barn. Opening the door, he exclaimed softly, "Who are *you*? And what are you doing *here*?"

A silver-gray mare with white legs and mane surveyed him with liquid brown eyes fringed by silver lashes. Then she gave a quiet snort and turned back to her bucket of oats. A note tacked to her stall said:

> *Hey, Doc Andy, we thought you'd enjoy riding Smoky.*
> *She's a real peach—anybody can ride her. You don't have*
> *to do anything for her—the Rawlins kids will do all of that.*

*They'll come morning and night. I'll drop in tomorrow to
say hello. Obadiah says you sing tenor.*

Mel Daniels

"Oh, aren't you a beauty!" Andy whispered. Taking some
oats from a nearby bucket, he offered them to the mare. Smoky
eyed him again and then munched on the oats, tickling his hand
with her tongue and lips. Eliza sniffed and approached the mare
with caution. Smoky gave a friendly grunt when she saw the dog.
Andy stood by her side half an hour, murmuring his admiration,
patting her neck and mane while she nuzzled his empty hand,
searching for more oats.

———

Sometimes Andy didn't sleep well. The long drive to Kentucky, moving into his new home, and his sudden attack of
homesickness had made him tired and restless. His mind was
on overdrive, thinking of medical school, home, and Louisa, and
wondering what challenges he would face in his new job. Why
hadn't he accepted the invitation to join a family practice clinic
in Cincinnati, where he would have knowledgeable colleagues,
up-to-date facilities, and regular hours? Or the one in Florida,
near the beach? What was he doing in isolated Hawthorn Valley,
Kentucky, trying to be a solo country doc? It certainly wasn't
about the money. He had chosen Hawthorn Valley because of his
sense of independence and the need to feel needed. He wondered
whether these would prove to be good reasons.

At midnight he opened the bedroom window to let in a fresh
breeze, switched on the lamp, and opened a box of books, finding
one of his favorites. At 2:15 a.m. he finally yawned, turned off the
light, and went to sleep.

He was a dreamer; it was odd how thoughts and events wove
themselves into his dreams. Sometimes they did play out later
in real life. At age nineteen, he submitted his application and
waited for his mission call, a packet of documents announcing
where he would spend the next two years as a representative of

The Church of Jesus Christ of Latter-day Saints. After mailing his papers, he dreamed he was dressed in a suit and tie with a name tag reading "Elder McBride," attempting to speak a new and strange language to a group of handsome, fair-haired people who couldn't understand a word he said. Three weeks after this puzzling dream, Andy opened a large, thick white envelope to learn he would serve in Finland. He struggled with the difficult language but eventually became reasonably functional in Finnish. During his time in Finland, he learned that the native Finns would take the time to listen to him simply because he was attempting to learn their language.

Though the work was hard, and success, if measured by conversions and baptisms, was modest at best, his time in Finland had been rewarding. Certainly he had returned home with more maturity and confidence, stronger in his convictions, with an increased sense of appreciation for others' beliefs and lifestyles. He had immersed himself in the Finnish culture for those two years, and at times he still missed it.

Another dream came to mind. In high school, he dreamed he had missed a goal in the last minute of a soccer game, ending his school's bid for a spot in the state playoffs. But he proved that dream wrong the next day, when his shot sailed in a perfect arc over the goalie's head and into the corner of the net, securing himself a brief golden moment in local sports history and his team a slot in the state tournament.

In tonight's dream he was with Louisa, sitting on a park bench that overlooked the carpet of lights twinkling over the Salt Lake Valley. She snuggled against him and nuzzled his earlobe.

"Umm, Louisa," he sighed, as her soft lips brushed his cheek.

He turned to kiss her but encountered prickly whiskers instead.

He awoke with a start to find the wet lips of a horse gently caressing his cheek, his ear, and his neck. With a yell he leaped out of bed, his heart pounding. Eliza burst into the bedroom, barking in alarm. Andy struggled to his knees, fumbled for the lamp switch, and found himself staring at Smoky, who was evidently in a tender mood. She must have nudged the screen off its track with her nose and poked her head through the open window above his bed.

"What the—" Andy sputtered. "How did *you* get out? I know I latched the barn door. You gave me a scare, you rascal!" Grumbling, he pulled on some clothes and shoes and opened the back door. "Come on, Eliza, let's take Smoky back to the barn."

"Come here, Smoky," he ordered. The mare whinnied and bolted. He gave chase, stumbling in the dark and bruising his shin on the pump, until the mare finally decided to head toward the barn on her own. Andy darted across the field, reached the barn first, and opened the door. Smoky regarded him warily, her ears flattened against the side of her head, but she gradually calmed and walked into her stall.

"After you, ma'am." Andy latched the door of her stall. "Was it something I said? I'm afraid I haven't got a great track record with women," he conceded, offering her a handful of oats. She nibbled them greedily and smelled his hand, looking for more.

"That's it for tonight," Andy said. He placed a tentative hand on her neck and rubbed softly. Smoky grunted with pleasure.

"Well, that's something to write home about, Eliza. An old gray mare getting fresh with me while I'm trying to sleep." He gave Smoky a final pat. "Good night. Sleep tight. And I mean that."

He turned to leave the barn and saw a movement at the edge of the woods bordering the road. A girl emerged in the soft moonlight, tall and dark-haired, hastily buttoning her shirt. Looking both ways, she sprinted across the clearing toward a small log home and disappeared. A few moments later a boy stepped out of the trees, tucking in his shirt, and sauntered away in the opposite direction.

Chapter Six

*If you should spot a red bird,
you will see your sweetheart before sunset.*

—Miss Carolina's Remedies and Advice

The next morning, after breakfast, Andy went to the barn and filled Smoky's water trough. Behind him, someone cleared his throat and rapped on the open door. Andy turned to see a stocky, balding man whose build suggested considerable strength. "I'm Mel Daniels," the man said with a warm handshake. "Postmaster, farmer, horse-lover. You know much about horses?"

"Some. My grandfather owns a ranch. We like to load the horses up and head into the Uintah Mountains in the summer. It's beautiful lake country there, high in the mountains."

"Good fishing?"

"Trout," Andy replied, his mouth watering at the memory of freshly caught rainbow trout, dipped in egg batter, dusted with cornmeal, and sizzling over a campfire.

"So you've spent some time in the saddle?" Mel asked.

"Some. Grandfather's got them well trained. Smoky's a beautiful animal. Gave me a scare last night, though. She got out of the barn and poked her head right into my bedroom window. Woke me up."

Mel laughed. "She's one smart woman, Smoky is."

The words played through Andy's thoughts all evening. He fixed dinner thoughtfully. "A smart woman, is that what Mel said, Eliza?" Hearing her name, the dog wagged her tail.

———

"Well, would you look at that!" whispered Andy's friend Jim Christensen with a nudge. It was the first day of medical school, and, as always, Jim was checking out their female classmates. "I think she's the genuine article."

"Who?" Andy asked. "Oh." One glance confirmed it. All the signs were there, the long hair pulled back tightly and carefully twisted into coils at the back of her neck, the ankle-length skirt and long-sleeved high-necked blouse, sensible shoes, and no makeup. The young woman sat alone in the back of the room, her head bent over a textbook while the other students chattered and exchanged stories of summer jobs, travels, and romances.

"I'll bet she wandered into the wrong classroom," Jim said, shaking his head as he looked at their odd classmate. "I can't believe her clan would even let her go to college at all. Someone should show her where the home ec classes are."

The socializing ended when the professor entered the classroom. He set three heavy books on the podium and said, "Before we begin, I'd like each of you to introduce yourself. Tell us your name and your hometown."

" . . . Cincinnati, Ohio . . ." said the young man in front of Andy.

Andy stood. "Andy McBride. Salt Lake City, Utah."

His lifelong friend stood. "Jim Christensen, Salt Lake City, Utah.

The last student stood from the desk in the back of the room. It was the girl in the old-fashioned clothes. "Louisa Martin," she said in a clear voice. "Gabriel's Landing, Utah." That caused a buzz of whispers and curious looks. The girl dropped to her seat, her face flushed, and focused on her book.

"Thank you, Miss Martin," was all Professor Lee said, and he handed out the course syllabus. That was enough to make anyone forget the presence of an unusual student. Anatomy was going to be tough. The girl from Gabriel's Landing did not look up for the remainder of the hour.

As a teenager, Andy had seen a polygamous family in downtown Salt Lake City. The bowlegged man wore jeans with a western-style shirt, a cowboy hat, and scuffed pointed-toe boots. He swaggered down the sidewalk, heels clicking, while several anxious women scurried behind him, outfitted in long, old-fashioned dresses, with bonnets over their braided hair. A large herd of children hurried behind the women, venturing an occasional suspicious, frightened glance at the unfamiliar environment and at the outsiders, who were to be feared.

"I can't imagine what those women see in him," was his mother's only comment. Andy always associated the curious family's behavior with his grandfather's flock of chickens, the rooster strutting ahead while the nervous hens and their chicks scuttled behind him.

Louisa Martin was quiet in class, but always had a concise answer when the professors called on her. When study groups were organized, Andy made sure he was in Louisa's, hoping he would benefit from studying with the brightest student in their class. He began to sit by her in class, but she ignored him. Though her appearance was deliberately plain, it couldn't disguise the fact that she was naturally lovely. Frustrated that she wouldn't acknowledge him, he finally left a note on her desk before class. *"Can you meet me half an hour before study group? I'd like to look at your anatomy notes."* In response she crumpled the note and left it on the desk, without a glance at him.

After the lecture she walked briskly down the sidewalk, by herself, as usual.

"Louisa, wait up!"

She turned in surprise.

"I know all about Gabriel's Landing." Andy caught his breath after his sprint. "And it's okay. Really."

She looked around warily. "What's okay?" Her voice was quiet.

"Gabriel's Landing. You don't have to avoid me."

She began to walk again. "I'm not avoiding you."

"Yes, you are. I really did want to see your anatomy notes."

"Sure you did."

"Really, I did. I mean, I do."

She shrugged her shoulders.

"Louisa, we've never even had a conversation."

"I didn't come to medical school to have a conversation. And if you know 'all about Gabriel's Landing,' you know why."

Andy shifted his backpack to his other shoulder. "Doesn't it get lonely?"

"I don't have to answer that."

"Listen. Please stop. Just for a minute."

She clutched her books to her chest. A soft flush crept up her cheeks.

"I think you're very bright and very interesting. I like being in your study group. I'd like to be friends."

She shook her head. "Not interested."

He changed tactics. "Do you play foosball?"

"Foosball? There was a foosball table in my dorm last year. What's that got to do with it?"

"I was the foosball champion of Highland High School."

She rolled her eyes. "Your parents must be very proud."

"Louisa Martin, I never took you for a coward."

"Who said I was a coward?"

"One game. One game of foosball. Please. Look, we're just a few yards away from the student center."

She hesitated. Then she sighed. "If you'll stop pestering me."

Andy gave a brisk Boy Scout salute. "On my honor."

One foosball game led to another. After a while, Louisa didn't mind walking to classes with Andy. Sometimes they would linger after study group, just talking. He offered to walk her home at night, for safety's sake, and she didn't refuse.

When he saw that her scores were consistently a point or two higher than his, he doubled his efforts and aced the next test. Louisa stared at his paper in disbelief. She was used to making the top score in class. Andy laughed at her reaction. "How about a wager on tomorrow's chem test? Loser buys ice cream for the winner." With a flash in her green eyes she accepted his challenge, and beat him by five points the next day.

Escorting Louisa to and from class and home at night led to meeting her half an hour before study group to get a head start on the evening's session. Then it was sharing a pizza. A hike in the canyon. Long conversations after study group. A G-rated movie, *Seven Brides for Seven Brothers*. The humor of the plot was not lost on her. "Almost like home," she said with a wry grin, "except of course in Gabriel's Landing it would be *Seven Brides for* One *Brother*." Andy only smiled in reply and offered to share his popcorn. In the darkness he waited until the last few minutes of the movie to tentatively take her hand, which stayed in his, warm and comforting. Then, at her door, a kiss, a mere brush of his lips on her cheek. Another evening, a bolder, gentle kiss on the lips. A longer kiss that she returned, shyly.

He was smitten.

Chapter Seven

Early one morning, Louisa climbed to the top of Gabriel's Point, a large, rippled red rock formation that loomed over the little town. Below her, Gabriel's Landing was a beehive of activity where life was organized and predictable. Joshua always joked that if he forgot what day it was, all he had to do was take a walk; by watching the daily activities of the women, one didn't need a calendar. Today was Monday, Wash Day, and already clean clothes waved cheerfully from clotheslines. Tuesday was Ironing Day, while Wednesday was Sewing and Mending Day. Delicious smells had wafted from the ovens on Thursdays, Baking Day, when the women would spend all day making whole wheat bread and rolls as well as pies from bottled or dried fruit.

Fridays were reserved for heavy cleaning, and Saturday was Getting-Ready-for-the-Sabbath Day. Sunday was the Day of Rest, after the usual morning worship services. And then on Monday it started all over again.

Life in Gabriel's Landing was overseen by the Council of Brothers, a committee of six men that directed community policies, settled minor disputes, and organized various sub-committees for social, cultural, and educational activities. This body also directed the affairs of the church, which was based on Mormon principles and doctrines along with the old tradition of polygamy, the issue that had initially divided the two groups in the late eighteen hundreds. Many residents of Gabriel's Landing could trace their ancestors back to early Mormon pioneers who made the historic trek to Utah.

Two members of the Council walked down the road this morning, deep in conversation, nodding their heads and emphasizing their points with emphatic gestures. Joshua and his son-in-law Henry loaded finished bookcases into the truck. This afternoon they would be delivered to Cedar City, twenty miles away.

Most of the men left the town every day to work in the neighboring communities, using their skills of carpentry, construction, or house painting. They also sold chickens, eggs, and produce from their orchards and gardens, as well as quilts and other handmade items the women contributed. The women rarely left town, staying home instead to care for their homes and families.

The sounds of hammering came from Mac Cheney's crowded house. Two of Mac's wives were pregnant. Louisa hoped the construction would be finished before the babies came.

Carrie Stewart scurried down the street. She always seemed to be in a hurry. The small, slight woman had been Rachel's closest friend, and Louisa knew Carrie still grieved for her. It would be comforting to talk to Carrie again about her mother, to hear Carrie's stories of their girlhood days together and their longtime friendship throughout womanhood.

Aunt Sarah tended to her hens while Aunt Hannah hung bright patchwork quilts on the clothesline for airing.

The large yellow county school bus arrived and the children of Gabriel's Landing piled aboard, lunch boxes in hand, headed for public schools in Cedar City. The bus would make three stops: elementary, junior high, and high school. Every morning the children were cautioned not to make friends with "outsiders"; they were not to reveal anything about their families to their teachers, the principal, or other students, for fear of prosecution.

After the state of Utah had essentially ignored them for more than fifty years, recent high-profile cases had placed polygamous groups under scrutiny. Then vocal dissenters who had been expelled for disobedience, or who had left various groups, sometimes with threats on their lives, began to meet with state prosecutors, describing abuse and other crimes that could not be ignored. Stories detailing "Utah's Dirty Little Secret" began to appear frequently in the media. As a result of this negative publicity, many polygamous groups were not allowing their children to attend public schools at all. While still trusting their own children to keep to themselves at school, every resident of Gabriel's Landing took special care to avoid outsiders and therefore preserve their way of life.

⁓

Louisa's childhood had not been colored by harassment from the media; nor had she been raised in an atmosphere of fear and mistrust of outsiders. Instead, her memories of home were punctuated by a collection of images and sounds: the thumping of her mother's loom upstairs as she wove blankets, linen, and rugs; Aunt Sarah's sewing machine humming at a furious rate as she made shirts, blouses, skirts, and pieced quilts; and Aunt Hannah's music flowing from the piano. Aunt Hannah could play almost anything by ear, and her repertoire included ragtime, light classical, old Stephen Foster songs, and hymns.

Louisa closed her eyes and recalled the sound of her mother's soft voice as she read aloud to the family from her favorite authors: Charles Dickens, Lewis Carroll, Victor Hugo, Emily Dickinson, Shakespeare, and, of course, the Bible. She recited Mother Goose rhymes to the little ones while the older ones looked on, secretly enjoying them, too. Father always brought library books home for her when he visited Cedar City.

More memories were scented by fresh pine shavings and varnish in her father's workshop, Hannah's wonderful wheat bread baking in the oven, and the sweet smell of Aunt Sarah's roses on a warm summer night.

For every Mother's Day and birthday, Sarah always received

a new rosebush and a plump new hen, and Joshua presented Hannah with fabrics in her favorite colors and packets of needle-work patterns. For Rachel it was always books and skeins of wool or flax.

They enjoyed most modern comforts, including electricity and inside plumbing, but by choice did not own televisions or telephones or take a newspaper. An old acquaintance of one of the Brothers owned a diner at the edge of town, and he didn't mind taking an occasional message or offering the use of his phone in emergencies. Those were rare, however; life moved at a slow, measured, and predictable tempo for this largely self-sufficient group.

There was plenty to do when the whole town got together: square dances, taffy pulls, sing-alongs, sack races, relays, and charades. Life had a pace more typical of a century ago. There were plays, musicals, dramatic readings, spelling bees, and games for all ages, all punctuated by the gurgles and occasional cries or snores of the babies, who were included in every occasion. And of course, everyone went to the Sunday church meetings and daily morning devotionals.

Looking down at the little town she loved, Louisa sighed. She would have to introduce change slowly; her people were tied to tradition, hesitant to embrace new practices, and suspicious of modern science and technology as well. But she wouldn't hesitate to consult specialists, and she would take her patients to nearby hospitals when necessary, despite their dread of outsiders. Gabriel's Landing protected its way of life with a fierce loyalty that sometimes overruled wisdom and prevented prudent decisions involving health care. Louisa knew that unnecessary deaths and suffering had occurred because her people would not seek outside help. As a woman physician in a patriarchal society, she would have to establish her role and her credibility slowly, one small step at a time. Her thoughts were accompanied by the rhythmic chirping of "Mormon crickets," a species of grasshoppers native to the area. *Who conducts the grasshopper chorus every summer night?* she wondered, for they sang in perfect unison. *How did they stay together, all on the same pitch? Did the insects have a governing council like the Brothers that dictated their music?*

"I'll make this work," she promised the jagged red mountains that pierced the darkening blue sky, deep shadows in their recesses. She had often drawn strength from their constancy and the sense of deep wisdom within them, knowing they would hold her promises sacred.

Chapter Eight

Stepping over a broom is bad luck. To reverse the spell,
step backwards over the broom and be on your way.

—MISS CAROLINA'S REMEDIES AND ADVICE

The Hawthorn Valley Medical Clinic held few surprises for Andy. The building and equipment were basic, organized, and clean. The best instrument at the clinic, however, was Olive Mason, his nurse. A tall, spare woman with short, wavy gray hair, she owned the confidence of his patients. In the absence of a doctor she had often been the only source of medical help in the valley. She welcomed Andy warmly and briefed him on his immediate cases. He found her to be calm, pragmatic, and resourceful; surely her experience and knowledge qualified her for a raise in pay. It would be his first official request to the County Board of Health.

He arrived home from his first full day at the clinic tired and overwhelmed. He'd had to explore the cupboards and closets for supplies and equipment, and he wondered if he would ever remember the names of all of his patients.

"It'll get easier," Olive had assured him.

He wondered. Two hours into his first day he had referred Harm Collins to the larger medical center in nearby Taylor's

Glen for X-rays; he suspected lung cancer. Harm had a hacking cough, weight loss, and a history of smoking. "You'll see lots of that, troubles with lungs," Olive told him. "Here in tobacco country some folks started smoking when they were nine or ten years old."

She unlocked a cupboard and showed him a generous supply of antibiotics and other medications. "They're samples the pharmaceutical boys leave here. Don't know what we'd do without them. If you don't have any insurance, medicine's right expensive."

The next day Andy pulled into the driveway to find Smoky on the front porch, looking at him as if to say, "Hello, there, how was your day?" He became accustomed to finding the mare grazing by the porch, next to the windows, peering in to see if anyone was home. Neighbors would bring her home when she strayed.

"Don't worry, Andy," Mel chuckled. "Sooner or later, she'll mosey along home."

Andy felt confident with Smoky after a week, so early one morning he walked into the barn, intent on saddling her and going for a ride. When he approached her with the bit, though, she raised her head in resistance. He moved closer, reaching up, and she promptly stepped on his foot. Andy yelped in pain, but Smoky only leaned forward, shifting even more weight on him. He had to push at her leg and force her to bend her knee to free his foot. He was grateful for his heavy boot that had given him some protection as he limped back into the house, made an ice pack, and watched the bruises develop. A trip to the County Board of Health was on his agenda later that day, so he scheduled an X-ray of his throbbing foot. No fractures, he was told, just a deep, painful bruise.

He decided not to let his neighbors know Smoky had gotten the better of him again, but for a week he couldn't wear regular shoes and had to resort to sandals. He did his best to hide his limp, but he suspected he didn't really fool anyone.

One night he checked on Smoky and encountered a tall, dark-haired boy who was brushing the mare's glossy coat.

"Hi. You must be—"

"Hugh. Hugh Rawlins," the boy said with a shy smile and a late-adolescent crack in his voice.

"Good to meet you. So you and your sister take care of Smoky?"

Hugh nodded. "Yeah. We feed her, give her some exercise, and groom her." He turned to Smoky. "You're a fine old girl, aren't you?" he crooned. Smoky licked her lips in response.

"Why's she doing that?" Andy asked.

"It means she's relaxed and happy. She likes it when you stroke her. You know my voice, don't you, old girl?" Hugh put his arms around the mare's neck and whispered a few words in her ear. Smoky gave a contented grunt.

"I guess I don't know as much about horses as I thought I did," Andy admitted.

"They've each got a personality," Hugh told him.

"She certainly does. My first night here, Smoky's personality got out of the barn. She shoved the screen out of the bedroom window and nibbled on my ear. Woke me up."

Hugh laughed and patted the horse. "Up to your old tricks, eh, Smoky?"

"Now, what else was unusual—oh, yeah, when we were headed back toward the barn, I said, 'Come here,' and she bolted."

Smoky jerked her head and shifted in her stall.

The young man glanced at Smoky. "Most likely someone who trained her said those words when he was about to do something hurtful. Maybe even hit her with a whip. I'd never do that, but some trainers might. She hears those words, she might think you're gonna hurt her."

"I see. Anything else I should know about Smoky?"

"Can't think of nothing."

Andy took advantage of Hugh's experience and asked him to put the bridle on Smoky, watching how he did it. Hugh leaned forward and extended the bridle toward Smoky's mouth with a long arm and firm voice, staying away from her feet, and, to Andy's surprise, the mare cooperated.

After another week, Andy successfully bridled and saddled Smoky, careful to avoid her feet, and set out to explore the forest west of the road.

He passed Obadiah and stopped to say hello.

"How's the cabin working out, Doc?"

"Oh, it's great, Obadiah. Not the rustic little cabin I was expecting. It's a *home.*"

Smoky's ears perked up. Then, without warning, she took off with a burst of speed and Andy clung to the saddle horn for all he was worth.

"Be careful with that word!" Obadiah shouted. "No matter what she's doing, if that mare hears 'home,' that's . . ." Whatever else Obadiah said was lost as Smoky and her owner galloped away. When Smoky reached the barn she slowed to a gentle trot. Andy dismounted shakily and led her to her stall.

"What was that all about, Smoky?" he demanded, for he hadn't heard Obadiah's belated warning.

"What did you say to her?"

Andy turned in surprise. A tall, dark-haired girl who looked like Hugh Rawlins and was dressed in jeans and flannel shirt walked up to Smoky and caressed her mane.

"Hello. You must be Molly."

She nodded. "What happened?"

"I don't know. One minute I was in the saddle, talking to Obadiah, and the next thing I knew, we were on our way back to the barn," Andy said, scratching his head.

"Oh," Molly said with a broad smile. "I'll bet you said . . ." she looked at Smoky and then back at Andy. "H-O-M-E."

At least Smoky couldn't spell. "As a matter of fact, I did say it."

"She knows that word. She's lived here a few months now, so when she hears it, this is where she'll come, to the barn. Won't nothing stop her, either."

Andy soon became acquainted with his neighbors: Obadiah
and his family and Sheriff Jed Thomas, who appeared to be mild-
mannered and soft-spoken. A short, wiry man with unruly gray
hair, his most pressing duties seemed to be giving directions and
friendly speeding warnings to visitors (never tickets, though, for
tourists brought business), chasing truant children back to school
with a firm lecture and a peppermint from his bulging pocket,
and ignoring poaching in the nearby woods. No doubt he was
friends with every dog in town, for his other pocket held a supply
of dog biscuits.

Mel Daniels was the postmaster and owner of the general
store, and his wife, Mary Alice, ran the local craft co-op. They
explained that cottage industries and cultivation of new crops
such as berries had boosted the area's struggling economy. Since
roads had improved and Hawthorn Valley was now on the "tourist loop," Mary Alice was kept busy stocking the shelves with
quilts, rugs, wood carvings, homemade jams and jellies, and
handmade jewelry.

"If it's tourist season," Mel joked, "why can't we just shoot
them?"

Chapter Nine

*It is bad luck to see the new moon through bushes
or the branches of a tree.*

—Miss Carolina's Remedies and Advice

Andy heard the clattering of hooves and hurried to the open window in time to see a brown mule trotting down the road with a small woman on its back and bulging leather bags secured behind the saddle. The woman was wrapped in a black coat and wore a man's gray felt hat. As they passed, an answering whinny came from Smoky in her barn.

Andy saw the same strange sight several times in the following weeks. Was this an apparition, one of the Smoky Mountain ghost legends? No, his friends assured him, he'd probably seen Miss Carolina, the Healer, one of the last of her generation. She didn't care to drive, they said, so she rode a mule, just as her mother and grandmother had before her. Miss Carolina lived in an old cabin built by her grandfather that was nearly hidden in a deep hollow; if someone needed her, they would simply tie a strip of red cloth on a designated tree, with a message rolled inside it.

Healers were a tradition in Appalachia, and Andy had heard tales of their cures and practices, as well as their tonics and potions made from herbs, plants, trees, and flowers. He hoped he would meet Miss Carolina, and he wondered what she would think of him, the new doctor, an outsider with a fancy college degree.

He finally met Miss Carolina, but not the way he'd expected.

Andy had enjoyed his ride through the forest, gazing at the scarlet, orange, and yellow fall leaves in contrast with the evergreens. Then Smoky balked at crossing the creek. Fuming, Andy decided she *would* cross it, even if he had to lead her. He dismounted, took her reins, and sloshed through the creek. She followed without resistance and Eliza splashed happily beside them. When they reached the creek bank, Andy climbed into the saddle again, soaked to the knees.

After a few more peaceful miles at a relaxed pace, he began to daydream. What did the canyons look like this year at home in Utah, he wondered. Logan Canyon was his favorite, but spots of stunning beauty could be found all along the Wasatch Front. If the seasons and weather cooperated, the brilliant fall colors would be at their peak when the first snow appeared on the mountaintops. With the blue sky behind them, he couldn't think of a more beautiful scene, with the autumn's splendor at its best when winter made its sly first appearance.

Following the dazzling displays in the mountainous canyons, the fall temperatures began to nip trees in the lower foothills and valleys, and a second show began. Who was raking leaves for his father this fall? It was usually a family effort that extended over a six-week period, raking and bagging the leaves from the three giant maples and other smaller trees in their backyard. When the last leaf would finally fall, dozens and dozens of bags sat by the curb, waiting for the city's recycling organization to pick them up.

What was Louisa doing right now, he wondered, and had she taken a drive to see nearby Cedar Breaks and Brian Head, which sported spectacular displays of fall colors? *Don't go there*, he reminded himself, but his imagination took him westward, to another fall day . . .

"You know all about my background," Louisa had said one glorious fall day as they hiked in City Creek Canyon. "What about yours? I mean, I know you come from a mainstream Mormon family."

Andy fingered a scarlet leaf. "I wonder if there is such a thing."

"You know what I mean. Your parents are LDS, married in the temple, and the whole family goes to church together every Sunday. So, what do your parents do?"

"Well, my mother taught school for twenty years, and now she sings with the Mormon Tabernacle Choir."

"Really?"

He nodded.

"They're wonderful. We have all their albums. Of course, you and I were brought up reading the same scriptures and singing the same hymns."

"We're all proud of Mom," Andy said.

"And does your father sing in the choir, too?"

"No."

"Is he a teacher, then, like your mother?"

Andy inspected a large granite boulder, the same kind of rock that formed the strong outer walls of the historic Salt Lake Temple. "No."

"What does he do?"

"He . . . he's in the legal profession."

Her eyes narrowed. "You're being evasive."

He fixed his gaze on a bald eagle circling a lone pine tree in the distance. "He's a . . . prosecutor. With the Attorney General's Office."

"And what kind of cases does he prosecute?"

Andy wiped his sweaty palms on his jeans. "Criminal."

He glanced at Louisa, who chewed on her thumbnail. "What kind of crimes?" she finally asked.

"Just your garden variety crimes."

"Wait a minute. Is your father Cole McBride?"

Andy massaged his temples and then jammed his hands in his pockets. "Yeah."

"I see."

"Please, Louisa, don't . . ."

"He's got a big case going on right now, doesn't he? His name's in the paper quite a bit." •

"I guess."

"He's prosecuting the Murray case, isn't he?"

He nodded.

"Andy, look at me."

He finally met her eyes. "This isn't about us," he said. "I mean, the Murray clan, they're nothing like your people."

"In one way they are," she said grimly. "One rather significant way."

"Well, yes, there is that."

"You can say the word, Andy. They're polygamists. And so are my people."

"But they—this girl escaped from home, bleeding and bruised, and someone on the outside took her in and then contacted the authorities. Her father, the head of the clan, their prophet, had beaten her with a belt and forced her to marry his . . ." A sour taste rose in his throat and he swallowed. "His own brother—her uncle. She was locked in a barn for days as a form of 'discipline.' In this one case alone, he's charged with physical abuse and for arranging a marriage involving a minor. Within the group, no one dares to question his decisions. He extorts money from the head of every family, and if they can't pay, the men are kicked out of the group and their wives and children assigned to someone else. There's another warrant out for his arrest, for embezzlement, because funds from their school district are missing. His response was to pull all their children out of public schools. And now he's missing, too, but his faithful will protect him. They claim they'd die for him. You tell me life in Gabriel's Landing isn't like that, and the town is governed by a committee of your father's peers, not a fanatical, cruel dictator like Murray. I believe you."

She traced circles in the rustling leaves with her toes. "But here's the bottom line: your father puts my people in jail."

"Not your people, Louisa."

"Let's not . . . let's not have this conversation again, all right?" she finally said in a low voice, turning to him and wrapping her arms loosely around his neck.

He closed his eyes and rested his forehead against hers. Threading his hands through her auburn waves, he gave a sigh. "Agreed."

⁓

Suddenly, Smoky reared up on her back legs, whinnying in fear. Andy made a desperate grab for the reins but only caught air. He couldn't keep his balance and fell into a thicket. As he landed, he caught a glimpse of a small white animal dashing down the path; a rabbit had probably startled his horse. All thoughts of his skittish horse and the innocent rabbit left his mind as a sharp pain shot through his left ankle. To make his situation worse, he couldn't free himself from the vicious tangle of long, sharp thorns that snagged his clothes, dug into his skin, and held him captive. Smoky grazed peacefully nearby, unconcerned with her master's predicament and her role in it, but Eliza, trained to protect her master, began to bark in alarm.

For ten minutes Eliza barked while Andy tried to break off the thorns and free himself, but every time he moved, more snagged his clothes. He finally resigned himself to waiting for someone to pass by and notice his plight, though on a quiet autumn afternoon deep in the forest, it might take a while before help would arrive.

Then he heard a rustle and crunching of hooves on the fallen leaves. He was about to call out for help when the animal in question appeared from behind a thick stand of trees. It was a mule, and on its back was the small wizened woman in black.

"Whoa, there!" she said, pulling off her gray felt hat, her clear, high voice piercing the autumn air. "I heard all this here barking and thought I'd better see what it was about. Well, hello there, Smoky!" She gave Andy a quick once-over. "Did you toss your master into the thicket?"

"I wasn't paying attention," Andy grunted, squinting up at the woman. "My mind was . . . somewhere else. I think a rabbit startled Smoky." He shielded his eyes with his hand against the bright sunlight illuminating the woman's face. Her silver hair was pinned back into a bun, under the gray hat, but stray hairs poked out at all angles. The sun touched every hair with light, while shadows played in the deep creases of her face. He decided the woman must be Miss Carolina.

The beginning of a smile twitched at the corners of her mouth. "You'd be the new doctor, then. In a bit of a fix, are you?"

"You could say that." Andy regarded her with interest, though it was hard to ignore the unrelenting pain in his ankle. "I'm stuck in this thicket, just like Brer Rabbit. I was about to peel off my clothes and ride home buck naked."

A smile spread over her wrinkled face. "Well, now, that would be the most excitement Hawthorn Valley's had in a month of Sundays! How bad does it hurt?"

"How bad does what hurt?"

"I can see it in your face. I can hear it in your voice. I'm thinking you twisted your ankle when you hit the ground. The left one." Without waiting for an answer, she slid down from the saddle with surprising agility, securing the mule's reins around a slender tree trunk and Smoky's to another.

"Nasty barbs," she said, methodically plucking the thorns from Andy's clothes with sharp twists, finally releasing him from his prickly prison. She found a sturdy branch lying by the skeleton of a dead tree and handed it to him. "Same foot this mare stepped on a while ago, isn't it?"

"How'd you know about that?"

The woman only smiled. "Now use this here stick like a crutch. Prop it under your arm on the good side. Put your other arm around my shoulder. Now see if you can stand."

"Ah!" Andy couldn't suppress an exclamation of pain when he tried to put weight on his ankle.

"Do you think you can get up on that there saddle?"

"Yeah, I think so—ugh!" he grunted as he mounted Smoky.

The woman eyed his wet shoes and jeans. "You been wading in the crick?"

"I dismounted and led her across. It was the only way I could get her to do it."

"We'll see about that later. Follow me."

"Where are we going?"

She mounted her mule. "Your place."

At the stream she took Smoky's reins from Andy, staying astride her mule. "Get on, now, Smoky," she ordered, and the mare walked obediently beside her.

"How did you do that?" Andy asked, dumbfounded at Smoky's compliance.

"You got a lot to learn, boy."

At Andy's house, the woman looped the reins of both animals around opposite posts of the porch, slung her leather bags over her shoulder, and helped her patient hobble inside.

"Sit," she ordered, and before Andy could protest, he was sitting on a kitchen chair, his shoe and sock were off, and gentle hands were probing his swelling foot and ankle.

"I don't think it's broke," she announced. "Off with the shirt and that funny undershirt, too. Now!"

Obediently, Andy stripped to the waist. Looking down, he saw that dozens of small wounds covered his arms, chest, and back.

"Poked you pretty good," she said.

"Looks like it. In the medicine cabinet you'll find some—"

She silenced him with one stern look of warning, and out of one pocket of a worn leather bag she brought a small white jar and began to rub its contents on Andy's cuts and scratches. Whatever the concoction was, it had a clean, familiar, old-fashioned scent. He looked over his shoulder, where she was busily dabbing at the spots on his back. Why was that smell so familiar? He gave another sniff and tried to connect it with a person or place in his memory. "Uh, what is that?" he asked.

"It's witch hazel, boy. Don't you know nothing?"

Witch hazel. His grandfather's shaving cream. Dr. Pierce's Witch Hazel Shaving Cream. As a little boy he used to sit on the edge of the old claw-legged bathtub and watch his grandfather shave, a lengthy and careful process. Interesting, how a smell could take you somewhere else in your mind. He recalled seeing several old barns in rural Utah that still bore the advertisements in large painted white letters: Dr. Pierce's Witch Hazel Shaving Cream, as well as a remedy no longer available, Dr. Pierce's Tonic for Women.

Researchers had recently discovered the reason Dr. Pierce's Tonic for Women had been so popular: its main ingredient was alcohol. When one barn promoting Dr. Pierce's products fell into disrepair, a group of citizens raised money to restore it. Tourists bought postcards and paintings of the barns at summer art fairs. The "Dr. Pierce barns" were landmarks, reminders of a slower life, when the speed limit was thirty-five miles per hour and Burma Shave signs dotted the roadsides, before the freeways cut up the land, before clusters of new homes and businesses began to eat up the fields, before farmers could make more money by selling their land than raising their crops.

Did Grandpa still use Dr. Pierce's Witch Hazel Shaving Cream? Andy couldn't remember. Who was Hazel, Andy had always wondered as a child, and why would Grandpa use shaving cream made by a witch?

Andy felt a cool, soothing sensation wherever Miss Carolina dabbed the cream. "So . . . tell me about witch hazel," he said.

"Stops bleeding and swelling, cleans the skin, takes care of the itch. Good for poison ivy. Keeps bugs away. Keeps these scratches from getting infected. Nowadays you'll see it in fancy face creams, twenty bucks a bottle. I could be a rich woman if I decided to sell mine. Ever seen witch hazel growing?"

"No, I don't think I have."

"Last thing to bloom in the garden at the end of the season. Queen of the winter garden, it is. Even when it snows, if it ain't too cold, you'll see witch hazel showing its purty blossoms, mostly red and yellow with little stringy petals, real delicate. In the morning they unroll like one of them paper horns you blow at New Year's and then they roll up again at night. Yellow and red blossoms, mostly. Some thinks God made the blossoms showy so's folks would notice the bush and figger out what to do with it."

"Why is it called witch hazel?"

"The leaves look like hazel tree leaves. And the witch part? Well, lots of folks, mostly women, used it for liniments and poultices and balms, just like what I'm putting on you, and some even claimed it had magical powers. When them doubters started calling these same people witches, the plant got its name: witch hazel. I heard it called winterbloom or epiphany tree. Ever had one of those?"

"What?"

"An epiphany."

"Guess I'd have to think about that." Spiritual experiences, yes. Perhaps that's what she meant.

She attended to his arms and face. "The fruit looks like a hazelnut. When it ripens it busts right open. Seeds go flying more 'n four yards. I seen it with my own eyes. Like the human cannonball I saw when the circus passed through one day. It was a purty raggedy circus but the human cannonball, a man curled up in a ball, hurtlin' through the air, well, I've never forgot it. Anyway, you pick the leaves and dry 'em. Then you crush 'em real fine with a pestle and a mortar and you mix the powder in your ointments and poultices. The bark's useful when you make it into a tea. Good for the runs and piles, too. Need any for them?"

"Uh, no. But thank you."

She began to work on his chest. "Indians used it. Said the Great Spirit left it here on the earth, specially for 'em to use. When the white folks came over on the Mayflower, they didn't have many cures with 'em, but the Indians showed 'em how to use a lot of plants to make tonics and cures. And look how we repaid the Indians for their kindness."

She walked down the hall, shaking her head, her heels clicking on the wooden floor, and found Andy's bedroom, where he heard dresser drawers open and shut. She returned with sweats and a T-shirt. "Here. Put these on. You'll be more comfortable. Besides, those jeans are purty damp. I'll turn my back while you change. I don't scare easy, though. Reckon I've seen it all. And then some."

Andy pondered " 'and then some.' "

"Now you hop over to this here sofa and we'll prop that foot up high," Miss Carolina said. Andy obeyed and soon his throbbing ankle was elevated with a pile of cushions, and one was under his head. "Gotta be higher than your heart to help with the swelling," she informed him. "Now, I'm just going to brew you some yarb tea and stir up a plaster for that sore foot. And here's a dry sock for your good foot."

The small woman in black moved about the kitchen efficiently, humming snatches of songs he had never heard, while peculiar odors began to fill the air.

He reasoned with himself. Hadn't he been curious about Healers and their methods? Now he could watch Miss Carolina in action; besides, although his ankle throbbed, it probably wasn't a serious injury. What harm could she do?

While the woman tended her brews, Andy examined his ankle himself, feeling for possible fractures and checking for range of motion, wincing this time under his own exploring fingers. No doubt the woman was right; it was probably a sprain. It wouldn't put him out of commission, but it would slow him down for a few weeks. He had experienced a sprain or two in sports, and this was behaving like one. He settled back on the sofa before she turned from the sink, fixing her piercing blue eyes on him. "Well, what's your diagnosis, Doctor?"

"What?"

"You look too young to be graduated from medical school, by the way, and I know what you were doing when you thought I wasn't looking."

"Uh—" Andy stammered, seeing the humor in his situation, "well, I believe you're right, Miss Carolina. It's just a sprain." He paused for a moment. "You *are* Miss Carolina, aren't you?"

"I am. And it's a durned good thing I found you."

He nodded soberly. "You may have saved my life."

"Don't get smart with me, boy," she snapped, but her bright blue eyes held a smile. "All right. First, drink this tea. It's good for the pain and swelling."

Witch hazel ointment applied externally was one thing. But drinking tea with unknown ingredients was something else entirely.

Miss Carolina seemed to read his mind. "Down with it," she ordered.

Andy sputtered with his first sip. "That's disgusting!"

"What, medicine's supposed to taste good? The best ones taste the worst. Just hold your nose and down it goes."

Andy found himself obeying. "Uh," he gagged as his eyes watered, "Miss Carolina, what did I just drink?" *This is crazy*, he thought, letting a backwoods practitioner take charge and treat him, a licensed physician who had just completed eight years of medical training. Yet there was something about Miss Carolina that made him feel like a schoolboy under the stern gaze of a strict teacher.

She showed him the little bottle filled with fragments of dried bark, neatly labeled in a precise, slanted script. "Slippery elm," he read.

"Oh. A natural form of aspirin."

"I'm impressed, Doctor. Maybe they did teach you something in that swanky school after all. Now I'm going to spread this here plaster on your ankle. When it's dry I'll bind it nice and strong. You'll be shuffling around in no time."

Andy's minutes-old resolve to be an obedient patient dissolved when he saw the old woman's concoction. Oh, no, she was not going to smear that putrid, lumpy pea-green mixture all over his foot like frosting on a cake. The paste she had mixed reminded him of the contents of his stomach last year when he lost his lunch after eating a questionable spinach burrito, and it smelled even worse. Just thinking about that miserable meal was nauseating. He sat up abruptly. "Thank you, Miss Carolina, but

I think I'll pass on that. In the linen closet, on the third shelf, you'll find an elastic compression bandage and an ice bag. There's ice in the freezer."

Miss Carolina sighed, shook her head over her dubious patient, and took a small wooden spatula out of her bag. "It's made from mashed up cabbage leaves. Good for sprains." No doubt the cabbage had begun to ferment and was well on its way to becoming sauerkraut, Andy thought, as another whiff assaulted his nose. His eyes began to water. Miss Carolina covered his ankle with the mess, an old towel spread on her lap to protect her skirt and another one under his foot. "Give it a few minutes to dry. Then I'll wrap it up snug with this here knitted bandage. It's got a nice stretch to it. I knit 'em myself."

"Yes, ma'am," Andy heard himself say.

Ten minutes later Miss Carolina had bound his ankle with swift, sure hands. Meekly, Andy ate the soup she heated on the stove. At least he knew what was in that; Mrs. Obadiah had brought him a pot of her famous bean and bacon soup the night before. Then, under the watchful eye of the Healer, he sipped something bitter from another mug, gagging again as he swallowed the second course of Miss Carolina's treatment.

She inspected the mug to make sure he had finished her tea. "Good. Now, keep that foot up all night and as much as you can for the next few days. Use this branch as a walking stick when you need to get around."

Miss Carolina wiped her hands on a kitchen towel. "Keep that foot dry. I'll come by every morning and change the binding. Any questions?"

Andy shook his head meekly. "No, ma'am."

"And when you get healed up, I think it's high time for me to come over and teach you a few things about that skittish horse of yourn. I don't imagine anybody's been too forthcoming about her ways."

"As a matter of fact, nobody has been. Not until after the fact. Not until after I've made a fool of myself, that is."

Miss Carolina shook her head with a wry smile. "I thought

so. Having some fun at your expense, are they? Don't worry, I'm on to 'em now. We'll shape up that horse and purty soon she'll know who her master is. It'll be our secret, yourn 'n mine."

"Thanks." He was decidedly drowsy. The last brew was taking its effect.

"I'll just be packing up, then. Here's another jar of ointment for them scratches if they give you any grief. There's more tea in the jar on the windowsill. Should help you sleep, too."

What on earth have I swallowed? Andy wondered, as two Miss Carolinas seemed to be giving him instructions. He wasn't sure which one to obey.

"Still a skeptic, boy?" The Healer raised two of her four eyebrows.

"No, ma'am. I'm a scientist. Just like you."

"Well, now, that's different. A little doubt's healthy, I always say. In the morning, put this here bag of slippery elm bark in boiling water. Let it sit for about five minutes. If you must, sweeten it with a bit of sugar or honey. I take it straight. Like my whisky. How about you?"

"How do I take my whisky? Uh, well, I don't take it at all, actually."

The woman chuckled. "Forgot you was a teetotaling Mormon. No drinking, no smoking, no coffee or tea, right? What do y'all do for fun?"

Andy knew her question didn't require an answer, and he didn't think he could compose one in his giddy state. He focused hard, and the two Miss Carolinas fused into one. "Whoa, Miss Carolina," he said, rubbing his temples, "either my forehead is too . . . low, or my eyebrows are too . . . high."

She grinned. "Well, now, nobody's quite said it that way, how that potion makes you feel. Reckon you'll sleep well enough."

Andy forced himself to focus. "So what's in this stuff I just drank?"

She showed him two little white envelopes, each labeled in small, precise handwriting. For the love of Mike, he'd followed her orders and downed a strong dose of a natural barbiturate!

Well, you've wondered about the Healers, he reminded himself. *Now you've been treated by one.*

He couldn't find fault with the binding on his ankle. Surprisingly, the throbbing was subsiding. Miss Carolina spread an afghan over him and tucked another pillow under his head. "Reckon you should stay right here on this here couch tonight. You'll sleep sound enough. I'll just take Smoky to the barn and get her settled before I head home."

Before Andy could compose a reply in his foggy brain, the woman was gone. "The besht ones taste th' worsh. Jus' hole your nose an' down it goes," he finally mumbled, amused at his slurred speech. He gave a wobbly salute in the general direction of the door. "You know where to sen' yer bill." A giddy sense of well-being washed over him, and he thought he would just shut his eyes for a moment.

The loud ring of the telephone woke him. Disoriented, he threw the afghan aside and sat up, blinking at the morning sun shining through the pinholes in the window shades. Shaking his head to clear it, he stood up and took a step toward the phone.

"Ah!" The sudden stab of pain in his ankle reminded him of the previous day's events. Grasping Miss Carolina's walking stick, he found his way to the phone.

"Just calling to see how you are, Doc." It was Obadiah.

Andy yawned and steadied himself against the table. "I'm just fine, Obadiah."

"How's your bum ankle?"

Andy rubbed his eyes. "How did you know about that?"

"We have our ways. I'll be over with your breakfast in a few minutes. The missus has it ready. Anything else you need? Olive said to tell you she can handle the clinic today and not to come in. Said she'd send you home if you showed your face."

Determined to follow Miss Carolina's treatment program as a scientific experiment with himself as the subject, Andy accepted her daily malodorous cabbage plaster, a fresh knitted binding, and more bitter aspirin tea. Olive came to visit, bearing bread pudding, crutches, a cane, and a report on his patients, and he gave her the other potion, the one that delivered a knockout punch, to send to the lab in Taylor's Glen for analysis. His ankle propped high on pillows, he worked from his laptop and read two books purely for pleasure. He didn't lack for nourishment, either, for his neighbors, whom he'd affectionately dubbed the "Hawthorn Valley Relief Society," delivered meals and other delicacies daily.

He knew there would be ribbing from his new friends for taking a spill off his horse and then allowing himself to be treated by a Healer and her homemade remedies, but as he charted his own progress, he was pleased to note that Miss Carolina's ministrations seemed to do no harm; in fact, the scratches had all but faded, and his ankle was healing well. He had also gained a new friend in the eccentric Healer.

Chapter Ten

Louisa arrived home and heard Joshua's voice coming from his study, the place where he could retreat from the demands of a large family, to meditate and read and occasionally "rest his eyes," his term for a brief nap. When the door of his study was closed, no one knocked. When it was open, so was Joshua—available to his wives and children, to hear of their joys, their concerns, and their thoughts (when they cared to share them), to reprimand when necessary, to make peace, and to counsel and advise, all in the tradition of the family patriarch.

But today the door was partly open and her father's voice was raised, unusual for him; perhaps he was arguing with someone. Quietly approaching the door, Louisa peered through the opening.

But Joshua was alone. "Absolutely not!" he sputtered. He held a piece of paper in his hand. Waving it in the air, he continued his angry monologue. "I will not allow it!"

Louisa decided to slip away. Perhaps later tonight she would ask her father what had incited his rare outburst of anger.

"Louisa!" her father's voice thundered as she tiptoed past.

She stopped, turned, and retraced her steps, feeling like a

child caught in some kind of mischief, and returned to the doorway. "I'm sorry, Father, I didn't mean to eavesdrop, but the door was open and I heard you—"

"Come in, please, and close the door." He began to pace, a sure sign he was wrestling with a dilemma.

Louisa sat on the love seat, hugged one of Sarah's needlepoint cushions to her chest, and nervously fingered its tassels.

"I've received an official notice from the Council of Brothers," he said, pacing back and forth on the old rug, worn in a straight path from years of pacing. A letter from the Council was serious. Had Joshua openly challenged a doctrine or practice again? Had he read a forbidden book?

"It's a letter, or rather a decree, about your . . . upcoming marriage."

Louisa's mouth went dry and her heart began to pound. Since girlhood she had assumed she would eventually marry, and had even joined her sisters in speculating about one man or another, discussing his potential as a husband. When she was older, however, on the rare occasions when she had pictured herself as a wife, she had never put a face on the imaginary husband by her side. When she was honest with herself, she admitted there were also no other women in the picture.

For the most part, she had deliberately forced thoughts of marriage from her mind since her early teens, when she knew she was destined to attend college and perhaps medical school. This meant a reprieve of eight years after college for her, also allowing her eight more years to deny the reality that she lived in a polygamous community; she would probably be a plural wife; and that she would probably have little say in the matter. On those nights when she couldn't force herself to put the thought away, she had whispered a plea into her pillow: "Please, let them choose someone good and kind for me, and please, don't let him be terribly old!" Today she couldn't ignore the subject of marriage anymore.

"Who?" her voice wavered. "Who is it—who have they chosen?"

Joshua sank into his worn armchair, shaking his head. "It doesn't matter."

"I don't understand."

Joshua methodically tore the document into small pieces, dropping them into the wastebasket. Louisa watched the scraps of paper float downward, wondering whose name had been written on them.

"It doesn't matter, because I find the match totally unsuitable."

"Oh." Louisa's heartbeat began to return to normal.

Joshua turned to her in mid-pace. "The fact is, I do not know a single man in Gabriel's Landing who would make a suitable husband for you."

Louisa couldn't think of a response. Joshua had often spoken of the joys of plural marriage and the eternal nature of the family. What was he saying?

"I suspect you still feel something for this Andy fellow you met at school. And while I can't say I approve of your relationship with this outsider, because I'm too entrenched in the old ways, I hope you can make peace with this matter in your own heart."

Louisa's heart began to race again as she looked down at her fingers, tangled in the fringe of the pillow. "About Andy," she finally said, avoiding her father's gaze, knowing her face betrayed her feelings, "it wasn't meant to be. It was over long ago."

Joshua raised an eyebrow but didn't comment any further on his daughter's romance with an outsider. "I also believe you are conflicted about plural marriage. You've never voiced it in so many words, but I can sense what is in your heart."

"You always could," she murmured with a trace of a smile and a trace of a tear.

"I don't agree with the rigid system of assigning women to men," he said, "without considering their individual natures. Not anymore. As a young man, though, I never questioned the decisions of the Council of Brothers, but now I don't believe that love necessarily follows marriage. I was blessed in my own marriages, and I didn't realize some others around me were miserable. Due to their strong belief in The Principle, they stay together, though, believing that their sacrifice and obedience to The Principle will guarantee them a place in the celestial kingdom, and that because the family is a sacred institution, those bonds must never be broken. I do believe the family is a sacred institution, as is marriage. As a young man, I was so happy when the Council and my parents arranged my marriage to your mother. I believe she loved me, too."

Louisa nodded.

"Last week we spoke of Zina. I thought I was acting in her best interests in arranging a marriage for her. That was my responsibility, as her father, to meet with the Council and come to an agreement about a suitable match, expecting unquestioned obedience as well as gratitude from Zina. At the time, I did find Cyrus Hamilton suitable for her in every way. He is a studious and generous man, and he treats his wives and children with kindness. Under his roof, Zina would never know cruelty or poverty.

"Obviously, I never considered her feelings at all. I never imagined she would be anything but pleased about the match, having been raised in the tradition of her fathers. But now I realize she was just a young girl, with aspirations and passions and dreams that would have been squelched, due to the expectations and the confines, yes, the confines, of plural marriage, had she married Cyrus. Zina was—is—a unique and sensitive girl, like a bird that sings beautifully in the wild, but dies in captivity. It has taken years for me to reach this conclusion and I know it contradicts all that we teach, but now I realize that marriage would have dimmed the light in my daughter's eyes and in her soul. And so, rather than defy me, or the Council of Brothers, she simply left us. I feel her absence keenly every day."

Louisa glanced at the shelves of albums filled with Zina's postcards, sent from all over the country.

"I'll not make that mistake again. As I told Amy at the family dinner last week," Joshua said, "when people ask, and of course everyone's speculating about who you'll marry, my response will be that you're too busy taking care of your own, as you always promised you would."

The muslin curtain gave a small flutter. A slight breeze caught the scent of fresh sagebrush and carried it through the open window, and a sudden wave of relief washed over Louisa. "Oh, Father," she faltered, "I don't know what to say."

"You don't need to say anything. The Lord gave you a splendid mind and a compassionate heart. I imagine He expects you to use them."

Chapter Eleven

Eat two ripe bananas a day to chase the blues away.

—Miss Carolina's Remedies and Advice

Andy was an eager student when Old Man Tucker's Bluegrass Band met for practices. After a few weeks he had already learned the lyrics and chords to a number of new songs: "Shady Grove," "Saro Jane," "Poor Wayfaring Stranger," "John Henry," "Little Maggie," "Blue Moon of Kentucky," "Grandma's Lye Soap," "Everybody's Gonna Have a Wonderful Time up There," "Danny Boy," and "I Saw the Light." Obadiah anchored them with his bass fiddle and strong bass voice and also played tambourine, accordion, and harmonica. Mel Daniels did indeed play "one heck of a banjo" as well as mandolin and twelve-string guitar, and Harm Collins, a violin maker by trade, was also master of many unique instruments: hammered dulcimer, spoons, and tin whistle. Bo Rawlins joined on piano, playing by ear, and even played the bagpipes on occasion. Spokesman and storyteller Jed Thomas added to the vocals with his fine baritone voice. Andy learned to improvise with the vocals and guitar and even took a few turns at solo when the lead singer would nod at him as if to say, "Take it from here!"

Andy also earned a few points with the group when he taught

them some songs from his own repertoire, including "Dance with Your Daddy," "Cottonwood Cowlick," "Bury Me in My Overalls," "Going Down the River," "The Water Is Wide," and "Don't You Marry the Mormon Boys."

After Andy mentioned he had taken violin lessons in junior high and then quit, much to his mother's disappointment, Harm showed up to practice with an old violin.

"Here," he said. "We'll get you going on this. I can always use a backup."

Thinking of Harm's progressing lung cancer, Andy felt a pang of sorrow that his friend would need a backup, but he was surprisingly happy to have a violin in his hands again. If it had been this much fun in junior high, he thought after his first fiddling lesson from Harm, he wouldn't have given it up.

One Sunday a month Hawthorn Valley held a Hymn Sing in the narrow little white church between the post office and the elementary school. Though Andy attended the LDS ward at Taylor's Glen on Sundays, he also looked forward to the community Hymn Sings. The pump organ was a bit wheezy but still had a sweet, pure voice. The piano was terribly out of tune, but so were some of the singers, so it didn't appear to be a hindrance; people came to sing just for the joy of it.

The church had uncomfortable wooden pews and simple, plain glass windows. A potbellied stove at the back heated the building, with a large black pipe that ran the length of the ceiling. The worn old floor was made of wood, so no one could slip inside quietly, as their steps echoed throughout the church.

First, Minister Jones would lead the group in several hymns. Then anyone who wanted to sing solos could take a turn.

On one particular Sunday evening the minister stood up and sang, accompanying himself on his guitar. He pushed his thick shock of brown hair out of his eyes, and it fell back into place. His glasses slid down his nose; he took them off and put them back on, and they promptly slid down again. Then he peered over the top of them and looked out over the congregation.

"Last week we had a youth outing to Liberty," he told them. "I'm happy to report that at the revival, two of our young people came unto Christ and were saved. Hugh and Molly Rawlins, please come to the front so everyone can see you."

Hugh and Molly shuffled reluctantly to Minister Jones's side. He put an arm around each of them. "These are fine young people. We welcome them to the fellowship of Christ."

There were smiles from all corners of the room for the brother and sister, who finally raised their eyes, looking abashed but pleased.

"And I've asked them to sing for you tonight." He strummed a soft introduction on his guitar and the two began to sing:

Amazing grace! How sweet the sound
That saved a wretch like me!
I once was lost, but now am found,
Was blind, but now I see.

They started softly, hesitantly, but by the second verse their voices were strong and sure and they began to harmonize.

What fine voices, Andy marveled. He hardly knew the Rawlins kids. They weren't very talkative; they just came and went from his barn, feeding and grooming and exercising Smoky every morning and evening. He wondered if they had plans for college; surely, from what he had seen, they had the potential. It was hard to imagine gruff Bo Rawlins as their father. Other than the musical talent they obviously shared, Andy couldn't see much of Bo in his son or daughter, but any man would be proud to have children like Hugh and Molly.

Andy was introduced to "shape note singing," where the notes "fa-la-ti-do" were represented by various shapes on paper rather than traditional notes. The singers sat in a square, one side each of tenors, altos, sopranos, and basses. Obadiah, the leader, made brisk up and down motions with his hand, and one section would start with a four-note theme. Then another would take it up, giving it the effect of a round. When the third and fourth sections joined, it became a rich and joyous musical free-for-all, but all the singers seemed to know their notes as well as the words, and surprisingly, everyone ended together.

Andy didn't know how to describe the music; he had never heard anything like it. He smiled when he compared it to the Mormon Tabernacle Choir, but this musical form was honest and vital and compelling in its own way. He vowed he would learn shape note singing and join in with the group.

He was asked to perform one Sunday night at the Hymn Sing and hastily declined, not used to singing solos. Someone handed him a guitar, though, so he sang the first hymn that came to mind: "Come, Come Ye Saints," which told of the Mormon pioneer trek to the West.

Some of his own ancestors had made that journey, walking most of the way. George Benjamin Craner did not survive the trek to Utah and was buried, according to the records, "on the plains, Kansas." Another, Thomas McBride, was murdered before the exodus to Utah, in an ambush at Haun's Mill, Missouri, by hostile anti-Mormon mobs. Arriving in the Salt Lake Valley on foot, his twelve-year-old son, Jamie McBride, had no shoes; they had completely worn out, and his bloody, frostbitten feet were wrapped in rags. This lad's story was in Andy's heart as he sang, his thoughts far away from Kentucky:

> Come, come, ye Saints, no toil nor labor fear;
> But with joy wend your way.
> Though hard to you this journey may appear,
> Grace shall be as your day.
> 'Tis better far for us to strive, our useless cares from us to drive;
> Do this, and joy your hearts will swell—
> All is well! All is well!

Chapter Twelve

For coughs, take the juice of one lemon, one cup of honey,
and half a cup of olive oil. Cook for five minutes. Cool.
Take one teaspoonful every two hours.

—MISS CAROLINA'S REMEDIES AND ADVICE

Andy had checked the clinic's old generator, remembering Obadiah's warning about power outages. In a bad storm, power lines could be knocked down by falling trees or limbs. "I think the old generator at the clinic needs some repairs," he told Mel Daniels one afternoon as he picked up his mail. "Is there anybody around who can take a look at it?"

"Bo Rawlins is your man. He can also fix just about anything with moving parts. Old cars, farm machines, you name it. As long as it's old stuff. The new cars, they've got computer parts in 'em that tell you when to turn on your lights and fasten your seat belt and when to blow your nose . . . well, he can't fix those, but he's kept a lot of old machines humming for years. Just don't expect the job to be finished for a good week or two. He'll get it done, always does, but on his own time. Depends on whether he's sober."

"Bo also . . . farms," Mary Alice hedged. "I mean, he's got a little plot of land. It can keep him busy."

"Tobacco?" Andy asked.

Mary Alice looked at her husband. "I guess we ought to warn Andy."

"Warn me? About what?"

"Well," Mel said, "you get a little deeper into the forests, you might stumble on some valuable crops of marijuana. It looks real pretty, the plant, I mean. Brings in good money, too."

"I see."

"Now, I've never seen Bo's little cash crop and I hope I never do, but rumor has it he does pretty well every year on what he earns from it. It's best to stay away from them little enterprises if you should spot them. Folks get a little . . . protective. If you get my drift."

"Right."

"Just make it real clear you're not the law if you do stumble across a little patch. Pretty soon folks'll recognize you, so I doubt you'll be peppered with much buckshot."

～

Bo Rawlins had taken the generator apart, tested each moving piece, replaced a few worn bolts and nuts, and smoothed worn edges. He cleaned and polished every piece and painstakingly reassembled and lubricated the generator, making small adjustments until he was satisfied with the sound it made when he turned it on. The project had taken more than a week, as Andy had been told to expect. Sometimes the smell of alcohol was strong as Bo worked. Andy never knew when Bo would show up with his tool kit, give him a brief nod, and resume his task.

Harm Collins often accompanied Bo on jobs when he felt strong enough. Concerned at the symptoms Harm exhibited on his first visit to the clinic, Andy had sent him to Taylor's Glen for tests and wasn't surprised at the diagnosis of advanced lung cancer. Harm had endured one round of chemotherapy, and though it had weakened him and robbed him of his hair, he still performed with the band. He didn't have the breath to sing anymore but still showed up for every practice and performance, accompanied by his portable oxygen canister, and still played the sweetest fiddle Andy had ever heard.

Harm was a fine violin maker, Andy was told, and only needed to make two or three instruments a year to bring in enough income to keep his family comfortable. Harm Junior, apprenticed since he was knee-high, now fashioned the hand-made treasures, bringing samples of wood and half-finished violins for his father's advice, for Harm couldn't handle the dust created from shaving and sanding the wood in his old workshop.

"This old girl should be purring like a kitten now," said Bo, wiping his hands on the rag tucked into the waist of his grease-stained overalls.

Harm coughed and nodded. "I think she's good to go for a good while."

"Where did you learn to repair machines, Bo?" Andy asked.

"Been tinkering all my life. Guess I just have a feel for it. You gotta have a good ear for it, too, so you know how an engine should sound. Taught myself most everything I know. My boy, he's going to be better than me someday. He's already rebuilt a truck for hisself. It's almost done. With a good paint job it'll be one fine-looking Chevy truck."

"You must be proud of him."

Bo gave a nod, wiping a streak of grease off the machine. "He's a good kid. Well, I think we're done here."

"Thanks. We really need a working generator here."

Bo gave Andy a cool, appraising look. "Not like what you're used to back home in the big city, huh?"

Harm rolled his eyes, but Andy smiled and met Bo's challenge. "I spent three months in Mexico as part of my medical training. We had dirt floors and no running water, and our beans and rice were speckled with little worms."

"Hmm." Andy thought he heard a note of approval in Bo's voice.

"I do a lot of camping, too, and I've even spent a few nights in a snow cave, so I'm used to doing without electricity. But here at the clinic I can't risk it."

"A snow cave? Now why would anybody wanna do that?" Harm asked.

"Looking back on that experience, Harm, I can't even tell you. It was just something the Boy Scouts did every winter back home in Utah. I don't want to even imagine how the tradition started."

"Didn't it get mighty cold in there?" Bo asked.

"No, if you dig it the right way and you have tarps under your sleeping bag, and plenty of warm clothes, it actually gets pretty cozy in the cave. The snow works like insulation and it contains your body heat."

"So you're a Boy Scout, huh?" Andy heard a trace of contempt in Bo's voice.

"I am. By the way," he said, changing the subject, "I heard Hugh and Molly sing the other night. They have wonderful voices. That's not surprising, though."

Bo's eyes narrowed. "You heard 'em sing? Where?"

"At the Hymn Sing the other night." Uneasy at Bo's reaction, Andy regretted volunteering this information.

Harm busied himself with giving the generator one last polish.

"Oh," harrumphed Bo. "Yeah. They do sing pretty well."

"Like their pa," grinned Harm.

"They're fine kids, Bo," Andy agreed. "And they're good with my horse."

Bo's eyes narrowed. "Your horse, you say?"

Andy's heart sank as he tried to maintain a casual, friendly tone. He'd evidently revealed more than one secret about Bo's children, and he hoped it wouldn't cause repercussions for them. Perhaps Bo didn't care for them going to church, and now, thanks to Andy, Bo knew they had jobs that paid them a little spending money. "Oh, they just help out once in a while," Andy told him, with an anxious glance at Harm, who gave a reassuring nod.

Bo nodded. "Handsome kids, if I do say so, and smart."

"They are."

Bo knelt, put each tool in its proper place, and shut the old battered metal tool case. Andy knew the man wanted to be paid in cash, so he handed Bo a stack of bills, the agreed-upon price, and pulled a receipt book out of his pocket. "If you could just sign here on this bottom line . . . I have to keep records of my expenses for the Board of Health."

Bo scrawled something on the receipt.

"Thanks very much, Bo. I'm glad to know this is working now."

"We'll see ya tonight, Doc Andy," Harm said. "We're practicing, right?"

Andy nodded.

Harm tipped the brim of his cap, and Bo gave Andy something that resembled a Boy Scout salute. Then he grunted, shoved the money in his pocket, picked up his tool kit, and left.

Chapter Thirteen

Joshua was all too familiar with the small, oppressive Council Room, where badly rendered oil portraits of past and present Gabriel's Landing leaders hung on the dark wood paneling, grim and imposing. Out of habit, he checked the condition of the pine floor he had installed years ago. It could use a good buffing and oiling; he would mention it to Henry in the morning.

Tonight the Council of Brothers was assembled, six solemn men in dark suits, around a heavy oblong table Joshua had also crafted in his shop. Scriptures, paper, and pencils were laid in front of each place. A pitcher of tepid water and scratched plastic glasses were arranged in the middle of the table. Light came from three tall yellow-shaded lamps, casting random jaundiced shadows over the assembled leaders. Soon the rising moon would offer gentle silvery light, but the windows and shades were tightly drawn against it. Disciplinary actions were conducted in private, and though it was a cool evening, the room was already warm.

Joshua stood before the Brothers, hat in one hand, scriptures in the other. He wore his only suit, worn and gray, with a neatly pressed white cotton shirt made by Hannah, and a narrow tie, a sign of respect. He would remain dignified and calm as he stood to be judged by the Council. It wasn't his first experience before the formal, solemn group, nor, he suspected, would it be his last.

Joshua's cousin Brother Lloyd Merrill presided. A serious man, strong and vigorous beyond his years, and dedicated to tradition, he nodded to Brother Lemuel Page and said, "Thank you for your heartfelt prayer, Brother Page. Brother Hansen, please record the proceedings of this council, the names of those present, our purpose for assembling this night, and the actions taken. Brother Joshua Martin, do you stand and face this Council of Brothers of your own free will?"

Joshua placed his hat carefully on the table as he reflected on the irony of his situation. Free will did not exist in Gabriel's Landing. It was understood that in order to live in Gabriel's Landing, a person had little agency, but Joshua finally answered with a quiet, resigned "Yes," and directed his gaze at the Brothers, one by one. His eyes remained on them until, reluctantly, each looked up in silent acknowledgment of his presence and their shared histories in Gabriel's Landing.

He knew them well: beside Brother Merrill sat Brother Lemuel Page, a lifelong friend, hard working and practical, who had often broken bread at Joshua's table. Brother Ernest Hansen, of Danish descent, his fair hair turning white now, shifted in his chair. He was a tall man who found that most chairs didn't accommodate his long legs. Ernest's daughter Beth was married to Joshua's son Evan; the two men shared four beautiful grandchildren.

Brother Eldon Kimball, a soft-spoken and patient man, had the same dark eyes and dark hair as his older sisters, twins Hannah and Sarah, Joshua's wives. A frequent visitor at the Martin home, Eldon was a gifted musician and often joined Hannah at her piano for an evening of music and singing, bringing his own flock of wives and children along to harmonize. Tonight Joshua detected a troubled look in Eldon's eyes.

Eli Young, Joshua's next door neighbor, doodled on his paper. Several times each summer, Eli's cow would break through the fence and flatten a portion of Joshua's vegetable garden, wreaking havoc with the bean trellises, tomato cages, and squash vines. The next day, fresh butter and cream and the promise of a stronger fence would be delivered as an apology for the destruction. "Good fences make good neighbors," Joshua would joke, quoting his favorite poem by Robert Frost. Joshua always planted more than he needed in the spring, with Eli's cow in mind, but Eli was still a generous, fair man and a good neighbor.

The final Brother in the formal meeting was Orson Richards, Gabriel's Landing's historian and biblical scholar. His failing eyes and trembling hands revealed the inevitable process of aging, which he had seemed to defy for so many years; however, six months ago he had taken to using a cane. Deliberate, dignified, articulate, and sober, Brother Richards commanded respect and admiration from all as the patriarch of Gabriel's Landing.

Brother Merrill cleared his throat. "This is not your first occasion to appear before this Council to account for your disobedience," he began.

Joshua focused his gaze on Brother Merrill's Bible and chose not to acknowledge the statement.

Brother Merrill glanced at Brother Young. "Tonight we have met to discuss the marriage of your daughter Louisa. As Brothers, we have given this matter a great deal of prayerful consideration. Since you have not arranged a marriage for her, we of the council have selected John Olsen to be her husband. He has indicated his willingness to join with her in the eternal covenant of plural marriage. You were informed of this decree by the delivery of the marriage document four weeks ago. Is that correct?"

"It is."

"And what was your response?"

"I destroyed it." John Olsen was only a few years younger than Joshua. He had five wives and more than thirty children, and, like Joshua, John was grandfather to a growing number of youngsters. He made a good living as a mechanic and was known to treat his family well. Joshua considered him an honest and hard-working man. But, in Joshua's eyes, those qualities did not qualify John Olsen to be Louisa's husband.

"And why did you choose to ignore this decree?" Brother Merrill inquired.

"I cannot sign such a document."

Brother Page tugged at his tie. Joshua resisted the urge to do the same. The temperature in the room was becoming more uncomfortable; still, the windows would not be opened to improve circulation. He and the Council of Brothers would share at least one uncomfortable situation with each other—the atmosphere of the sweltering room.

"Brother Martin, explain to this Council why you do not support this marriage."

"It's quite simple. My daughter does not love John Olsen."

Brother Hansen spoke. "Love grows within the marriage, nurtured by a kind and righteous husband. Your daughter will learn to love this good man and find happiness as his wife."

" 'And, ye fathers, provoke not your children to wrath: but bring them up in the nurture and admonition of the Lord.' Ephesians, chapter six, verse four," Elder Page counseled.

" 'I have no greater joy than to hear that my children walk in truth.' Third John, chapter one, verse four," was Joshua's reply.

"John Olsen is only a few years my junior. He is twenty years older than Louisa."

" 'Children's children are the crown of old men; and the glory of children are their fathers,' " boomed the deep voice of Orson Richards. "Proverbs, chapter seventeen, verse six."

The Brothers nodded in agreement with their senior member. Brother Hansen turned to his own shabby Bible, worn over the years by faithful study, with many passages underlined and notes penciled in the margins. " 'Children, obey your parents in the Lord: for this is right. Honor thy father and mother; that it may be well with thee, and thou mayest live long on the earth.' Ephesians, chapter six, verses one through three."

" 'Whoso findeth a wife findeth a good thing, and obtaineth favor of the Lord.' Proverbs, chapter eighteen, verse twenty-two," added Brother Merrill.

Joshua nodded in agreement. "I have been married to three

remarkable women. We still grieve over the loss of Rachel, my first wife. I loved her dearly. As I love Hannah and Sarah," he turned to Eldon Kimball, "my surviving wives—your sisters."

Brother Kimball sighed. "We are speaking of your rebellion, Brother Joshua Martin, in the matter of your daughter's marriage."

"I have been commanded on other occasions to take young women to wife," Joshua said, "women the ages of my own daughters. I will not do so. Nor will I encourage Louisa to marry into such a relationship. My conscience is troubled by such a thought. I also believe it is immoral to compel our fine young men to leave the only homes they have ever known so that the older men can choose young brides for themselves. No one speaks of this openly, but we cannot deny that this is what happens to many of our young men."

Brother Page shook his head, but Joshua continued, "And might I remind you of the great service Louisa provides for our people. Medical care in Gabriel's Landing is improving. Mothers are healthier now when they give birth. No infants have died at birth or shortly after birth since Louisa has been caring for the women of Gabriel's Landing, using her God-given gifts and the education she worked so hard to obtain. When you were ill, Brother Young, Louisa correctly diagnosed the underlying cause. The treatment has restored your health, has it not?"

Brother Young looked up, gave a slight nod of acknowledgment, and then looked away.

"She has set the broken arms of our children with care and precision; they will heal straight and strong. There is no one in this room who has not benefited from her care. 'Let all bitterness, and wrath, and anger, and clamour, and evil speaking, be put away from you, with all malice: And be ye kind one to another, tenderhearted, forgiving one another, even as God for Christ's sake hath forgiven you.' Ephesians, chapter four, verse thirty-one and thirty-two."

The authoritative tone of Brother Richards caused all eyes to turn toward him. "I believe we have discussed this matter in enough detail."

Brother Merrill sighed and gestured to Brother Page. "Brother

Page, please note in the minutes that Brother Joshua Martin remains disobedient. I suggest another disciplinary hearing in three months. If you do not heed the commandments of this body of Brothers at that time, Brother Martin, you will lose the right to worship with us. You will also face further disciplinary action. 'Woe to the rebellious children, saith the Lord, that take counsel, but not of me; and that cover with a covering, but not of my spirit, that they may add sin to sin.' Isaiah, chapter thirty, verse one. Brother Martin, you will take our counsel and ponder and pray about it, and if you are humble and worthy, you will be given direction to obey it."

Joshua knew he was on shaky ground by defying Brother Merrill and the rest of the Council, but he couldn't help replying, " 'Blessed are they which are persecuted for righteousness' sake: for theirs is the kingdom of heaven. Blessed are ye, when men shall revile you, and persecute you, and shall say all manner of evil against you falsely, for my sake. Rejoice, and be exceeding glad: for great is your reward in heaven: for so persecuted they the prophets which were before you.' Matthew, chapter five, verses ten through twelve."

Brother Merrill's eyes flashed. "Brother Joshua Martin, you stand rebuked by this Council. May you repent of your rebellion and disobedience."

Joshua looked at each man in turn, as he had at the beginning of the meeting. "With all due respect, I believe my presence is no longer necessary in this assembly. 'I am a man more sinn'd against than sinning.' " He picked up his scriptures and his hat and turned toward the door.

Brother Page flipped through his Bible, a puzzled frown on his face. "Where's that verse, Brother Orson?" he asked Brother Richards, " 'More sinned against than sinning'?"

Joshua looked back from the doorway. "Shakespeare. *King Lear*, act three, scene two. Good night."

Chapter Fourteen

Joshua turned off the porch light and closed the front door carefully.

"Good evening, Father." Louisa closed her book.

"Louisa?"

"I couldn't sleep."

Joshua sat on the sofa across from her, lamplight etching weariness in the lines of his face. "I've been walking around the outskirts of town for a couple of hours, but I doubt I'll be able to sleep much tonight either." He rubbed his beard, a sure sign he was perturbed. "I have met with the Council of Brothers tonight."

Louisa nodded. "I know."

"We did some scriptural sparring," Joshua said with a slight smile that threatened to become a grin of satisfaction. "I held my own."

Louisa didn't doubt that.

"I'm on probation, so to speak. If I don't repent in a timely manner, which means if I don't follow their decree, they will take further sanctions. But we've been down that road before, the Brothers and I. They won't expel me from Gabriel's Landing; the Council would never go to that extreme. Besides, we're told in the scriptures to forgive each other seventy times seven. They haven't exhausted their supply of forgiveness." He shrugged with a tired smile. "And they can't kick me out. I'm related to each of them in some way, and there's not a better carpenter around, so my skills are in demand. But I will not agree to this decree, this marriage they have determined will take place."

Joshua raised his hands in front of his chest, palms out, as if defending himself against an invisible, yet very real, force. A muscle in his jaw twitched under his silvery beard. His eyes, usually mild and thoughtful, blazed as he declared through clenched teeth, "I know that stand is in defiance of The Principle, but they will not usurp my role as head of this family." One hand reached for his desk for support, absently resting on his Bible. The other was clenched by his side. "I will not give in to the pressure of the Brothers." He smacked the Bible with his fist.

Louisa stared at her father, wide-eyed. The floor under her feet seemed to give a slight shift.

"Father!" she finally gasped. "The Bible!"

Joshua looked down at his hand, inches above the sacred book. "Oh. I had no idea I—well, I guess I've just sworn on the Bible. Vehemently. But I believe the good Lord understands my dilemma." He thrust the offending fist into his pocket. "As your father, I believe I am acting in your best interests to refuse this marriage."

Louisa took a deep breath.

"Of course, I'll have to reason with your aunts. They've been looking forward to your wedding, you know, for so long. They'll be mighty disappointed. What will they do with all those quilts and dish towels?"

Louisa sighed. Dear Aunt Sarah and Aunt Hannah; they hadn't been subtle in pointing out the virtues of various men in Gabriel's Landing. And of course there was her hope chest bulging with quilts, linens, and kitchen towels embroidered with the days of the week, and the traditional long white cotton nightgowns adorned with tucks and ruffles. The pine chest displayed Joshua's handwork and had been filled with loving care by her mother and aunts over the years.

"You've come home to your family and your people, and all

our strange ways, after living in the outside world with the Gentiles. You've kept your promise to us, but I've begun to wonder if the sacrifice has been too great."

"Father—" Joshua silenced her with a raised hand.

"My sacred authority as your father surpasses any other earthly authority."

Louisa had a sudden image of her father standing at a pulpit, speaking to a congregation that absorbed every word, as if he'd just received it from the burning bush. He seemed taller and stronger, his voice powerful, stern, and uncompromising. He could have been a great leader in Gabriel's Landing if he had been more obedient to the Brothers and The Principle in matters both temporal and spiritual.

"Again, I forbid you to marry." He met her eyes and his voice softened. "Unless, of course, you find a man you truly love, who is worthy of you."

Louisa gasped. The vision faded, the imaginary pulpit and attentive congregation vanished, and the man who stood before her was just Joshua, her father, steady, wise, and introspective. Small crinkles formed around his eyes, and one corner of his mouth made a slight upward twitch. He met her eyes and spoke not as the stern patriarch but as her loving father, his powerful voice deep and calm now. He extended his hands, calloused and stained from work, strong and reassuring, and raised her gently to her feet. "Times are changing. Even in our little hamlet."

She kissed his cheek and stroked his tidy beard. She could not remember a time when he had ever been clean-shaven, and she wondered if she would even recognize him without his beard. A sudden tear appeared in the corner of his eye. He cleared his throat and blinked. The tear vanished, but a soft glint remained in his eyes.

"I believe," Joshua said, tall and straight, squaring his shoulders, the old quiet, composed authority restored to his voice, "that we—or I—have said all that needs to be said. Good night, my dear."

Chapter Fifteen

*Squeeze a little juice from a dandelion stem onto a wart
and let it dry. Do that for a few days and the wart should
shrink and dry and fall off. But if you leave a wart alone,
it might just go away by itself in a few months.*

—Miss Carolina's Remedies and Advice

Andy had found an old canoe in the barn, and after a trial dip
in the lake to assure its water-tight condition, he began taking it
out on Hawthorn Lake, a picturesque lake surrounded by pines.
He had even caught a fish or two, though the pole and tackle
box were mostly for show. Eliza loved being a passenger as Andy
rowed.

One Saturday afternoon after a satisfying morning on the
lake, Andy put the red vest on Eliza, walked into Big Granny's
Diner, sat on a battered wooden chair, and picked up the grease-
spattered menu. He'd heard about Big Granny's Diner, and
Edna's famous trout, and it was time he'd sampled it. Clad in her
red service vest, Eliza settled at his feet, her nose working over-
time. "Yes, old girl," he said with a pat, "I'll share a bite of trout
with you, if you promise you won't tell anybody."

He looked around with interest at the wooden tables and
benches and the gingham curtains. If the aim of Big Granny's

was to make one feel at home, it certainly succeeded. The juke-box at his table offered only country music, a nickel a song. The dishes were blue-and-white speckled tin, like Grandpa's on the ranch at home. The most interesting features, though, were the hats, all shapes and sizes, that covered nearly every free space on the rough log walls. Under each was a hand-lettered card indicat-ing who had worn the hat in his lifetime. He read "Omar Thorn-ton, 1956," "Jedediah Morris, 1942," and "Bear Mason, 1931." The oldest belonged to "Greenberry Gibbs, 1914."

"Greenberry and his family built this place," Edna said, steaming coffeepot in hand. "When he died, the family hung his hat on the wall. Soon other folks brought in hats when folks died, and added to the collection. Even had a magazine come and write up a article about it, with colored pictures and all. Put this place on the map, I tell you."

She reached for Andy's coffee cup, but when he covered it with his hand and shook his head with a smile, she said, "Oh, that's right, you'd be the new doc. I heard you don't drink coffee. What gets you up and going in the morning, anyway?"

He only smiled, knowing Edna didn't need a reply. "I've come for your famous trout dinner, Edna."

She gave a pleased nod and said, "Grits with the trout?"

"Sure." He wasn't certain about the grits. Edna must have caught the doubt in his face because she grinned. "Wait'll you taste mine."

"All right. And a piece of greenberry pie. What is greenberry pie, anyway?"

"Not bitter at all. Greenberries grow wild here, especially near the lakes and creeks. You've never tasted anything like my greenberry pie. Named after old Greenberry Gibbs," she said, with a nod toward the oldest hat on the wall, "the original owner of this place."

"And who was Big Granny?"

"His wife. Their picture's on the back of the menu."

Andy turned over the menu. Big Granny did justice to her name and had probably eaten a good deal of her famous cooking over the years. Greenberry was lean and dour looking.

"They say Greenberry could tell a story good as anybody in Hawthorn Valley, even if he does look a tad grim in the picture. Hated having his photo taken."

"Ah."

"It's about time you came in to try my trout, Doc."

Andy nodded. "Definitely."

"You like trout?"

"Oh, yes." He hadn't tasted trout since his last camping trip with his grandfather, father, and brothers. He stared out the fly-specked window at the beautiful Kentucky fall and thought of that weekend, more than four years ago, just before his last year of medical school . . .

If there was a more beautiful tree than the quaking aspen, Andy had yet to see it. Slim, white-barked trunks supported its uplifted branches while small, gray-green leaves, shaped like spades, fluttered on their thin stems and reflected the sunlight like silver coins. The sweet, wistful sigh of the wind passing through a stand of aspens sounded almost human. "Quaking" described the movement of the leaves and not the nature of the tree, for though quakies were quick to grow, they were also robust enough to withstand strong winds and the stress of high altitude winters.

The trout sizzled in the pan as Grandpa tended to them. Andy's job was to pitch the tent he would share with his father and brothers, who were still fishing. He hammered the last stake into the ground and gave an appreciative sniff. "There. Smells great, Grandpa."

"I hope there's trout in heaven. If there isn't, I might reconsider my options." Grandpa spoke of heaven often since being widowed, although he still maintained a firm grasp on earthly life. Raised on a farm, where weather determined daily routines and awarded annual profit or loss at whim, Grandpa was keenly attuned to the moods of the sky and sensed its variations as accurately as a barometer. "The outdoors adds flavor to anything you cook," he said. He checked the coals on top of the Dutch ovens, arranging them evenly around the lids with long-handled tongs. One held his famous potatoes with onions and cheese. Biscuits baked in the other. Andy's mother had sent fresh fruit and gingerbread for dessert.

When the rest returned with more fish for breakfast and put them in a cooler, they sat around the fire and ate Grandpa's banquet. There were five of them, three generations of McBrides: Grandpa Andrew McBride, his son Cole, and Cole's three sons.

When they all declared they were stuffed and the dishes were scraped and rinsed and plunged into hot, soapy water, Cole and Grandpa settled the horses for the night. Then they sat around the campfire for the tenth annual McBride storytelling contest. Each tried to outdo the other with outrageously funny tales, but, as usual, Grandpa's was voted the best. This year his yarn was about the grizzly bear who played "Camptown Races" on the harmonica to lure sheep away from the flock.

"I'm impressed, Pete," Grandpa said to Andy's younger brother. Pete had told the story of a moose who collected unwary hunters' hats and wore them on his own "hat rack" of antlers. "Another year or two and you'll give me some real competition. Cole, I'm not sure your story was up to snuff."

Andy glanced at his father, who seemed tired and preoccupied. "Next year," Cole promised.

"Listen," Grandpa said.

"I don't hear anything," said Pete. "Only the crickets."

"That's just it. No noises except a lonely cricket or two, a log shifting in the fire, or the breeze in the pines. Nothing else. And look at the sky. With no city lights for competition, the stars are twice as bright."

They gazed at the sky in silence and then started to point out constellations: Orion, Taurus, Gemini, Leo. Here, too, Grandpa was in his element. His Navy training served him well as he found Ursa Minor and the North Star. "For as long as ships have sailed the seas Polaris has been an essential guiding star," he said. "Your grandmother was mine for forty-eight years. I like to think she's still watching over me." Grandpa had been widowed for seven years now; Andy knew he felt the loss keenly. Several people Andy admired and respected made up his personal North Star, including his father and grandfather.

When Andy awoke at dawn his father's sleeping bag was empty. He glanced at his younger brothers, still sleeping. His two sisters had joined their mother, aunts, and female cousins for the annual McBride Women's Retreat. Andy wasn't sure what that included, but he'd heard snatches of conversations about yoga classes, shopping, spas, theater, and a new French restaurant.

Andy slipped on his coat and shoes and joined his father, who was perched on a boulder at the shore of the deep blue lake, watching the last faint pink and yellow fingers of the sunrise disappear.

Cole glanced up with a brief smile. "Morning." He was whittling, hollowing out a short section of a thin fallen pine branch.

"Morning, Dad. Are you feeling all right? You were kind of quiet last night."

Cole blew the shavings away and continued whittling.

"Something on your mind, Dad?"

"I have five children. Something's always on my mind," Cole said with a tired smile. "You didn't come with instruction manuals."

"So who's on your mind this morning?"

The little piece of wood was now a hollow cylinder. With a few finger holes it would turn into a primitive flute with a sweet, plaintive sound. Cole did not look up from his task. "You're on my mind."

"Me? I'm about to start my last year of med school. I know I'm going to graduate. Why would you worry about me?"

Cole hesitated, blowing shavings off his sleeve. "Your cousin Christine told your mother about a girl you've been seeing."

Startled, Andy jammed his hands in his pockets and tried to assume a casual tone. "She did?"

"So why haven't we met her? You've always brought your friends home."

"Well, she's in med school, too, and we have to study all the time. You know how it is."

"So, tell me about this girl. Where's her home?"

"She's from . . . a little town near Cedar City."

Cole's tone sounded carefully casual. "Is that right?"

"Uh-huh."

Andy felt a sudden blast of chilly wind off the surface of the lake. *He knows. Dad knows Louisa's from Gabriel's Landing.*

"Andy, your mother and I came from similar backgrounds. When we met, we had the same goals in life. We still do. We've built a partnership. Marriage should work like two NBA basketball players, like Stockton and Malone. Stockton knows exactly where Malone's going to be. Then he makes a no-look pass to Malone, who takes a thirteen-foot jumper, and in it goes."

Dad and his sports analogies. Andy could see where this was going.

"No matter how tight the defense is," Cole continued, "sooner or later Stockton steals the ball and passes it to Malone. Malone hits a sweet thirteen-foot jumper or sails in for a lay-up. They do it play after play, game after game, year after year. The NBA will never see the likes of them again when they retire. That's the way a marriage should work, Andy, with the partners always trying to be in synch with each other. Your mother and I do that pretty well."

The wind died down as quickly as it had come up. Andy bent and collected a handful of small rocks, sorting through them. "And your point is?"

"What I'm trying to say about marriage, and I'm not saying this very well, is that when you choose your partner, it's for life."

"I know. You and Mom have a good marriage. Solid. Lots of . . . Stockton-to-Malone moments."

Cole gave a brief smile. "We've had our hard times, and there are a few things we'd change if we could go back, but we've worked hard at it. Nothing's more important to us than our family."

"I know this is leading somewhere, Dad."

"The small town where this girl lives, would it happen to be Gabriel's Landing?"

Andy found the perfect stone, smooth and rounded from years of being hurled against other rocks, and rubbed it between his thumb and forefinger. "Yes, as a matter of fact."

"She comes from polygamy, then."

With an expert sideways toss, Andy skipped the rock across the glassy surface of the lake. "Seven," he said. "My all-time record."

"Andy." His father put a gentle hand on his knee.

Andy threw another rock, but this one landed with a soft "plunk" and disappeared in the center of a widening circle of rings on the smooth surface of the lake. "That went nowhere," he said.

"Uh-huh." Cole set his whittling down on the rock beside him.

Andy recognized the tone. Underneath his father's "uh-huh" was a question waiting to be answered. Andy ignored the invitation.

Cole glanced at him. "Christine says the girl is beautiful."

"She is."

"No doubt she's also very bright, if she's in med school."

Andy nodded, staring straight ahead.

"And she's a polygamist, right?"

"No, she isn't."

"She isn't?"

"No, Dad. She isn't married."

"Not yet. But she will be, won't she? Surely you know I'm prosecuting three polygamy cases right now."

"I know."

"One goes to trial next week. That's one reason I wanted to come up here, away from my office and phone, from the reporters and the anonymous and not-so-anonymous threats. I needed to clear my head, but it hasn't worked too well so far. Andy, what were you thinking, getting involved with her? Crimes are being committed by these people, especially crimes against women and children, and we're uncovering more evidence all the time. More victims are coming forward. It's ugly. And it's going to get uglier."

Andy took a deep breath. He knew what was coming next.

"A hundred and fifty years ago," his father said, "there were reasons, economic, practical, and spiritual, for plural marriages, but only a small percentage of the men actually took plural wives, you know. And they provided for their own families. They didn't live in poverty and ignorance. They didn't perpetuate welfare fraud the way many of them do now, putting a burden on every taxpayer in the state—'bleeding the Beast,' their term for defrauding the government and forcing the rest of us to essentially subsidize their illegal lifestyle. In 1890—"

"The Manifesto. Utah couldn't join the union without enacting a ban on polygamous marriages. I know my Utah history, Dad, and I know some people still practice polygamy today." He paused, studying his father's troubled face. "You're worried I'll be . . . seduced by these people, isn't that the word, that I'll join them and practice a lifestyle that opposes everything I've been taught all my life, and that I'll sever all ties with my family and hide from the law, just to be with her."

Cole was silent and tight-lipped as he gazed over the lake.

"Don't worry, Dad. She's committed to her people, and I could never live that way. It can't go anywhere, this . . . friendship. We both know that." He stooped and collected another handful of rocks, but he didn't find a skipper. "We have no future."

"But I can tell you care for her. Very much."

Andy sighed. "It will run its course." Now he had made his relationship with Louisa sound like a disease, a medical condition to be treated. "In a week I start my last year of med school. In May I'll start four years of residency. And so will she—somewhere else. You don't need to worry about me."

"I do, son. I'm afraid you'll get your heart broken."

Andy stood. "Maybe I'll go into cardiology, then, and devote my life to finding a cure for broken hearts. Let's get the fire going."

Chapter Sixteen

When your child is just four weeks old, make a thin braid from several strands of the new mother's hair. Pierce a dime and thread the mother's braid through. Tie this medallion around the neck of a baby while she is teething and she will have strong, straight teeth throughout her whole lifetime.

—Miss Carolina's Remedies and Advice

"Well, hello, Molly," Andy said to the tall, gangly teenage girl in the examining room. "Haven't seen much of you or your brother lately—but you two are great with Smoky. Thanks for taking care of her."

She nodded. Her eyes were fixed on the faded chart on the wall that illustrated the human digestive system.

"How's school?"

She looked down at her hands, the nails bitten down to the quick. "Oh, the usual. You know." Her heavy dark hair fell over her face, obscuring most of it.

"I've been wanting to tell you how much I enjoyed your singing the other night. 'Amazing Grace' is one of my favorite songs. You and your brother have very good voices."

"Thanks."

"And I don't know what I'd do without your dad's help

around here. Bo can fix just about anything, can't he?"

"He sure can't fix this," she murmured.

Small talk was getting him nowhere, and Molly was clearly distressed. Andy consulted her chart. According to Olive's notes the girl's temperature, blood pressure, and pulse were normal. "So what can I do for you today?"

The girl flushed and finally raised her eyes. The only resemblance he had ever noticed between Molly and her father, Bo Rawlins, was her dark eyes. But today, instead of the shy, friendly look he was accustomed to seeing in them, he saw sadness and . . . yes, maybe even desperation.

"Could we talk . . . alone, Doc Andy?"

"Of course," said Olive, and slipped out of the room.

Andy pulled up a chair and opened Molly's folder, idly doodling in the margins. "Why don't you tell me what's on your mind?"

Molly pulled a plastic bag out of her pocket. It contained the test strip of a home pregnancy test with a positive sign in the window. She handed it to Andy, and tears began to run down her cheeks.

Andy gave her a box of tissues and gave her a few minutes to compose herself. He busied himself at the sink, getting her a drink of cool water. She took a few gulps.

"When was your last period, Molly?"

She took another swallow and then a deep breath. "About three months ago."

"And you've been regular until then?"

She nodded.

"You're probably ten weeks along, then. That's two and a half months."

She took a deep breath. "That's about what I figured."

"Have you told the father?"

She shook her head, studying the scuffed toes of her shoes.

"Don't you think you should?"

"To tell the truth, I'm not exactly sure . . . who the father is."

Andy suddenly remembered . . . a tall dark-haired girl

slipping out of the woods late at night, followed a few minutes later by a young boy, his first night in Hawthorn Valley.

"There are tests that can tell us who the father is."

With a determined set to her chin, she met his eyes. "I don't want to know."

Andy leaned forward. "Listen, Molly. We both know it took two people to make this baby. The father is legally responsible for supporting the child until it's eighteen."

"I didn't even love any of the guys I had . . . I was with. I don't want them to know about the baby, either. I wish it would just go away."

Andy gave her a sharp look.

"I won't have an abortion. I don't think it's right."

He gave a mental sigh of relief.

"You must think I'm a bad person," Molly said.

"Molly, no. Never. You made choices."

"Lousy ones."

"And choices have consequences."

"At the Hymn Sing the other night, what the preacher said—well, I haven't been saved at all. I'm a sinner."

"Look at me, Molly. We're all sinners. I'm your doctor. You've hired me. I work for you."

She gave a shaky sigh.

"What about your parents?"

"My pa's wife—well, I don't get along too well with her. And Pa will go plum crazy."

It was clear the girl had considered her options as she told Andy she knew she couldn't take care of a baby; she couldn't even support herself. She was a junior in high school, and her grades were good enough to earn a scholarship, but now that would be impossible. A baby should have two parents who wanted it and could give it a good and loving home, she told him.

"Do you know of a convent, or someplace like that I could go to have the baby, and then let someone adopt it?" she asked.

He closed her folder. "I know a family you could probably live with until the baby's born."

"You do? Where?"

"Out West, where I come from."

"I've never been more than a hundred miles away from Hawthorn Valley."

"I think you'd like it. It's not as green as Kentucky, but it's beautiful country in its own way."

"So how does this work?"

"Well, since you're a minor, you'll need your father's permission."

"I can't tell him," was her flat response.

"He'll probably take it hard at first—most parents do—but you know he loves you."

She shook her head. "Sometimes I'm not so sure."

Andy paused, chart in hand. "You know who else will stand by you?"

"Who?"

"Olive. In the next room. She's your dad's cousin, right? Olive is a very understanding person, or she wouldn't be working for me."

Molly took a shaky breath. "I guess it's okay. All right."

Andy opened the door. "Olive, could you come in, please? I think my patient could use some . . . comfort."

One look at the girl's face confirmed Olive's suspicions. She gathered Molly into her arms and held her close, murmuring softly, giving Andy a slight nod over the girl's heaving shoulders as he backed out of the room.

Half an hour later Olive opened the door. "Doc Andy, Molly's ready to be examined. I told her I'd stay with her. Then we're going to dinner at Big Granny's. She's craving . . ."

"Trout," Molly flushed, her eyes still damp and her voice shaky. "The way Edna cooks it, with cornmeal, crisp outside and tender inside. With a slice of lemon." She managed a weak smile.

"Ah, Edna's trout. Delicious," Andy said.

"And she's having a salad and a glass of milk," coached Olive. "She's going to have a healthy baby. It takes courage to do this, and you'd better believe I'm going to stand by her. And if Bo Rawlins tries to give his girl any grief, I know how to handle him. He'll come around."

Olive held Molly's hand as Andy performed a routine prenatal exam. "You're healthy, Molly," he said. "The baby seems to be healthy, too." He rummaged in a cupboard and found a bottle of prenatal vitamins. "Take one of these every day. And I want to see you every month. More often if you have any questions or problems. And here's a book about pregnancy. Your body will go through a lot of changes. They're normal, but you should understand what's happening."

Olive put her arm around Molly. "This girl will do the right thing by the baby, and then she'll go back to school. She's gonna make something of herself."

Molly managed a weak smile.

Andy nodded. "I believe she will, Olive. I know it's hard to see beyond this, Molly, and I'm very sorry, because you're going through one of the most painful experiences a young girl can have, but you're doing what's best for the baby. That takes courage. And you'll have our help every step of the way. The blood I took today will be checked to make sure I didn't miss anything, and it will also be tested for HIV and sexually transmitted diseases."

"I never even thought of that," Molly said. "How could I have been so stupid?"

"If you didn't use a condom—"

Molly shuddered. "Obviously, we didn't."

"We'll test you again in three months and then six months."

"We'll be praying it's negative, dear. Come on now, get dressed so we can go to Big Granny's. We're eating for three," said Olive.

In his private office, Andy dialed a series of numbers on the phone. "Hey, Karen! This is Andy. McBride . . . Andy McBride . . . Yes, *the* Andy McBride . . . Uh-huh. The boy next door who fell out of the walnut tree trying to spy on you. The one who took you to the prom when your date stood you up. By the way, you were the prettiest girl there, did I ever tell you? How's Roger?

And the kids? Really? That's great. Say, Karen, I'm calling from Kentucky, and there's a girl here who needs your help . . ."

⁓

A week later, loud pounding on his door roused Andy out of a sound sleep. He stumbled to the door in his pajamas and bare feet, squinting at the clock and fumbling for the light switch. On the doorstep stood Hugh Rawlins, white-faced and worried.

"Hugh! It's past midnight. What's wrong?"

Hugh jammed his hands in his pockets and rocked back and forth on his feet. "I got my sister in the pickup. She's banged up good. I snuck her out of the house."

Andy hurried outside to Hugh's truck, opened the door, and looked at the shivering, bleeding girl. Then he ran back inside and grabbed a stack of blankets. Thrusting them in Hugh's arms, he told the boy to keep his sister warm, dressed in haste, and called Olive.

In the driveway, Hugh rolled down his window as Andy dug his keys out of his pocket. "Follow me, Hugh. Take it easy on the bumps in the road." He jumped in his Jeep, started it with a roar, and headed for the clinic.

Easing the girl onto a backboard and neck brace, Hugh and Andy lifted Molly's limp body from the truck and carried her inside. She closed her eyes

"Doc, is she—" Hugh grabbed Andy's arm in fear.

Though Molly was still and very pale, Andy was reassured by a regular pulse at her wrist. "No, I think she fainted from pain and shock. She'll come around." The door opened. "Olive, thanks for coming at this unearthly hour."

The nurse gasped when she saw the battered, beaten girl. Her face hardened. "Bo Rawlins, you brutal, pitiful excuse for a . . ." she muttered.

Hugh rubbed his sleeve over his eyes. "I've never seen him so mad, so mean."

Olive threw her coat aside and tucked another blanket around the girl. "I underestimated his temper."

"Pa don't usually hit her so hard."

Andy gave Hugh a sharp look. "This has happened before?"

"He's a nice enough guy when he's sober. We've had some good times working on my truck. He's . . . he's taught me a lot. But he's got a short fuse when he's been drinking. It gets ugly. Molly finally told him about the baby, I guess. I've known for a while, but I never said nothing."

Molly opened her eyes. She looked around the examining room in confusion, and then at Andy, Hugh, and Olive. Her hand wandered toward her abdomen. "Is the baby all right?"

"Did he hit you there?" Andy asked.

"I don't think so. He hit my face and my nose started bleeding, and—ugh, my arm—it hurts, and it hurts to breathe. I put my hands over my stomach, but he grabbed my arm and he—he twisted it really hard. It made a noise. Like a twig snapping. I must've passed out. Is that what happened, Hugh?"

"Guess so. That's when I came in from the barn." Hugh looked at Andy. "Jessie, our stepma, she was screaming at him to stop. I gave Pa a good shove and he fell onto the couch. Hit his face on the table on his way down. Guess he passed out himself, then, drunk. So I picked Molly up and took her out to my truck. I could see her arm was hurt. It looked crooked, so I was real careful not to bump it."

"I'm going to call the sheriff, Hugh." Andy examined Molly's cuts and bruises. "I want you to tell him what happened."

"No, sir. I won't talk to no sheriff. I'm already in big trouble if Pa finds out what I've done."

Andy exchanged glances with Olive, who nodded grimly. "All right, Hugh, I understand. You'd better go home, then—for now. We'll take care of your sister. Be very quiet so you don't wake anyone. You did the right thing. Molly's lucky to have you for a brother."

"Reckon I'll lay low a few days. I'll pack what I need in my truck and stay away from the house 'til he sobers up and cools off. There's a place I can hole up. Down an old dirt road I don't think even Pa knows about."

"Stay out of his way," Olive warned. "You can come to my place anytime. You know where I keep my extra key."

"Yeah," Hugh said with a nod. "Molly, you OK?"

She gave a feeble nod. "Don't get in any trouble on account of me."

"I'll be all right. Pa's still probably passed out on the couch."

"I've found her a foster home, out West," Andy said.

"Yeah, she told me."

"She was going to leave in a month or so, but now, as soon as she can travel, I'll put her on a plane. Go, Hugh. And take care of yourself. Call me or Olive, so we know you're all right."

"Maybe it's time for me to leave, too. Without Molly around, well, she's my best friend. Guess I should think about moving out on my own."

"I saw an ad for a job in Taylor's Glen. Three Meadows Stud Farm," said Andy.

"Thanks, I'll check it out."

Molly nodded. "Go, Hugh."

Andy swore under his breath, dabbing at Molly's cuts and gently examining her for obvious injuries. She was nearing the end of her first trimester, so the baby was still well protected within the pelvis. So far there were no signs of miscarriage.

Andy splinted the girl's arm and slipped it in a sling, tucking an ice pack inside the sling to help with pain and swelling. Then he and Olive helped Molly out to the Jeep. "We're going to the emergency room in Taylor's Glen, Molly. You need X-rays. I'm going to call an obstetrician for the baby. And an orthopedic specialist for your arm." He reached for his cell phone.

"But what about the bill?"

"Don't worry about that. We can apply for state assistance since you're a minor."

"What if my pa comes after me?" she shivered.

Andy signaled and turned onto the highway. "He won't. He'll be arrested. He could get out on bail, but—"

"I'll go to court and get appointed as your guardian. And we'll get you out of here fast," Olive promised her.

Molly's dark eyes were dull with pain. "It won't do no good to call the sheriff."

Andy's eyes left the road for a moment. "Your father broke the law. If I don't report this, *I'm* breaking the law."

"Everybody in Hawthorn Valley is related, Andy, you know that," Olive explained through clenched teeth. "Sheriff Thomas is Bo's brother-in-law."

In the back seat, Olive comforted the girl, who winced at every bump in the road, though Andy drove as carefully as he could in the darkness. *If she miscarries, I'll see that he's charged with manslaughter. What kind of a brute could do this to his own daughter?*

The fracture was consistent with Molly's account. In the emergency room, they'd had to apply traction to set the bones in her wrist. Andy winced at the pain in the girl's face. The staff physician took photographs and dictated a statement detailing Molly's injuries. Besides the fractured arm, she had two bruised ribs, a broken nose, and numerous bruises that were turning light purple now. In a few days, when they darkened, she'd be even more of a sight.

The obstetrician performed an ultrasound and showed Molly an image of her developing baby. "See," Andy said, pointing to the wiggling black and white image on the monitor, "here's the head, and . . . did you feel that kick? We could see it right here on the screen. And look, he's sucking his thumb."

Her eyes widened. "I didn't know babies did that before they were born. Did you say . . . he?"

Andy shook his head with a smile. "Sorry. I can't tell."

The O.B. agreed. "Actually, your baby's not cooperating at the moment. We can't tell right now if it's a boy or a girl. Maybe when you have your next ultrasound."

Both E.R. doctors recommended that Molly remain overnight for observation, so Olive settled into the reclining chair next to the bed; Molly wouldn't be alone, and when she was discharged she would stay with Olive. Andy stayed to see that his patient was calm, told her he'd check on her tomorrow, and drove home. First thing in the morning, he would call Karen in Salt

Lake City and see if Molly could come as soon as she was well enough to travel.

~

Olive persuaded Molly to make a statement to the sheriff at Taylor's Glen, who promptly issued a warrant. Bo was arrested, charged with assault, and jailed. Andy hoped he wouldn't be able to make bail until Molly was safe in Utah. Olive took the girl shopping and bought her some maternity clothes. Hugh brought a backpack of books and a few of her belongings from home. Three days after her father's brutal beating, Molly's bags were packed. The bewildered girl had never been on a plane before, and Utah seemed so far away. "It's very different country," Andy told her, when Olive brought her to the clinic to say good-bye, "and the people will sound funny when they talk."

"Like you, Doc Andy?"

He smiled. "I guess so. But you'll be the one with the accent. Here's a long distance phone card. I want you to call Olive or me at least once a week, promise? I already gave a card to Hugh so you can call each other. And I hope he looks into that job in Taylor's Glen. He's so good with horses. Maybe they'll hire him."

Molly nodded. "Doc Andy? I don't know what I'm supposed to do, I mean, on a plane."

"Don't worry. They'll tell you everything to do, believe me. And if you have any questions, the flight attendants can answer them. You'll be all right," he said, squeezing her good hand.

As Olive pulled out of the driveway, Molly turned and looked out the back window. She gave him a halfhearted wave before they turned the corner and drove out of sight.

~

Restless, Andy decided to take the canoe out on Lake Hawthorn. It was cool and breezy, but he worked up a sweat with smooth, brisk strokes of the paddles. Then he let the canoe drift, gazing across the lake at the migrating ducks and the lightly swaying trees. He began to sing:

The water is wide, I cannot get o'er;
Neither have I the wings to fly.
Give me a boat that can carry two
And both shall row, my love and I.
There is a ship, it sails the sea,
She's loaded deep as deep can be,
But not so deep as in love I am;
I care not if I sink or swim.
Must she be bound, and I go free,
Must I love one who loves not me?
Why should I act such a childish part,
And love a girl who'll break my heart?
Where love is planted . . .

Chapter Seventeen

Louisa buried her nose in one of Aunt Sarah's roses and sang softly to herself.

> *Where love is planted, O there it grows,*
> *It buds and blossoms like some rose;*
> *It has a sweet and pleasant smell,*
> *No flow'r on earth can it excel.*
> *O love is gentle and love is kind,*
> *The sweetest flower when first it's new;*
> *But love grows old and waxes cold,*
> *And fades away like the morning dew.*
> *The water is wide, I cannot get o'er*
> *Neither have I the wings to fly,*
> *Give me a boat that can carry two,*
> *And both shall row, my love and I.*

She looked at her watch with a sigh; it was time to open the clinic.

Libby Morgan broke down and wept for five minutes before she could even speak. Louisa had waited patiently, her arm around the girl who married at sixteen and was already the mother of two. "I can't have another baby," Libby sobbed. "I just can't. Not now. I think I might go crazy. Levi has threatened to call me before the Brothers for disobedience. Please, Louisa, tell me how I can—how I can keep from getting pregnant. Without my husband knowing. So it seems like . . . like it's God's will."

"Libby, I know motherhood is the highest calling a woman can have, but we must consider your health. Surely Levi understands how tired you are?"

"I don't think he's noticed."

"It would be good," Louisa said carefully, "if you could tell him."

"He'll be angry."

Louisa nodded, waiting for Libby to speak.

"And he has five other wives, you know. I have less time with him than the others, who have more children."

He seems to have time to make babies with her, Louisa thought grimly. "It's not recommended that women have children closer than two years apart. There can be problems for the mother and the baby. You're still breast-feeding, right?"

Libby nodded, looking down at her swollen breasts. "I've heard that keeps you from getting pregnant," she said, a hopeful look on her face.

"There's a name for people who tell you that," Louisa said.

"What's that?"

"Parents."

"What?"

"Sorry. It was just a joke from med school. A woman can ovulate while she's breast-feeding."

"What's ovulation?"

Louisa sighed. *Where do I start?* she wondered. *Slowly, carefully,* the voice of caution warned her.

"It's the time of the month when your body produces an egg, the time you could get pregnant."

"Oh."

They had a frank discussion, the younger woman showing a shocking lack of knowledge about her own body and reproductive system. "There are some ways you can avoid getting pregnant," Louisa told her. "They're not fool-proof. But if you take your temperature every morning and keep track of it on a chart, you'll know when you're fertile. If you can arrange for Levi to sleep with one of his other wives when you're fertile, that may prevent you from getting pregnant. But it's not a guarantee."

Libby nodded. "I guess it's God's will, anyway. And I'm Levi's property."

Ignoring the last comment, Louisa chose to address the first. "I believe it's God's will that we take good care of our bodies. You want to be healthy."

"So I can be a good wife and mother. That's my calling in life." Libby sounded rehearsed, mechanical.

Louisa nodded, suppressing a sigh. "Let's look at your labs. Hmm. You're slightly anemic, Libby. It wouldn't be wise for you to get pregnant for at least another six to eight months while you get your strength back. You have many childbearing years ahead of you."

"I know. That's what I'm afraid of. Some days I just don't want to get out of bed, and the other wives call me lazy. I'm not, but Junior still doesn't sleep through the night and sometimes, even though I love my children, I feel so hopeless, even numb, and there's no way out. I don't feel like I'm contributing enough. I'm letting everybody down. I'm letting myself down."

"Have you heard of depression?"

"No."

Of course not.

"You've described it very well."

"I have?"

"Some of your symptoms are physical. You're anemic and you're sleep deprived. Your body hasn't fully recovered from two pregnancies. You've lost some weight. And you don't need to.

And some of your symptoms are psychological. Do you know what that means?"

"I'm crazy?"

"No, psychological refers to how our minds work, how we think, and how we feel. You tell me you don't feel worthy. That's called low self-esteem. You don't want to get up in the morning. Life looks hopeless, and it seems there's no way out."

Libby nodded. "You mean this is real? I really thought I was going crazy."

"No, dear, it's very real."

"Levi said to snap out of it."

"There's more to it than that. Now, I know many people here don't know very much about depression. But here's a pamphlet about it," Louisa said. "You know everything we talk about is confidential?"

"Yes, I'll never tell Levi or the Council."

"I'm not sure they know very much about depression yet. It will take a while. So maybe it's best if you and I talk together, and you can ask me any questions you may have. So I'd like you to read this material and then . . . leave it here. Does that sound like a good idea?"

Libby nodded. "I want to read it. And I want to read more about taking my temperature every morning. But I wouldn't want Levi to know about any of this."

Louisa nodded. "You can take these pamphlets into the next room and close the door. I'll see that you're not disturbed."

Soon other women came with the same questions and complaints; Libby must have shared some information with them.

Louisa began to hold a weekly class. "Healthy Pregnancy" was the name of the class, and the women did indeed discuss healthy pregnancies. They also discussed depression, its causes, and some ways they could begin to cope with it. It was understood that the men were not privy to this information, and Louisa sent regular handouts on pregnancy home with the women in the class. That would keep the men happy, she thought with a sigh.

Had it always been this way in Gabriel's Landing? Had she just not noticed? Troubled, she took a detour on her walk home, to the little weedy cemetery at the western edge of town.

She stood at the foot of her mother's grave, deep in memories. Beside it was the small grave of Rachel and Joshua's firstborn, Rose, who died in infancy. Louisa had never paid much attention to the other graves and their markers, but now she gave them some close scrutiny: Girls dead at the age of sixteen, seventeen; infants buried beside them, birth and death dates on the same day, told a tragic and troubling story. The infant mortality rate was three times greater than the state's average.

There were also children buried who did not live beyond their fifth or sixth birthdays. She made note of the names and would look at family records when she went to the clinic in the morning. Were these the little ones whose deaths were "God's will"? She had seen at least six young children in various stages of kidney failure since returning home. She had requested a study from the University of Utah on genetic defects that resulted from close intermarriages, and she had no doubt that these children reflected the statistics pointing to severe familial kidney defects.

Careful, casual questioning at home had also caused her great concern. When asking about a family and their children, she realized that in some cases she did not know all of the offspring. More inquiries revealed responses of "he wasn't quite right in the head, you know," and other similar comments.

Then, once in a while, a mother would bring in a child with numerous disabilities, apologizing for taking Louisa's time and nervously mentioning that her husband was "out of town for the day," and then asking Louisa, timidly, if anything could be done for the youngster. In some cases, medications could help with the symptoms and make the child more comfortable. In others, early intervention programs offered by the state could have made significant differences, but Gabriel's Landing residents chose which governmental services they would use and which they would not.

Over the next week, further research into genealogical, medical, and cemetery records revealed that other such children in her own generation had lived to their teens, and yet she had no memory of them. They had simply been hidden from public view. From all the information she had been able to gather, and from the cases she was now seeing, these children received loving care from their mothers; this love was obvious when Louisa began to see more of the "hidden children" in her practice. She appreciated the trust of her patients but was devastated by the revelations she had uncovered.

Reeling from shock, she wondered how she could have been so unaware of the secrets Gabriel's Landing had been keeping, at least from the prying eyes of the government. If the authorities had been made aware of the numbers of birth defects not reported, indeed, of births and deaths not even reported, no doubt state investigators and doctors and social workers would have come around snooping, asking for census information, and trying to account for every birth and death and every living resident of Gabriel's Landing. The numbers, Louisa knew, would not add up. No doubt that was one more reason Gabriel's Landing had wanted one of their own to treat them, someone who would keep their secrets and, now, who might offer some treatment for children with disabilities whose existence had largely been a matter that was not discussed.

Stunned, she began to pace up and down in her bedroom. She stopped when she realized it was a habit she was picking up from her father. One pacer in the family was enough. She grabbed her jacket and flashlight and left, headed for Gabriel's Point, where she hoped she would find the quiet and privacy she needed to deal with the information she had uncovered.

She had never imagined that so many stillbirths and birth defects existed in Gabriel's Landing. Why had she never known? *Because I didn't want to know. Because I was protected from knowing.* Away from home for college, medical school, and residency for years, she had only visited infrequently. She had also never realized the number of women and children who were victims of abuse, received at the hands of husbands and fathers who took their authority to extremes and treated family members as possessions they could handle in any way they chose.

She had treated numerous cases of abuse during her medical training, physical, verbal, and emotional, and had seen shocking cases of neglect and cruelty, but somehow she had been in a state of denial that it could exist to any extent here, in the close-knit community where she had been raised. And sheltered.

Gabriel's Landing was not the peaceful, harmonious community she had always imagined, though members of her family continued to be, as far as she could tell, kind and loving to each other. But now she knew her family was probably unusual in that respect, that Joshua's wives and children were more fortunate than others.

All these years, she had simply not been privy to information not meant for her ears. Until now.

Chapter Eighteen

Andy's first Christmas in Utah since moving to Hawthorn Valley was nothing short of culture shock. To add to that, his younger sister Lindsay was married a few days before Christmas, and he found himself wearing a tuxedo and standing in a reception line.

"Andy, it's wonderful to see you!"

"Hello, Sister . . ." Memory clicked . . . "Morgan."

The woman shook his hand vigorously. "We haven't seen you for so long! Where are you living now?"

"Hawthorn Valley, Kentucky. It's a little town, not far from Lexington."

"That's right, your mother told me. Well, it must be great to be home for the holidays and your sister's wedding. Doesn't Lindsay look lovely?"

Andy glanced at his radiant sister, standing beside her new husband, greeting other guests. "Yes, she does."

"They look so happy together. Are you married?"

"No, not yet. Thanks so much for coming. Sister Morgan, you remember my brother, Pete." Andy passed her along to his brother, turned to greet the next person in the line, and a similar conversation ensued.

He felt out of place in a tuxedo, shaking hands with so many people he knew or should have known, and meeting others he would probably never see again. He tried to handle the "still single, are you?" questions with grace but kept looking at his watch, hoping this long day would be over soon. After the guests had left, Andy sat in the corner sipping a cup of punch, slipping out of his shoes.

Following Lindsay's wedding, Andy had enjoyed Christmas at home in Salt Lake City. He took his grandfather to Temple Square to see the lights, more magnificent this year than ever. The misty evening fog, snow on the ground, and thousands of twinkling colored lights on every branch gave the square the illusion of a fantasy world.

Then they went to the annual Tabernacle Choir Christmas concert to see his mother sing. The Tabernacle was decorated with wreaths and garlands of evergreen and banks of red, pink, and white poinsettias. Dozens of trees with small winking lights clustered on either side of the massive pipes of the famous organ. Mom had been in the Choir for five years now and she loved it, even though the time commitment was substantial. She had a beautiful voice; she had studied music and taken lessons for years, and it had been her lifelong dream to sing in the Choir. Andy watched as her face glowed and her eyes never left the conductor as they sang traditional hymns and carols.

The family New Year's party started with great food and ended with the traditional games, jokes, laughter, and outrageous resolutions. Andy also managed to go skiing half a dozen times, attacking the slopes with his usual intensity and energy.

He was a bit rusty, but he was smug to see that he could still ski circles around Jim, his longtime ski buddy. Jim had been witness to one of his less graceful moments during their medical school years, and he rarely missed an opportunity to describe it to their friends and classmates. Over time it had become something of a legend.

"Andy, you're getting in over your head," Jim warned during a break from school as they stepped off the ski lift, looking down at Andy from his superior height of 6'4". The lanky young man with dark, curly hair and angular features had been plagued all his life by everyone's assumption that he played basketball. Actually, tennis was his sport. When it came to skiing, though, he could never keep up with Andy.

"Unless, of course," Jim continued, "you plan to convert to her way of life, move to Gabriel's Landing, take a dozen wives, a couple of them underage girls, build a ramshackle house that you never finish so you won't have to pay property taxes, let your wives sign up for welfare and defraud the government. Let's see, don't they call it 'bleeding the Beast?' Of course you would have to hide from the authorities so you wouldn't be charged with bigamy and non-support, or worse. But here's a thought: you *could* have a very lively practice in obstetrics, and deliver, I don't know, maybe three or four babies a week."

"Don't start with me, Jim."

"Well, then, *she* could always leave *her* family and the nineteenth century to join you. But then, of course, she could never go home again. Unless a couple of men from her clan break in and abduct her in the night. They'd have her married to someone else and hidden away before you found her, if you ever did. You never know. I read the papers."

It was Christmas break, and Andy had put his studies aside. He missed Louisa. If he had ever doubted his feelings for her, being apart confirmed them. He gave a mighty lunge and sped down the slope. He was a blur of red, navy, and white as he whooshed down the side of the mountain, leaving a cloud of snow behind him.

"Hey, wait up!" Jim wiped snow from his face. Andy stopped a hundred yards away, by a large pine tree, and shoved his goggles onto his forehead. Here on the top of the mountain the world was white and clean and unsullied as far as he could see. Today he had pushed his worries into a little box in his mind and locked it. Now Jim was trying to pick the lock.

"The worst cases get in the news. You know how the media will pounce on stories like that," Andy told Jim when his friend skidded to a stop beside him. "They're not all that way. Louisa comes from a very close, loving family. There's been no abuse. She'll be a great doctor."

"Of course she will. She'll be the best, and of course the only doctor in all of Gabriel's Landing. Listen, Andy, we've been friends since first grade. You've always been honest with me, and I'm being honest with you."

Andy stiffened and looked up. "And you're about to say this is for my own good? Want to reconsider?"

Ignoring Andy's warning, Jim persisted. "I mean it, man. She's a great girl—brilliant and beautiful. Believe me, I've noticed, even when she wore those old granny dresses and cinnamon-bun braids. I can see how you fell for her. But her family, the town, the lifestyle—," he jammed the tip of his ski pole in and out of the snow with the beat, "that means trouble, BIG Trouble, with a capital *T*, and that rhymes with *P, Po-lyg-a-my!*"

Andy took off, executing a skillful turn.

"She'll never leave her people! You know that!" Jim shouted when they skied side by side again.

Andy took the next curve slowly, letting inertia take over his body and mind.

Jim navigated the turn, too, his technique a little wobbly, and finally caught up with Andy. "Don't get involved. Move on. Find someone else."

Andy took off, leaving another cloud of fine powder behind him. "It's too late for that, Jim!" he shouted, gearing up for the moguls ahead.

"What? I can't hear you! Slow down!"

"I said, it's too late!" Andy looked over his shoulder at his friend and lost his balance. Narrowly avoiding a clump of tall pines on one side and a huge boulder on the other, he took a spectacular fall.

When the holidays were over, it was time to go back to Hawthorn Valley, to his comfortable log home, his new friends, Eliza, who had stayed with Mel and Mary Alice, and his practice. When he pulled up to the driveway, a feeling of contentment filled him; it felt like coming home.

Chapter Nineteen

*With the gushing self-sufficiency of youth I was feverish
to plunge in headlong and achieve a great reform here—
until I saw the Mormon women. Then I was touched. My
heart was wiser than my head. It warmed toward these
poor, ungainly and pathetically "homely" creatures, and
as I turned to hide the generous moisture in my eyes, I
said, "No—the man that marries one of them has done an
act of Christian charity which entitles him to the kindly
applause of mankind, not their harsh censure—and the
man that marries sixty of them has done a deed of open-
handed generosity so sublime that the nations should stand
uncovered in his presence and worship in silence."*
       —*Mark Twain,* Roughing It

The late winter storm had stranded Andy at Mel's. He didn't
mind; Mel and Mary Alice were good company. They treated
him like family, and Mary Alice was a fine cook, almost as good
as his mother.

"So how are you and that horse getting along, Andy?" Mel
asked after dinner.

"Oh, just great." Thanks to Miss Carolina's private coaching,

Andy had learned how to handle the mare's quirks, and Smoky now responded like the docile horse Mel had described in his welcome note. "You were right. She's a wonderful animal. Well-trained. Anybody can ride her."

Mel raised an eyebrow, shifting in his chair under Andy's knowing gaze. "Well, now, that's good to hear. Your ankle all healed up?"

"Oh, yes. That was my fault. I wasn't paying attention when a rabbit ran in front of us. I want to thank you for lending me the horse, Mel. And for making me feel so welcome. Everyone's been so helpful."

Mel cleared his throat and leaned over to scratch Eliza between the ears. "Uh, yeah, people are always . . . happy to help."

Miss Carolina was right. They had given him an unpredictable horse and then had sat back to see what would happen to the new doc from "the big city." Thanks to his friend the Healer, he and Smoky were getting along famously. *But I'll never give Mel and Obadiah the satisfaction of knowing I needed help*, he thought.

"So," said Mel, squirming a bit in his chair. He cleared his throat. "On another subject, if you don't mind my asking, how many wives has your pa got?" He propped his feet on the old footstool.

"Let's see . . . sometimes I lose track."

Mel's feet and the legs of the chair hit the floor with a thump.

Andy smiled and ran his hand through his shaggy brown hair. "Let's see. Counting my mother, only six."

"Only six?"

"One for each day of the week."

"One for each day of the week?" Mel's voice cracked.

"Well, of course, the Sabbath is a day of rest." Andy added marshmallows to his steaming mug of hot chocolate and stirred it thoughtfully.

Mel cleared his throat. "Does he . . . ever get 'em . . . mixed up?"

"Oh, no."

"Then how the he—how does he keep 'em straight when it comes time to—I mean—I mean—"

"You're referring to conjugal rights?"

"What's that?"

"Sleeping arrangements."

"Uh, that, too."

"Well," Andy explained, "that's really quite simple. We have a very large home with seven front doors."

"Seven?"

"Uh-huh." Andy sipped his chocolate, gazing into the fire.

"Why seven?"

"Well, there's the big front door that everybody uses."

"Why do you need six other front doors, then?"

"You see, each wife has her own outside door to her own private bedroom. Then we have half a dozen big rooms for the kids, like dorms. We all share the rest of the house. There's a huge community kitchen, living room, family room, and dining room."

"Really?"

"Dad calls it the Best Little Doorhouse in Utah."

"Best little what?" Mel sputtered.

"Just a little family joke. My dad has a wicked sense of humor."

"Well, any man with six wives has gotta have a sense of humor!"

Andy nodded. "I'd say so. Anyway, above each door there's a sign with one day of the week painted on it. That's how my father knows where he'll be sleeping each night. On Sunday he sleeps on the couch."

"Well, I'll be!"

"My mother is Aunt Monday. Then there's Aunt Tuesday . . . you get the idea. That's what we kids call them, but only behind their backs, of course. Otherwise, they're Aunt Violet, Aunt Lily, Aunt Iris, Aunt Petunia, and Aunt Hyacinth. My mother's name is Fern. He couldn't find any more women named after flowers so he had to settle for a plant."

"And just how many kids are there?"

"At last count thirty-five, with another on the way. I'm the oldest."

"Holy mackerel! Thirty-five, and another on the way? Your father must have—"

"Stamina." Andy grinned. "We are also a very fertile people."

The snow was falling again, and Andy knew he'd be spending the night at Mel's. He had learned to accept hospitality rather than brave rutted, slushy, unlit county roads at night. His first winter in Hawthorn Valley was proving to be a challenge, but he was used to snow and ice and bitter cold. He also knew when to stay off the roads.

"So the other wives, you call them your aunts?"

"Uh-huh. They're really our stepmothers. But it's a title of respect. Each wife calls the rest of us her 'adopted' children. So my mother has eight children of her own and twenty-seven 'adopted' children."

Mel rocked in silence for some time, a frown deepening on his face. "Do they get along with each other, all them women?"

"They do. They call themselves 'sister wives.' They all banded together right from the first and set all kinds of rules. Nobody can get away with anything. Can you imagine having six mothers? When my father sees any signs of mischief, he hollers, 'Just wait until your mothers get home!'"

Mel laughed until tears filled his eyes. "I've always been interested in genealogy, but this takes the cake!"

"It gets complicated. Since Aunt Lily and Aunt Iris are sisters, when it comes to their children, they're each other's cousins as well as half-siblings, and my father, their father, is also their uncle."

"Holy cow! I'd like to see your family tree!"

"I'm afraid there are a few branches that don't fork. When we studied genetics in medical school, we had an assignment to chart our family tree. Mine was mind-boggling. The professor was speechless when he saw it."

"Bet he was. Sounds like the old song, 'I'm My Own Grandpa!' Ever heard it?"

"Ever heard it?" Andy rolled his eyes. "That's my father's favorite song. Every night, we have to stand around the piano and listen to him sing it. And he makes us sing the chorus with him."

Mel drummed on the arm of the rocker and sang the song with gusto.

"Gee, thanks, Mel, haven't heard that since I left home. Makes me homesick."

Mel grinned. "So, about the wives, with this Sunday, Monday business," he persisted.

The sister wives liked that arrangement just fine, Andy explained. Keeping company with a man once a week was quite enough for them. Then someone else had to put up with him for the rest of the week. How else could they get their work done? Andy's mother and aunts felt sorry for a woman who had to live with one husband all the time, day in and day out. Couldn't imagine how anyone could do it.

Mel digested this bit of information as he hooked his thumbs in his belt loops. "So you really grew up in—"

"The word's *polygamy*, Mel."

"I know what the durned word means, just never knew anybody who really, well, you know . . ."

Andy sighed and searched Mel's kind gray eyes. "I'd appreciate it if you'd keep all of this under your hat. People might be uncomfortable if they knew their new doctor is the son of a polygamist."

"Sure, Doc, I understand."

"Thanks, Mel."

"Besides, a man should be judged by his works, so the Good Book says."

"The Good Book says a lot of things," said Andy with a wry smile.

Mel put another log on the fire. "So, if you don't mind my asking, how come you're single? Seems to me you should have a passel of wives and children by now."

Andy winced. He leaned forward and spoke in a quiet voice.

"Mel, very few people know this, but I . . . uh . . . well, when I was playing high school football, I meant to tell you, they sent us to the high school in the nearest town, I got injured in the . . . you know . . . and so I can't—"

"Well, now, that's a real shame, a healthy young man like you. Happened to my Uncle Howard, fighting World War II in France."

"A man who can't father children isn't too—useful, where I come from, so I'm a bachelor."

"Ah, so you're celebrate. Kinda like a monk."

Andy suppressed a grin and took a sip of hot chocolate. "Yeah, I'm celibate; we have a very strict moral code. Still, I have to wonder, sometimes, what it's like, you know . . ." He studied the planks of the wooden floor.

"Oh, right. Well. It's like, it's like—" Mel's face was the color of the mulberries on the wallpaper.

Andy shook his head. "That's all right. You don't have to explain. I've read the books."

"Well, I can tell you this much. There's nothing like it."

"So I'm told. I—I wouldn't know," Andy sighed. "Anyway, without a wife and children, I can devote more time to being a good doctor."

"Well, folks here have taken a shine to you, that's for sure. How long has it been, now?"

"Since August. When I first came, everything was still so green. And then the fall colors were beautiful. So . . . it's going on eight months now. Hawthorn Valley's starting to feel like home."

Mel scratched the few remaining hairs on his shiny scalp. "Uh, speaking about home and family and all, there's something else I'm dying to know, I mean, since we was talking about polygamy and all."

"And what's that?" Andy projected the picture of innocence.

"Did you have 'em taken off?"

"Did I have what taken off?"

"The horns."

"Horns?"

Mel put his hands to his temple, pointed his index fingers upward, and wiggled them. "Those horns."

Andy imitated the gesture. "*Those* horns?"

"I always heard them Mormons had horns growing out of their heads. You must've had yours taken off, like we do with our calves when they're little."

"Oh, of course. It's quite simple."

"Don't it hurt?"

Andy explained that the whole horn business was painless. "Immediately after birth, the midwife puts little bandages on the spots where horns would normally grow. The bandages contain an anti-horn herbal compound. If the bandages are changed every day, the tiny bumps that are supposed to grow into horns go flat as a pancake, and the hair grows right over the spots with no scars." To demonstrate, he bent his head forward and sifted his fingers through the thick, straight hair at his temples, and sure enough, there were no bald spots where horns might once have sprouted.

"Well, now, that's pretty clever!" Mel marveled.

"On the tenth day of life, we have a party to mark the occasion. Horny Joe goes out to the town square and gives ten blasts on his trumpet, kind of like Joshua in the Battle of Jericho."

Mel cleared his throat. "Did you say 'Horny Joe'?"

"It's just a nickname, of course. His name is really Joe Toad. But he's the official horn-blower for special occasions, so people just started calling him Horny Joe. And since he has nine wives and forty-seven children, I guess he's earned it. He's a good sport. Anyway, that's the signal for everybody to come to the house to take a peek at the new baby. They bring gifts and casseroles and pies and cakes. There's music and singing and parlor games like Charades and Musical Chairs, and we all have a grand time."

"Ah," Mel nodded.

"It's sort of a 'coming-out party.' And that's when the parents announce the baby's name. If it's a boy, they might call him Brigham, Parley, Omni, Mosiah, Himner, Nephi, Orson, Orrin, Ammon, Amulek, Lehi, Heber, or Laban."

Mel raised an eyebrow. "Unusual names, aren't they?"

"I was very lucky to be named Andrew. That's from the New Testament."

"Oh, yes, a good solid name." Mel told Andy he was sure to meet plenty of folks named Maisie, Daisy, Bobbie Jo, Mary Jo, Jim Bob, Billy Bob, Billy Joe, JoJo, Billy Ray, or Billy Jack—lots of variations on Billy and Bob and Joe. "Most folks in Hawthorn Valley are related to each other some way or another. Or more'n one way. They say Kentucky is made up of five million people with fifteen last names."

Andy was glad he'd only have to learn fifteen, then.

"Did you know you're living in the old stomping grounds of the McCoys?" Mel asked.

"The McCoys? The family that feuded with the Hatfields? Those McCoys?"

"Yep. I come from the McCoy line on my pa's side. And Alice comes from the Hatfields."

Andy blinked, open-mouthed.

"But we're peaceful now. Mostly. I mean, the two families are. Not that Mary Alice and I aren't . . . another time I'll tell you the whole tale, 'cause it takes all night. Why, we even went to the Hatfield and McCoy reunion couple of years ago."

"They have a reunion?"

"We check our weapons at the door, of course."

"You *what*?"

"Ha! I got you on that one! No weapons. The only competition was on the softball field. The McCoys won the game, which was all right, because the Hatfields won the feud all those years ago. What I'm saying is, Andy, you aren't the only one with an unusual family history. Nothing to be ashamed of. Now, my family tree, well, I like to think it's at least in the forest somewhere."

Andy grinned. "I'm glad you're broad-minded. I guess we have more in common than I knew—famous or notorious ancestors, unusual names, that kind of thing."

"Speaking of names, you mentioned Brigham Young. Wasn't he the fella who led the pioneers out to the West?"

"He was."

"And didn't he have a lot of wives?"

"He did. My mother can trace her ancestry back to one of Brigham's wives."

"No kidding? You're related to Brigham Young?"

"A long way back."

"And Steve Young, the football player? I seen him interviewed on TV. He said he was a Mormon, and that Brigham Young was his great-great-great-great grandfather. I think it was that many greats, anyway. You related to him?"

Distant cousins, Andy told him, though they'd never met. Many Mormons could trace their ancestors back to the same pioneer stock.

"Well, I'll be!"

"Mark Twain visited Utah once and wrote about the Mormons. He said Brigham had a huge bed made for him and his wives, seven feet long and ninety-six feet wide. But it didn't work out."

"I wouldn't think so!" Mel exclaimed.

Andy kept a straight face. "All that snoring made such an infernal racket, it kept him awake all night. Shook the very foundations of the house. He was afraid the roof might cave in."

Mel burst into laughter. "Oh, now, that's choice."

"According to Twain, Brigham said, 'Take my word for it, ten or eleven wives is all you need—never go over it.' "

"Even ten or eleven wives—I can't imagine it!"

"Brigham couldn't remember all their names to save his life, according to Twain, so he just gave each one a number. At least *my* father knows his wives' names." A sudden yawn caught Andy off guard. "Well, I suppose I should be turning in. I'm very grateful for a warm place to sleep tonight." Much better than last Wednesday night after he had delivered Cassie Talbot's twins, slid off the road, and spent the night in the ditch because he couldn't pick up a signal on his radio or on his cell phone. He was always prepared, of course; he kept a sleeping bag and emergency supplies in his Jeep, but he was always glad to stay in a real home.

As busy as he was with his practice, loneliness and an occasional feeling of isolation were also part of his life in Hawthorn Valley.

They were glad for his company, Mel told him, because it was downright lonely since Junior went away to school and Katie got herself married and moved to Virginia. On Sundays, Frank came to visit with his wife and kids, and they surely looked forward to that. Mel nodded toward a door on the left. "That's Junior's old room. You can sleep there. The bath's on the other side. We've had indoor plumbing for more'n forty years now."

"A great invention. Good night, Mel."

Andy put his toothbrush into the toilet kit he always kept in his truck and looked at himself in the mirror of the plain, functional pine-paneled bathroom. A hand-stitched sampler on the wall read:

The Beauty of the House Is Order.
The Blessing of the House Is Contentment.
The Glory of the House Is Hospitality.
The Life of the House Is Love.

You need to stop telling stories like this, he scolded himself. *You really do.* The frank blue eyes that met him seemed to agree, though a sly gleam lurked in their depths. *Hey, don't you start with me!* Andy warned the image, and then shook his head ruefully. *Andy McBride, you're incorrigible.* His reflection agreed.

And he needed a haircut.

Within five minutes, his conscience temporarily quieted, Andy drifted toward welcome slumber. Sleep was precious and best taken when he could get it, sometimes in little snatches after assisting with a long labor and difficult birth or coming home late at night at the end of his rounds.

He dreamed someone was scratching at the door and whimpering, and woke with a start.

"Eliza, wasn't the warm hearth good enough for you?" he mumbled, groping his way to the door. The dog's white-tipped tail wagged with enthusiasm, thumping against the doorframe. Andy could swear she was smiling. In one bound his pet, protector, confidante, and traveling companion was at the foot of his bed.

"Hope Mary Alice doesn't mind."

Eliza gave a contented grunt and settled herself comfortably for the night. Andy pulled three layers of soft, faded handmade quilts over his shoulders and fell into a deep, dreamless sleep.

Andy's nose woke him in the morning. Something delicious was happening in the kitchen. Mary Alice was famous for her pies; a hint of sausage spiced the air, as well as cinnamon and cloves and the aroma of hot coffee. Andy slipped into his clothes, let Eliza outside, made a quick trip to the bathroom to make himself presentable, and found his way to the kitchen.

"Morning, Andy."

"Morning, Mary Alice."

"How did you sleep?"

"Like a baby."

"Glad to hear it. Nice having you here."

"I'm glad to be here, believe me." Andy smiled and sat at the heavy oak table with its red and white checkered oilcloth covering. "Uh, Mary Alice?"

"Yes?"

"I have a confession to make."

"Another one?" The gray-haired woman's eyes widened in surprise. Andy imagined the late night conversation she and Mel must have shared, all about Andy's scandalous family history. He grinned, meeting her gray eyes. With a guilty flush, she turned back to the stove, stirring something vigorously. "I mean, whatever would you have to confess? You practically live a monk's life."

"Forgive me, Mary Alice, for I have sinned."

She turned, coffee pot in hand. "You have?"

"It was no accident that I showed up on your doorstep last night, a weary traveler in need of shelter. Truth is, I planned to get as far as your place before I gave up on the roads. There isn't a better cook in all of Hawthorn Valley."

"Oh." Mary Alice wiped her hands on her apron and tried to conceal a pleased smile. "Well, I reckon a bachelor probably appreciates home cooking whenever he can get it."

Andy nodded. "Yours in particular."

"Coffee?"

"No, thanks."

"Oh, I'm sorry. I forgot—"

"No need to apologize for offering me coffee. I like the smell of it anyway."

"How about hot cider?"

"Thanks. That's what I smelled, too, when I woke up, the cinnamon and cloves. Your kitchen is a little piece of heaven."

Mel opened the door, stamping the snow off his boots, and Eliza followed him into the house. "Last night's storm was the kind that teaches you to cuss," Mel said. "That dog sure loves a romp in the snow." Eliza gave a vigorous shake, sending snow all over the hearth.

"That's how she got her last name. Uh, Mel?" Andy cleared his throat. "Speaking of names . . . and families . . ."

"Yeah?" Andy saw the interest in Mel's face as he joined him at the table. Mary Alice brought steaming plates of breakfast to the table and took her chair, looking every bit as interested as her husband.

Andy hesitated and then gave sigh of remorse. "I've always had this streak of pure mischief in my character, I'm ashamed to say, and sometimes I just let it run rampant. I'm not Irish; the McBrides came from Scotland, so I can't blame it on the Blarney Stone."

"What are you getting at?" Mel stroked his salt-and-pepper beard.

"Last night, most of what I told you about my family was a bald-faced lie."

"It was?"

"I told you some whoppers. I need to set the record straight."

Mel started to take a bite of hot apple pie but put his fork back on his plate instead. "Well, now, young man, I reckon you've got a heck of a lot of explaining to do, then."

Andy confessed, over hot apple pie, sausage, eggs, and the inevitable grits, that he was not the son of a polygamist at all. Yes, he was from Utah and his people were Mormons. That part was true. However, it was his great-great-great grandfather who had six wives, not his father. Polygamy was a part of his heritage, though. He was of pioneer stock and proud of it.

"We've been hearing about polygamy in the news lately," Mel commented.

Andy nodded. "I know. But those are the extreme situations, where there's been abuse of women and children. Those cases *should* be prosecuted. But they're not all like that, not that I agree with their way of life. I've known some polygamists who were good people, a little odd in their views, but decent and hard-working and devoted to their families. They've kept the traditions of their fathers, and their fathers before them. Society around them has changed but they haven't. The whole issue's very complicated." If Mel only knew how complicated.

Mary Alice cleared the table.

"Well, I can't imagine having a handful of wives," Mel said. "One is enough for any man to deal with."

Mary Alice threatened him with a spatula. "Kindly rephrase that, dear."

Mel reconsidered. "With a wife like Mary Alice, why would I want any others?"

"Thank you, dear." She kissed his balding head.

"Oh, and there's one more thing I need to set straight," Andy continued. "I—um—mentioned that I—was not capable of—"

Mel coughed. The look on his face told Andy that was one piece of information Mel had kept from his wife, something that should be kept among the menfolk.

Andy flushed. "There's no reason I can't get married and have children." An image of Louisa appeared, unbidden, in his mind. He imagined her sitting at the dinner table with her sister wives and a large brood of children. No doubt she was married and even pregnant by now. He winced inwardly and forced the picture back into the mental box that held his memories of Louisa. "Brigham Young said that a single man over twenty-six was a menace to society. I don't know about that, but I haven't found a woman who'd be willing to put up with me."

"I'm awful glad to know that, I mean, to know you're a regular guy and all," Mel grinned.

Andy finished his breakfast. "Well, I've overstayed my welcome, Mary Alice, all because of some tall story I told your husband last night, in a perverse state of mind. I surely led you on and I do apologize."

"No harm done, son."

"And thanks for your hospitality. Eliza and I should be on our way." He nodded at the brace on Mel's wrist. "See me in a week so I can check on this. Are you doing the exercises the therapist taught you?"

"When I remind him," Mary Alice said.

"Good. You should see some improvement, then, with the exercises and the medication. And the next time I'm in the neighborhood again, you can fill me in on the local gos—I mean—happenings. Take it easy for a while and that wrist will heal faster."

"All right, Doc. Stop by anytime."

When Andy rose from the table, a bright piece of colored paper caught his eye. It was taped above the door of the bedroom Mel and Mary Alice shared. It read, "Tuesday."

He turned to Mel and Mary Alice, who burst into laughter.

"You didn't think I swallowed all them tales last night, did you?" Mel asked, wiping tears of mirth from his eyes.

Andy was speechless as he looked from one to the other and then the sign above the door. "I think I've been had," he finally groaned.

"Son, you've met your match. Better watch your back. I'm kinda famous in these parts as a practical joker. I've pulled a few good ones in my day."

Chapter Twenty

Joshua grunted under the weight of the pine boards. Easing them back onto the sawhorses, he decided to wait for Henry. A strapping young man, his son-in-law could lift heavy loads with ease, while Joshua had begun to feel aching joints at the end of the day. He had always revered and respected his elders, but now he seemed to be joining their ranks.

"Brother Martin?" A hesitant, plaintive voice interrupted his thoughts.

"Oh, good morning, Sister Stewart. What can I do for you today?" The moment the words left his lips, Joshua regretted them. He knew what Carrie Stewart wanted. She wanted to be adopted into his family as his third wife, and for her children to live with them as well. She also hoped he would marry her two oldest daughters, a practice not uncommon in polygamous groups.

Since plural marriages were illegal and therefore never registered, divorce wasn't necessary. If differences couldn't be resolved within the family unit or by the Brothers, a woman could be reassigned to another husband, and would take her children with her. Carrie had never approached Joshua directly, but more than once she had asked Hannah and Sarah to consult with him. Joshua was happy with his two wives, and he had no desire to take any more. To complicate matters, Carrie was married to his cousin.

Carrie bore a loaf of zucchini bread wrapped in a checkered cloth. "Still hot from the oven," she said. "Ellie baked it." Joshua gave it a sniff and smiled at the woman. Ellie was Carrie's eldest unmarried daughter. Though Carrie had borne seven children, five living, if she stepped on his industrial scales she wouldn't clear a hundred pounds. People always said a strong wind would whisk her away to the clouds, her long skirts ballooning as she sailed higher and higher in the sky.

There was something about Carrie that always troubled Joshua. She seemed to have the ability to make herself even smaller, almost disappearing into herself at times. On those occasions she often had a split lip or a black eye, and when she smiled, which wasn't too often as the years passed, he could see two chipped teeth and a missing incisor. Joshua knew the source of the injuries and the broken teeth. It was Harrison Stewart's substantial fist and the substantial temper behind it.

"Harrison's in Cedar City, isn't he, getting those tires replaced?" Carrie nodded.

"And how are the children?"

They were doing well, she told him, except for Micah. "He's taken to slipping out at night. I've smelled tobacco smoke on his coat. I hang it out on the clothesline first thing in the morning, before breakfast, so the fresh air can get rid of the smell. By the time Harrison and the boys head out to work, Micah's secret is safe."

"I'm sorry to hear he's taken to smoking," Joshua said. "Hard habit to break if he gets hooked. Have you talked to him about it?"

She nodded, her eyes watering. "I told him we'd only have one conversation about it, and that's all I would ever say. He knows how I feel about smoking; it's bad for his health and against our religion. I asked him to never let me see him," she faltered, "with a cigarette in his mouth. He promised. But if his father finds out . . ."

Joshua sighed, absently sanding a curved piece of pine. "I hope Micah comes to his senses before that."

"Perhaps you'd have a word with my boy. He looks up to you," the woman said, her soft gray eyes pleading.

"Well, now, he's a fine young man, probably just going through a stage. I . . . wouldn't want to interfere with my cousin's family. I don't imagine Harrison would take too kindly to that."

Carrie seemed to shrink. "No," she said in a low voice, "I suppose that wouldn't be right." Even her clothes seemed to fade.

Joshua scratched his head. "But my garden could use a good tilling, and if you could spare the boy and your husband's tiller for an afternoon, we might just have a chance for a conversation." They both knew Joshua didn't need help with his garden; a perfectly sound tiller sat in his own shed.

The gratitude in the woman's eyes pierced him. He recalled the day three years ago, when she had knocked softly on the window of his study, startling him as he read the Bible late into the night. She was seeking refuge from his cousin's wrath. Careful to avoid any hint of impropriety, Joshua had awakened his wives, asked them to see to Carrie's bruises and cuts and to make a bed for her on the sofa. In the morning Carrie was gone, the bedding was neatly folded, and the incident had never been discussed.

Joshua noticed that Sarah frequently took a basket of fresh eggs to Carrie, and he knew she insisted they would go to waste if Carrie didn't take them. Hannah gave the Stewart children piano lessons in return for a half a dozen loaves of Carrie's whole wheat bread each week, which Hannah said was the best in Gabriel's Landing. In Joshua's opinion, no one made better bread than Hannah, but he held his tongue, touched by the women's kindness to their neighbor.

Henry's return to the shop eased Joshua's awkwardness at being alone with someone else's wife. *A woman who wanted to be his wife.*

"Henry, I'm relieved you're back," Joshua told his son-in-law. "I'm too old to be of much use in the shop anymore. It must have something to do with becoming a grandfather again."

Henry grinned. "Growing like a weed, that baby. Morning, Sister Stewart."

Joshua glanced at Carrie. "I'm glad those days are long gone for me, with little babies coming right and left. I'm contented to be the doting grandpa. I know some men my age are taking young wives and having more children, but they've got more fortitude than I do."

Carrie seemed small enough to fit the child-sized rocker Joshua was making for Amy's birthday. "Well," she said, "I should be going."

"Thanks so much for the zucchini bread, Sister Stewart. It's always appreciated."

Joshua was rewarded with a quick hesitant smile, the gap between Carrie's teeth showing briefly. The door closed with a quiet click.

"One word from you, Henry," Joshua warned.

"I know. She'd be ever so grateful if you would take her off Harrison's hands. Since she can't give him any more children, he might be ever so grateful, too."

Joshua sighed. "And then there are her unmarried daughters."

Henry nodded. "Fine girls. But I'm not looking to marry again, either. I have a lot of mouths to feed."

Joshua picked up his hammer and went back to work. Thinking of the quiet, submissive woman's plight and his cousin's frequent bad humor, though, he put extra force into the swing of the hammer, missed the nail, and hit his thumb instead. He yelped in pain.

Henry screwed open the water jug, grabbed the ladle, and fished out some ice cubes. Wrapping them in a clean cloth, he handed them to his father-in-law. "It's a good thing you aren't a cussing man."

Joshua closed his eyes and held the ice pack on his throbbing thumb. "A man who resorts to profanity . . ." he began.

". . . has a woefully inadequate vocabulary," Henry finished the sentence, one of Joshua's favorite sayings. "Still, that must hurt like—"

Joshua glanced out the window as the tiny, round-shouldered woman turned the corner and disappeared. "Indeed it does."

Chapter Twenty-one

*Two spoons accidentally placed in a cup or saucer at the
table means an upcoming marriage in the family.*

—MISS CAROLINA'S REMEDIES AND ADVICE

"What can I do for you, Miss Calloway?"

"Jemimah," the blonde, dimple-cheeked young woman said in a
husky voice, crossing her legs so her black skirt hiked even further
up her thighs, and attractive thighs they were. She leaned forward
and smiled, her ample bosom exposed by her low-cut red sweater.

"Olive!" Andy called.

His nurse took one look at the situation and smiled at Andy.
"Yes, Doctor? Sorry, I was on the phone with a patient."

"Does she have to be here?" Jemimah complained.

"Regulations," said Andy. He knew what Jemimah wanted.
His tone became increasingly dry and detached as he conducted
a brief examination. Throat, ears, nose . . .

"Does everybody in your family have beautiful blue eyes?"
Jemimah asked, as he peered into hers, checking her pupils.

Andy stepped back and shook his head. "Contact lenses."

Olive concealed a smile.

"I get this pain," Jemimah said, "here." She fingered the
scooped neck of her sweater.

Andy stifled a sigh as he listened to her heart. "No murmurs, that's good. I think it's a simple case of gastritis."

"What's that?"

"Heartburn. Upset stomach. Olive, can you get the pamphlet on heartburn for Miss Calloway? Follow the suggestions on it for a couple of weeks. But if you don't feel better, we'll want to do some tests. You can get an over-the-counter antacid at the pharmacy and use it as needed." He gave his patient a half-smile. "And lay off the chili peppers and I think you'll be feeling better soon."

The woman smiled again, a suggestive look in her eye. "I already do."

"Well," said Andy, offering a businesslike handshake, "you take care, now, Miss ..." He glanced deliberately at her file, "Miss Calloway."

He ducked into his office and shut the door. When he thought the coast was clear he opened the door and called, "Last patient for the day, Olive?"

Olive stood by the window, watching Jemimah leave in a huff. "Uh-huh. Better face it, Doc Andy."

"Face what?"

"You're a handsome young man. A good catch. Every single woman within a hundred miles has probably checked you out by now."

"You're exaggerating, Olive."

"And soon the next round will be making appointments to see you, with something as minor as a hangnail, willing to drive two hours just to see you. And they'll be so grateful for your medical skill, they'll be bringing casseroles and cookies."

Andy knew he had a guilty look on his face.

"I thought so. Most of those dishes were made by their mothers, by the way. Tell you what. Invent a story about a girl back home, the love of your life, who's coming out here to marry you as soon as she finishes school or can leave her job or whatever."

Andy took a deep breath and admitted what he'd never told anyone in Hawthorn Valley. "Well, there is a girl back home. Was. No doubt she's married by now."

"I'm real sorry about that. But my advice to you is to put her picture where people can see it, here in your office and at home on the mantel. It'll be a hint that you're taken."

Andy shook his head. He had pictures of Louisa in an album he hadn't unpacked.

Olive gave him a sympathetic look. "Listen, my sister in Tennessee's got a beautiful daughter. I'll get a couple of pictures of her, and you can put 'em anywhere you like. That ought to break a few hearts, or at least discourage some of 'em."

"Thanks."

"Seems to me you've got a case of heartburn, yourself."

Andy shrugged, put the attractive Miss Calloway's file in the cabinet, and locked it. He hung up his stethoscope and fished for the keys to his truck. "Guess so. G'night, Olive."

"I don't think an antacid will do him any good, either," Olive murmured as Andy drove away.

Chapter Twenty-two

*When you blow the seeds off a ripe dandelion, they can
carry your thoughts to someone you love who is far away.*

—Miss Carolina's Remedies and Advice

Miss Carolina was free with her advice to lovelorn bachelors.
"Why don't you hold a Dumb Supper, Andy?" she said. "Can't
do any harm."

The old tradition of the "Dumb Supper" offered single girls a
chance at true love, or so the story went. It made sense for a single
man to try his luck, too, the Healer reasoned.

There were certain rituals to be followed. Nine different kinds
of food had to be prepared. The table was set just so, with one
empty place, and total silence prevailed (thus the term "Dumb
Supper"). Then, with chairs turned backwards, the lonely soul
waited for the clock to chime the magic hour of midnight. If
everything was done according to the rules, at the stroke of
midnight a young man would materialize. Looking around the
room, he would meet the gaze of one of the girls, the one who was
meant to be his, and a happy marriage would result.

One lonely summer evening, Andy had even tried his own
version of the Dumb Supper, and eaten alone in silence, with a
place set for a guest. Then he sat in his chair and waited, finally

dozing with his head resting on his arms, until the clock struck midnight.

A sudden thumping sound on the porch was matched by the pounding of his own heart. What mischief had he caused by his lighthearted venture into black magic?

With a creak the front door opened slowly, pushed by some outside force. In the dimness of the candlelit room, a massive shadow moved across the wall. Then the being turned slightly in the doorway and the light reflected off its large, liquid eyes.

Smoky.

When Andy had wiped his tears of laughter away and his pulse had returned to normal, he escorted the lady back to her barn, giving her a hug and an extra ration of oats.

So much for the Dumb Supper.

Chapter Twenty-three

Made into a poultice, mustard can lift a black mood.

—Miss Carolina's Remedies and Advice

Once in a while Andy scanned the headlines of the Salt Lake City newspapers on the Internet. He noticed that *The Salt Lake Tribune* was running an in-depth series on polygamy, Utah's "dirty little secret." He sighed when he spotted a common error: national news reports continued to link modern-day polygamy with The Church of Jesus Christ of Latter-day Saints. The Church would quickly respond with a disclaimer: polygamy is not practiced by Church members, and any member who chooses that lifestyle is excommunicated. Then another story about polygamy would feature a news reporter standing in front of the Salt Lake LDS temple, visually suggesting an LDS connection again to viewers who weren't familiar with Utah's culture and people. It was painful to read and uncomfortable to know that many readers would be misled.

There were significant differences between various polygamous groups, more than fifty in the country. Many were connected with a particular religion, but others were not. Some, like Louisa's, were peaceful and hard-working people, preferring to raise their children without the influence of the Gentiles or the outside world. Others were not so amicable with rival groups and outsiders.

As a prosecutor in the Attorney General's Office, Andy's father was heavily involved with several high-profile cases in which serious crimes including spousal and child abuse, sexual crimes, and welfare fraud were alleged. Cole McBride had seen the backward ways and ugliness of polygamy in his practice but rarely had contact with the peaceful groups like Louisa's, who were simply dedicated to the old ways and traditions, in stark contrast with the rest of society.

There were also ugly, long-standing rivalries between some fundamentalist groups—rivalries that had even involved kidnapping and murder. Andy decided to skip over any articles related to polygamy for a while and clicked to the sports page. Unbidden, though, he recalled a scene in Louisa's kitchen, when she was packing her dishes the day before medical school graduation.

"The only real difference between us, Louisa," he had said, "is that my family stopped practicing polygamy more than a hundred years ago. Yours didn't."

Louisa continued to pack a stack of plates, wrapping them in newspaper.

Andy picked up a sheet of newspaper and glanced at the *Deseret Morning News* headline: "Polygamist, 53, charged with incest, child rape."

Louisa reached for it and read it silently. "Not in my home," she said, with a pointed look at Andy. "Not in my family."

Chapter Twenty~four

If your right eye itches, you will cry.
If your left eye itches, you'll laugh.

—MISS CAROLINA'S REMEDIES AND ADVICE

One Saturday afternoon when the clinic was closed, Andy took Smoky for a ride in the hills. He returned in the mid-afternoon, hungry, happy, and muddy, his pouch filled with "yarbs" and flowers, and led Smoky to the barn. The Talbot boys, Smoky's new caretakers, would come by tonight, but he needed to dry her sweaty coat and give her water.

He sang a song the members of Old Dan Tucker's Band had taught him. It was one of his favorites, plaintive and soulful. He drew out the *O* on the end of the alternating lines to add to the melancholy sound, while he experimented with a southern drawl.

I am a poor wayfaring stranger,
Traveling through this land of woe,
There'll be no sickness, no toil nor danger
In that bright land to which I go.
I'm going there to see my mother,
I'm going there no more to roam;

I'm just a-going over Jordan,
I'm just a-going over home.

"Step away from that mare, Doc," whined a familiar voice from the doorway. "I'd hate to see a fine animal get in the way of our business."

Andy looked up with a jerk. It was Bo Rawlins who stood in the barn, his face flushed, a rifle in his hand. A wave of apprehension threatened to overcome Andy, but he tried to stay outwardly calm and casual, keeping his movements slow and deliberate as he finished brushing Smoky's coat. Giving her a final pat, he stepped out of her stall and latched the gate.

"What's on your mind, Bo?"

"Getting even with a Boy Scout." Bo raised the rifle to his shoulder and took aim.

Andy stood still, his heart pounding, his hands sweating, and his mind racing for some way to reason with the man, but the strong smell of whisky suggested Bo wasn't in a mood to be reasonable.

"Bo," he said, his voice even and quiet, "put that down and we'll talk this over."

"Interfering with my family, that's what you did. Kidnapped my daughter and sent her away. Now my son's got himself a job in Taylor's Glen, a job *you* told him about. You put uppity ideas in their heads, Doc, and you're going to regret the day you ever set foot in this place. Ever spent any time in jail? It ain't exactly the Travelodge. What I do with my family is my own business, and calling the sheriff was a big mistake, Dr. McBride. They should both be home working around the place for me, where they belong. That song you were singing was right pretty, though, and it fits the occasion real nice, as you're headed home to meet your Maker."

Andy calculated: if he made a quick dive to the left, he could shield himself behind a large metal drum the Talbot boys were saving to make into a water trough. It might serve as a shield. And then what? He couldn't think beyond diving for cover as he inched to the left, calculating the distance between himself and the drum.

He heard a bark in the distance. Out of the corner of his eye he saw a flash of black and white streaking through the meadow. Eliza was heading toward the barn with a burst of speed. His heart sank. *Stay away, Eliza! Stay away! There's no way of knowing what this man might do, but I don't think he'd hesitate to shoot you in his condition, especially if you startle him.*

He kept his eyes focused on Bo, though, giving him no reason to think there were more than two players. He could tell that drink had slowed Bo's reflexes; he hadn't reacted at all to the barking, still focused on Andy as his target. Eliza had the advantage as she rushed into the barn. With a snarl the dog leaped at the man from behind and sank her teeth into his calf. Bo yelped in pain and astonishment, the rifle waving wildly in his grasp. A shot pierced the wooden roof and echoed through the valley. The force of the rifle's kick made it fly out of his unsteady hand. With Eliza still firmly attached to his leg, he yelled and struggled to reach for the weapon, no doubt to dispose of the dog.

Andy grabbed a pitchfork and in one desperate lunge jammed it into the floor, the tongs just missing Bo's fingers but preventing him from reaching the rifle. Keeping his eyes on Bo, he felt with his foot for the rifle on the floor and gave it a mighty kick backward, well beyond Bo's reach.

Bo roared in pain and fury and turned to strike the dog. Growling, Eliza let go of Bo's leg but kept a firm grip on the man's overalls from behind. He couldn't turn around to get a good swing at her. He was the prisoner of a forty-pound border collie.

A soft click sounded behind Bo. "Nice and slow, put your hands up." It was Miss Carolina, stepping into the open doorway, her rifle aimed at the man's back.

Mel appeared, rifle in hand. "You heard the lady," he said. "It's over."

"You might as well give up." It was Olive, a rifle poised on her shoulder, her finger on the trigger.

Three rifles were trained at Bo's back by three people who meant business. Slowly, he raised his hands and uttered a string of oaths. Andy saw hatred kindling in the man's eyes, mixed with pain and drunken confusion.

"That kind of language ain't proper to use in front of a pure-bred mare, Bo. I don't much care for it either," Olive said.

Eliza growled, still tugging at Bo's overalls.

"Eliza. Off," Andy said, amazed he could find his voice. "Come. Good girl." Eliza came to his side and sat but kept her eyes trained on Bo, giving a low, threatening growl through bared teeth. Her tail flipped back and forth, but it wasn't a friendly wag.

Mel found a nasty-looking hunting knife in the side of Bo's boot and a pistol in his pocket. "Bo, you know better than that. Somebody could get hurt. Now, turn around and walk back to the house real slow. We'll all be right behind you."

The silent group walked single file to the front of the house, Eliza at Andy's side. Their progress was slow as Bo limped on his injured leg.

Obadiah roared up in his truck, stopped it with a screech, and jumped out. He stared at the odd procession. "I heard a shot," he said. "Everybody OK?"

"Sure," said Mel, following Bo to the front porch. "Come and set with us for a while, Obadiah."

Mel pointed to a chair. "Sit down, Bo, and cool your heels. In fact, let's just all sit here on the porch real friendly like until the sheriff gets here. No, not our sheriff, Bo. Not your brother-in-law. Jed Thomas is a fine man, but this is a case of conflicted interest or whatever they call it, being he's your relation and all. Olive called the county boys. I believe you're acquainted with them. They take this kind of behavior more serious anyway."

Miss Carolina surveyed the group. "Seeing as you gentlemen are getting settled all nice and comfy, I'll just make us some good, strong coffee—oh, I forgot, Doc Andy won't have any. I'll find something in his kitchen."

"You had no right to take my daughter from me!" Bo snarled, glaring at Andy with hate and malice.

"Nobody took her," Olive said. "She left. You lost all rights to your daughter when you left her so battered and bruised she passed out from the pain."

"She's my daughter, and I'll make her behave as I see fit."

Mel scratched his head. "The law doesn't see it that way these days, Bo. The court made Olive her guardian."

"Didn't you learn nothing from being in the pokey, Bo? Seems to me like you have yourself a little probation violation problem," Obadiah said.

"The girl was pregnant. How do we know *he's* not the father?" Bo pointed an accusing finger at Andy. "Yeah, I bet that's it," he spat. "Got an innocent girl pregnant and sent her out West to have his brat. Wonder how many other girls he's done wrong, ever thought of that? *He's* the one you should be calling the law for. And you'd better believe I'll tell them all about it when they come. Then we'll see who goes to jail."

Miss Carolina returned, carrying a tray of glasses and a pitcher of orange juice. She poured a glass for Bo. "We're all going to pretend you never said any of that, Bo. You'd best keep your trap shut. And drink your juice. You'll sober up faster. And where you're going you'll need to be sober."

"I should take a look at that bite. When did you have your last tetanus shot, Bo?"

Everyone looked around in amazement, but the most amazed was Andy, for he heard himself utter the words with cool, professional detachment, as if Bo were a regular patient at the clinic, coming in for a scheduled appointment.

Mel's lips suppressed a wry grin. "Pull up your pant leg, Bo, and let's have a look at it."

"I'm going to sue that dog for violating my—my bill of rights!" sputtered Bo when he saw the deep puncture wounds and the blood trickling slowly down his leg and onto his sock.

Andy eyed Bo's leg. "Don't worry, she's had her shots. Olive, the peroxide is in the bathroom cabinet, if you wouldn't mind."

Bo howled as the peroxide bubbled in the wounds. Olive dabbed at them, applied antibiotic ointment, and bound his leg securely with thick gauze and a compression bandage.

"There's some tetanus serum in my bag," Andy said. "In the truck." He handed the keys to Olive.

"Hey, she's not touching me with no needle!" protested Bo.

"I just might have something in my bag, Bo, to stave off the lockjaw. But don't know as I'd want to waste it on you," Miss Carolina said.

Olive returned with the bag.

"Bo, shut your mouth or I'll do it myself." Mel took the syringe from Olive. "I've watched it done a few times, but you'll be my first real patient. Can't be too hard to do, just poke the needle in and push this here little plunger thing. Or maybe you'd rather let Olive do it."

Olive gave the injection. Bo winced. "Ah!"

"Your arm will be sore for a few days. You'd best start moving it around. Gently," she advised.

"Call the vet in the morning, Andy," Mel suggested. "You might want to take precautions with your dog, seeing as how she"—he glared at Bo—"bit a snake." He stroked the dog's head. Eliza stretched out at his feet and rolled onto her back in complete submission as he scratched her stomach. "Quite a fierce animal you got here, Doc," Mel grinned.

Andy shook his head in disbelief. "She's never—"

"Didn't know you had it in you, Eliza. That was some performance," Mel told the dog.

Bo's eyes were glazed and the fight had gone out of them. "That was some bite," he mumbled. "Dangerous animal."

Two patrol cars pulled up, lights flashing. Four officers emerged. The county sheriff climbed the steps to the porch.

"What's this I hear, Bo? You pulled a rifle on the Doc? Can't you keep yourself out of trouble? Well, you'll have time to think while you're sitting in jail. Public defender will be there to meet you. Ernie, cuff him. Fred, read the man his rights and we'll be on our way. Bud'll stay behind and take statements from all of you. Evening, Miz Olive, Miz Carolina. Evening, gentlemen."

When the last deputy left, Andy took a deep breath and stared at the hills and the darkening sky. The sun must have set.

"How did you know I was going to be in trouble?" he asked his friends.

"We know Bo. He's been working himself into a state of drunken righteous indignation ever since he got out of jail," Obadiah told him. "There's been at least one of us shadowing you all the time for two days. Us four and my two oldest boys. Bet you didn't know that."

"I never even—"

"And we never let Bo out of our sight, either," said Mel. "Well, we did lose him for a couple minutes there. Didn't know he'd followed you into the barn till I heard the shot. That gave us a little extra steam to get here in a hurry."

"And I'll bet you didn't know I'm the best shot in Hawthorn Valley," said Miss Carolina. "Target shooting, that is. Don't care to hunt. I'm on the side of God's creatures. They've never done me any harm."

Andy shook his head in disbelief. "I don't know what to say."

"You don't have to say anything. Well, I'd best be getting along. Gentlemen, Olive, Miss Carolina, it's been a pleasure. G'night," said Obadiah. In a few long strides he reached his truck, started it with a roar, and lurched down the road, grinding the gears.

"He shoots better than he drives," Mel commented.

"I'll see you in the morning, Doc Andy," said Olive. "G'night."

"Good night, Olive."

"Mel, I—" Andy began when Miss Carolina had left and the two men were alone.

"It's our way, Andy. We protect our friends. Hopefully Bo will settle down. Best thing you ever did was get that girl out of town and tell Hugh there about the job in Taylor's Glen. He's a natural with horses, and word is he's never been happier. Bo's wife Jessie will move back in with her folks; she'll be all right. Reckon Bo will be in jail for a while, so you can rest easy. Wish it didn't have to be this way. He's a decent enough fella when he's sober. They have AA meetings for the prisoners if they care to go, but the rest is up to Bo. Aw, shoot. We'll have to find somebody to replace him in the band."

"Mel, if you hadn't been here—"

"But we were. Besides, he was drunk. He was shaking too much to be very accurate."

"He was?"

"But we weren't going to take any chances neither. We took him right serious. I guess you were a bit shaky yourself. Looks like you still are."

"Yeah." Andy tried to quiet his trembling hands.

"I'd recommend a stiff drink, but I guess that's out of the question."

"I think I'll take Eliza for a long walk. I need to clear my head."

"Take a lantern with you so you don't step in any rabbit holes. And you're still coming for dinner tomorrow, aren't ya?"

"What? Oh, yes. Thanks. I mean, thank you very much, Mel. For everything."

Mel nodded. "You'd best see why your dog is standing in front of you, barking like you're the mailman. G'night."

It was amazing, the way a trained assistance dog could predict a seizure. It had been so long, more than four years, Andy thought something else must have set her off, but she never whined unless . . . the alarm in Eliza's eyes and in her bark left no doubt. Andy walked inside and shut the door with a sigh.

Chapter Twenty-five

Within a few months of Libby Morgan's tearful visit to the medical clinic, another Martin was summoned to appear before the Council of Brothers. If Louisa had listened to the nagging voice she had managed to ignore all through medical school, she would have predicted this very scenario. Instead, she had squelched it, determined she could overcome any resistance or ignorance she might face as a woman physician in Gabriel's Landing. Now she stood with quiet dignity before the Brothers, just as her father had, in the same stale room with the stern portraits on the walls.

After the usual prayer and other formalities, Brother Merrill cleared his throat and began. "Sister Louisa Martin, have you advised your patients, specifically Libby Morgan, Beth Richards, and Flora Card, about contraception?"

How did they know? It didn't matter, but she knew the three women mentioned had probably faced very unpleasant consequences for attending her "Healthy Pregnancy" class.

"With all due respect, doctor-patient confidentiality prevents me from answering that question," she said, her hands turning clammy.

"You have advised women not to get pregnant. That is

the husband's decision, and his alone," Brother Richards said sternly.

"And you have advised against first cousins marrying," said Brother Kimball with a frown.

"That's because close relatives, such as first cousins or double cousins, have a significantly higher rate of birth defects when they intermarry. I didn't realize the extent of this concern until I returned home to Gabriel's Landing, but we have a significantly higher rate of children with intellectual disabilities, I mean, mental retardation, than the average population. I have also recently seen six children with an inherited kidney condition. Their life expectancy is very short. In fact, the University of Utah did a study—"

Brother Richards interrupted. "We do not need a university to meddle in our affairs. And if it is God's will that they are born with less than perfect bodies, and these children die before the age of accountability, their place in the kingdom of heaven is certain. These valiant spirits do not have to tarry on this earth very long to earn their celestial glory."

"I know they are valiant spirits," Louisa said. "I truly believe that. But if we could provide more healthy bodies for those spirits waiting in the spirit world, wouldn't that be wonderful? God has allowed great scientists to discover many wonderful things that lengthen and improve our lives. These children, especially the ones with the kidney condition, they suffer. And there is little I can do for them, beyond prescribing medications and special diets that will relieve some of their discomfort and improve their quality of life. I'm attending a convention in Chicago in a few months, and I hope to learn more about how to treat these children."

"These children with perfect spirits and less than perfect bodies are a manifestation of God's will," Brother Hansen said, his tone clearly closing the subject.

Brother Merrill continued, "It has also come to our attention that you have diagnosed several women with . . . melancholy."

Louisa glanced at Brother Young, whose own wife suffered lengthy episodes of severe depression. "The medical condition is called depression."

"There is no such condition," he said, his eyes flashing with sudden anger. "When women are obedient to their husbands, read their scriptures faithfully, and put their families' welfare before their own, any imagined sadness will disappear, and they will know deep and abiding happiness as wives and mothers, the most glorious of all callings in God's kingdom."

Louisa pulled a folder from her briefcase. "I've brought some articles on depression for any of you who'd like to read them."

"Preposterous!" Brother Orson Richards sputtered.

Brother Lloyd Merrill said, "There is no purpose in further discussion. We will not read these lies!" He swept the articles onto the floor, a reaction that didn't surprise Louisa.

Brother Lemuel Page continued, "A man is to command his wife in all things. She is to keep nothing from him, and submit to him in all matters. You have interfered with this sacred relationship."

And when the wife is exhausted, her day filled with unending household tasks and the demands of two young children, one of whom is barely weaned and not yet walking, as well as a handful of other women's children, would a loving husband even think of forcing her to have another child? Louisa knew this response would only further anger the Brothers. They would never know that three "miscarriages" she had treated were not miscarriages at all; the women had succeeded in aborting their own pregnancies, but all three had ended up in a Cedar City emergency room to be treated for hemorrhage, infection, and other serious complications. The Brothers, she suspected, knew nothing of the desperation these women felt. It wouldn't even register on their religious radars.

"My responsibility is to my patients," she repeated. "I hold this information in strictest confidence. I will not violate this trust."

"For the record, you are stating that you will continue to counsel wives to disobey their husbands?" Brother Merrill said.

"I will continue to give my patients the best care possible."

"Sister Louisa Martin, you are hereby rebuked by this Council. You have brought shame to your community and family. You will cease these objectionable practices and repent of your wrong-doing. We will meet in one month to determine your status, to decide whether you are worthy to practice medicine among the righteous people of Gabriel's Landing."

"What takes place between a doctor and a patient is privileged information," Louisa said again. "I have taken an oath."

"This Council answers to a higher authority than any oath you may have taken as a doctor," Brother Merrill declared.

"Have you heard of the Hippocratic Oath?" Louisa asked, her voice quiet but determined.

Brother Merrill frowned and looked up at her under bushy gray eyebrows. "That has no bearing on your offenses before the Council."

"Indulge me, Brethren, please," said Louisa, and took a deep breath.

"I swear to fulfill, to the best of my ability and judgment, this covenant: I will respect the hard-won scientific gains of those physicians in whose steps I walk, and gladly share such knowledge as is mine with those who are to follow. I will apply, for the benefit of the sick, all measures that are required, avoiding those twin traps of overtreatment and therapeutic nihilism. I will remember that there is art to medicine as well as science, and that warmth, sympathy, and understanding may outweigh the surgeon's knife or the chemist's drug. I will not be ashamed to say 'I know not,' nor will I fail to call in my colleagues when the skills of another are needed for a patient's recovery."

"Dr.—Sister Martin!" Brother Merrill sputtered, outraged. "This is most inappropriate!"

"You will hold your tongue—"

"I will respect the privacy of my patients," Louisa continued, her voice louder and stronger as she reached inside her soul and drew on strength she had never imagined she would find there *"for their problems are not disclosed to me that the world may know. Most especially must I tread with care in matters of life and death. If it is given me to save a life, all thanks. But it may also be within my power to take a life; this awesome responsibility must be faced with*

great humbleness and awareness of my own frailty. Above all, I must not play at God."

"Sister Martin! You will hold your tongue!" shouted Brother Page, his face poppy-red.

Louisa looked directly into Brother Page's cloudy blue eyes and concluded:

"I will remember that I do not treat a fever chart, a cancerous growth, but a sick human being, whose illness may affect the person's family and economic stability. My responsibility includes these related problems, if I am to care adequately for the sick.

"I will prevent disease whenever I can, for prevention is preferable to cure.

"I will remember that I remain a member of society, with special obligations to all my fellow human beings, those sound of mind and body as well as the infirm.

"If I do not violate this oath, may I enjoy life and art, respected while I live and remembered with affection thereafter. May I always act so as to preserve the finest traditions of my calling and may I long experience the joy of healing those who seek my help."

Nearly palpable electric tension of escalating anger charged the atmosphere air in the small room, already miserably oppressive. Surely, Louisa thought, a sudden thunderstorm would burst on them any moment, with a bolt of lightning aimed specifically at her.

"Are you quite finished?" demanded Brother Young, darts of fury in his eyes, his hands shaking.

Strangely calm, Louisa replied, "Yes, I believe I am. Good night, Brethren."

～

Louisa left the Council room, walked home to change into her hiking boots, found a flashlight, and climbed to the top of Gabriel's Point, where the gentle full moon shone benevolently on the little town and its odd collection of homes. Within many of those homes were patients who trusted her and who had confided the most personal and troubling facts about themselves as a result of that trust. She knew there were many ways their lives could be improved, and that because of her training, she could be instrumental in making some of these healthy changes happen for them. Even though she had been careful and taken small, gradual, conservative steps in educating and treating her patients, it had been too much for the Brethren, who seemed to think their authority and control were being directly challenged and even defied.

You're fooling yourself if you think the Brothers will change, Louisa. The mocking words seemed to emanate from deep within the hills themselves. Then she sensed a certain strength and calm as the red cliffs seemed to add, *But good for you, Dr. Martin, for taking on the Brothers!*

⁓

Louisa slipped inside the back door, boots in hand, and tiptoed toward the stairs.

"Good evening, Louisa," said a deep voice in the shadows of the room.

"Father!"

Joshua turned on a lamp. "You didn't expect me to sleep when you were tangling with the Council of Brothers, did you?"

Louisa swallowed. "Tangling?"

Joshua grinned. "I'm so proud of you! Oh, how I wish I could have seen the righteous indignation of the Council of Brothers as you recited the Hippocratic Oath!"

"How—how did you know about that?" Louisa gasped.

"There are very few secrets in Gabriel's Landing," said Joshua, a twinkle in his eye.

"It was out of line. I don't know what came over me."

"They are good men, Louisa, all of them. They're just not used to open opposition, especially from a woman. You took an enormous step for womankind tonight, my dear."

"But, Father, somehow they found out what we talked about in our weekly groups, and it wasn't all about a healthy pregnancy. And now that their husbands know, I'm a little worried about my patients."

"I know."

"I think . . . I think my days as a physician in Gabriel's Landing are coming to an end."

Joshua sighed. "And that will be our great loss."

"But Georgia and Emma are very competent. They'll know when something is too serious to for them to handle here."

"They lack your discerning eye and your years of training. But we'll have to accept what they can offer."

"And I've disgraced my family."

"I've never been more proud," Joshua said.

Louisa tried to process her father's last remark when he asked, "When do you appear before the Council again?"

"Four weeks."

"Four weeks? That's when I'll be meeting with them. I think we should go together, don't you? Just imagine the team we'd make! Like father, like daughter!" he rubbed his hands together with relish.

"Father!"

"Louisa, this is all about years and years of frustration I have known as a member of this community. I believe in plural marriage, and I try to live it the way my own father did, with respect and dignity and . . . and patience. I do not think we should take advantage of the government, and I believe we should take care of our own. We were given our brains and our agency to learn first-hand whether our choices were good or bad. Now, the Council of Brothers worries about anyone defying them or slipping out of their control. It brings to mind a scripture, though, in the Doctrine and Covenants, section one hundred twenty-one, verse thirty-nine:

" 'We have learned by sad experience that it is the nature and disposition of almost all men, as soon as they get a little authority, as they suppose, they will immediately begin to exercise unrighteous dominion.'

"And," Joshua said, standing up and heading for his study, dropping a fatherly kiss on her forehead, "just in case you've been shocked by my words tonight, you can rest assured that I will spend the night repenting."

Chapter Twenty-six

*Feathers attract lightning, so in a thunderstorm you must
keep away from your feather bed.*

—Miss Carolina's Remedies and Advice

"Olive, would you be able to be my . . . chauffeur . . . for a while?"

"Can't say as I've ever done that, Doc Andy. Is your car on the
blink?"

"I wish," sighed Andy, sitting across from his nurse.

"What's wrong?"

"I'm invoking doctor-patient confidentiality here," Andy said.

Olive leaned back, giving him a long look under arched eyebrows. "When my son was arrested for driving under the influence, we had to drive him around a bit until he paid his fine and
did his community service and got his license back, that is, when
he couldn't use his bike, but somehow I don't think you've been
driving drunk."

Andy managed a brief smile. "No, but the other night I did
drink a bottle of juice I found in the cupboard. It said 'elderberry'
on the label. How was I to know it was elderberry wine? I was
thirsty and it was delicious, and I drank the whole thing before I
realized there was a warm glow that started in my chest and just sort
of radiated outward from there. Pretty soon I was feeling mighty

fine and very generous toward all mankind and womankind."

"Saints preserve us!" laughed Olive.

"I had one heck of a hangover in the morning. Fortunately, it was Saturday, so I nursed it at home and no one was the wiser."

"Well, I'm glad you got that off your chest, Doc Andy. So I take it you need a driver but you haven't been arrested for DUI?"

"That might have been easier, if I'd been driving impaired. Alcohol leaves your system in a few hours. The problem is, for the next three months I'll be impaired, or at least potentially impaired."

"Well, now, you've confused me there."

Andy clicked a ballpoint pen, stared at the tip, and then clicked it again. Sure enough, the tip was gone. He continued to manipulate the pen as he told Olive, "Nobody here knows this. I mean, it wasn't relevant. You see, Eliza is a service dog. That's why she has a red vest, when I remember to put it on."

"And?"

"She's trained to anticipate epileptic seizures."

"I still don't see—"

"My epileptic seizures."

"Oh."

Andy met her sympathetic eyes and looked away. "I had a closed head injury in college. They thought it was just a severe concussion until I had a seizure. And then, a few days later, another . . . anyway, I was on medication, and I also got Eliza. She's trained to anticipate my seizures. She's amazing, and a wonderful companion, besides."

"Just what does she do?"

"There is evidently a chemical that's released before a seizure occurs. Originally service dogs were trained to help people with balance and mobility, and to help them open doors and many other tasks. But they found that these dogs also began acting strangely before their owner would have a seizure. They realized the dogs could detect that chemical, one humans can't recognize. So some dogs were trained especially for people with seizure disorders. In my case, Eliza starts barking and whining, and there's a certain tone to her voice that I only hear if there's going to be trouble.

When she warns me like that, it gives me time to find a private place, loosen my shirt collar, and lie down . . . if I don't respond to her warnings, she herds me into an empty room, leans on my legs until I lie down, and even tugs at my shirt collar. Then, if I'm not lying on my side, she nudges me and rolls me on my side and stays with me until I wake up. Usually, when I do come out of it, she's licking my face. Of course, I'm pretty disoriented for a while, and she hovers over me like a mother over her young." He took a deep breath. "I had a seizure last night. I haven't had one for more than four years. I had no clue it was coming on, but Eliza did."

"Last night? You mean after we all went home?"

Andy nodded. "Just as Mel was leaving, Eliza started to bark and whine. She got pretty frantic before I paid attention. I mean, we'd all been through a scary time, and she'd even bitten a man. I thought she was just letting off a little steam or something when she started to bark. It took me a while to recognize that particular sound in her voice. But when I did, I went inside and straight to bed.

"I'm not required to report this according to Kentucky law. I mean, as a physician, I don't have to report myself. If that makes any sense. But on Monday I'll check in with Sam Oliver—he's the neurologist in Taylor's Glen—and start on some meds. After three months without a seizure, the law says I'm safe to drive. Then I'll gradually wean myself off the pills and see how it goes."

"Well, now, Doc, you can depend on me. We won't say nothing and most folks probably won't notice you're not driving for a while. And I imagine you can ride Smoky around here. Nobody will have a second thought about that, either. I'll drive you to Taylor's Glen whenever you need to go. I know you go to church there. I haven't been to church myself for years, but what the heck, I'll take you to your Sunday meetings. Maybe the good Lord'll forgive me for a few of my shortcomings. I might even visit your meetings as long as I'm there."

"Olive, you are a gem."

"Just take care with that elderberry wine. It's mighty potent, Doc."

Chapter Twenty-seven

After the disciplinary hearing, Louisa was very busy at the clinic, though the number of patients she saw dropped sharply. She knew many were afraid to come, since she had been rebuked by the Council of Brothers. But she still opened the office faithfully every day, saw a few patients, and worked on her records.

One day, just as Louisa was ready to lock up, a timid knock at the back door surprised her. It was Carrie Stewart, holding her side and gasping. Blood trickled from a gash in her scalp. Louisa put her arm around the woman and helped her into an examining room. When Carrie lifted her blouse, Louisa was shocked to see bruises and welts forming across her back. When Louisa told Carrie she would drive her to the nearest emergency room for X-rays, Carrie did not resist.

On the way, Carrie told Louisa, slowly, shame and humiliation in her face and voice, what had happened. It was no different, she confessed, than the numerous other occasions when Harrison had lost his temper over a small matter.

"He's usually sorry afterwards and treats me nice for a while, but then his temper starts to get uglier and uglier. But I realized tonight, for the first time, that I hadn't done anything to deserve this."

"It's never right for a husband to strike his wife or children, no matter what they do, Carrie."

"That's something I never knew, really, until you came home. I thought about it a lot, and I believe you're right. That's why I'm willing to tell them what happened. I don't care if it humiliates my husband. He had no right to hit me, and if I don't do something about it, he'll do it again. But, I don't have a way to support myself or the children. They love their father. I'd be breaking up a family. Still, it's not right, what he does."

"All of that can be worked out, Carrie. Right now we need to get you treated and make sure you're safe. There are places you can stay where he isn't allowed to see you, and counselors who can provide you with the help you need. By law, you know, I must report this. If I don't, I'm breaking the law. Do you understand that, Carrie?"

The small woman nodded. "Yes. I know this is only the beginning. It's probably going to get uglier, isn't it?"

Louisa sighed. "I'm afraid so, when Harrison finds out, when he's arrested for assault. But don't worry. I'll be with you every step of the way."

Four hours later, after Carrie had been treated and had made a statement to police in Cedar City, she was taken to a safe home. "There are phones for you to use. Call me anytime at the office, even if you just need to talk, all right?"

"Yes," Carrie said. "You know, I've taken this for a lot of years, but I began to realize that's what my daughters will expect from their husbands. They'll think it's their fault, the way I have all these years."

"Then you may break the cycle. You're doing a good thing for your family, remember that."

State and local authorities had maintained a simple policy toward Gabriel's Landing: Let them take care of their own. However, Carrie's "betrayal" of her husband and the criminal charges against him caused a flood of media attention, focused on Gabriel's Landing. She and her unmarried daughters were driven from one safe house to another under cover of darkness. Harrison Stewart, outraged, was soon out on bail.

Reporters from newspapers and television stations camped around Gabriel's Landing, clamoring for interviews. "No comment," was Louisa's reply as she hastily shut the door in their faces. A virtual hostage of the press, her every move outside her home was followed and documented. She was grateful they didn't have televisions in Gabriel's Landing; she realized her picture would show up on the six o'clock news across the state. No doubt, she thought grimly, the story would also be picked up by national wire services.

There was plenty of material for the press without her cooperation, as the media took pictures of some of the poorer homes and their inhabitants, if they were unlucky enough to step out for a moment. Finally, a team of men with shotguns blocked the only road in and out of town, preventing the intruders from getting any more glimpses of life in Gabriel's Landing, so the reporters merely backed off and took pictures with powerful zoom lenses instead. They also found ample information by interviewing former residents of Gabriel's Landing and other polygamous communities, people who had left, been invited to leave, who had lost their property, or in some cases, had actually escaped. They were only too happy to answer questions in detail.

~

There was one more thing she could do on behalf of her patients, and without a pang of conscience, during the quiet days at the clinic, Louisa had altered her medical records. It was clearly unethical but completely justifiable in her mind. In some cases she even destroyed her patients' records that had references to birth control, depression, abuse, or suspicious miscarriages, because she knew the records would eventually become the property of the Brothers. It was her last act, as their physician, to protect her patients.

Her purge was thorough. She recopied handwritten notes

and revised them as necessary. She secured a post office box in Cedar City and mailed all the originals to it. She reviewed every document on her computer, including the billing and records, and, after copying them onto disks, systematically deleted the same material she had expunged from patient folders.

Making a backup disk of her remaining programs and her "cleansed" data, Louisa put the clinic's computer tower in a trash bag and drove to Cedar City.

"Louisa! Louisa Martin! Gosh, it's been a long time since high school!" Ken Hammond said as she entered his computer store. "You haven't changed a bit."

She noted Ken's thinning hair, the reading glasses perched on the end of his nose, and his expanding waistline, and smiled at him. "Neither have you. This is quite a business you have here."

"We work hard. Being a geek in school paid off. So, what can I do for you?"

"If someone wanted to . . . give their computer to someone else, and they didn't want any information left on it, they should reformat the hard drive, right?"

Ken nodded. "But fragments of information will still be on the hard drive, even after you reformat."

"Really?"

"It takes an expert to find them and reconstruct the data, but it can be done."

"You mean you can't really erase everything?"

"Technically, nope." Ken shook his head.

"So, what would you advise this person to do, then?"

"To be safe? Get a new hard drive. Destroy the old one."

"Do you have any new hard drives on hand, Ken?"

"Sure do. In fact, I can even install it for you right now; it'll just take a few minutes. Did you bring your, I mean, the other person's backup disk and software? And is your computer in your car?"

Louisa flushed. "Was I that obvious?"

Ken smiled. "It doesn't matter to me where this computer's been or where it's going. It just needs a new hard drive, and that's easily remedied."

Louisa sighed in relief. "Thanks."

When the new hard drive was functioning and all her data and programs transferred to it from the backup disk, Ken said, "What shall I do with the old hard drive?"

"What do you recommend?"

He found a hammer and gave it to her. "Give it a few good whacks."

Louisa hit the hard drive with the hammer.

"You can do better than that. Harder."

After five more blows with the hammer the old hard drive, and anything that might have been on it, was destroyed.

"You're relieved," Ken said, tossing the dented metal box into a box marked "recycle."

"I am. I imagine you've got a television. I understand I've been on the news."

He nodded. "I'm sorry about everything that's happened. But I'd expect nothing less of you."

"What do you mean?"

"You were always a person of principle. No pun intended. You would always put your patients' needs first. I'm proud of you, Louisa, and proud to know you, for what it's worth."

Louisa smiled gratefully at her old classmate, one of the few kind faces she had encountered that day. "Thank you, Ken. That means a lot to me."

He carried the computer to her car and slipped it into the empty garbage sack. "If anyone saw you here today and asks me about it, I repaired your printer." He shook her hand firmly. "That's my story and I'm sticking to it. Take care, Louisa."

Louisa took the computer back to the clinic and plugged it in again. Then she headed home for dinner. To her dismay, Amy had come home from school in tears, having been disciplined for causing a disruption in class. The disruption, Louisa determined after careful questioning, occurred because Amy defended her oldest sister when others shouted taunting insults. Her younger brother Danny had a black eye but refused to talk about it. The quilts Aunt Hannah had hung on the clothesline that morning had been slashed in broad daylight, but no one knew a thing about it.

The next morning, Sarah's roses had been hacked to mere pathetic twigs, petals and leaves and blossoms littering the garden, and all that remained of her prized chickens was a pile of bloody feathers. A hand-lettered "closed" sign was taped to the clinic's front door.

Chapter Twenty-eight

Louisa still had a key to the clinic, and that night she made a stealthy trip to retrieve a few belongings. She packed her stethoscope in her medical bag, looked around the clinic one more time, turned off the lights, and locked the door. On the desk was a letter addressed to the Council of Brothers. It contained a check, covering the final installment of the $30,000 they had invested in her education. Her modest salary had been applied to this loan from the first day she began practicing in Gabriel's Landing; she had also saved money from her stipends as a resident, and the Martha Hughes Cannon award of $50,000 had been a godsend. Now she was debt-free.

What would Dr. Cannon think of her? Louisa wondered. Dr. Cannon had apparently balanced it all: professional, personal, family, and even her political activities that were very controversial in her day. Still, Louisa liked to think that Martha Hughes Cannon would have advocated education and enlightenment and spoken out against cruelty and narrow-mindedness.

It was a short walk home, and she was nearly there when she remembered the picture of Andy, face-down in the bottom desk drawer. No doubt he had met another girl, a good Mormon girl, and was married by now. Still, she couldn't bear to leave his picture behind.

She walked back to the clinic, retrieving the picture from the desk drawer. Wiping a bit of dust off the glass, she studied the photo—Andy with his engaging smile, straight light brown hair, and blue eyes. The picture was, how old now? Probably six years or so. But she doubted he'd changed very much. Andy. Another heartache.

She shut the drawer and heard the shattering of glass, quickly followed by the smell of smoke. She dropped to the floor and waited, her heart pounding, until the back door slammed and she was reasonably sure the intruder had left. The reception room began to fill with smoke. Coughing, she crawled on the floor until she found the source of the blaze, a stack of paper towels burning in the restroom. She grabbed the fire extinguisher and put out the blaze quickly. Then she opened the windows and doors. Rushing outside to catch a breath of clean air, she waited until most of the smoke had cleared before she went back inside to investigate. The cause was evident; someone had broken the bathroom window with a brick, ignited a pile of paper towels, and fled out the back door.

Heartsick and exhausted, she locked the clinic for one last time. She would report the fire and the broken window in the morning and let someone else handle the mess. She took her key and slid it under the door of the small room in the church where she had been formally disciplined by the Council of Brothers. Her one comforting thought was that Andy's picture was probably responsible for saving the building.

Chapter Twenty-nine

A dead snake hung on the fence will bring rain.

—Miss Carolina's Remedies and Advice

Andy opened the door and slid out of his Jeep with a heavy heart. This was the worst part of his job, delivering bad news to patients and their families. Harm Collins had advanced lung cancer by the time Andy sent him for X-rays and scans in Taylor's Glen, when he had first come to Hawthorn Valley. Surgery and chemotherapy had followed, but Harm had still played with the band as long as he was able to muster the strength to practice and perform.

Today Andy held the latest fax from Harm's oncologist in his hand. The news was grim, and he prayed he would be able to give Harm and his family some comfort. Harm's face held the look of death. He was pale and thin; chemo had robbed him of his hair. The oxygen machine ticked rhythmically as it delivered measured doses of oxygen through the nasal tube.

"Well, Harm, Cora, how's it been going?"

"Can't get him to eat," Cora said.

"Nothing tastes good. I'm not hungry," whispered Harm.

Andy nodded. "I have the latest reports from the specialists in Taylor's Glen and Lexington, from the blood tests and X-rays. Your tumors aren't any bigger, but they're not any smaller, either.

It appears the chemo isn't shrinking them, and it's only making you sick and anemic. We're all very sad and very discouraged. I'm sorry I don't have better news or any other treatments to offer."

Harm nodded. "Figured as it wouldn't be good news, or I'd be feeling better."

"We can give you a blood transfusion in the morning in Taylor's Glen. It's just a temporary boost to get more oxygen to your brain for a couple of days, so you can make decisions with your family."

Harm shook his head and timed his speech to the pace of the oxygen the machine delivered to his lungs. "We've talked about all that. Cora knows my wishes. Saw the lawyer, and the will's in order. Visited with the minister and took care of a few matters on my conscience. Harm Junior has finished the last of the two fiddles we started together, and they're beauties. Over the years, them fiddles has made it so Cora will be comfortable for the rest of her life. Guess I'm ready to move on."

"Then," said Andy, "what we need to do now," he put his hand on Cora's shoulder, "is to make Harm as comfortable as possible. It won't make a difference if he eats or not. If something sounds good to him, by all means, fix it for him. If he doesn't want to eat, it's all right."

"Well, that's a relief," said Cora. "I've been trying so hard to find something he'd eat."

"How's the pain, Harm?"

Harm gave a grim smile. "It's like an in-law who won't go home."

"It's getting worse?"

Harm nodded.

"It keeps him awake at night," said Cora.

"We can start you on morphine patches, Harm. I brought some today. Cora, I'll show you how to use them. They deliver a constant amount of morphine through the skin. And you can add another patch if the pain gets too bad. I'm not worried about addiction at this point."

"Only addiction I ever had was cigarettes," Harm's whisper

was raspy. "And to tell the truth, I'd sure like one now. Even though I know it's cigarettes that done this."

"But he can't, with the oxygen and all, can he?" Cora asked.

Andy shook his head. "No. But we'll try to make you more comfortable, Harm. Olive will stop by in the morning and I'll come at night to check on you. And you can call me anytime, Cora. You know that."

The woman's tired, drawn face showed the toll Harm's illness had taken. Their oldest daughter walked into Harm's room, saw Andy, and fled to the kitchen.

"She's not taking this well," Harm said.

"Who's taking care of Cora?" Andy asked, searching her face.

Her eyes held a look of determined pride. "Oh, I can take care of myself," she said, straightening her shoulders.

"You're worn out. You need a break. Is there somebody who can come and stay with Harm for a while, so you can take a walk, or a nap? What about the kids?"

"Well, as you know, they're all grown up. But they all live within a stone's throw from us. Harm Junior's real good to come every evening and read to his pa. Harm looks forward to that. And of course Harm Junior's taken over the violin making business. Harm thinks he's right capable. Even shared all his trade secrets so the family tradition can continue."

Andy nodded. "Good."

"But our oldest daughter, well, you saw her. She can't handle it. I guess I ought to set 'em all down and have a talk," Cora said.

"And surely there are neighbors who can help?"

"Oh," said the woman, "they've offered. Maybe I could use a little help."

"A pot of soup now and then?" suggested Andy.

She met his eyes with grim resolve. "It's hard to be on the receiving end."

"It is. But you've been a good neighbor to them. They'd like to do the same for you."

"I'll speak to the kids tonight and we'll . . . set up a schedule. And when the neighbors call, Doc Andy . . ."

"Let 'em help," whispered Harm. "You're working too hard, Cora."

Cora nodded.

"Doc Andy?"

"Yes, Harm?"

"Guess you'll have to be thinking of a replacement for me in the band."

Tears stung Andy's eyes. "Harm, I—"

"Be sure to teach 'em all the new songs, the ones you brought all the way from Utah."

"There's no replacing you, Harm."

"Whoever you get, they'll be second rate, I know, but teach 'em anyway."

Andy mustered a smile as he took the man's hand, cold and weak.

"That," he said, "I will promise to do."

As Andy opened the door to leave Cora said, in a low voice, "How much longer do you figure he's got, Doc?"

"A couple of weeks, maybe, if he's not eating. It's all right, Cora. That's the body's way of shutting down, one system at a time. It's hard to watch, but this will run its course. You just keep him comfortable and gather your family around you, and we'll see Harm through to the end."

The end came ten days later. Cora called, and in a trembling voice said, "I think he's passed, Doc Andy. I can't feel a pulse or nothing."

"I'll be right over."

The church bell rang seventy-two times, once for each year of Harm's life. "It's Harm," people said, stopping their work to listen. "Godspeed, old friend."

Two days later Harm Collins was lowered into the ground in a pine box while Harm Junior played "Amazing Grace" on his father's favorite fiddle. The fierce March wind cut through even the warmest of coats, so the preacher's brief remarks were warm, followed by an earnest prayer for the soul of Harm Collins and the loved ones he left behind. Mourners laid flowers on the casket and began to slowly make their way home.

Cora approached Andy. "I want to thank you," she said. "For everything." Andy always felt helpless when he lost a patient, and wished he could have done more. It was hard to know what to say.

"As you know, we called all the family together, after you told us the end was near. Everybody came around, Doc. We all had some good visits with Harm. There was a good feeling in the house. He went peaceful. That's a blessing."

Andy took her hand. "It was. Now, you take care of yourself."

She looked at the flower-covered coffin and nodded.

"Godspeed, Harm," Andy murmured, and turned his back against the bitter wind.

Three weeks later Andy opened a knock at his door and found Cora Collins at his doorstep, holding a large box in her hands. "Cora, it's good to see you. Come in."

The woman looked tired, he noticed, but seemed to have an air of acceptance about her.

"I miss Harm more'n I can say. Some days is worse than others."

Andy nodded.

"Harm left you something, Doc Andy."

"He did? That wasn't necessary."

"Harm wanted you to have it." She handed him the box. "Open it."

Inside the box Andy found a violin, worn from years of being played, and a bow. "Harm's old fiddle? Oh, Cora, I can't accept this. You're very kind, and so was Harm, but this should stay in his family."

Cora shook her head. "No, the kids each have their own. Harm said you needed to take some lessons but you'd get the hang of it real quick."

Andy traced the curved lines of the instrument with his hand.

"It's his way of staying in the band, you know."

"Well," Andy cleared his throat, "I'm honored, Cora. I promise you, and Harm, that I'll learn to play this old violin. And when I'm good enough, I'll play fiddle in the band. In Harm's memory."

"That's all he wanted, Doc. Thank you for everything. Oh, and look inside."

Newly printed, inside, under the bridge area, were Andy's initials and the date. His eyes misted over. "Thank you, Cora," he said, kissing her wrinkled cheek. "And thank you, Harm," he murmured, with an upward look.

"I think he heard you, Doc."

Chapter Thirty

After the clinic was closed, Joshua spent the better part of two days in his study with the door closed. Then Louisa did what no one had ever done before when Joshua closed the door to his sanctuary—she knocked. Without a word, Joshua opened the door and then closed it behind her.

She left Gabriel's Landing the next morning. Breakfast was a silent meal, punctuated by a few sniffles and nose-blowings, but Louisa was touched when Aunt Hannah served her favorite cinnamon rolls, fresh and warm, a gesture that said more than Hannah could express in words. She had also filled a cardboard box with a dozen more, and Hannah had packed a picnic basket with sandwiches and fruit.

Few words were exchanged that morning, but more than a few tears were shed.

Louisa hugged her brothers and sisters one by one and promised to write. Then she inspected Samantha's chubby baby, who had a slight rash. That's all it was, she reassured Samantha, and told her where to find the over-the-counter hydrocortisone ointment. Rachel Louisa grinned, revealing two small, even white teeth.

I'll probably never see little Rachel Louisa again. I won't see any of you again.

Her immediate family, her brothers and sisters and their spouses, had supported her through the ugly times. They would never know how much strength she had drawn from their loyalty.

Sarah and Hannah had not blamed her for the destruction of their quilts and chickens and rosebushes. If they had, Louisa thought, maybe she could have summoned some anger toward the people who had hurt her family, and then she could have drawn upon that anger to maintain her own composure, so saying good-bye wouldn't have been so painful. She hugged her aunts, who gave her a bit of loving motherly advice, as they always did, to take care of herself. They assured her again that everything could be replaced. Sarah wasn't certain the old rosebushes had been completely destroyed; with some tender attention, they might recover and bloom again. Joshua had already ordered a flock of fine hens, they told her, a dozen new rosebushes, and new fabric for quilts. They would be very busy quilting this winter. The first one would be a Grandmother's Flower Garden in their favorite blues and yellows, and it would be for Louisa.

Louisa wasn't sure her aunts fully understood why she had taken the actions that had torn the town apart and put it under the media's intrusive microscope, but their support and belief in her had never wavered. When Louisa thought of forgiveness, she had only to remember the unconditional love of Hannah and Sarah. And Father.

The last and hardest farewell was with her father, who met with her in the privacy of his study, where he gave Louisa her mother's Bible. They knelt on the worn carpet, and he offered a quiet, humble prayer for her safety and protection as she embarked upon this new journey in her life. "We ask Thee to bless Thy daughter, Louisa, that she might continue to minister to Thy Children, to relieve pain and suffering according to Thy will. Bless her with peace in her heart and help her to find a joy and contentment in her new life. Help her to know of Thy love and to seek Thy guidance in all that she does."

When they rose to their feet he startled her by saying, "And when you get settled in Salt Lake City, I'm coming to visit you." Normally, only the men left the community, and then only for work and essential shopping trips. No one ever ventured as far as Salt Lake City. Louisa hadn't expected any contact other than letters, but Joshua would defy the Brothers yet again on her behalf. He reached into a drawer in his desk and pulled out a check. "I know you've paid all your debts, but that hasn't left you with very much. Rent can be expensive in the big city, and you'll need this to get started. And yes, you can pay me back, if you must. Interest free."

The media had painted shocking stories about polygamous families, some of which contained sad truths, but if they had only lived in Louisa's home, where harmony and affection dwelt, where differences were resolved with the kind guidance and wisdom of her father and his patient, gentle wives, they could have depicted a polygamous family that functioned well, a family that did not know poverty, a home where abuse did not occur, an environment where she'd been taught everything that was good and true in her own character.

The red dirt-packed roads were deserted, but Louisa knew she was being watched from behind the folds of the heavy drapes protecting the windows of the houses she drove past on her way out of town. Though still dressed in her traditional outfit, she had only packed her "outside world" clothes to take with her, leaving the rest of her old-fashioned dresses hanging in the closet. No doubt they would be shared with other women her size, as nothing was ever wasted in Gabriel's Landing.

An hour after she left, when the tears and sobs had subsided, she stopped at a service station. In the restroom she splashed cold water on her puffy eyes and washed her face, patting it dry with a paper towel. She took a small bag out of her purse and applied a light layer of foundation, a little mascara, and a subtle shade of lipstick. She unzipped her gym bag and pulled out jeans and a University of Utah polo shirt. Quickly shedding her old Gabriel's Landing attire, she changed her clothes and slid her feet into soft white crew socks and high-tech running shoes.

Now for the hair. Down came the braids, which needed little prompting to separate into single wavy strands. She held her hands under the running tap and ran them through her hair to dampen it. Then she brushed it and left it loose, flowing over her shoulders and down her back. She would shorten it by a few inches, maybe even six or eight, when she was settled. "A woman's hair is her crowning glory," Rachel had always said as she brushed and braided her daughters' hair. What would Rachel think of her now? Louisa had lost any crown she might have worn and had driven out of Gabriel's Landing in a cloud of dust and disgrace, not glory.

But when she looked at herself in the mirror, she liked what she saw, for the serious woman who regarded her had courage and determination in her eyes, though they were reddened from crying.

She arranged her hairpins, rubber bands, and assorted hair clips in a neat line on the counter next to the sink. She took her ankle-length high-necked dress and draped it over the paper towel dispenser. Her oxford-style shoes, with the long black stockings stuffed inside, went on the floor below the dress. After a moment's hesitation she arranged the homemade constricting brassiere that was more like a corset, the modest camisole and knee-length white cotton bloomers, next to the hairpins. All she needed to complete the picture was a sunbonnet. Too bad she had left that home—at her father's home, she corrected herself. It was her home no longer.

Chapter Thirty-one

Louisa soon found an apartment in Salt Lake City, small and comfortable, and a new job at the Highland Medical Clinic. She had felt awkward during the interview, certain that the clinic administrator knew all about the trouble in Gabriel's Landing, but he never mentioned it. He simply reviewed her resume and offered her a job in obstetrics, where they were short-staffed.

On her first day at work, anxious and a little apprehensive, she stepped out of the elevator and heard someone call her name.

"Louisa? Louisa Martin! Is that you?"

"Jim! Jim Christensen!" What a welcome sight, a familiar sight, an old friend from medical school. But something about Jim was different. It took Louisa a moment to decide what was missing. Andy, Jim's sidekick all through school, was missing. She forced herself to put aside the mental picture of Andy and Jim, fast friends, the Mutt and Jeff of her medical school class.

"Hey," he said, giving her a hug, "It's so good to see you! What are you doing here?"

"Same thing you are. I'm employed here. Actually," she looked at her watch, "I start in about twenty minutes. You know how I am about punctuality."

"You're working here?"

"Didn't you read all about the trouble in Gabriel's Landing? I had to leave."

Jim shifted his weight from one side to the other. "Yeah, you were big news, Louisa, but just for a while. I'm sure everyone's forgotten about it. Well," he said in response to the disbelieving look she gave him, "most people have forgotten. I'm so sorry you had to go through all that."

She nodded.

"So you're living in Salt Lake City? Why didn't you call me? I could have helped you find a place and move all your furniture in."

She gave a wry smile. "I've always carried a lot of baggage, Jim, but not that kind. There wasn't much to move. It all fit in my car."

"Baggage goes there," Jim said with a nod toward a closet marked "storage."

Louisa smiled.

"Well, you'll be a great addition here. I'm in sports medicine."

"Of course." She looked up at him; she had forgotten how tall he really was. "You look great, Jim."

"So do you. Listen, can you meet me for lunch? We have a lot of catching up to do."

"I think my social calendar is open for lunch. Sure."

"Then meet me at noon right here by the elevator. The food in the cafeteria isn't half bad."

Over the course of the next few days, Louisa was introduced to most of her colleagues by Jim, who made the transition to her new job much easier.

"Louisa's my old pal from med school," he told everyone. "Top of our class." If anyone recognized her from the news or knew anything else about her background, they kept it to themselves. For that she was especially grateful.

"You look so familiar," one of the internists said at lunch one day, sitting across from Louisa, "but I can't place you." He gave a slight wince and shot a questioning look at Jim, and Louisa knew Jim had administered a swift kick under the table. The internist would recall soon enough, she knew, but it was all right. Hopefully her new colleagues could move beyond her background and focus on the present. Three other physicians on staff were also from their class at the U, and Louisa found herself invited to dinner at Market Street Grill that night. When she hesitated, thinking of her modest bank account, one of her old classmates quickly invited everyone to an impromptu potluck dinner instead. Louisa appreciated the warm welcome, and the paychecks, and soon she felt comfortable in her new job.

"Come to a musical on campus with me tonight," Jim said one day. "At Kingsbury Hall. It will be like old times. You haven't been back to the university yet, have you?"

"No," she admitted.

"Maybe it's time."

She looked into his kind hazel eyes and gave him a grateful smile. "You know I can't resist a musical, and oh, Jim, it's been so long! I've missed the theater so much."

———

The orchestra was tuning up as Jim and Louisa found their seats. She looked around with a smile at the familiar murals on the wall of the historic old theater. She opened her program and began to read about *Joseph and the Amazing Technicolor Dreamcoat*.

"Do you remember the last time you were here, Louisa?" Jim asked.

"I haven't been here since graduation."

"I know. I can still see your face, the way you looked that day, when they called your name, when they gave you the Martha Hughes Cannon award. I think I was the first one on my feet."

"So it was you!"

"What do you mean?"

"The standing ovation. You started it? I was overwhelmed. That was the first, and hopefully last one I'll ever have."

"If I hadn't jumped to my feet, I know a hundred other students in our class who would have."

"That award made all the difference," she admitted. "Financially, of course, it was more money than I'd ever seen in my life. It still is. Was. You know what I mean. Anyway, I was pretty thrifty during my four years of internships and residencies, and by the time I left Gabriel's Landing, I was completely out of debt."

"That's admirable. Most of us are just starting to repay our student loans. But I don't regret going to medical school at all. Do you?"

"Oh, no. I can't imagine doing anything else. I guess I was programmed to want a career in medicine since I was a little girl, with my father telling me all about the remarkable woman named Martha Hughes Cannon. But in the end I had to want it, and I did. Even if I couldn't complete my father's dream for me."

The lights flickered and then dimmed, and an expectant hush fell over the audience.

"I don't know when I've laughed so much," Louisa said as they walked across the campus afterward.

"I've seen *Joseph and the Amazing Technicolor Dreamcoat* at least four times," Jim said, "and I always find it hilarious. What did you think was the funniest scene?"

"I think it was . . . when Joseph was showing off his coat and naming all the colors in it. He said something like, 'I am handsome, I am smart . . . ' "

" 'I am a walking work of art.' It's so therapeutic to laugh, isn't it?"

"Oh, yes. And of course it's touching when Joseph is reunited with his family."

"I'm so sorry you had to leave your family."

Louisa shrugged. "At least happy endings are possible in the theater."

"I can't offer you a happy ending, either," Jim said, "but I can offer you a pizza. Will that do?"

She smiled. "Yes. But only if it's pepperoni."

Chapter Thirty-two

One morning, when she had been at the Highland Clinic a month, Louisa paused at the examining room door and read the name on the folder. Molly Rawlins. She smiled. Molly was a young girl, pregnant, due any day, who was going to give her baby up for adoption. It was one of the most painful experiences a girl could have, she imagined. But despite her difficult situation, Molly had an engaging personality, a frank manner, and a charming Kentucky accent. She loved her new life in Salt Lake City, and Louisa could identify with that.

"My doc at home is from Utah, too," Molly told Louisa. "Maybe you know him."

Louisa smiled. "Utah's a pretty big place."

Molly laughed. "That's true. I've never been in such a big city. It's beautiful here. And I love the mountains. They're so tall. Taller than anything I've ever seen. Anyway, Doc Andy from home, he's the one who found me a place to stay here."

"Your Doc Andy sounds like a great guy."

"Oh, he's the best. Everybody really likes him, even though he talks funny—well, I mean, he talks like most people in Utah do. I guess I'm the one with the accent. He told me I'd be, but

I keep forgetting. Anyway, he plays in a bluegrass band. And he even has a dog with a middle initial and a last name."

Louisa froze, pen in hand. "He does?" she asked carefully.

"Yep. Her name's Eliza R. Snow."

Louisa closed Molly's chart. "And does your Doc Andy have a last name?"

"Uh-huh. It's McBride. Andy McBride."

But Louisa already knew that.

So Dr. Andy McBride was practicing medicine in Kentucky. The mention of a border collie's name was all it took for their mutual patient to innocently supply that information. Information easy enough to find, of course, but Louisa hadn't wanted to find it. And now what was she going to do with it?

Nothing. Andy had moved on, she was certain. It was all too painful to relive. But what did she counsel her patients to do? "Face your grief," she would tell them gently. "It's the only way to get through it." Finally, more than four years' worth of tears burst through the dam Louisa had so carefully constructed. She bent over her desk, buried her face in her folded arms, and wept for an hour. Her tears finally spent, she sat quietly and watched the sun go down behind the Oquirrh Mountains. Soon the city lights started to twinkle, and still she sat, staring out the window.

She heard someone fumbling with her doorknob. Jumping to her feet, she grabbed for the nearest object to use to defend herself, which turned out to be her stethoscope.

Someone reached for the light switch. "Louisa!"

"Jim!"

"I'm so sorry. I didn't know anyone was here, and I had to borrow a text from Dr. Franklin. I saw a shadow in your office and I thought I'd better check it out."

She sat on a corner of her desk, heaving a sigh of relief. "I was just . . . thinking, and I guess I lost track of time."

"I take it you were ready to defend yourself," he said with a nod at the stethoscope in her hand.

She looked down at the useless weapon and then, seeing the merriment in Jim's eyes, she said, "Don't tempt me, partner. I wield a pretty mean stethoscope."

They both laughed. Then Jim said, "Just let me know when you're ready to leave and I'll walk you to your car."

"Thanks," she said, grateful for his offer. The parking terrace was well lighted and patrolled by security, but she was always glad to be safely in her car with the doors locked. "Actually, I'm ready now." Quickly turning her back, she dabbed at her damp eyes and took a long drink from the bottle of water on her desk. She found her purse and keys and said, "All right, let's go."

Jim's company on the way to the parking garage was comforting. He had been to a conference on sports injuries and was enthusiastic about the new developments in sports injury rehabilitation. Louisa was happy to listen and glad she didn't need to say much. She found her car on the third level and unlocked it. "Thanks so much, Jim."

"Louisa?"

She looked up at him. "Yes?"

"Back in your office. When I startled you in the dark. That was about Andy, wasn't it?"

Louisa looked down at the keys in her hand. "How did you know?"

"Your eyes are a little red. I think I interrupted something."

Louisa sighed. "I just found out, inadvertently, that Andy's in Kentucky. I didn't know it would hit me so hard."

"Ah."

"Jim, please don't tell Andy where I am."

He shook his head. "I won't."

She looked up. "And don't tell me how he's doing, either."

"If you can reach my shoulder," Jim said, "feel free to cry on it."

An hour later, over dinner, Jim said, "I have a confession to make."

"What's that, Jim?"

"I had a crush on you in med school," he admitted with a boyish smile. "We all did."

"Me? With my old-fashioned—"

"Your old-fashioned beauty? Your mind? Your place at the top of the class? Shall I go on?"

"I . . . never imagined. I don't know what to say."

"You don't have to say anything. For you, it was always Andy," he said with a quiet sigh.

"But I have to move on. I'm not that girl anymore. I've had to reinvent myself."

"And you have. Just look at you, Louisa: new job, new apartment, new friends . . . you're doing a great job."

"Some days it's hard to remember who I was when I started med school. I'm sure everyone thought I was odd and shy and quiet and aloof."

"You *were* odd and shy and quiet and aloof."

She smiled. "And I didn't think it was wise to form any attachments. I was going back to Gabriel's Landing to practice, anyway. Other than my roommates, Andy was my first real friend at the U, and he had to work hard just to get me to play a game of foosball. But I have a new life now and new friends." She smiled at him. "Old friends, too."

"I hope you count me as one of them."

"Always, Jim. I can't imagine what these past few weeks would have been like without you. There could have been some awkward moments for everyone. But because of you, everyone has accepted me. I can't tell you how much that means to me."

He fiddled with the last bit of quiche on his plate. "I'm glad I could be there for you."

She thought for a moment and then asked, gently, "Is there a woman in your life, Jim?"

"No," he said, catching the waiter's eye. "Check please." Fumbling for his wallet, he said, "There's no one."

As he filled out the credit card slip she thought she heard him murmur, "No one like you, anyway."

Chapter Thirty-three

Andy read Molly's letter for the third time.

Dear Doc Andy,

I'm feeling stronger every day and I'm back in school now. My arm is all healed, too. Hugh is real happy in his new job in Taylor's Glen.

Giving up the baby was the hardest thing I've ever done, and they tell me I need to grieve. I guess I'll learn what that means. All I know is I'm very sad and there's an ache in my heart that won't go away.

Did I tell you about my doctor? Her name is Dr. Martin. When I told her about your dog's name, she seemed surprised. She knows who the real Eliza R. Snow was, too. Did I tell you how pretty Dr. Martin is? I've never seen such beautiful red hair. Not carrot red, but darker. She wears it in a French braid sometimes, and it looks so fancy. And she has the nicest smile.

I can hardly believe I'm in school. I'm wearing regular clothes like the other girls now, but I feel like somebody very different inside. I miss the baby and I'm sad. Did you know

it was a girl? Seven pounds, lots of dark hair. She was beau-
tiful. So tiny. They said she was perfect. Some days it's worse
than others. Dr. Martin said it would be like that.

  I decided to go to church with Karen's family. And I
met the bishop—he's like the minister. I guess you already
know that. He said he wanted to get acquainted, so we
had—what do you call it?—an interview. Anyway, I told
him who I was and why I was there and about the baby. We
talked about repentance. I didn't know much about repent-
ing, but I heard plenty about sin and going to hell from
my pa and the preachers at home. I feel like maybe God's
forgiven me because I did right by the baby and gave her
to good parents, and now the bishop says I have to forgive
myself. That's hard. But he says he knows I can do it and
I can talk to him anytime I want to. When our interview
was over he shook my hand and I felt—I felt better about
myself. It's hard to explain. But I like my new life here. It's
because of you, Doc Andy, and Olive and Karen and her
family and everyone who's been so good to me. School is
hard, but I'm catching up and I'm studying real hard.

                                        Love,
                                        Molly

Andy folded the letter and replaced it in the envelope. So
Louisa Martin was Molly's "beautiful lady doctor" in Utah. She
was probably doing an obstetric rotation in Salt Lake City, then.
No doubt her practice involved many obstetric cases.

He grabbed his coat, whistled to Eliza, ran to the barn, and
saddled Smoky. "Come on, old girl, don't hold back. We can both
work up a sweat." He buried his nose in the horse's mane. "And
maybe you ladies can give me some advice. About how to get
somebody out of my head. I'd be much obliged."

Chapter Thirty-four

Louisa twisted the strap of her handbag and fidgeted as she sat on the edge of her chair. The window of the LDS Church Office Building in Salt Lake City offered a splendid view of the multi-spired granite temple with the golden angel on top, the surrounding colorful gardens, and the busy city beyond Temple Square.

A middle-aged woman with a pleasant voice answered the phone at her desk and then smiled at Louisa. "He'd like to see you now."

Louisa stood as the office door opened. Elder Harris smiled and grasped her hand in a firm handshake. A tall silver-haired man with a slight stoop to his shoulders, he was dressed in the expected dark suit, white shirt, and conservative tie of an LDS leader. When she met his dark eyes, she felt he was looking right through to her soul. In a way, he reminded her of Joshua. He pulled two chairs away from the desk and gestured toward one.

"Tell me about yourself," he said, sitting in the other chair, "and why you're here today."

Louisa found herself telling him all about her upbringing, her education, her relationship with Andy, her expulsion from Gabriel's Landing, and her new job at the Highland Clinic.

"I was too idealistic to think I could honor my Hippocratic

Oath when it conflicted with The Principle. You do know what The Principle is?"

He nodded.

"And I'm sure you know the rest. It was in the news. About what happened."

"That must have been very difficult for you and your family."

She nodded. "I knew I could never live The Principle, and so did my father. During my four years of residency, I went to LDS meetings when I could. It just felt right. I made it the subject of prayer and my choice was confirmed. I didn't reveal my background to anyone—we're so good at keeping secrets anyway—but I imagine a few people suspected. Anyway, ward members were always kind and friendly. And then, when I moved to Salt Lake City, I decided to take the missionary lessons. The sister missionaries said I was a quick study."

He chuckled. "I'll bet you were. We share a common heritage, of course, and most of our religious beliefs are based on the same doctrines."

"That's what Andy always said when we argued, that if it wasn't for my upbringing in polygamy, I would have made a good Mormon."

Elder Harris smiled.

"My bishop and stake president have been wonderful, but they thought, given my unusual background, that I should have an interview with a General Authority—to get permission to be baptized," Louisa explained.

Elder Harris took an envelope off the edge of his desk and handed it to her. "I wrote this as soon as I received your note requesting this appointment. There was never any question in my mind. I just wanted to meet the remarkable young woman I'd heard about, and to give you a proper welcome to the Church."

Louisa's eyes brimmed with tears.

"Now, when are you going to make things right with Andy?" Elder Harris asked.

"What?" she gulped, her tears vanishing.

"I'd be delighted if you'd send me a wedding announcement."

Chapter Thirty-five

For burns:
Make a poultice of raw grated potatoes or turnips and
bind to the burn. Change poultice and apply a new one
each and every hour.

—Miss Carolina's Remedies and Advice

Andy reviewed the registration packet for the medical convention sponsored by Northwestern University School of Medicine in Chicago. The conference had not disappointed him; it had been time well spent. He loved the city, with its compelling architecture, great museums, old theaters, and famous restaurants. Walking to his room at the old Palmer House, he looked around appreciatively at the wood paneling, ornate moldings, crystal chandeliers, and elegant carpeted stairways. Music floated to the lobby from a grand piano played by a man in a tuxedo.

It was certainly strange to be in a big city after Hawthorn Valley. It was exhilarating, but Andy also felt a bit dazed, trying to process the sensory overload. He saw small groups of people, obviously attending conferences, as indicated by their name badges. Then his eyes rested on a lovely auburn-haired woman wearing a badge that said "Louisa Martin, MD."

Maybe the sensory overload was making him delusional. He

blinked, but the woman was still there, looking as surprised as he felt.

"Louisa?"

"Andy?" She clutched her folder to her chest.

"What are you doing here?" they asked in unison.

"Well," Andy said, "I guess it's obvious what we're both doing here. Attending the convention on family practice."

Louisa nodded.

Andy thought of a hundred things he wanted to say, but only one sentence came out. "So you've kept your maiden name?"

She nodded.

"How unusual, how very un-pluralistic of you."

"Un-what?"

Andy warmed to his interrogation, stepping back to take in the whole picture. "And where are the long dress and sensible shoes? I don't see a wedding band, but no doubt you were married the evening you arrived home in Gabriel's Landing."

A look of pain crossed her face, but once he had started, he couldn't stop. After all, she had walked away from him when they graduated from medical school. His eyes rested on her waistline. "Surely you're pregnant by now? If so, you're hiding it well, Doctor. But however did you get your husband's permission to leave the compound?"

"That," Louisa said, green flashes of anger in her eyes, "is enough, Dr. McBride."

"Yes, Dr. Martin, I suppose it is." Andy took a deep, shaky breath. He was shocked at his tone and his biting remarks, but his resentment had festered for nearly five years now, and all it took was one look at Louisa to cause it to explode.

"I have an engagement for dinner. You'll excuse me, I'm sure," she said, and walked away, her shoulders squared, head held high, and disappeared into the throng of conference attendees.

"Wait! Louisa, I didn't mean, well, I did, but I really didn't—" A few people had turned, suspending their conversations, and were staring at him. He jerked on his necktie, which was suddenly very confining. Then, to his relief, he saw a familiar back.

The back belonged to a tall man with dark, curly hair. Jim. Jim Christensen, his friend since boyhood. What great timing, to see a friendly face. "Jim! I didn't know you'd be here! Say, it's great to—"

Hearing his name, Jim turned his head and looked over his shoulder, a curious look on his face. Andy walked toward him, his arms open for a hug. But when Andy darted around a woman who had stepped in front of Jim, he saw that his old friend was already hugging someone: a woman with auburn hair. Jim's grip tightened on the woman, and the woman lifted her head from his chest. Her eyes met Andy's, a look of shock on her pale face.

Andy stood rooted to the floor in astonishment and confusion. Louisa Martin, the only woman he had ever loved, was wrapped in the tender, comforting embrace of Jim Christensen, his best friend. Without a word he wheeled around and headed toward the nearest door, nearly upsetting a waiter balancing a large tray of drinks. He found himself in a kitchen, hot and steamy, smelling like a dozen delicious dishes at once. A stocky cook looked up and said, "Hey, buddy, maybe you've had too much to drink. This is the kitchen."

"Sorry," Andy muttered. "But if I ever needed a drink, now would be the time to get good and drunk." He left the kitchen, spotted the nearest exit, and escaped into the night.

He walked up and down Michigan Avenue, oblivious to the traffic and the elegant storefronts and restaurants. Finally he strolled to the Chicago River and stared at the city lights reflected in it.

Did Jim like the citrus scent of Louisa's shampoo? he wondered.

Chapter Thirty-six

When Andy's grandfather turned eighty-five, the family held a party for him. Andy flew home to Salt Lake City for a brief weekend. Spring in Salt Lake City was always uncertain. Although the weather could be capricious, ranging from sunny to snowy in a single day, the sunny moments made him forgive the blustery ones. At Temple Square all the flowers were in bloom, more beautiful than ever. He knew their appearance was carefully timed by the gardeners who controlled the heated pipes below the beds, so that they bloomed for April conference, no matter what kind of spring had been sent to the valley.

The day after the party Andy drove to the Highland Clinic. He needed to apologize to Louisa. And to Jim. He found their names in the directory by the elevator and rode to the second floor.

"May I help you?" a pleasant woman said.

"I would like to see Dr. Louisa Martin." He began to sweat.

"I'm sorry, Dr. Martin is out of town until Friday. I can take a message if you'd like."

Andy shook his head.

"Would you like an appointment with one of our other physicians?"

"Is Dr. Christensen in, Dr. Jim Christensen?"

She consulted her computer. "Sorry, he's in surgery all day."

"Thanks."

Andy wandered forlornly out of the clinic, to the street where he'd parked Grandpa's new car, and smacked his hand on the hood in frustration. An earsplitting, shrieking wail made him cower, hands to his ears. Up and down the scale the alarm screamed, like one of Macbeth's witches, the echoes bouncing off the hard surfaces of the tall buildings and concrete sidewalks.

"It's the alarm, mister," said a skateboarding boy with multiple piercings and tattoos, dressed in baggy pants, the crotch nearly reaching his knees. He made a skillful jump over the curb. "Don't you know nothing?"

"No, I don't know nothing," Andy muttered, fumbling with the remote to disable the alarm.

When the wailing stopped, he unlocked Grandpa's car and slid in. He thumped his head against the steering wheel in irritation, and the horn blared. A nearby pedestrian jumped, and then flashed a universally unfriendly gesture. Andy slumped back in the driver's seat, closing his eyes.

Bad timing. Lately, he was all about bad timing. First there was the fiasco in Chicago, on the last day of the medical convention, when he had seen Louisa for the first time in nearly five years and, giving in to some impulse that had evidently been lurking in his soul for the whole five years, he had lashed out at her, and what he said was irrational, cruel, and humiliating. He had followed her, intent on apologizing, only to find her in the arms of his old friend. Then he had two people on his "apologies owed" list, but he hadn't found either of them before the convention ended. Now, a week later, there wasn't a place in Salt Lake City that didn't remind him of Louisa in some way. She was out of town and he was flying home in the morning. He smacked his forehead with his fist, buckled his seat belt, turned on the radio, and pulled out of the parking space.

"Jeremiah was a bullfrog," belted Three Dog Night. Andy jabbed at the radio controls and hastily changed the station. All he needed was to hear "Joy to the World," which Louisa had called "our song." She knew it was a drinking song, but it always made her smile. "You've exposed me to the devil's music," she had teased Andy.

He pulled into his parents' driveway. What he needed now was a swift ride into the hills on Smoky, with Eliza dashing along beside them. Today, however, he would have to be satisfied with a good run around the streets of his boyhood. No, he decided, he would change into his jogging clothes and drive to a neighborhood where nobody knew him. The last thing he needed was friendly neighbors stopping to greet him and ask him how life was in Kentucky, and was he married yet?

An hour later, hot and sweaty, he drove back home and headed for the shower. He reached for the shampoo and lathered his head vigorously. The shampoo had a familiar scent. Where had he smelled it before? It reminded him of oranges and lemons and spring rain . . . He opened his eyes, squinted at the bottle of shampoo, and read the label. Louisa's favorite shampoo. Suds dripped into his eyes, stinging them. He turned on the cold water full force and yelped when it hit his skin.

Chapter Thirty-seven

*Drink a cupful of strong coffee to remove the odor of
onions from the breath.*

—Miss Carolina's Remedies and Advice

"Yes!" Andy tore open the envelope. "Finland, here I come!" He
quickly scanned the list of participants in the exchange program,
twenty physicians from all over the country. He didn't recognize
any of the names. "I'll bet I'm the only one who speaks Finnish,
though."

He reached for his phone and called the physician's assistant
in Taylor's Grove, who often covered for him.

"Tim, can you and your partner arrange to cover my practice
for a month? Yeah, a whole month. Thanks a million. I owe you.
I'll leave you notes on any ongoing cases. Otherwise, you know
the drill. Where am I going? Oh, I have an opportunity to spend
a month in Finland, to learn about their health care system. We'll
get to visit some hospitals and shadow some physicians in various
specialties. Then they'll spend a month here in the states, doing
the same thing. No, Finland isn't frozen all the time! It's beautiful, and I can't wait to go!"

Two weeks later Andy stood in line at the airline counter, grunting as he lifted his heavy bag. His passport and tickets were examined and boarding passes were issued. There would be layovers in Cincinnati and Amsterdam. He calculated that it would take twenty-four hours in transit from Salt Lake City to the International University in Jyvaskyla, Finland. In his carry-on bag was an English-Finnish dictionary and a small case of CDs to practice his conversational skills. His Finnish was rusty at best; it had been nearly ten years since his return from his mission. He hoped his comprehension and reading skills would help him through, too.

He filed through security, taking off his shoes and belt, emptying his pockets into a small container, and putting his carry-on bag on the conveyor belt. Then he had to sit down, put on his shoes and belt, and account for his passport, boarding pass, and other carry-on items. He headed toward the gate, buying a cinnamon roll and a small carton of juice for his breakfast. At the gate he put on his earphones and listened to conversational Finnish, muttering to himself as he tried to brush up on the difficult language.

Finnish words tended to be long, with many syllables and vowels with dots over them and absolutely no similarities to Latin-based languages. The closest languages to Finnish, he had been told, were Hungarian and Estonian. How they had kept the language from being influenced by Russians and Swedes who had invaded the country in their earlier history, he didn't know, but there were no similarities to languages in nearby countries. His language instructor had told the class that the Finnish were fiercely independent, focusing on taking care of their own and staying out of other countries' affairs.

He listened to the phrases and repeated them quietly, feeling the unfamiliar words on his tongue, trying to regain some of the competence he had learned while in Finland.

The CD advanced to the food section, and he could almost smell the fresh grilled salmon and the small steamed yellow waxy potatoes that seemed to accompany every meal. There would be fresh fruits and vegetables and jelly-filled doughnuts, too. As a hungry young missionary he had even learned to like herring. Sounding more and more familiar, the food vocabulary words made him smile: *pannukakku* (pancake); *kaneliassat* (cinnamon cookies), *Karialanpiirakat* (Karelian pies with rice filling), *letut* (crepes), and *vispipuuro* (porridge).

He had a whole month to be a visitor instead of a missionary. During his two years in Finland, sightseeing was limited to excursions on P-Day, Preparation Day, when they also took care of laundry, letter writing, shopping, and cleaning their apartments. Then they could explore the city, always in pairs, never separated from their assigned companions. This time he could immerse himself in learning about the country's health care system and seeing as much of the country as he could.

When he took off his earphones, the gate attendant was announcing the final boarding call. Grabbing his possessions, he hurried to the counter, showed his boarding pass, and dashed down the tunnel to the plane. It was an enormous plane and, of course, his seat was in the middle of the row, where he would have to climb over people to get in and out. He jammed his larger carry-on bag into the overhead bin, found his seat, and shoved his backpack under the seat in front of him. The passengers on either side were settled, reading books and magazines. He tugged on his seat belt, fastened it, and leaned back with a sigh.

He was vaguely attentive to the usual safety presentation, and then they were moving on the runway. When the plane was in the air he decided to close his eyes and take a brief nap. It would be a grueling trip, and he should try to get a bit of sleep when he could. With the nine-hour time difference between the two countries, he knew he would probably suffer some jet lag anyway.

In Cincinnati, where he had a two-hour layover, he walked briskly up and down the terminal corridors, stretching his cramped muscles. Then it was on to Amsterdam and finally Helsinki. At Helsinki he cleared customs, got his passport stamped, and saw a man holding a sign: "Physicians International Exchange Program." Andy shook hands with their guide and struck up a conversation in Finnish. The man was surprised and responded with a smile. Where had Andy learned the language? he wondered, and one question led to another. The bus pulled up, and they were ushered onto it. The last to board, Andy took the seat behind the driver, across from their guide, who still wanted to talk.

Now it would be a four-hour trip to Jyvaskyla, where they would stay in a hotel for the first night. Or was it the first day? With the time difference, it was already tomorrow.

Their guide passed out their ID tags, which they were to wear at all times during lectures and clinical settings. He also advised them to keep the tags handy in case they got lost. The information on the picture ID would help others direct them back to the university or hospital, or to the home of their host families. Andy watched with interest as each name was called, a hand was raised, and a tag was given. He couldn't see many of the faces that belonged to the hands since the seats had high backs.

"Dr. Hatch, Dr. Weinstein, Dr. Wells . . . Dr. McBride." He raised his hand, and the guide handed him his tag. He slipped it around his neck. "Dr. Martin," said the guide, and walked to the back of the bus, where a hand was raised.

He sighed. When would he think of Louisa whenever something, as simple as a common surname, jogged his memory? He turned to the passenger next to him and introduced himself. Soon they were engaged in lively conversation.

"You speak Finnish?" one of the others asked, overhearing, incredulous.

"It's been years, and I've forgotten a lot. No doubt my accent will be terrible. But I'll probably understand a good portion of what people say. In Finland, though, just about everyone under age thirty speaks English, and they'll be anxious to practice their English on you."

"Well, I'm sticking with you," said the man on his left. "I imagine you'll be our official translator."

"Oh, no, they have plenty of those, and we'll manage just fine in English. But I'll be happy to translate whenever I can, if you have questions. I also have an English-Finnish dictionary, and that's really helpful."

"How did you learn the language?" the man behind him asked. That led to another explanation of Andy's mission. The man on his left stiffened a bit when the LDS faith was mentioned and casually picked up a magazine, while the woman on the right peppered him with questions about Mormonism. Andy began to feel like a missionary again. He tried to steal glimpses of the countryside as they traveled. It was as green and clean as he remembered. Pedestrian and bicycle paths paralleled the roads, and the wildflowers were in bloom. Andy marveled at these. In Utah, sagebrush and weeds grew next to most of the freeways, and once in a while were simply mowed down. Here, beautiful flowers sprung up voluntarily.

Four hours later, as they reached Jyvaskyla, their guide gestured to an old European-style building and said, "Tonight you will stay in this hotel. Tomorrow after breakfast in the hotel you will each meet your host family. Our first session will begin tomorrow evening. Here are your hotel keys and room numbers." He walked up and down the aisles, handing out keys.

At the hotel, Andy got off the bus with a tired sigh. At last they were here, and it felt so familiar. He collected his bag and then noticed a woman struggling to pull hers out of the pile of suitcases on the sidewalk.

"Here, let me get that for you," Andy said, and grasped the handle of the suitcase. He tugged and soon the luggage was free.

"Thank you, Andy," the woman said. She must have looked at his ID tag.

"You're welcome." He straightened to smile at her.

Then he froze. Surely it was not Louisa. He took in the auburn hair, green eyes, sprinkling of freckles . . . the name on her ID tag . . . Chicago flashed through his mind . . .

"Louisa? What are you doing here?"

She patted her ID badge. "The same thing as you, I imagine. I was a last-minute replacement for someone at the Highland

Clinic who couldn't go. Luckily I had a valid passport because I studied for three months in Mexico a few years ago."

"I don't know what to say."

She raised a warning hand. "I think you already said it."

"Chicago. That was . . . I was an idiot."

"Yes," she said, her face pale, as if she expected more abuse. "You were." She turned and picked up her bag.

"I was a stupid idiot. I was out of line. I tried to find you to apologize, in Chicago and then in Salt Lake, but I never found you. I thought about writing a letter, but I just couldn't even think of how to start it."

He studied her face. The look was cautious.

Finally she nodded. "I saw you at the Salt Lake airport. I didn't know you were headed for Finland, but here we are."

"I didn't know you were even here until two minutes ago."

"I've had a little time to get used to the idea that we were both going to be . . . here . . . for a month."

"You've had about twenty-four hours to get used to the idea. I'm still wondering if it's just let jag. Louisa, we're both exhausted, at least I am, but would you meet me for breakfast in the morning, please?"

"All right, breakfast."

She gave another nod, looked at her room key and the numbers and arrows on the wall, and turned to the left. Andy checked into his own room, phoned in a wake-up call, and within ten minutes he was sound asleep.

In the morning, when the phone rang, he rolled out of bed reluctantly, wishing for another eight hours of sleep, and headed for the shower. Ten minutes later he was in the dining room, waiting for Louisa. She walked in with a group of other doctors, and they were all laughing at something. They lined up at the buffet, exclaiming over the appealing spread. The breads and fresh fruits looked wonderful, and though it was surprising to see cucumbers and tomatoes at a breakfast buffet, they were eager to begin sampling Finnish cuisine.

Andy stood at the end of the buffet, his plate filled, and waited for Louisa. "Will you join us, Andy?" she asked, and introduced him to the others.

"Sure," said Andy, disappointed, and sat at a table with four other physicians. There would be no chance to apologize this morning.

After breakfast, host families arrived at the hotel and were introduced to the Americans who would be spending the next month with them in their homes, and within half an hour they had all left the hotel. Before leaving, Andy was approached by two of the other doctors.

"Uh, Andy, I have a question about the toilet in my bathroom, one of them said. "It has two buttons that flush the toilet, and some labels. . . Why are there two buttons, and does it matter which one I use?"

Andy grinned. "Yes, it does. Finland is ahead of most of the world when it comes to conservation. Use the button on the left if you need a . . . light flush, and the button on the right . . ."

"Oh. I suppose that does make sense. Thanks!"

He would find a time to talk with Louisa alone soon, he vowed. At least he could repair a bit of the damage, and perhaps they could feel less awkward.

The next few days were busy as the American physicians met the Finnish physicians and attended lectures and toured hospitals and clinics. Finally, when they had a free afternoon, Andy asked Louisa to go for a walk with him. Alone. He saw reluctance and caution in her eyes. She finally shrugged and nodded.

"Wear sturdy shoes and bring a coat," he told her.

Their destination was a grass-covered hill, much smaller and smoother than many they had climbed in Utah. "This is the only ski lift in Jyvaskyla," Andy said.

"You're kidding! They ski on this . . . little hill?"

"You won't find tall mountains around here. Cross country skiing is more common than downhill in the winter. But in the summer, well, just look at the view from this hill." He nodded toward the scene below them and Louisa gazed at it, her eyes widening.

"Beautiful, isn't it?"

"Well, if you like forests and lakes and forests and lakes," she finally said. "And wildflowers. It's breathtaking."

Andy determined that the grass was dry and sat, patting the grass beside him. Louisa sat a safe distance away.

"I need to explain about Chicago," he said.

She was silent, looking down at the beautiful sight below them.

"I was stunned to see you. I didn't even know you'd left Gabriel's Landing."

"That's hard to believe," she said. "It was all over the news."

"That's just the thing," he told her. "I'd check the headlines of the Salt Lake papers, mostly sports, I'm afraid, on the Internet. It was too painful to read about what was happening with the polygamy . . ." He wanted to say "mess," but knew that wasn't appropriate. "With the polygamy situation. I honestly didn't know anything that happened at Gabriel's Landing."

"Well, you missed some sensational stories. The press loved it. I understand I even showed up on CNN."

"I know. I did some research in the newspaper archives when I got home from Chicago. I'm so sorry about what happened. You could have done so much good for your people. And I'm sorry you had to leave your family. I know you were so close to them."

She shrugged. "I thought, since your parents knew about me, they might have said something to you."

"Louisa, look at me."

She gave him a sideways glance.

"That was a subject I wouldn't discuss with them, so I wouldn't have expected them to mention anything about it. Do you believe me?"

"I guess," she said. "All right, I do. It was a terrible time in my life."

"I can't imagine. Anyway, when I saw you in Chicago, I was . . . surprised. Astounded. Shocked. Confused. Clueless. Speechless."

"Angry and bitter."

"I didn't even know I'd harbored that much bitterness so long. I even thought I was starting to forget you. But there you were, looking so, well, so like yourself, you know, but instead of being happy to see you, and at least being civil, I was, well, it was unforgivable. I had no right to say any of that."

She nodded.

"And I realized I still cared for you, after all this time, after everything that's happened."

Louisa was silent for several minutes, weaving a slender wreath of wildflowers. Then, in a quiet voice she said, "If you really cared, why did you give up on us, Andy?"

"Why did I give up? *You're* the one who went home to Gabriel's Landing! That said volumes about how you really felt. Didn't it?"

She shook her head. "You could have come for me."

"Come for you?"

"Yes!" She stood, her eyes blazing with anger. "You could have, Andy!"

He opened and then closed his mouth several times. "I . . . didn't know I was supposed to come for you." What unspoken rule about relationships had he missed?

"If you loved me, you wouldn't have given up on us so easily. You could have come for me," she insisted stubbornly.

"How could I come for you? First, I thought you'd get married right away . . . that would be something of a deterrent, you have to admit."

"I didn't get married. But that's another story."

"Being reasonable, Louisa, how was I to know? Outsiders are hardly welcome in Gabriel's Landing. To come after you, when I assumed you were married, and even if you weren't, well, I guess I'm something of a coward. I mean, what if I had shown up, pursuing their beautiful lady doctor? I've been on the business side of a rifle, Louisa, and I don't recommend it."

"You could have written."

"And incurred your husband's wrath? I would never go after a married woman."

"But I wasn't," she insisted stubbornly. "I wasn't married."

He threw up his hands in frustration.

"And Molly," she said, "I asked Molly, in a roundabout way, if you had someone . . . someone special in your life, and she said yes, she knew you did, but she hadn't met your sweetheart. So I just assumed . . . that you'd found someone else, the way I always said you would. And I tried to be happy for you."

"Well, that's where *you* assumed wrong. *You* were the special person in my life, and of course Molly didn't know. I tried to meet other women, honestly, I did; I went to a singles ward and went to the singles firesides and dances, and I met some nice women. But I never felt about them . . . the way I felt about you. And as I said, I've avoided reading articles about polygamy in the Salt Lake City papers. It was too painful. But I hoped you were happy to be home among your people and that you were doing well in your practice."

"For a few months. Then it all fell apart. Ugly doesn't describe it. You were right all along. I should have known I couldn't practice real medicine in Gabriel's Landing. I couldn't meet the needs of my patients without crossing the Council of Brothers. And then when I contacted someone at the University of Utah about some of their research on birth defects, the kind you see when relatives intermarry, they saw it as a betrayal. When a child is born with deformed kidneys, it's God's will. It's God's will that they suffer, too. They didn't want to hear that if close relatives who wanted to get married would at least seek genetic counseling, they could avoid some of these birth defects. And that, of course, was heresy, too. I treated women for depression. I advised them, when they asked, about how they could delay pregnancy."

Andy winced.

"Yes. It didn't go over well." She sighed. "Anyway, I have a new life in Salt Lake City. And I like it. And I guess . . . I guess . . . I guess we've had one big misunderstanding."

"And bad timing. We met in Chicago and I thought Jim . . . well, why shouldn't he want to be with you? He's a good man."

"He's a wonderful man."

"So that's it?"

"No," she said quietly. "Again, you're jumping to conclusions. When you saw me in Jim's arms, it was because—"

"Because I'd said such terrible things?"

She nodded. "I was trying not to weep in public. I don't do it well, and you'd hurt me terribly."

"I know. And I'm sorry. I thought you'd hooked up with my best friend, and I was furious with both of you."

"I know. But Jim and I don't have a romantic relationship. He was so helpful when I started at Highland Clinic, introducing me to everyone, making everything smooth, and we've had some good times together."

"Did I tell you I was on my high school track team?"

"No."

"My best event was jumping to conclusions."

She smiled.

Andy took the wreath from her hands and set it on her shining hair. Tilting his head, he decided he liked it. "Louisa, I think I've missed some fundamental rule about communicating, I mean, communicating with women. I didn't know you wanted me to come after you. I don't own a rifle, but I would have bought one and taken it with me if I'd known."

"Next time . . . I'll try to be more clear," Louisa said.

"So you forgive me for . . ."

"For everything. I made assumptions, too. Will you forgive me?"

"Of course. You know, I just haven't been the same since John Stockton retired from the Utah Jazz."

She giggled. It turned into a laugh. He joined her, seeing the ridiculous mistakes they'd both made, and he laughed in relief that they were even in a position to share a laugh. Finally he wiped his eyes and offered his hand. She took it with a smile. Then he couldn't let it go. They sat in comfortable silence for a few minutes, and then they began to talk about their lives in the years they had been apart since medical school graduation. It felt like old times, Andy marveled. They had just clicked into place like the old friends they had always been. He wondered if they had another chance, another chance to fall in love again. Today had been wonderful, though, just spending time with Louisa, the pain and misunderstanding between them finally laid to rest.

She looked at her watch. "I'm afraid it's nearly time to head down."

He stood and helped her to her feet.

"Can I, would you, I mean, would you come on a walk with me again?" he asked.

She smiled. "Of course."

One walk led to others. Soon, all their free time was spent together, sometimes alone, sometimes with the other physicians, talking, laughing, sightseeing, and trying new foods.

Surprisingly, Andy reclaimed some of his competence with the language and tried to use it whenever he could. That seemed to impress the staff in the hospital, and they allowed him special privileges because of it.

One day Dr. Rheo caught him in the hallway. "Dr. McBride, a woman is about to deliver triplets. Would you like to . . ."

"Assist? Of course!" Andy ran after him. Hurriedly he scrubbed, and then he was wrapped in a sterile gown, mask, and cap and then pushed through the swinging doors.

"Labor is progressing well. How would you like to deliver the babies, Dr. McBride?"

"Me?"

"There are two obstetricians beside you if you need assistance. I just thought, since you speak the language well, that you could handle it."

Two hours later Andy held three small, healthy babies, one after another, and handed them to their happy, overwhelmed parents. A nurse took photos so he could tell everyone at home about the remarkable experience. It humbled Andy to know that the first human hands ever to touch these precious newborns were his. He breathed a silent prayer of gratitude, looking at the parents and their babies, and blinked away tears.

"Well done!" Dr. Rheo clapped him on the back.

"*Kitos! Kitos!*" Andy thanked the man, and impulsively gave him a hug.

The parents announced that the triplets, all boys, would each be given a middle name of one of the three physicians who had delivered them. "Andrew is my name. That's 'Antero' in Finnish," he told them, grinning.

From the glassed observation area Andy heard applause as some of his new friends and colleagues, both American and Finnish, smiled and gave thumbs-up signs.

Soon Andy found himself in a leadership position, as a liaison between the Finnish and American doctors. He quickly learned Finnish medical terms and taught them to the Americans. When there were miscommunications, he was often called to resolve them.

Two weeks after arriving in Finland, Andy and Louisa sat alone in a small restaurant.

"I've been thinking," Andy said. "A lot."

"And?"

"I've never been so happy."

"I feel the same," she said with a radiant smile.

"I don't imagine your family would approve of me, being a Gentile and all."

She nodded. "A moot point, because I can't go home again, anyway."

"And my family wouldn't approve of you, because of your background. As you said, my father puts your people in jail."

"Yes, I understand."

He took a deep breath. "So, since we've resolved that our families wouldn't approve anyway, let's just get married."

"Married?"

"Yes. Here. We'll find an LDS bishop."

"A bishop?" Her eyes widened.

"Do you have reservations about a bishop marrying us? I

could find a judge, if you like, and there's a wonderful old church in the town square. We walked by it yesterday."

"No, I don't have reservations about being married by an LDS bishop. In fact, I was supposed to see my bishop at home for an interview, but I took off for Finland in a hurry instead."

"Your bishop? Interview?"

"I attended LDS meetings all through my residencies, wherever I was. Even though I knew I'd go home to my family's way of life . . ."

"Really?"

"Over time, all of the teachings made sense and it felt right. I've had a . . . a witness, in my heart, that I've made the right decision."

"And what is that decision?"

"To be baptized."

"Baptized? Louisa, that's great! I didn't know!"

"That's all right. You said all the right things."

"What did I say that was right?" Andy asked cautiously. "I need to write it down for future reference."

She took his hand. "You wanted me before you knew I was going to join the Church. You wanted me as I was." Her eyes filled with tears.

He leaned over the small table and kissed her. "Of course I did. I never stopped wanting you. I hoped that someday, because our belief systems were so similar, polygamy set aside, that you might have a positive feeling toward Mormonism. But when or how it developed didn't matter."

"Well, the when is now. And the how . . . do you think we could arrange a baptism here?"

"Give me one day and I'll have it all set. The bishop here will need to talk to your bishop at home."

"Of course. I'll give you his phone number. I have it in my room."

"And, if you'd like, I'll ask him to perform the marriage for us, too."

"This is a lot to absorb."

"But it's never felt so right. I love you, Louisa. I've loved you since you beat me at foosball."

She smiled, her green eyes warm. "I tried not to love you, but when you ran into the goal post in that soccer game and got knocked out, I was so terrified of losing you. By the way, how are your seizures?"

"Only one, recently, after four years with no problems. I think it had something to do with skipping a couple of meals and being at the business end of a shotgun. Long story. But I'm back on my meds and after three months, well, you know the drill. I'll taper off and see how it goes. I'm all right."

"And Eliza?"

"She saw it coming. She didn't forget a bit of her training."

"Good old Eliza." Louisa took Andy's hands in hers. "I love you, Andy McBride."

"And I love you, too." They kissed again, long and tenderly.

"Oh, I almost forgot." Andy dug into his pocket. "It was the best I could do on short notice at the marketplace." He held up a polished silver band. "Louisa Martin, will you marry me?"

She gasped and then nodded, her eyes brimming with tears.

He reached across the table and slipped it on her finger. "I had it engraved. It says 'Love forever' in Finnish."

"I love it," she said, admiring how it looked on her finger. "I really do."

Suddenly their world, which had only contained two people this evening, was interrupted. On cue, the waiters, who had been in on the plan, began to sing a traditional Finnish love song. One brought a bouquet of wildflowers and presented it to Louisa. The other customers caught on quickly, applauding and lifting their glasses to the couple. The manager appeared with a bottle of champagne. Andy had a quiet conversation with him in Finnish. The manager looked surprised, but smiled and nodded. He returned with a bottle of sparkling cider.

The band struck up a waltz. Andy stood, holding out his hand. "Shall we?"

Louisa took his hand with a smile. "I love you, Andy

McBride," she said. And there, in front of everyone, she put her arms around Andy and kissed him. That brought more applause as they walked to the dance floor.

The restaurant began to empty and Louisa looked at her watch. "I think they're ready to close. Will you come to my host family's home so we can tell them about our plans? Maybe Jani would like you to ask his permission."

Andy chuckled. "Sure."

"And speaking of permission . . . how will we tell our families?"

"I think I'd like to write my parents a letter tonight. And after the wedding we can send a few pictures. They should arrive home before we do. Maybe they'll have a little time to get used to the idea. I know eloping isn't fair to families, but given our circumstances, they wouldn't have been happy for us anyway . . . once they get to know you, Louisa, it will be fine."

"Father knows a little bit about you. I doubt he'll be terribly surprised. He won't be thrilled, but for my sake he'll try to be happy about it. That's asking quite a bit, coming from a fundamentalist Gabriel's Landing father."

"I'll write to him tonight, too, and tell him how much I love his daughter."

She smiled.

"But what about your job, Louisa?"

"I only signed a short contract. I was due to renew this week, but here I am instead. So I'll be free to leave. I've heard Kentucky is beautiful."

"I think you'll love it. Louisa Martin, will you share my life with me? And will you share my medical practice with me?"

She kissed him. "Yes, yes, and just to be sure, yes."

Chapter Thirty-eight

Andy's host family offered their home when he told them he was getting married. "We insist," they told him. "We want to share this happy day. Don't worry about flowers or food. Just call your guests."

Louisa's host family called Andy's, and together the two families planned a party.

Most of their new friends and Finnish colleagues didn't know much about the LDS faith, but Andy and Louisa invited them to the baptism anyway. They had chosen a small lake for the occasion, and though the water was cool, the setting was beautiful. The group assembled and watched respectfully as Andy baptized Louisa and then, assisted by the bishop and missionaries, confirmed her a member of the Church. The missionaries beamed, because baptisms were rare in Finland, where few people were interested in hearing about the LDS faith.

Later that day the bishop officiated at the wedding. The women in the group had done some quick shopping and found a simple lacy white dress for Louisa. Following a quick sewing session to adjust the hem, she pronounced it perfect.

Louisa met Andy in the garden, carrying wildflowers in her

arms. A few more flowers were wound in her hair, which fell in shining waves down her back. The bishop spoke English, but for the benefit of all the guests, he conducted the ceremony in both languages, one paragraph at a time, joking that it he had never performed a "double wedding." The ceremony was brief and heartfelt, and the couple's answers were evidently satisfactory, for they were soon pronounced husband and wife and Andy kissed his bride. The host families served a buffet dinner in the shady garden. After much laughing and congratulations, singing and dancing, the guests finally left and Andy's host father handed him a key. "This is to our summer cottage. You can stay there for your honeymoon."

"Oh, we'd planned to stay at a hotel—you don't have to—I mean, you've already loaned us your second car and thrown us a wonderful party . . . I can't impose."

"This is our wedding gift to you. We've had a wonderful time, too. Thank you for allowing us to share your happiness. You'll find the kitchen stocked with food and plenty of wood to fill the stove." They embraced the newlyweds and said, "Go! Have a wonderful time! And when you come back, Andy, your wife can stay here with you!"

They spent three days at the summer cottage, enjoying the sauna and then, when they were so hot and sweaty they could hardly stand it, running outside to jump in the clear lake. They paddled the canoe around the lake, and Andy even caught a couple of salmon.

"This was the perfect honeymoon," Louisa said as they locked the cottage, preparing to drive back to Jyvaskla. "I just wish we could stay . . . away from all the cares of home, here in this beautiful place."

"We will come back," Andy said. "The temple is nearly finished. When we've been married a year, we can be sealed in any temple we choose."

"Our letters and pictures should arrive before we do."

"There's nothing we can do but pray they accept this, in due time. I'm determined to enjoy every day we have here. And when we get back home, yours will be the first face I see in the morning and the last thing I see at night. Together, I think we can face just about anything."

"Together," Louisa mused. "What a lovely word."

Chapter Thirty-nine

*Morning grouchiness can be cured by placing your head
under the cold water tap and letting the water run full
force for five minutes.*

—MISS CAROLINA'S REMEDIES AND ADVICE

THREE MONTHS LATER

Andy read his mother's latest letter with a smile. It was amusing
and newsy, as usual.

After their trip to Finland, they had made a quick visit to Salt
Lake City to pack Louisa's belongings, and they had also stopped
in to visit Andy's parents. Cole was at work and away from his
office, Margaret said, but she appeared happy to see them and
welcomed Louisa with a warm hug. His mother had responded as
Andy had known she would, with grace and acceptance, keeping
any reservations she might have had to herself.

Cole, he knew from what his mother had not explicitly said
that day, or in the past three months, had not accepted the marriage at all. He doubted his father's feelings had changed since
their tense conversation years ago on that camping trip in the
Uintahs. Cole was still actively prosecuting polygamy cases,
Andy knew, and no doubt his feelings were even stronger now.

For Andy to marry a woman who came from that environment would be completely unacceptable to Cole.

"Give your father time," was all his mother had said in reference to his father as they sat in the home of Andy's boyhood. "Now, tell me all about the wedding. And thank you so much for the wonderful pictures."

Andy glanced at Louisa, whose wide eyes were fixed on the mantel. Andy followed her gaze and saw one of the wedding pictures they had sent, in a silver frame.

"Your mother is president of your fan club, you know," Margaret had often said during his growing-up years. "It's in the job description." She had confirmed that many times.

He met his mother's eyes, nodding toward the mantel, and gave her a smile of gratitude.

They visited a few minutes more, and then Andy looked at his watch with reluctance.

"I'm afraid we've got to run, Mom. We have to see Grandpa and then pack Louisa's things and clean her apartment, and our flight is in the morning."

"It was wonderful to meet you, Louisa," his mother said, and Andy knew she meant it.

Grandpa's reaction had been heartwarming as well. "When you find that person you want to share your life with," he said, "don't waste time." He had a gift for them, he said, and brought out one of his wife's quilts.

"I'm afraid it's a bit worn," he apologized.

"Oh, no, that makes it even better," Louisa said. "Quilts are made to be used, and this one is lovely."

"I think this wife of yours is a keeper," Grandpa said with a wink for Andy.

Joshua had written a letter following the wedding, wishing them well. It had a cautious tone, Louisa said, but she knew

Joshua would support her choices, even if it meant marrying a
Gentile. Since then his letters came weekly, with news of family
and Gabriel's Landing, and expressing his desire to meet Andy.

Louisa arrived home from her shift at the clinic and dropped
a kiss on Andy's rumpled hair. "Can you believe it's our six-month
anniversary today?"

"It is?"

She laughed at his expression. "It's all right. I wasn't expecting flowers."

"But you should have flowers—just because."

"All right, surprise me with flowers one of these days."

"I'll do that," he said with a smile. "As soon as I figure out
how women's minds really work."

"Now that," she said, "would take away all the mystery."

Andy thought it best to nod wisely.

"Obadiah's out of work for a while. I guess a project fell
through," Louisa said.

"I'm sorry to hear that."

"I think he's a little worried. But then I've been thinking . . ."

"It's dangerous when you say that."

"Do you think he could do some work for us here?"

Andy thought for a moment. "The barn could use a new roof."

"And we need to turn one of the bedrooms into a nursery."

"All right, I'll give him a call." Andy picked up the phone
and then put it down. He pondered their casual exchange. "Did
you say a nursery?"

"But I don't know what color to paint the walls yet. And we
really should add another bath."

Andy stared at her. "A nursery?"

"Do you think he could have it done by July?"

Andy felt blindly for the sofa. "How long have you known?"

"I took a pregnancy test after you left this morning. I've
been so smug all day, just waiting until we could be alone, to tell
you."

"You're *pregnant?*"

She sat in his lap. "Married people do have children. We haven't exactly been celibate."

"Holy mackerel!"

She blanched. "Please . . ."

"Nausea?"

"It comes and goes."

He placed his hand on her flat stomach. "There's actually a little person growing in there?"

She nodded. "I'm going to get fat."

"Oh, Louisa!" He held her close. "I'm going to be a father!"

"A good one."

"I don't remember stuffing hazelnuts in my pockets," he said.

"Hazelnuts?"

"Miss Carolina swears by them. She says they're a sure guarantee of fertility."

Louisa laughed. "I don't think we needed any help."

"We'd better think of names," Andy said suddenly. "Names. Yes."

"There's plenty of time for that," Louisa said. "This calls for a celebration, don't you think? Tim's on call for us tonight. Let's turn off the phones and pagers. I'm sure we can think of something to do."

In one swift move he unplugged the phone, swept her up in his arms, and headed for the bedroom.

~

Across the road, Obadiah turned from the window. "Lights just went out at Andy's. Again."

His missus laughed and came to his side. He put his arm around her shoulders and she leaned into his strong, familiar frame.

"What's so funny?" Lizzie wanted to know.

Obadiah winked at his missus.

Lizzie looked from one parent to the other. "Why won't anybody tell me what's so funny?"

Chapter Forty

For asthma:
Put a handful of dry wild turnip leaves in a quart of good
whisky. Let stand three days and take one tablespoon as needed.

—Miss Carolina's Remedies and Advice

"Well, Father, Aunt Sarah, and Aunt Hannah, this is home," Louisa said as they pulled up to the cabin at sunset. "I hope you aren't too tired from the flight."

"Oh, no, dear, I'm not, even though I'd never been on a plane before. It was exciting!" Hannah said.

"What a lovely place," added Sarah.

Andy set their bags in the hallway. "Joshua, there are two bedrooms made up for you and your wives . . ."

Joshua nodded. "Thank you. Ummm, what do I smell?"

"Soup in the slow cooker," Louisa said. "Dinner will be ready in a few minutes."

There was a knock at the door. "Mel, come in," Andy said. "This is Louisa's father, Joshua Martin. And Sarah."

"Pleased to meet you," said Mel.

"And Hannah."

"Happy to meet you, too." Mel looked from one woman to the other. "Are you—?"

"Yes, they're sisters," Andy said hastily. "Twins," he added.

"You've come a long way to see your daughter and her husband, Mr. Martin."

"Call me Joshua. Yes, we have come a long way. I understand you've been very good to them."

"I've never seen two people so much in love, except my Mary Alice and me."

"It's beautiful country here," said Sarah. "So different from the desert!"

"So green!" added Hannah. "And we'll be back to visit after the baby's born, to help out."

"Glad to hear it," said Mel. "Well, Mary Alice sent a cake. I'd better be getting home. G'night, folks."

Later that evening Obadiah stopped by with a load of firewood. Joshua sat on the swing with his arm around Hannah. Sarah emerged and sat on a rocking chair, needlework in hand. Louisa introduced her family, and Obadiah welcomed them with his customary bashful smile. He invited them to the next day's dance at the high school gymnasium.

"What type of dancing?" Joshua asked.

"Old-fashioned, mostly. Square dancing, round dances, waltzes."

"Then we'll look forward to it."

"And of course our band's playing," Obadiah told them. "Andy's and mine. We call ourselves Old Dan Tucker's Band."

"That will be lovely," said Hannah. "We've never heard Andy sing or play before."

"You haven't? You're in for a treat. See you later, folks."

"Well, Louisa's parents and her aunt look right comfortable doing square dances. Even brought their own costumes," observed Mary Alice, sitting on a folding chair and propping her feet on another as she watched the lively dancing.

"I don't think those are costumes," Mel said. "That's how they were dressed when I met them yesterday. I think they're just sort of old-fashioned."

"The ladies have lovely long hair, too," said Mary Alice, "all braided up and wound around their heads. Like my ma used to wear hers. Now, Louisa told me her mother had passed on. I know Hannah and Sarah are sisters, but which one is married to Joshua?"

"Hannah," Obadiah said.

"Sarah," Mel corrected him.

"No, it's Hannah. She came out of the bedroom with Joshua when I was over yesterday morning," Obadiah said.

Mel shook his head. "It's Sarah," he insisted. "This afternoon Joshua was sitting on the porch with her, and he had his arm around her."

"Mighty affectionate with his sister-in-law," Obadiah commented.

"Oh, my gosh!" Mary Alice looked from one to the other with wide eyes. "They're both his wives!"

"What?"

"Where did you say they live, honey?"

"A little town in Utah. Out in desert country. Louisa says she has a big family, lots of brothers and sisters."

"I'll bet she does," said Mary Alice. "Louisa's mother, who passed on a few years ago, was Joshua's wife. And so are Sarah and Hannah, evidently."

"*What*?"

"You heard me."

"No! You mean he's a polygamist?"

"Reckon so. Remember what Andy told us? How he knew some college students who'd come from them little towns? I'll bet Louisa was one of 'em. She told me she and Andy met at medical school. It all fits, don't it? I mean, look at the three of them, the way they get along. They're *both* his wives."

"Well, I'll be!" sputtered Mel. "I do believe you're right. He's married to 'em both! He's a real live polygamist!"

"Here in Hawthorn Valley, imagine that! The most excitement we've had here in a long time!" Obadiah exclaimed.

"Let's keep this under our hats, Obadiah," Mel said. "Can't say as I approve or understand, but we'll show 'em courtesy. For Andy and Louisa's sake."

"You're right," Mary Alice said. "I won't have anybody saying anything unkind about them. Heaven knows we have our own odd ways."

"But not as odd as that," Obadiah said, shaking his head.

"I wouldn't know about that. But while they're here, we'll show 'em a good time. And they're one man short in the square dance. Guess I'll join in," Mel said.

And so the evening went. Joshua danced with his wives and daughter and nearly every other lady at the dance. Sarah and Hannah did not lack for partners either.

The Martins thoroughly enjoyed the Sunday night Hymn Sing. When Andy was asked to sing "Come, Come, Ye Saints," he said, "Only if my wife and her family will join me. Hannah, will you play the organ?" and they sang the traditional old hymn in four-part harmony. After all, it was as much a part of Louisa's heritage as Andy's.

By the end of the week Joshua's wives had acquired new recipes and quilt patterns, promising to send some of their own back to their friends in Hawthorn Valley. Sarah took some native plants home with her, their roots gently cushioned in damp sponges and wrapped in plastic. She hoped they'd survive in the desert with some extra care.

On the way home from the airport Louisa said, "They know."

"What?"

"They know my father's a polygamist."

"I imagine a few of them figured it out. But, you know, in the end it didn't matter. Your family charmed them anyway."

"I was so apprehensive, but it couldn't have turned out better. If only . . ."

"I know. If only my father could be as accepting. Especially with the baby coming." He placed his hand on her abdomen, slightly rounded now.

"I've been feeling little flutters today."

"Really? You've felt the baby moving?"

"Like a tiny butterfly. At first I wasn't sure. Then it happened a second time, and a third."

"I can't wait until I can feel it."

"Be patient, Daddy. In a month or so little Junior will be thumping hard enough for you to feel it."

An ultrasound in Taylor's Glen confirmed what Andy and Louisa suspected. "Twins!" said the obstetrician, beaming. "Congratulations!"

Louisa wept all the way home. "It's all these hormones," she sniffled.

"Then what's my excuse?" Andy rubbed his sleeve over his eyes.

"You *have* no excuse! This is all your fault!"

"Sweetheart, it's a little late to place blame on anyone."

"You delivered triplets in Finland!"

Andy wisely decided not to reply to this accusation.

Louisa hiccupped and felt her bulging stomach with wonder. "It feels like a soccer game's going on in here."

"Maybe they'll grow up to play soccer, like their dad."

"Oh, Andy, what are we going to do with two babies?"

He squeezed her hand, his own trembling. "Love them."

Chapter Forty-one

For healthy hair:
Make a strong tea of wild cherry bark and twigs.
Rub this on the hair after washing.

—Miss Carolina's Remedies and Advice

Mel chuckled. "Twins, you say? Well, I guess the good Lord saw fit to send you two at a time."

"I hope the good Lord knew what he was doing," Louisa said, her hand on her enlarging abdomen.

"You'll want to keep an eye on these wee ones when they come," Mel said.

"That goes without saying, Mel," Andy told him.

"Oh, Mel's just remembering something that happened a long time ago." Mary Alice winked at her husband.

Louisa paused on her way to the kitchen. "What happened? Don't start your story without me! I'll be right back with lemonade."

"Well, surely you've heard tales of the baby-swapping that happened in our neck of the woods years ago?" Mel settled in his chair, nursing his lemonade. Andy and Louisa were a new audience for his yarns, and he delighted in the telling.

"Oh, Mel, that was fifty years ago," Mary Alice reminded him.

"How time flies!" he mused.

"What happened?" Louisa asked, settling in a rocking chair.

"Well," explained Mel, ever the storyteller, "folks was in the habit of getting together at somebody's house for a chickery and music and dancing on a Saturday's night."

"A chickery?" Louisa asked.

"A party where they cook fried chicken. There might be five or six families gathered at one place. They'd wrap the babies snug in their quilts and put them on the big feather bed. Usually they'd snooze through the whole party."

"But one night," said Mary Alice, the corners of her lips twitching, "some mischievous boys slipped into the bedroom."

"I'm telling this tale, Mary Alice. Anyway, ever so quiet, they took the babies and unwrapped them. Then they switched their quilts and blankets and wrapped 'em up all snug again. It wasn't 'til folks got home that they realized something was amiss. Mrs. Thomas down the gully never got over it, they say. She went to change little Mattie's diaper and fainted on the spot. Seems her little Mattie had turned into a Matthew," Mel grinned.

"Fortunately, we'd just got telephones, so everybody started calling everybody else. It was pretty wild, all them folks yapping all at once on the party line. Finally they decided to meet at the church and trade babies."

"Did they ever find out who did it?" Andy asked.

Mel inspected his boot for a speck of dust. "Folks had their suspicions."

"I heard tell as a few lads had extra chores every night for a month. Seems all the families whose babies were switched had the biggest woodpiles ever seen in these parts," laughed Mary Alice. "Oh, it was rich! Six families with the wrong babies!"

"Thanks for the warning," said Louisa. "We'll be sure to take the right ones home."

Chapter Forty-two

For the flu:
Boil sassafras bark in a pint of water for twenty minutes.
Strain and add one pint of good whisky. After it cools,
adults may take one teaspoon four times a day.

—Miss Carolina's Remedies and Advice

Little Bo Peep's sheep would not line up correctly. One panel of wallpaper was a quarter of an inch off. Louisa brushed her hair back from her forehead, a thin smear of paste grazing her eyebrow. Working with care, she pulled the panel free from the paste-smeared wall and repositioned it. The border strip would eventually cover any uneven seams at the top, she hoped.

The day had turned humid, and her energetic determination to transform the bedroom into a nursery was wilting. She climbed down from the stepladder, taking each step slowly. As she inspected her work, the mismatched panel detached from one upper corner and fell to the floor in a slow whispering spiral.

That was it. She'd just close the door and think about it tomorrow. It was time for a long, cool drink of lemonade, a shower, some relaxing music, a good book, and pillows under her feet. As she reached into the refrigerator for the pitcher of lemonade there was a knock at the door. She sighed again. Andy was at the clinic, she'd tell whoever it was, and it would be best to meet him there.

A well-dressed middle-aged couple stood at the threshold. With a shock, Louisa recognized Margaret McBride, who gave her a warm hug.

"This is my husband, Cole," Margaret said.

Louisa nodded, too surprised to speak. She took an involuntary step backward, holding on to the doorframe with one hand, as the shock of the McBrides' presence registered.

"We only stopped by to say hello," Margaret said. "We noticed Andy's Jeep isn't here, so we'll just call back later." She fumbled for a card in her purse. "This is where we're staying. In Taylor's Glen."

Louisa blinked. "Please . . . stay. Andy will be home soon. You've—come a long way."

"I think we've come at a bad time," Cole said.

"No, I was just trying to hang some wallpaper." Louisa looked down at her shirt, an old one of Andy's, as she'd outgrown all of hers. She was perspiring and disheveled, with gobs of wallpaper paste on her clothes, a streak of it across her face, her hair frizzy from the humidity.

"Cole," Margaret said, "let's take a walk. Louisa can freshen up before Andy gets home, and we can use the exercise." She took his arm, and he nodded.

They turned, went down the front steps, and were halfway down the front path when Louisa found her voice again. "Andy will be surprised," she faltered.

Andy's parents turned around. "Yes, I believe he will," Cole said.

"And—and pleased," Louisa added.

Margaret gave her a grateful smile.

"Thank you," was Cole's reply.

"Look, there's Andy!" Margaret said as they came out of the barn, having met and admired Smoky. "Let's give them a few minutes alone before we descend on them."

As they watched, their son stepped out of the Jeep. Louisa

met him in the driveway. They kissed and Andy caressed her abdomen under the flowing shirt, clearly revealing a bulge.

"She's pregnant," said Margaret. "Oh, my goodness."

"Are you sure?"

"A woman knows."

"Good heavens. I'm going to be a grandfather again?"

"I believe so. Andy will make such a great father."

"I hope he won't make the same mistakes his own father made."

"No," Margaret said, rubbing his arm, "I think each generation invents their own batch of mistakes as parents. But Andy will be fine. He was raised by a good man."

"That's kind of you to say," Cole said, "after I turned my back on him."

"But now we're going to make it right," Margaret said. "I mean, we can start today. To be better parents."

As Cole and Margaret watched, Andy gestured toward their rental car. Louisa told him something that made him stiffen. A brief conversation followed. He took her face between his hands and kissed her forehead. Then he gathered her into his arms and held her close, rocking her gently as if to comfort her. She nestled her head against his shoulder. They joined hands and walked inside.

Cole and Margaret looked at each other. "Well," Margaret ventured, not sure of her voice.

"Yes. What a mess I've made of things."

"But she invited us to stay, and she said Andy would be pleased to see us. That's awfully generous of her. And no doubt she was embarrassed to be caught off guard and covered with wallpaper paste the first time she met her father-in-law."

"Paste or not, she is lovely, isn't she? Even prettier than her pictures."

"She's beautiful," Margaret agreed.

"Well, should we knock on the door again, and see how Andy's going to react?"

"That's why we came, Cole, to make things right. To try, anyway."

Andy's reaction was to hug his mother and greet his father with a hearty handshake. "What a surprise!"

"I'm afraid we gave Louisa quite a surprise, too. We're sorry. We should have called, but we didn't know if you'd want to see us. I mean, we just decided to . . . show up," his mother said.

"Come in," Andy said, "and see our home. How long are you staying?"

"Well, we're staying in a nice little hotel in Taylor's Glen, and we thought we'd visit the area . . . for a few days," Margaret said.

His parents admired the home and Margaret exclaimed over the quilts and afghans.

Louisa appeared in the bedroom doorway, wearing a flowing emerald green dress, her eyes picking up the color of the fabric, her shower-damp hair woven in an intricate French braid. "Will you stay for dinner?"

"Oh, we couldn't impose," began Margaret.

"Andy's cooking. He'd be very disappointed."

His parents exchanged glances. "Andy's cooking? Now that," Cole said, "I want to see."

"And I'm putting you to work. You can set the table and light the fire," Andy told them. "It's getting a little cool tonight."

The conversation at dinner was safe and casual, filled with news of family and friends back home. Louisa was quiet as she listened to her husband and his parents; Andy gave her knee a reassuring nudge under the table.

Margaret and Cole insisted on doing the dishes while Andy tended to the fire. Soon it was crackling again, sending a friendly glow into the room. His parents dried their hands and sat in armchairs across from Andy and Louisa, who shared the sofa.

"So, Dad, Grandpa tells me you're the bishop of our ward now," Andy said.

"It's been almost a year," Margaret said. "He's a wonderful bishop."

Cole cleared his throat. "In a way, that's why I'm here."

Andy tensed and put a protective arm around his wife.

"Last week," his father began, looking down at his hands, "a couple came in to see me. They were devastated because their only daughter is marrying a man of another faith. They wanted to know how they could change her mind. They wondered what they'd done wrong as her parents, for her to even think of marrying outside of the Church. They were desperate to stop her. Well, I sent a quick silent prayer heavenward for guidance, and I found myself counseling them to do what I haven't been able to do myself: to trust their daughter and respect her choice, and to accept this young man for all the fine qualities he has."

He cleared his throat. "I have never been so humbled," he finally managed to say. Margaret reached for his hand.

Andy's grip on Louisa's shoulder tightened.

"Your mother and I talked late into the night after I got home," Cole said. "I knew I had to right the wrong, but I wasn't sure how to, after all this time. Even if Louisa hadn't joined the Church, I had no right to withhold my love from either of you. I should have had more faith in my son and trusted him to make a good choice, which he did."

"Thank you," Andy said. Louisa nodded, too overcome to speak.

"You know," Cole said, "we talk about unconditional love almost every week at church, but when it came to showing it, I changed the concept to fit my own narrow reasoning: 'I'll give you my love and approval as long as you do what I want you to do.' I realized I was the one who needed forgiveness. Not you, Andy. And certainly not you, Louisa."

Louisa took a deep breath. "It was good of you," she said, "to come all this way."

"I hope someday you'll be able to forgive me, both of you," Cole said. "Maybe today can be a new start for us, a place to begin again."

"I do forgive you, Cole, and I understand why you opposed our marriage. There are friends and family at home in Gabriel's Landing who will never forgive me for marrying an outsider," Louisa said quietly. "My father was resigned to the idea that I would marry someone from 'the outside world,' and he's even come to visit us here in Kentucky. That's most unusual. I've never felt any bitterness toward you, and I'm very glad you came here today. It means the world to me. And to Andy."

Andy nodded and squeezed her hand. "And we eloped. As I said in my letter, I knew it would come as a shock, and you'd feel cheated, but at the same time I knew you couldn't be happy for us."

"You should only have happy, supportive people at your wedding," Margaret said. "I do understand."

Cole looked at his wife, relief on his face. "I can see why Andy loves you, Louisa, and why he couldn't get you out of his heart, even when you were apart and he didn't think you had a future together."

"Speaking of something special," Andy said, his hand on Louisa's rounded belly, "we're expecting."

"Your mother thought so," Cole beamed. "That's great!"

"Twins," Andy said with a grin, watching for his parents' reaction.

"Twins!" The McBrides didn't disappoint Andy and Louisa. "Wonderful!"

"Believe me, discovering Louisa is carrying twins was a shock to us, too. I was trying to find a clever way to tell you Louisa was pregnant, Mom, but I wasn't sure . . ."

"How I'd react?" Cole asked. "Well, I'm thrilled."

"Just wait until we tell everyone at home!" Margaret took Cole's hand. Talk of babies and nurseries and plans for the future brought smiles to everyone's faces.

Louisa looked at Andy and smiled. "We're going to the temple a few months after the babies are born," she said. "After I've been a member for a year. We'd like you to be with us when we're sealed to each other and the babies. That's the ceremony that really counts, for eternity."

"We'll be there," said Cole. "Nothing could keep us away. You two have something very special."

"Do you know the gender of the babies?" Margaret asked. "Two boys or two girls or one of each?"

"They didn't cooperate for the ultrasound. We couldn't tell for sure. So it will be a surprise. And we're all right with that," Andy said. "We've got two boy names and two girl names ready, just in case."

Louisa nodded.

"Well, we'd better be going," Cole said half an hour later, helping Margaret to her feet.

"Thank you, both of you, for coming to see us," Andy said.

Andy pulled his parents into a hug. Then Cole kissed Louisa's cheek. "Welcome to the family," he said. "Finally."

Margaret held out her arms to Louisa, and the two women embraced.

"Oh, Louisa, before we go," Cole said. "I was thinking . . ."

"What, Dad?" Andy asked.

"Margaret and I have hung a lot of wallpaper in our day. We'd be happy to finish the nursery for you."

"Really? I'd be so grateful."

Two hours later the job was done, Little Bo Peep's sheep had lined up correctly, and the nursery began to look like a room waiting for two special babies. Andy's parents would visit again, they promised, and if Louisa wanted to hang more wallpaper, they hoped she'd save it for them.

Chapter Forty-three

For insomnia:
Eat two or three small raw onions with a
little bread lightly spread with fresh butter.

—Miss Carolina's Remedies and Advice

Louisa would never, ever, be condescending to women in labor again. She had never meant to be, but now that she was surrounded by patronizing, condescending, arrogant know-it-all doctors and nurses, she was ready to throttle all of them. Their platitudes made her furious. The stupid picture on the wall, where she was supposed to focus—they didn't believe it when she told them it changed with each contraction, from a rose to a cow to an American flag to a rose.

It *hurt*, this force that took possession of her body and seemed determined to rip it in two, and it was exhausting. Human beings breathed every day of their lives without being told to, so why was everyone telling her to breathe? She knew how to count, but these idiots in green scrubs couldn't count beyond four to save their lives. "In two three four, out two three four, in two three four, out two three four," was as far as they could go, and they were so proud of this accomplishment, they wouldn't shut up. Didn't these dimwits know there were three thousand two hundred fifty-eight tiny flowers on the wallpaper?

"Ice chips!" she yelled.

The nurse looked at the monitor. "Another contraction's coming, Dr. Martin. Get ready. Take a deep cleansing breath."

"Tell me about it," gasped Louisa. "I can feel them long before this stupid earthquake machine can register anything."

"Sorry."

"Just don't do it again."

"No, of course not, Dr. Martin."

"Andy!"

His face came into focus. She relinquished his hand, and he massaged his fingers. "What is it, sweetheart?"

"Sing to me!"

"What?"

"To distract me. Sing to me!"

"Uh," Andy cleared his throat. "What would you like to hear? Hey, everybody, we're going to sing for the lady!" Half a dozen green-clad doctors and nurses paused and looked at him. "You heard me, sing! The lady wants music, and music she shall have!"

"Uh, what shall we sing, Dr. McBride?" one of the nurses asked.

"Joy to the World!" gasped Louisa as another contraction gripped her midsection.

"Joy to the world, the Lord is come," a half-hearted chorus sang.

"Not that one! It's not Christmas, you idiots! Our song, Andy, you know, the one by Three Dog Night!"

"Oh. Well. Jeremiah was a bullfrog, Was a good friend of mine . . ." He waved his hands as if conducting the choir and nodded vigorously at his colleagues.

This time everyone in the delivery room joined Andy in Three Dog Night's lusty drinking song.

"Don't You Marry the Mormon Boys!" she yelled after the next contraction.

"What did she say, Dr. McBride?"

"Uh, it's just a little old folk song. I guess she wants to hear it." Andy leaned over and sang quietly in Louisa's ear:

Gather round, girls, and listen to my noise,
Don't you marry the Mormon boys.
If you do your fortune it will be,
Johnnycake and babies is all you'll see.

"Excuse me, Dr. McBride," said the pediatrician, "I couldn't quite hear that. Sing it again, will you?"

"Phil," Andy muttered through clenched teeth, "another time."

"No, Andy! Sing it again!" Louisa insisted. "The man wants to hear it! Nice and loud, so everyone can hear!"

Andy obliged and was rewarded by muffled applause from rubber-gloved hands.

Louisa grabbed his hand again. "Listen, everybody, can I have your attention please? I'm in transition. That means it's almost time to start pushing. And when I want to push, I am going to push. Is that clear? And I am not a girl. I do not want to hear 'good girl, atta girl, that's my girl,' or any other phrase with the word *girl* unless I give birth to one. I am a woman. W-O-M-A-N. Are there any questions? Now, will somebody please shut me up before I make a complete idiot of myself?

"All right, I'm ready to push. Andy, support my back. AAAAAAAAaagh! . . . Now I'm going to sleep for a few seconds. Be quiet, everybody, the *woman* needs her rest . . . Aaaaaaaaaagh!"

Ten minutes and ten quick catnaps later a small, wet, squirming infant gave a wail of protest at being expelled from the safe, dark, quiet environment she had known for so many months. After a few quick wipes with a soft towel made her presentable, she was wrapped in a soft pink blanket, and a pink knit cap was placed gently on her head. Nestled in Louisa's arms, the baby gazed vaguely at her mother, quieting at the familiar sound of her mother's voice. "Oh, she's finally here, and she's beautiful!" Louisa whispered. "Just look at her, Andy!"

Andy had already counted fingers and toes and watched the infant turn a lovely, reassuring shade of pink. "She's perfect." The baby opened her eyes wide and turned at the sound of his voice. "She already knows her daddy!" He placed his finger in her tiny palm, and she grasped it with surprising strength. Like her mother, Lauren was exhausted. Within a minute she was asleep, still holding onto his finger.

Her mother didn't have that luxury. Lauren was taken from her arms and the pushing began again. Five minutes later another blinking, squawking bundle was placed in her arms as a reward for her efforts, this one wrapped and capped in blue. Fingers and toes were counted again, his parents and everyone in the delivery room declared Alex and Lauren the most beautiful, remarkable babies in the world, and then he was handed to the pediatrician for more indignities.

An hour later Louisa opened her eyes. "Why do I keep hearing Three Dog Night songs in my head?" she mumbled.

Andy leaned over and kissed her. "Drugs. They'll do that. Here, have a sip of juice."

"How are the babies?"

"One of each," he said. "We did good work."

"We?"

"Uh, you did good work. I'm just the culprit who caused all this commotion eight months ago."

"You certainly did."

"They're beautiful, Louisa, just under five pounds each and healthy. That's great for being a month early. Good lungs. The nurse will bring them in for a visit soon. Do you think you're ready for this?"

Louisa gripped his hand. "Now's a fine time to ask."

"I think I'm supposed to say something reassuring here."

"Then say something reassuring."

"I think they're both going to have red hair."

She smiled. "I love you, Andy McBride."

Chapter Forty-four

The bee, he is an insect small,
And cunning as a weasel;
If he should land upon you all
He'll leave a little measle.

—Miss Carolina's Remedies and Advice

FOUR YEARS LATER

"Alex! Lauren! Wait!" Andy shouted.

The twins looked back and smiled at him, hand in hand. Then they vanished into the fog.

"Wait!" Andy sat bolt upright in bed, drenched in a cold sweat.

Louisa rolled over, awake now, too. "What is it?"

He took a deep breath and slowly exhaled. His heart was still pounding. "Bad dream. Sorry I woke you."

She yawned. "What was it about?"

Andy hedged. "It was kind of vague. Foggy. I'm just going to get a drink." He got out of bed and strode down the hallway, opening the door to the twins' room. They slept soundly in their new beds, tousled red curls on the pillows, their favorite stuffed toys tucked in with them. He straightened a blanket, caressed a lock of hair, and gave the casement window an extra crank to make sure it was closed. He walked through his home, checking every door and window. Then he mopped his face with a towel and took a long drink of cool water.

He didn't tell Louisa any more about his dream; he didn't want to worry her. He'd had this dream more than once, chasing the children, being within an arm's length of them, and then, helpless, seeing them vanish with a giggle into the fog. He supposed it was natural for a father to worry about his children's safety. An occasional dream didn't mean anything. The twins would celebrate their fourth birthday next week; that was probably why they found their way into his dream.

He'd also dreamed that Louisa was living in polygamy in Gabriel's Landing, he reminded himself, and that had never happened. She was here, she was his wife and the mother of his children, and she was keeping his bed warm. He drank another glass of water and returned to bed. Louisa pulled him close and stroked his hair.

"You haven't been yourself since John Stockton retired from the Utah Jazz. Life moves on, Andy."

He sighed and relaxed against her.

"I'm the one who just found out she's pregnant again. I'm supposed to have bizarre dreams, not you," she reminded him with a kiss. "Go back to sleep."

Chapter Forty-five

It is unlucky to have clothes mended while wearing them.

—Miss Carolina's Remedies and Advice

"Hugh!" Jeremiah Reese called.

Hugh Rawlins looked up from grooming Chester, his favorite horse, whose coat shone like a polished chestnut.

"Yeah?"

"Somebody here to see you. Says he's your pa."

Hugh didn't think so. Last he'd heard, Bo was doing time, but Hugh didn't want his boss to know anything about his father.

"My pa? You sure?"

"Says his name's Bo. He's waiting by the front gate. It's OK, take a break."

No way. Pa's in jail. Did he escape? Is he on the run? Hugh gave the gelding a few final strokes with the brush, led him to the stall, filled the bucket with feed, and latched the gate. He washed his hands and splashed cold water on his face. Tossing the paper towel into the trash, he said, "Be right back, Jeremiah."

"No hurry." Jeremiah turned away, absorbed in his task. He never asked questions, and took a man at face value. He had hired Hugh on impulse, he said, because he thought the boy had potential. And Hugh hadn't let him down.

Hugh's boss was his hero. With his first paycheck Hugh got a short, tidy haircut like Jeremiah's and bought good working boots, long-sleeved denim shirts, and decent jeans. He lived in the bunkhouse with room and board taken out of his check, the cheapest housing around. He was saving his money for a new truck to fix up and sell for a little profit.

There were books and magazines in the bunkhouse. Never one to care for reading before, Hugh discovered *Popular Mechanics*, and he found a dictionary to keep in his footlocker. He even checked out a couple of books Molly told him about from the library. Sure, he got some flack for reading in his spare time, but he didn't mind.

He kept five hundred dollars in his mattress, neatly stitched under the ticking. In case he found a promising truck in the want ads, he wanted ready cash for a down payment. He'd never had so much money, nearly three thousand dollars in the bank now.

Life at the stud farm was good. They worked him hard but treated him fair. The grub was regular and better than home. One night he went into town with some of the other hands and found himself at a bar. He was underage, but Chuck knew the owner, so Hugh had a beer with the guys. And then another. He lost count of how many tall, froth-topped mugs they shoved in front of him, but he'd been horribly sick in the bathroom, just puked his guts out. In the morning, he found himself back at the Three Meadows Horse Farm, sprawled across his bunk, with no memory of how he got there.

Jeremiah had evidently noted the boy's blanched face and red eyes and the knowing grins of the other hands. "Hot day," he told Hugh. "Drink a lot of water. You look a little peaked. Go inside and ask Sue for a couple of aspirin. Then take Chester in the shade to groom him." By afternoon Hugh felt much better. Lunch had tasted surprisingly good, and he'd taken in a lot of water, as Jeremiah recommended. Never again, he promised himself, remembering his own father's drunken, sloppy nights, when he'd pass out on the couch and his kids would have to clean up the mess in the morning.

After that night, Jeremiah always had something for him to do on Friday nights, a chore that couldn't wait, and would he mind not going to town with the others? Hugh was grateful for an excuse that allowed him to save face with the other guys.

These and other thoughts flashed through his mind as he approached the front gate, which was freshly painted white. The grass was green and lush and clipped, and the arched sign stood tall and proud, announcing "Three Meadows Horse Farm."

There stood Bo, grizzled, looking a little older.

"Hello, son," Bo said, his loose yellow dentures clicking.

"Hi." Hugh folded his arms, hugging his chest, and leaned against the fence post.

"I'm out."

"Uh-huh."

"Sprung me. Early release. Good behavior."

"Oh."

"Came to see my son." Bo eyed Hugh from head to foot. "You're bigger by a couple of inches and about twenty pounds. Getting broad across the shoulders, too. Looks like they're making a man out of you."

"Guess so."

"Ever hear from your sister?"

"Once in a while," Hugh lied. He and Molly emailed each other nearly every day, and he was planning to spend Christmas with her in Utah.

"Know where she's living?"

Hugh hesitated. "She moves around a lot."

"Well, you tell her that her pappy's coming to see her one of these days."

"You can't!"

Bo's eyes narrowed. "What do you mean, I can't? I'm her pa. I can see her when I durn well please."

Hugh hesitated. "I mean, she's out of the country."

"Out of the country?"

"She'll be gone for a few months. It's part of her college

program." Molly was spending a semester in Scotland as part of an exchange program, and having a wonderful time.

"College?" Bo frowned.

Hugh nodded.

"How's she paying for it?"

"Scholarships. Loans. She has a job. She works hard."

"Well, now. Little Molly in college. Whatever happened to her brat?"

Hugh's hands formed fists. Then he took a deep breath, shrugged at his father, and glanced back at the corral and bunkhouse. No one seemed to notice him standing by the gate with Bo.

"You heard your stepma divorced me?"

Hugh nodded.

"Went back to live with her folks. Found another man. That's women for you."

Hugh shrugged again. "So . . . what are your plans?"

"Treat you well here, do they?"

Hugh looked over the green fields, the tidy buildings, the corrals of purebred horses, the grounds shaded by proud, old trees. "Yeah."

"Pay you all right, don't they?"

Hugh tensed, on guard. "It's OK."

"How much you got on you?"

Hugh's hands dropped down to his sides, his left hand straying to his back pocket, as if to protect it. "A few bucks."

"Let me see your wallet."

Hugh sighed and pulled out his wallet. Bo took it and pocketed the ten and two ones. He checked the rest of the wallet. "Credit cards?"

"Nope."

"How much," Bo's eyes glinted as he leaned forward with his hand on Hugh's shoulder, "can you get your hands on in, say, five minutes?"

"Well, I . . ." Hugh hedged.

"You always was a good kid," said Bo, delivering a punch to

Hugh's shoulder, too hard to be playful. "Man's lucky to have a son who'll stand by him in thick and thin." His eyes hardened and he dropped his voice. Hugh smelled whiskey on his father's breath. "I know where you'd be keeping it. Just like I always did, in the mattress. Let's us just take a little walk."

Bo left with Hugh's five hundred dollars and another playful hard punch, his steps crackling on the gravel walkway. Hugh watched him until the drive curved and he couldn't see his father anymore.

He was relieved that the bunkhouse had been empty; to his knowledge, no one had seen him with Bo, except Jeremiah. "There goes my down payment for a new truck," he muttered. "From now on it all goes in the bank. I'll never keep more than twenty bucks out of my paycheck, just enough to take Debbie out for a burger and the dollar movie. I bet that's the last I'll see of him, anyway. He thinks he got everything I had. Guess I forgot to mention my savings account." He sighed, straightened his shoulders, and walked back to the tack room.

"You OK?" Jeremiah asked.

Hugh shoved his shaking hands in his pockets. "Yeah."

Chapter Forty-six

To relieve a toothache:
Take some bark from the south side of a red oak tree.
Boil and add a pinch of salt. Dip a cloth in it and
hold against the aching tooth.

—MISS CAROLINA'S REMEDIES AND ADVICE

But Hugh hadn't seen the last of his father. The next day he was summoned again to the front gates. The man who stood there had some resemblance to his father, but Hugh had never seen Bo Rawlins in a suit. It was cheap and it fit him poorly. His shirt collar looked too tight and his tie was askew. He smiled, showing a broad row of large, straight white teeth.

"Picked up my new dentures," Bo said with a new hiss in his speech. "Got fitted for 'em a while ago. A friend's been sending me a little cash to help out while I was in jail, and I been paying on 'em every month. When I got sprung I owed just about three hundred dollars. Good thing I ran into you. Money well spent, don't you think?"

Hugh blinked. With his son's money, Bo had bought a new suit and new teeth.

"Somebody I want you to meet," Bo said. He put his thumb and index finger to his lips and gave a piercing whistle.

A small smiling woman appeared from behind a large chestnut tree. She was probably forty, not over five feet tall, and thin. She wore a ruffled summer dress and a straw hat decorated with fake cherries and green leaves. She took off her hat, patted her mousy upswept brown hair, and gave Hugh a shy smile.

"My new wife, Jane," said Bo, giving her an affectionate squeeze. "Ain't she a peach?"

"How do," giggled Jane, extending her hand, nearly as small as a child's. There was a rhinestone *J* on the lower edge of one lens of her glasses, and her hair . . . where had he seen a style like that? Jane's hairdo was just like the housekeeper's on *The Brady Bunch.* What was her name? Alice. He'd seen a few reruns on TV. Hugh took Jane's soft, small hand, speechless. She smelled like magnolias.

"Met Jane in prison," Bo explained.

Hugh's eyes went swiftly to the woman's face. Jane looked like the kind of woman who'd take in stray dogs and cats and hang bird feeders in her yard. She probably belonged to clubs like the Daughters of the American Revolution and would even turn herself in to the police for accidentally running a stop sign when nobody was around. They'd met in jail?

"Her and me was pen pals," Bo chuckled. "Wrote each other for a year."

Pen pals? Bo was basically illiterate, depending on his wife and kids to read important letters and documents to him. He could sign his name and he recognized traffic signs, so he had somehow managed to pass the driver's license test.

Bo put his arm around Jane and gave her a squeeze. "Jane's a kindergarten teacher."

"Assistant kindergarten teacher," she corrected with another girlish giggle.

"Born and raised in Louisville. Loves kids. Wanted to meet mine. Been telling her all about you."

Jane blushed. "I met Bo for the first time in person yesterday morning. He's every bit as sweet as his letters." She held out her left hand with a slim gold band on the ring finger. "We were married just this afternoon."

Hugh swallowed, his mouth suddenly dry. Was Jane the "friend" who'd been sending Bo money for the last year? Did she know she'd been paying for his dentures?

"Headed on our honeymoon," Bo said. "Going out West. I'll be in touch. Well, sugar," he said, putting his arm around her again, "let's get this show on the road."

"Bye," Jane said, her voice soft and happy, trilling like a bird's. "It's lovely to meet you, dear. I hope we'll become good friends."

Mr. and Mrs. Bo Rawlins walked to a silver car Hugh hadn't noticed, parked behind a cluster of trees. It was new and cost more than Hugh hoped to make in a year. Jane took the keys out of her bag and opened the door. Bo turned, showed his new teeth in a broad white grin, and gave his son a wink.

Chapter Forty~seven

*If a lady's apron becomes untied while she is preparing a
meal, someone is talking about her.*

—Miss Carolina's Remedies and Advice

Louisa turned from the phone. "That was Mary Alice. Her
daughter's been in a car accident. They think she's going to be all
right, but Mary Alice is headed to Lexington to stay with her for
a few days. So the twins can't visit her this morning while you
take Eliza to the vet."

"I can take them with me," Andy said.

"That," Louisa said, "would be a circus."

Their other regular sitters were in school or otherwise occu-
pied, and Miss Carolina didn't have a phone.

"We'll be fine. You won't be gone that long," she said.

"I hate to leave you alone."

"Millions of pregnant mothers do this every day."

"But they're not *my* wife. And they're not pale and dizzy. I'd
better cancel Eliza's appointment."

Louisa insisted they would be fine. Andy gave in and told
the twins he would be gone less than an hour; he was just taking
Eliza to the vet. No, she wasn't sick. It was a "well dog checkup,"
just like they had "well child checkups."

"Now, stay inside and play quietly and do as your mother says," he told them.

The twins nodded.

"Go on, get out of here." Louisa smiled, though she was feeling queasy.

Alex and Lauren headed for the playroom. Louisa went to the refrigerator and got out the clay and cookie cutters so the twins could play at the kitchen table when they tired of the building blocks in the playroom. She sat on the couch and nibbled on a soda cracker. This pregnancy was already taxing her more than her first. Sometimes the drowsiness was so overpowering . . . she closed her eyes. Just for a moment.

"Shh. Mommy's asleep," said Lauren. "Don't wake her up."

"But I want to go outside." Alex headed for the door.

"Mommy said to stay inside. So did Daddy."

"I'm going outside," announced Alex.

Where one twin went, the other was bound to go. Lauren sighed and followed her brother out the back door.

"Alex!" Lauren called, looking up from the sandbox. "Don't go out of the yard! Mommy said so!"

"Look what I found! A puppy!" Alex said. "He likes me!"

Lauren ran to the fence where a small black and white puppy licked her brother's outstretched hand. "What's his name?"

"Dunno."

"Then think of one."

"He's black and white like a skunk. Let's call him Skunk," Alex said.

"OK. Hi, Skunk! How did you get through the gate?"

"Oh, there you are." A man's voice came from the other side of the fence. The twins looked up in surprise. "I see as you've found my puppy."

Alex and Lauren continued to stare at the strange man.

"It's all right." He opened the gate and smiled, his white teeth flashing. He bent and picked up the puppy. "I'm your Uncle Bo. Your grandpappy in Salt Lake City wants you to come with me. We're going to get on a jet plane and visit him."

Lauren's eyes widened. "We're going to visit Grandpa Cole?"

"But what about Mommy and Daddy?" Lauren asked, looking back toward the house.

"Oh, they're coming to Utah too," the man said with a smile. "We're just going a day or two early, to surprise your grandpa."

"Our mom's asleep," Lauren said, looking at Alex.

"And we shouldn't wake her up," Alex told her.

A silver car pulled up with a woman in the driver's seat. She smiled and rolled down the window. "I'm your Aunt Jane. How old are you darlings?"

Alex held up four chubby fingers.

"Well, now, isn't that nice! Are you identical twins?"

Lauren shook her head. "Uh-uh. We're eternal twins. He's a boy and I'm a girl."

"Oh, yes, of course. Well, come on, dears," Jane trilled, "we're all going on a trip to see your grandpa!"

"Do my mommy and daddy know?"

"Of course! They're the ones who asked us to take you to Utah."

Without a backward glance, the children followed the puppy and the man to the car.

Chapter Forty-eight

In our lovely Deseret
Where the Saints of God have met,
There's a multitude of children all around.
They are generous and brave;
They have precious souls to save;
They must listen and obey the gospel's sound.

Hark! Hark! Hark! 'tis children's music—
Children's voices, oh, how sweet,
When in innocence and love,
Like the angels up above,
They with happy hearts and cheerful faces meet.

"The first Eliza R. Snow wrote that," Andy told her namesake as they bumped along the rutted gravel road. "You really should learn it, too. Then again, Eliza R. Snow never had children of her own." Eliza didn't seem to mind his singing; in fact, her tail wagged to the rhythm of the old pioneer song. "Well, we're home. That wasn't so bad, was it? No more shots for a year. Hop out."

The front door slammed behind Andy. "Sorry," he apologized, seeing Louisa on the sofa. "Didn't mean to wake you."

Louisa yawned and stretched. "I just closed my eyes for a moment," she murmured.

"First trimester," Andy smiled, kissing her forehead. "It's awfully quiet here. Where are the twins?"

"In the playroom."

The playroom was empty. Andy checked their bedrooms and took a quick look outside. "And your next guess would be?"

Louisa leaped to her feet and then grabbed the arm of the sofa, her head spinning. "Alex! Lauren! Where are you?"

Andy dashed outside, calling for the twins. He raced to the barn, where Smoky regarded him with placid eyes, but no children greeted him. "Lauren! Alex!"

Eliza's barks of alarm bounced off the hills and echoed through the valleys.

Andy ran to the back porch, where Louisa stood in the doorway, grasping the frame for support.

"Andy," she whispered, her eyes wide with fear. "They're gone."

Chapter Forty-nine

When you first take off your shoes to go barefoot in the spring, wash your feet in cold water and you won't catch a cold all summer long.

—MISS CAROLINA'S REMEDIES AND ADVICE

Sheriff Jed Thomas, normally calm and unhurried, didn't waste any time organizing a search in Hawthorn Valley. Neighbors combed paths and meadows around their homes. Miss Carolina took her mule into the hills on paths only she knew about. Obadiah borrowed Lauren's sweater, let his hounds sniff it, and headed for the banks of the creek. School was dismissed for children over age twelve, and each group of students was given an area to search. The sheriff's department was out in full force, and a crew of deputies from Taylor's Glen was quickly dispatched. Authorities scanned the children's pictures, jotted down their age, weight, height, and other identifying marks, and sent the information via the Internet to the media and the Department of Transportation, which flashed missing child alerts on electronic highway signs.

Thomas placed a call to the FBI. "An agent will be here from Lexington in half an hour and more are on their way," he said, hanging up the phone.

Louisa clutched Andy's hand. "FBI? Do you think they've been—?"

Thomas's normally affable face was grim. "We've learned not to waste a moment when children are missing. The word's out all over the state and the FBI will probably take it national."

⁓

FBI Agent Percy, whose eyes looked too old for his face, opened his briefcase. It was meticulously stocked with new sharpened yellow #2 pencils, a calculator, tape recorder, extra batteries, a digital camera, cell phone, and yellow legal pads. He pulled out one of these, dated it, looked at his watch, and recorded the time, 1400, military style. "Dr. Martin, you go by your maiden name, is that correct?"

"Yes," she said, "it would be too confusing with two Dr. Mc-Brides here in Hawthorn Valley, so I use my maiden name as my professional name, too. I always have."

"All right, Dr. Martin, tell me everything you can remember before you discovered the children were missing."

"They were in the playroom. I was going to make some soup for the slow cooker. But first, I got out the clay and cookie cutters so they could play here in the kitchen when they were through with the building blocks. That was about nine this morning. I decided to sit down for a moment before I started the soup, and I guess I fell asleep. When I woke up it was about nine thirty and they—they were gone."

"Do the children often play alone in the yard?"

"No, not unless I'm watching from the kitchen window. They know they're supposed to stay inside the fence, and our dog is very protective. But she wasn't here."

"She was with me," Andy explained. "At the vet. If she had been here—"

Eliza paced through the house, sniffing, restless. She gave a little whine and sat at Andy's feet.

"You expect the family pet to supervise your children, Dr. Martin?"

"Of course not!" Louisa snapped.

Percy turned to Andy. "And when did you get home, Dr. McBride?"

"It was about nine thirty. I woke Louisa when I got home."

Louisa shook her head, her face pale, the light freckles more evident across her nose. "I just sat down for a minute," she explained again. "I was suddenly very, very tired. I must have dozed off because when Andy got home I was asleep on the sofa." Her voice faded. She swallowed hard and then leaped from the sofa, rushing to the bathroom.

Andy turned to Agent Percy, flushed, his teeth clenched. "*She's pregnant.* I know you're doing your job, but please, ease up on her. We haven't told anyone about the baby yet. She's about eight weeks along, and she's at risk. Her blood pressure's already elevated. Stress can be dangerous for her health and the baby's. Drowsiness isn't unusual in the first trimester. It can come on very suddenly and just overpower a woman. I think that's what happened this morning. Our children are missing, and you're *grilling* her, *interrogating* her, challenging her competence as a mother, suggesting she's responsible. Well, if anyone's responsible for not watching them, it's me. *I* shouldn't have left her alone, knowing how ill she was. I should've remembered my dream . . ."

Percy's eyes narrowed. "Your dream?"

Andy berated himself. *That was stupid, bringing up my nightmare when the twins disappeared into the fog.* He shook his head. "It's nothing. Sometimes I have dreams. Sometimes they're nightmares. About six weeks ago, I had a dream where they were running and I couldn't catch them. That's all. Listen, I'm a parent. I'm protective of my children, and I worry about them. Any parent would."

"Humph," was Percy's response as he wrote on his legal pad in precise capital letters. Andy strained to see what Percy had written, but the agent looked up from the pad and frowned.

"Agent Percy," Andy said, "we'd arranged for a friend to stay with them this morning, but she canceled at the last minute. I know you have to consider everyone a suspect initially, even the parents. I understand that. Ask me anything, but *leave my wife alone.* Please."

Percy rubbed his eyes. "I think we've covered everything

with your wife for the moment. I do have some questions for you. Have you been having marital problems?"

"No."

"Any infidelity?"

"No."

"Mental illness?"

"No."

"This pregnancy, was it planned?"

"Why would you even ask that kind of a question?"

"Has your wife been behaving irrationally?"

"What?"

"Women's hormones, when they're pregnant, well, there have been cases where the mother . . ."

"No irrational behavior."

Percy cleared his throat. "We know Dr. Martin comes from Gabriel's Landing, Utah. A polygamous community."

"And?"

"Do you have more than one wife, Dr. McBride?"

Andy forced himself to count to five before he said, through clenched teeth, "Absolutely not!"

"Do you plan to take another wife?"

"No, I do not plan to take another wife. Ever!"

Percy raised an eyebrow. "We do know there are . . . problems . . . with some of those groups. You do associate with Dr. Martin's father and his plural wives, don't you, Dr. McBride?"

"They're *family.* When Louisa reported abuse in Gabriel's Landing, she had to leave. I assume you've done your homework, and you know about the trouble and why she had to leave. It's a very . . . closed community. She can never go home again. But yes, her father and his wives write letters, and we also exchange letters with all of her brothers and sisters. Mr. Martin and his wives do come to visit us. We welcome them into our home and our family. I know it's unconventional, but they are the children's grandparents. And they are wonderful grandparents."

"Dr. McBride, would anyone from Gabriel's Landing or a rival polygamous clan have any reason to take your children, anything to gain? Something related to the incidents that forced Dr. Martin to leave?"

"I can't imagine that anyone would have that kind of hatred. Not that kind, to take our children. The group she comes from, in Gabriel's Landing, they keep to themselves. They don't have any rivalries with other groups. No enemies that I know of."

"No ongoing feuds with other clans?"

Andy shook his head. "Perhaps all of this is hard for you to comprehend, but Louisa and I share a common heritage, a pioneer heritage, and . . . Joshua Martin is a fine man. I'm proud to know him. And Sarah and Hannah are two of the kindest women I've ever known. Do you understand what I'm saying?"

Percy was evidently a man who did not answer questions. He only asked them. "I know it's . . . complicated," he conceded. "We will be interviewing Dr. Martin's father and his wives."

"I understand." Andy gave an anxious glance down the hall-way, toward the bathroom.

"Do you use drugs, Dr. McBride?"

"No."

"But you have access to them?"

"I'm a physician. I have access to a certain number of sample medications from the pharmaceutical companies, but I don't have any controlled substances at the clinic."

"How about alcohol?"

"We don't drink. You won't find any in the house. Please, go through the cupboards. Be my guest."

"Recreational drugs? Marijuana?"

"No." *Get a grip, Andy. Stop being so defensive. Keep calm. Keep Louisa calm.*

"What drugs will we find at the clinic, Dr. McBride?"

"Samples from the pharmaceutical companies, prenatal vita-mins. Antibiotics. All legal. There's nothing with any street value, if that's what you're asking."

Louisa appeared in the hallway, looking pale and weak. Andy hurried to her and guided her back to the sofa.

Percy checked his watch again and noted the time on the

legal pad. "No more questions for the moment, Dr. Martin, Dr. McBride. Anything that comes to mind, no matter how trivial, please tell us. Any piece of information could be critical. We have to investigate the family thoroughly. Standard procedure. Our job is to recover your children."

He went into the kitchen to brief the other dark-suited agents. For a moment, they reminded Andy of Mormon missionaries. Dark suits, white shirts, and short, conservative haircuts . . . they only needed name tags. Forcing himself to clear his mind, he focused again on the scene in his kitchen.

Agent Matthews stood by the table, in charge of four other men who would be gathering information by interviewing possible witnesses, neighbors, or any suspicious persons. He was a nervous man, constantly chewing gum; he was trying to give up cigarettes, Percy had said. Matthews took a sheaf of papers from Percy and gave each of his men instructions. They nodded and left. No doubt friends and neighbors and patients would be asked endless questions about Andy and Louisa and their children.

Myers was the technical expert, Percy explained. A tall, gangly young man with acne who looked like he'd just graduated from high school, Myers gave a brief nod when introduced to Andy and Louisa, but he didn't put his laptop down to shake hands with them. He quickly set up his computer at the kitchen table and put on his headphones. Within a minute his long fingers were flying over the keyboard. The fax machine churned out more papers that Percy read with a frown.

Percy returned to the living room. "Dr. McBride, I'm going to ask you again: Is there anyone you can think of who would want to harm your children?"

Andy shook his head. "I've been thinking all morning, racking my brain."

"Or anyone who would want to harm your wife?"

Andy's grip on Louisa's hand tightened. "No."

"Dr. Martin?"

"No," she said.

"Is there anyone who might have a reason to hurt you?"

"No."

"Think of your medical practice, both of you, please. Have you lost a patient recently? Malpractice suits?"

"No."

"Any miscarriages, still births, infant deaths?"

Andy recalled one miscarriage, but surely the Kelseys didn't hold him responsible.

Percy gave Matthews orders to interview the Kelseys. Andy winced; being questioned about their personal loss would be distressing for them. He gave Percy the keys to the clinic, where Olive would unlock the file cabinets and provide the FBI with complete access to their records.

"What's he doing?" Andy asked, as Agent Myers carried the family's computer tower into the kitchen and connected it to his laptop.

"Standard procedure. He'll review emails, Internet sites you've visited, everything on your computer. Even items you thought you'd deleted. Myers will find them. He'll find everything."

"There's nothing to find. Nothing objectionable, nothing illegal. Just emails, medical sites, ESPN . . . like any other home computer, I'd imagine."

Percy gave a wry smile. "Myers will find everything." Myers started a download and put a tap on the phone.

Percy answered the knock at the door. It was Miss Carolina, who had tethered her mule to the porch. Percy looked beyond her and gaped at the strange sight of a mule. Miss Carolina brushed past Agent Percy and strode inside, going straight to Andy and Louisa. Percy shut the door and stared at the peculiar woman. Ignoring the agents, Miss Carolina was direct, as usual. "Doc Andy, Doc Louisa, I been thinking."

"And you would be—" Percy asked, pencil and legal pad in hand.

The woman drew herself up to her full height and looked at him with narrowed eyes. "Miss Lily Carolina Bates."

Percy blinked and responded with a nod, almost the beginning of a bow.

Andy had never heard the Healer's full name. The small

woman stood in the middle of the room, working her floppy hat with her hands. Tapping the toe of her small black boot on the wood floor, she began to interrogate Percy. "I hear the little ones have gone missing. It's possible someone took them?"

"Yes, ma'am," Percy said, "I'm afraid so, ma'am." Evidently he did answer questions.

Miss Carolina turned to Andy. Her blue eyes were intense as she said, "Think, Andy. Somebody does have a grudge against you. It's been, what, five years since he cornered you in the barn with his rifle?"

Percy broke the lead on his pencil, tossed it in his briefcase and grabbed another. "A rifle? In the barn?"

"Bo Rawlins?" Andy asked incredulously.

"Makes sense, don't it?" Miss Carolina said.

"Who is this Rawlins?" Percy demanded.

Miss Carolina's voice hardened. "Bo's all right when he's sober. But when he's liquored up he can get downright ugly. Went after Doc Andy 'cause Andy took care of his girl and sent her away so her pa couldn't beat her anymore. She was in the family way, and Bo blamed Andy for that, too."

Percy looked at Andy. "The girl was pregnant?"

Andy nodded. "She was my patient."

"What was your relationship with this girl?"

Andy gritted his teeth. "She was my patient."

Miss Carolina stamped her foot. "Stop making insinuations, young man. You're interrupting what I have to say."

"Sorry, ma'am," Percy said.

"Then Hugh, that's Bo's boy, he left home and found a new job in Taylor's Glen, and Bo blamed Andy 'cause he told Hugh about the job. Then, after he got out of jail the first time, for hurting his own girl, and her in the family way and all when he did it, Bo got stinking drunk, loaded his rifle, and followed Andy into the barn. We was right behind him, three of us following him with our rifles, 'cause we knew Bo was in a drunken state of righteous indignation, but this here dog, Eliza R. Snow, she got to him first. Bit him in the leg."

Hearing her name, Eliza wagged her tail. Her dark eyes shone as she gave Miss Carolina her full attention.

"And the dog, you say, this dog, she—"

"Yep. Bit him in the leg. Eliza R. Snow is a good judge of people."

"Who?" Percy's face showed his confusion.

"The dog, of course, who did you think I was making mention of? The dog's name is Eliza R. Snow."

Percy's pencil traveled quickly across the page.

"Bo's in jail, Agent Percy," Andy said. "He was convicted of attempted assault with a deadly weapon and parole violations."

Miss Carolina persisted. "Maybe he's out." She glared at Percy. "Ever think of that? Or he might could of escaped." Percy straightened his tie. "Find Bo Rawlins," Miss Carolina ordered. "He's the only person in this valley's got a bone to pick with Doc Andy."

Percy called to Matthews, who presided over the organized chaos in the kitchen, which had been taken over by fax machines, phones, printers, and laptop computers. "Run a check on Bo Rawlins." Percy turned to Andy. "R-A-W-L-I-N-S?"

Andy nodded.

Percy turned to Louisa. "Dr. Martin, has Rawlins ever threatened you or the children?"

"I've never even met him," Louisa said.

"The trouble with Bo happened before Louisa and I were married," Andy told him. "Louisa wasn't even living here then."

Miss Carolina brewed peppermint tea for Louisa and served it to the agents as well, telling them they probably had sour stomachs in their line of work. "Now, there's no caffeine in it in case you're wondering. Otherwise Doc Andy and Doc Louisa wouldn't drink it. It's agin' their religion."

They sipped their tea obediently. Miss Carolina made a soothing lavender compress, insisted that Louisa lie down, and put it on her forehead. "Gotta be careful in your condition, honey," she whispered.

Louisa's eyes flew open. "My condition?"

Miss Carolina took her hand. "In the family way, aren't you?

Not much gets past me. Now you stay put." She slipped a pillow under Louisa's head and covered her with an afghan. Louisa tried to sit up, but Miss Carolina stopped her with a gentle hand. Then she turned to the agents. "She needs her rest," the Healer announced.

They nodded.

"See that she gets it. Now, I'm just going to get back on Harold. That's my mule," she said. "You might want to write that down, too."

Percy started to write and then looked down at the Healer, who gave him a wry smile. "Got another path or two to check. You know how to find me, Andy." She glared at Percy. "But it's Bo Rawlins you need to find. You'd best send your boys in them fancy suits after him." She crammed the old felt hat on her head, walked to the door, and closed it behind her with a slam.

Sitting on the edge of the sofa, holding Louisa's hand, Andy saw the puzzled look in Percy's eyes and anticipated the next question. "Miss Carolina is our good friend. I wish I had half of her common sense. She's a Healer. She looks after us. That's right, she looks after us, even though we're physicians, and we love her dearly. She takes care of everybody. The twins call her Grandma Miss Carolina. They think they have half a dozen grandmothers here in Hawthorn Valley."

"Could she be right about this Bo Rawlins?"

Andy sighed and ran his fingers through his hair. "He probably hates me, and Miss Carolina explained that very well, but surely he'd never take it this far. Anyway, he's in jail, so—"

"*Why wasn't Dr. McBride notified?*" bellowed Matthews into his cell phone, pacing up and down the kitchen floor. He turned and gestured to Percy, picking up a fax with his free hand. Waving it vigorously, he yelled into the phone. "*Paperwork?* The man holds Doc Andy, I mean, Dr. McBride, at gunpoint and threatens his life, he gets released from jail, and nobody even thinks to notify Dr. McBride? *Paperwork?* Find a better excuse. No, don't waste your time on a flimsy story, and don't blame some other department. Find Bo Rawlins *now!*"

Chapter Fifty

Fresh marigolds in any room will heighten the energy within.

—Miss Carolina's Remedies and Advice

Before Andy could react to the news that Bo was indeed out of jail, there was another knock on the door. Percy opened the door and stepped out onto the porch. Andy heard a familiar voice. "Rawlins. Hugh Rawlins."

Andy jumped to his feet. "Hugh!"

Hugh stepped into the doorway. For a moment, Andy hardly recognized the boy; he was taller and broader and there was a new air of confidence about him, despite the distress Andy saw in his face. Hugh licked his lips nervously. "Doc Andy. I heard about Alex and Lauren on the radio, and I had to come. To see if I could help or anything."

"Rawlins? You're Bo Rawlins's boy?" Percy asked.

Hugh looked at Andy in surprise and then nodded at Percy. "Yes. How did you know about my—"

"When's the last time you saw him?"

"It's all right, Hugh," Andy said. "Tell him everything you know about your father."

"I, uh, well, I saw him yesterday afternoon." Hugh gave an account of his last two encounters with his father: Bo's first visit

267

to the horse farm after he was released from jail, and again on the following day, when he returned as a married man, with his magnolia-scented new wife in tow.

"Do you know where he is?"

Hugh shrugged. "On his honeymoon, I guess."

"You guess? Did he say where they were going?"

"Out West. That's all he said. They drove off in her car. I can tell you the make and model and color. Silver Lexus RX 400h coupe. Brand new. 268 horsepower, custom wheel hubcaps."

Percy leaned forward. "Silver Lexus 400h coupe?"

"Yeah. Cars are sort of a hobby for me. I mean, I like to read about them."

"Good. Tell me more."

"It has . . . yes, it has a sun roof. And Kentucky plates. Wait, I think they were custom license plates. You know, the ones where you can put a name or something on them. I'm not sure, maybe they said 'Jane,' that's her name. I wish I knew more, Doc Andy, Doc Louisa. I wish I—"

"Matthews, check out the car this boy just described. Can't be too many of them around here. Did you know your father was going to be released from jail?"

"No, sir. I was surprised to see him when he showed up at Three Meadows, where I work."

"You had no contact with him before then?"

Hugh shook his head. "No, sir. Just a postcard about six months ago. That's all." A light sheen of sweat glistened on his forehead. Andy was certain Percy made note of that, too.

"But your father knows you're friends with Dr. McBride?"

"Yeah—yes, sir."

"Would you agree to a polygraph test?"

Hugh looked at Andy in confusion. "What's that?"

"They just ask you questions and monitor your heart rate while you answer, Hugh. It's one way to tell if someone could be lying. Louisa and I both passed. You'll be fine."

Hugh's eyes widened. *You think my pa took the twins?*

"We have to investigate every lead," was all Percy would say.

"Doc Andy?" Hugh's voice cracked. "Do you think my pa did this?"

Andy put his hand on the boy's shoulder. "I don't know. It's possible. They have to investigate any possible leads."

"It's all right, Hugh," said Louisa, sitting up. "We know you had nothing to do with this."

Hugh's face held a look of anguish. "Doc Louisa, I'm so sorry about the twins."

Louisa nodded, tears in her eyes.

"You say your father's headed out West?" Percy asked Hugh. "Does he know anybody there?"

"I don't know."

"Didn't you say your sister lived in the West?"

"Yes, sir. She goes to Utah State University. Got a scholarship. She works in a greenhouse part time."

"We will need her contact information." Percy handed a fresh legal pad and pencil to Hugh.

Hugh pulled a slip of paper from his wallet. "She's in Scotland now, for a semester, but here's a phone number where she's staying. My boss sold me his old laptop, and me and her have been emailing back and forth."

"Do you have it with you?"

Hugh nodded. "In my truck."

"Matthews! Go out to this boy's truck and get his laptop. Give it to Meyers."

Hugh fished for his keys in his pocket and gave them to Matthews. He turned back to Percy. "Like I told you, sir, I haven't heard very much from my pa for the last few years, just a postcard now and then. He's—what's the word?—he's pretty much illiterate."

Then Hugh gave a description of Jane, working with the sketch artist, but he didn't know much about her, either—even her last name. He supposed it was Rawlins now. Then he submitted to the polygraph test and passed. He stood up with a sigh of relief.

"Wait." Hugh sat down again and closed his eyes. "Wait. There was something else about Jane. Pa said, he said, yes. He said she was born and raised in Louisville. Does that help?"

"Matthews, look up a Jane Something from Louisville with a brand new silver Lexus RX 400h, custom plates; they may have her name on them."

"That's all for now," Percy told Hugh, "but don't leave town."

"No, sir, I hadn't planned to. I'm staying in Hawthorn Valley until you find Alex and Lauren. I'll call my boss in Taylor's Glen, and he'll give me time off, no questions asked. I can bunk at Olive's." He turned to Percy, grim torment in his dark eyes. "I'd do anything for Doc Andy and Doc Louisa and the twins." He swallowed hard and looked at Andy and Louisa and licked his lips again. "If my pa's taken them, I—I'm so sorry."

Andy put his arm around the young man's shoulders. "Listen, Hugh. You came right away. You've told us everything you know, and I know you've told the truth. They have more leads now because of you. They may find our children because of you. I pray they will. And if your father had anything to do with this, we know you're not involved. Do you understand what I'm saying?"

Hugh wiped his forehead with his sleeve. He nodded.

Percy handed him a pencil and pad. "Write down a number where we can reach you." Hugh scrawled Olive's phone number on the pad and handed it back to Percy, who gave the boy a piercing look and then, grudgingly, an approving nod. "You've given us some helpful information. Maybe even the information we need to find these missing children. You came as soon as you heard, didn't wait for someone to come and find you. That saved us time. Every minute counts, son. You think of anything more, you call this number, all right?"

Hugh put Percy's card in his pocket. Suddenly, Percy extended his hand. Hugh swallowed hard and shook it. He looked back at Andy and Louisa, who nodded their thanks and their trust. With a sigh, he left.

The president of the county jail's Pen Pal Club told the FBI agents everything she knew about Jane and promptly submitted her resignation.

Jane's silver Lexus was found in the long-term parking lot at the Lexington airport.

Chapter Fifty-one

Jane's silver credit card made a quick swipe as she paid for their Wal-Mart purchases. She had been surprised that the children didn't have suitcases with pajamas, clean underwear, and extra clothes (what was their mother thinking, she wondered), so after landing at the Las Vegas airport and renting a minivan, they made a trip to Wal-Mart (after the Happy Meals and McDonald's Playland). In addition to clothes, she also bought toys and books for the children and looked for slippers for Bo, who had padded around barefooted the night before. Giggling, she found large furry bear slippers in his size. The animals had silly grins and crossed eyes designed to jiggle with every step.

To his credit, "You're a real crack-up, sweetie" was all Bo said as he dropped the grinning bear slippers in the shopping cart.

The children had to have fuzzy animal slippers, too. Lauren chose orange and black striped tigers and Alex fell for the shaggy lions. Then they persuaded Jane to buy some for herself. "Oh, what should I choose?" she squealed. "They're all so adorable!"

Lauren pointed to the pink bunny slippers. "Get these, Aunt Jane!"

Jane stroked the soft fleecy ears. "I shall name them Flopsy and Mopsy, after Peter Rabbit's little sisters."

Alex laughed. "You're funny, Aunt Jane. Isn't she, Uncle Bo?"

"Yeah. A real crack-up."

After piling books and toys into the cart, Jane turned practical and bought toothbrushes and toothpaste for the twins, who were so enamored with their new slippers they insisted on wearing them out of the store.

"Come on, Uncle Bo, Aunt Jane, put yours on, too," Lauren urged.

Bo sighed as he sat on the bench outside the store and put on his slippers, but he found some comfort knowing that in another twenty-four hours or so he'd dump these little Chatterboxes on their grandpappy, in return for a tidy nest egg of his own. He didn't mind being temporarily supported by Jane, who had a healthy savings account and an inheritance from her late husband, dead more than fifteen years; he'd soon have it all in his own name if he played his cards right. Speaking of cards, once his bride and the Chatterboxes were settled in the motel, he'd put his shoes back on and head out to make some serious money of his own. The stills and marijuana crop had been neglected in his absence, but he'd soon be making money off them, too, when he was back home and settled again.

Bo played a mean game of poker, and he was feeling lucky. He fingered the wad of bills in his pocket with satisfaction. On their wedding day, Jane had withdrawn five thousand dollars in cash from the bank, a loan to cover his "temporary cash flow problem." She gave him a thousand dollars and stashed the rest in her bosom, where, as far as he knew, it remained. In the morning he'd be sure to flash a few big bills at the restaurant and make a show of offering to pay for breakfast, but he'd let his little wife pick up the tab.

"Come on, sweetie, let's get this show on the road. We need to find a motel so I can find me a good game of—I mean, so the Troublemakers can go to bed."

"Of course, dear. It is getting late." Jane buckled the twins in their booster seats, opened a box of graham crackers and two bottles of juice, and pulled their new picture books out to occupy them on the way to the motel. She had insisted on renting a van with all the extras after they landed in Las Vegas, so the children could watch Disney videos on the little television mounted on the ceiling behind the front seats.

While Jane struggled with the cart and bags, Bo hopped in the van and started the engine, which responded with a satisfying roar when he stomped on the accelerator. Jane took a quick inventory of their purchases. "Oh, Bo, darling, we forgot one of our bags, the one with the toothbrushes and toothpaste. We mustn't neglect the children's oral hygiene, not for even one night. Would you be a dear and go back for it?"

Bo swallowed his customary retort ("Get it yourself, woman!") which had always worked with his other wives, who'd always been dirt poor. "Sure, honey."

Jane wheeled the squeaky cart to the return rack a few yards away. Anxious to get to the poker tables, Bo left the keys in the ignition and the motor running, slamming the door in his haste to retrieve the bag. As Jane reached for her door handle, a soft "click" automatically locked the children safely inside and everyone else out. It was one of the extras she'd requested, automatic locks that activated within sixty seconds.

"Oh, dear! Oh, dear!" The children were buckled in their booster seats, crunching on graham crackers and guzzling juice. "Darlings, please unlock the door!" Jane knocked on the window and waved to get their attention. They waved back. Using exaggerated gestures, she pointed hopefully to the lock button on the driver's side, but they couldn't even see it, and they wouldn't know how to open it anyway, she realized to her dismay. They probably thought she'd invented a new game, with all her gesturing and head-bobbing.

Tears formed in her eyes; she seemed to cry easily these days. It must be all the excitement of meeting and marrying Bo, who had charmed her with his dazzling smile. Their first night together, though, when the smile plopped into a glass of water on the nightstand, she fled to the bathroom where she shut the door, turned on the tap to mask the noise, and wept. It was just nerves, she told herself, for Bo really was a dear, though he wasn't at all like her first husband, timid balding Walter, who passed away after only a year of wedded bliss, leaving his young widow with a sizeable bankbook.

When she had composed herself she powdered her nose, secured her upswept hairstyle and angel curls with a couple of hairpins and a generous spritz of extra-hold hairspray, fussed over her new modest pink negligee, opened the bathroom door, and tiptoed to the bed. "Bo, darling," she whispered.

Bo was asleep, his caved-in mouth open, his snores shaking the bed. Jane stared at him for a full minute. Then she stuffed cotton in her ears, slipped under the bedspread and inched to the outer edge of the bed, pulling the spread up to her chin. Exhausted, she finally closed her eyes and slept.

The next morning Bo had been in a hurry to drive to Hawthorn Valley and pick up his niece and nephew, so the marriage hadn't been consummated yet, and, of course, with the children sharing their room now, that would have to wait. It was probably just as well, she was beginning to think, after the first disappointment wore off; after all, she and Bo had hardly met in person before they became man and wife.

Now the tears slid down her cheeks and splashed onto the crisp white linen collar of her pastel flowered dress. "Oh, the children, the children!" she wept, though they waved and smiled from their booster seats.

"Can I help you, ma'am?" A blue-vested young man whose name tag read "Lionel" approached her.

"Oh, yes, oh, yes, indeed! I'm in dire need of assistance. You see, the doors locked automatically, and the motor's running, and my little darlings are locked inside. You must help me, sir!"

"I'll see what I can do, m—" the lad stared at her feet.

"Oh!" Jane managed a giggle and gave a little hop in her bunny slippers. "We all got new slippers, and the children insisted we put them on. We're on our honeymoon, you see."

"Yes, ma'am," Lionel responded politely. "Of course. I'll just go inside and get the manager."

~

"What do you mean, you can't break in?" Bo sputtered, holding the bag with the oral hygiene items, stamping his bear-slippered foot.

Eli the manager's eyes rested on Bo's unusual footwear for a moment. A grin started to appear on his face, but he pressed his lips together and kept his composure. "No, sir, you see, that would damage the van. We can call for assistance, though. We're happy to do that, and you and your grandchildren will be out of here in no time."

"I'm their uncle," Bo set him straight. Then he flashed an engaging smile. The lights in the parking lot caught the stunning whiteness of his teeth, and the surveillance video cameras documented it as well. "I'm taking them to see my older brother, their grandpappy. In Salt Lake City. He's the Mormon bishop, you know. Runs the whole church. Like the Pope."

"I see. Well, sir, we'll have a locksmith here in no time."

"Just give me one of them extra-long screwdrivers from Hardware. I'll give it back soon's I'm done. You won't even need to take the price tag off. All you gotta do is—well, I've done it myself plenty of times. A couple minutes with a screwdriver and we're ready to get this show on the road."

"But, sir, that would damage your new van!"

"No problem. It ain't mine, anyway," Bo told him. "So just get me the tool. You see," he confided, as Jane pressed her nose against the window to smile at the children through her tears, "I'm in a hurry." He lowered his voice. "A business investment, if you know what I mean."

Eli gave a respectful nod. Bo felt compelled to elaborate. "There's a deck of poker cards with my name on 'em, just waiting for me."

An ominous rumble drowned any response Eli might have

made. Rain clouds were gathering quickly, darkening the sky. "Uh, tell you what, sir," he looked from Bo to his employee, "I'll have Lionel bring out a couple of umbrellas. Wouldn't want to get your . . ." he saw the fluorescent pink of Jane's bunny slippers in the lights ". . . your feet wet. Or—or your heads, of course, either. I'll just go back inside and call the locksmith."

The faithful Lionel headed to the store for umbrellas and then turned back to Bo. "Anything else I can get for you while you wait, sir?"

"What a marvelous young man!" Jane thanked him, sniffing. "You are so very kind, sir."

Bo put a friendly arm around Lionel. "I could use a visit from my old friend, Jack Daniels."

"There's nobody here by that name. But I've only worked here a month. I could ask."

"I mean," Bo gave Lionel's arm a little squeeze for emphasis, "booze."

Lionel took a step away from Bo. "Oh. Well, I'm sure that's against company policy. Besides, you're going to be driving, aren't you?"

"What's that got to do with it?"

"Uh, I'll just get those umbrellas."

Chapter Fifty-two

Two hours later the twins dozed, graham cracker crumbs smudged on their faces. They were warm and dry in the van while Bo, very damp, paced and swore and ruined his new slippers. Jane had stood faithfully by the window nearest the children, holding a Marge Simpson umbrella over her head, alternating from one side of the van to the other so that each child received equal attention, repeating nursery rhymes and singing songs to them long after they had fallen asleep.

"Would you stop that infernal racket, woman?" Bo finally snarled. A glance at Jane's stricken face suggested he'd said something wrong. "Uh, I mean, my dearest, um, cupcake, they're asleep, you see, the Graham Cracker Kids, they're snoozing away, so you can stop singing. Rest yourself, sugar. Don't get your knickers in a knot."

After the nice service station attendant gave Jane a lift back to the van, which had run out of gas ten miles away from Wal-Mart, he put two gallons of gas in the tank and followed them back to the station, where he filled the rest of the tank at the pump. Then Jane's magic silver card got them a room with two beds at the Lucky Inn.

Jane blotted her soaking hair with a towel and helped the twins into their new pajamas, bundling up the damp and dirty clothes. "Bo, dear, I'll just take these down to the laundry, sweetheart," she said with a little shiver, reaching for a dry sweater. "I won't be gone long."

Bo grunted and looked up from tying his boot lace as the door closed behind Jane. "Huh? What'd she say? Where'd she go?"

He heard the toilet flush. Evidently the Chatterboxes were exploring the new bathroom. Lauren poked her head out of the door. "We want a bath in the big tub, Uncle Bo!"

"Sure, why not? Go ahead. Help yourself." Bo looked at his watch in irritation. Then he found the remote control and channel-surfed until he found a bowling tournament on the sports network.

In the laundromat Jane had already made a new friend, Lucy from Oklahoma. When Jane confided with a blush that she was a new bride, Lucy begged for all the details of the courtship and wedding. "Well," said Jane with a little flutter, "it all began about year ago when I got the most wonderful, romantic letter . . ."

⌒

The twins tossed their pajamas on the bed and dashed back to the bathroom, where they grabbed the hotel's little bottles of shampoo, body wash, mouthwash, conditioner, and lotion and dumped them all into the jetted tub, which was soon filled with warm, bubbly water and splashing children.

"Soap! Soap! Soap! Don't forget the soap," chanted the children from a story Miss Carolina had told them.

"Rubber duckie, you're the one, you make baftime so much fun," Alex sang, squeezing the yellow rubber duck Jane had bought at Wal-Mart. Lauren belted out a song from her father's favorite oldies CD, "Splish splash, I was takin' a baf, on-a on-a Saturday night!"

"Let's sing the song Uncle Bo taught us last night, while we were riding in the van," Alex said, and the twins gave an enthusiastic rendition of the old Irish song:

What do you do with a drunken sailor,
What do you do with a drunken sailor,
What do you do with a drunken sailor,
Early in the morning?
Put him in the bed with the captain's daughter,
Put him in the bed with the captain's daughter,
Put him in the bed with the captain's daughter,
Early in the morning . . .

An hour later Jane returned, her new best friend's name and address tucked in her pocket. An infomercial for a gadget guaranteed to find fish in any lake or your money back blared from the TV in the empty room.

Jane sneezed. "Bo, darling, where are you? Alex? Lauren?"

She found two pairs of size four pajamas on the bed. Suddenly, water gushed from under the bathroom door, forming a large dark stain that spread quickly over the carpet.

"My heavens!" she shrieked, and opened the bathroom door. The pink bunny slippers were flooded as the water rushed over her ankles, the floppy rabbit ears bobbing in the current.

"It's OK," Alex told her, sporting a beard of bubbles on his chin. "We took a bath. All by ourselves."

"I can see that," Jane placed a nervous hand over her fluttering heart. "Well, let's just rinse off, darlings, and get nice and dry. What strange smelling soap!" She sneezed again.

The mint-scented children were tucked into bed with their new stuffed animals when a sharp, insistent rap brought Jane to the door. Soggy towels in hand, she opened it to face the red-faced manager. Did she know they'd flooded the room downstairs? With many "oh, dear's" and "we're terribly sorry's" and "you see, my dear husband . . . 's" and "you are so very kind, sir's," she gave him her silver card, paid for the damage to both rooms, and charmed him into renting them another.

An hour later, established in the new, dry room, Jane sat on the bed, exhausted. Her eyes rested on the bunny slippers, matted and soaked, huddled sadly by Bo's soggy cross-eyed bears.

"I miss Skunk," Alex said, on the verge of tears. "I miss the puppy."

"He couldn't go on the plane with us, honey," Jane told him.

"Do you think he's happy?" Lauren's lower lip quivered.

"Oh, yes, I'm sure he is," said Jane, with a little frown on her face as she glanced at Bo.

Driving through a residential neighborhood on their way to the airport, Bo had told her to stop beside a group of children playing basketball, where he got out of the car, holding the puppy in his arms. "Hi there," he said. "Would you like to win a contest? Who can tell me the name of the President of the United States?"

"George W. Bush," said a little girl with short blonde hair and glasses.

"Close enough. Congratulations! Here's your prize!" Bo put the puppy in the girl's arms, hopped back in the car, and said, "All right, Jane, let's go."

"Mommy, Mommy, look what the nice man gave me! Can I keep him, can I keep him, please?" they heard as they drove away.

Now the twins had a new worry. "I miss my mommy and daddy," Alex quavered.

Lauren nodded. "Me, too," she said, on the verge of tears.

"Oh, sweethearts," Jane said, putting her arms around them, "we're going to see them soon, at your grandpa's, in Salt Lake City. Remember, Uncle Bo promised?"

After a while the children were consoled. Jane read stories to them, and within a few minutes they were asleep, curled back to back like two matching bookends. It had been a long, exciting day for them. Little angels, they were, such precious darlings. Jane kissed their cheeks, tucked the blankets around them, folded their freshly laundered clothes, changed into her own flowered pajamas, and blew her nose. She found a music station on the television and heard the first verse of the big band classic "Gonna Take a Sentimental Journey" before she fell asleep.

Chapter Fifty-three

"Cheating fools, all of you!" Bo bellowed as the security men hauled him out of the Dicey Casino. A pair of furry stuffed dice hung around his neck, bobbing, as he resisted the guards' grip on his arms. "You don't know who you're dealing with! I'm a very important person. See here, got something a rich grand-pappy in Salt Lake City's gonna pay big bucks for. Two some-things he's gonna pay big bucks for. And I'm gonna be rich, too, and you'll be real sorry you cheated me and made me hock my solid gold wedding ring, didn't give me half what it's worth, just you wait 'til I talk to the police about that, and just wait 'til my bride hears about this, she'll be broken-hearted 'cause she paid for the rings, and it's all your fault, you skunks, you lousy, dirty, stinking—"

Bob the bouncer fished in Bo's pocket and found the keys to the van and the motel room. Beckoning to a waiting taxi, he opened the door and before Bo knew it, he was deposited in the back seat.

"Hey, wait a minute! My van!" he sputtered.

Bob handed the motel key to Bo but kept the keys to the van in his pocket. "Come back and get them in the morning when you're sober, sir. Ask for Bill at the front desk. He'll have the keys. Can't let you drive home in your condition."

"But—"

"Oh, no problem, sir," grinned Bob, who probably weighed three hundred pounds and competed in those oily bodybuilding contests Bo had seen on TV. "The taxi's on us. Good night."

It was after 2 a.m. when the taxi deposited Bo at the Lucky Inn, where he stubbed his toe on the curb and limped up the stairs. In the dim light he peered at the number on the room key, 208, and found the matching number on the door. He turned the key and pushed the door open. He fumbled for a light switch. Turning on a lamp, he saw two rumpled beds, soggy carpet, and piles of sodden towels, but no Jane and no Chatterboxes.

"I've been robbed, I tell you! My wife and the Chatter—the Graham—the kids, they're twins, there's two of them, they've been kidnapped! Call the FBI!" Bo yelled, stumbling down to the manager's office.

"Keep it down, will ya? Some of us are trying to sleep!" yelled a man, slamming his door.

The sleepy manager looked at Bo's room key. "Your wife and grandchildren moved next door. Room 210. You didn't know?"

"I'm their uncle." Bo straightened his shoulders and assumed a posture of wounded dignity. "I was out on business. Not that it's any of your business."

"There was a . . . a water incident. We had to move them to a dry room. Here's a key. You *are* leaving in the morning, right?"

"You bet, buddy. Can't wait to get out of this low down leaky place. Wouldn't be surprised if old Noah himself showed up, leading the animals two by two. Whole lousy town's full of cheaters and low down varmints and—" The window slammed shut and the manager disappeared.

After three tries Bo opened the door to room 210. Staggering to the nearest bed, which happened to be Jane's, he collapsed on it.

"Heaven help us!" shrieked Jane, sitting bolt upright. "An intruder! Help! Oh, help!" In the darkness, she fumbled for the nearest weapon, and grabbed a Gideon Bible from the nightstand drawer. Flailing around with it, she managed to give the intruder a solid whack on the head.

"Ouch! Hush, woman! It's me, your husband!"

In the morning a small hand tickled Bo's whiskery cheek. He grunted. "Go 'way."

Alex patted Bo's shiny balding head. "You're a real crack-up," he said.

~

Jane was glad there was a restaurant next to the motel, as they had no transportation. She bought breakfast-to-go for herself and the twins: scrambled eggs, sausage, pancakes with syrup, and orange juice. For Bo she brought a large mug of coffee, black. "Here's your coffee," she said.

Bo looked around the room and his eyes rested on his slippers. The bears, though soggy, continued to grin.

"Stop smiling at me," Bo muttered. He picked up his mug of coffee.

Alex paused, his fork in midair. "Uncle Bo! Stop! Don't drink that!"

"Why not?" Bo frowned, looking at the mug of coffee and then at Alex. With his other hand he held ice cubes wrapped in a washcloth at his temple, where a purple bruise was darkening.

"Heavenly Father says it's bad for us."

"Well, then, we just won't tell Heavenly Father."

Lauren gasped. "He sees everything, Uncle Bo, just like Santa."

Bo set the mug on the nightstand and stood up. For a moment the world rocked a bit but then returned to its normal orbit. "Going for a little walk." On his way to the restaurant he decided that even Heavenly Father could use a strong cup of coffee once in a while.

Half an hour later he sat at a booth in the café, nursing his coffee. Other than last night's water incident and the whack on his head from the Bible, so far so good. He had claimed Jane's affection, made an honest woman of her at the courthouse, charmed her out of some money, and now her handy credit card was paying for everything else. She would never know the romantic letters that had won her heart were written by his cell-mate, Cecil, who wept often and wrote reams of poetry. "Make it flowery. Lovey-dovey," Bo had instructed, and the letters had done the trick. Cecil also had a friend on the outside who found out everything about Andy McBride that Bo wanted to know. He had printed it on index cards in large letters: names, addresses, and phone numbers. "Write it slow, Cecil," Bo had instructed. "I can't read very fast."

When Bo walked into the Dicey Casino later that morning, Bouncer Bill had bad news. The van had been towed.

"What? Towed? You said you'd keep it here for me!" Bo sputtered.

"Yes, sir, until the police saw that it was parked in the fire lane."

"Well, I don't see as you've had any fire!"

"Say, that's a nasty bruise," Bill said, looking sympathetic, touching his own forehead and nodding at Bo.

"Wha—? Oh, that." Bo touched the goose egg on his forehead and winced. "My wife takes her religion seriously," he said, recalling the wallop from the Gideon Bible in the wee hours of the morning. For a scrawny little assistant kindergarten teacher, Jane was a woman of surprising strength.

Bouncer Bill handed Bo a card with the tow company's phone number and address. Bouncer Bob flashed him a friendly smile. Bo rubbed his arm, which was sore from last night's encounter with Bob.

"Listen here," Bo growled, "I ain't never coming back here! You'll be sorry, manhandling a man like me, gonna be rich soon, and one more thing, you big bullies . . ."

Bo shook his fist at them and stomped away, venting his opinion of Las Vegas, the Dicey Casino, and bouncers who man-handled decent people.

"Now, there's some new cuss words. I thought I'd heard

them all in this business," commented Bill as Bo left, shaking his fist at them.

A new round of curses followed, for when Bo stepped outside the casino, his taxi was gone.

Chapter Fifty-four

The doorbell rang, and with a sigh, Cole opened the door. A silver-haired, bearded man in an old-fashioned suit stood on the front porch.

"I *said,* no comment." Cole slammed the door.

The man rang the doorbell again. Cole turned back in frustration. How did the reporter get through the FBI blockades? The whole neighborhood was cordoned off; all traffic had to be cleared to gain entrance, and the press was held at bay. He opened the door. "Listen, I *said*—"

"Mr. McBride. I'm Joshua Martin. Louisa's father."

It took a moment for the information to register. "Please," Cole said, "come in. Forgive my rudeness. I thought you were a reporter. They've been so persistent, the police are controlling access to the whole neighborhood. We've been under terrible stress. So have you."

Joshua nodded. Cole hesitated for a moment and then extended his hand. "I'm glad you're here."

The men shook hands. "Margaret!" Cole called. "Louisa's father is here! Come and meet him!"

"Joshua, it's good to meet you," Margaret said, dusting flour off her hands to shake Joshua's. "But such a terrible time for all of us. We're so worried about the children."

Joshua nodded. There were dark circles under his eyes. "I don't have a phone, so the FBI contacted the owner of the diner on the outskirts of town. My car needs two new tires, and I was going to drive into Cedar City tomorrow and have them put on. My cousin said he'd drive me here instead, all the way to Salt Lake City. The agents said they talked to Bo Rawlins's old cell-mate, a man named Cecil, I think, and he told them everything. They think Bo's headed here with the twins, is that right? And the agents said something about a ransom?

"That's what they tell us," Cole said. "But he hasn't called. We're so worried about the children."

"The agent said I should be here, when they find the children, so they'll see their grandparents and they won't be frightened."

"Yes, of course," Cole said.

A timer rang in the kitchen. "I think dinner is just what you need," Margaret said.

Chapter Fifty-five

"Just one more quarter before I leave this lousy state," muttered Bo. He put the coin in the slot of the antique machine at the Last Chance Mini-Mart and jerked its heavy silver arm down. Three lemons lined up, one, two, three, across the window. Bells rang, buzzers blared, lights flashed, and Bo's hands flew up in the air. "Wait! Wait! I can explain! I can explain everything! I didn't do it. I mean, I was just on my way to Salt Lake City, see, I'm taking the Troublemakers to see their—"

"We have a big winner on aisle seven!" announced an animated voice over the crackling intercom. "Step right up, sir, so you can collect your winnings!"

Bewildered, Bo dropped his hands. Silver quarters were pouring out of the one-armed bandit, spilling onto the floor. He knelt and started to grab them and stuff them in his pockets.

Two clerks hurried over with plastic buckets in their hands. "Oh, no, sir, we'll do that," they said. "You just get to stand here and watch us!" Suddenly, Bo was in the middle of a celebration as other customers clapped him on the shoulder and shook his hand. Bo heard a familiar pop and fizzling sound as someone opened a can of beer from the cooler and gave it to him.

"Ladies and gentlemen, this old machine hasn't paid off in more than a year. We thought it was maybe broken, but folks just kept putting quarters in it, and the grand total is . . . three thousand five hundred dollars!" boomed the loudspeaker.

The manager shook Bo's hand and held up a Polaroid camera. "Now, you stand here by the slot machine and let's have a big smile for the Sinners and Winners Hall of Fame! And your name is . . . ?"

"Bo. Bo Rawlins." Bo could not take his eyes off the shimmering, jingling waterfall of quarters that flowed in a steady stream from the slot machine.

"Well, Mr. Bo Rawlins," the manager gave the camera to a clerk, put his arm around Bo and grinned, "give us another big smile."

Momentarily blinded by the flash, Bo was even more dazzled when his quarters were exchanged for a hefty cashier's check. The manager had been obliging and given him two hundred dollars in quarters, which Bo had stuffed in his pockets, his socks, and even inside his flannel shirt. A large stuffed bear was thrust into his hands, a gift from the management.

"Bo! Bo! We've been waiting in the van! Surely it doesn't take that long to use the men's room! Come on!"

It was Jane. The day was already hot, and his bride looked like a wilted spring flower, from her limp linen collar to her straggly hair and baggy hose falling in wrinkles around her ankles. She pulled a wrinkled handkerchief from under her belt and blew her nose.

"Would this be your better half? Congratulations, ma'am!" The jovial manager pumped her hand.

"What? Oh, thank you, sir, yes, the wedding was just—"

Bo crammed the check into his pocket. "Let's go, honey."

The manager maneuvered Jane between himself and Bo. "Smile for another picture, this time with your wife, Bo!"

Jane smiled automatically, blinking at the flash. Then she turned to her husband. "Bo, dear, if you're buying something for the children, be sure to get two. After all, there are two children," she fretted, and the manager obliged with another teddy bear. After a few more flashes of the camera, Bo smiled and waved at his new friends. "Well, I'd like to stay and celebrate with y'all, but like the little woman said, we gotta go. Gotta get this show on the road." He took Jane's arm and hurried out of the casino, trying not to jingle as he walked. He felt very heavy and very contented, the weight of the quarters in his socks adding a happy shuffle to his stride.

"What was that all about?" Jane asked.

Bo gave her a resounding smack on the rear. "Happy Hour!"

The quarters made Bo's suitcase heavier, and he had hoisted it into the van the next morning with a contented grunt. After a long day of driving, frequent potty stops for the Troublemakers, and listening to Jane's entire collection of kindergarten songs as she entertained them, they had arrived in Salt Lake City. On the map it looked like Las Vegas and Salt Lake City were just a few miles apart. He pulled over at a small park with a children's playground. "Listen, honey," he said to Jane, "I need to make a few calls at this here phone booth. Gotta call the Graham Cracker Kids' grandpappy." He patted the shirt pocket that held Cecil's helpful index cards.

"Yay!" yelled Alex and Lauren. "Swings!" Jane unbuckled them from their booster seats and they ran to the playground. "Watch me, Aunt Jane! Watch me!"

Bo fiddled with the cord of the pay phone. After two rings a man answered. "Let me talk to Cole McBride. Oh, it's you, McBride? Yeah. I got something you want. Two somethings, if you get my drift. Two redheaded Graham Cracker Kids. Now you listen close 'cause I'm only going to say this once. Put ten thousand dollars in a box, wrap it up real nice like a birthday present, and leave it outside the back door of the church. No tricks. No funny stuff. No police. Eight o'clock tonight. Yeah, I'll find the church just fine. Hey, now that I think of it, add another ten thousand for pain and suffering. Them little Chatterboxes . . . well, just put the whole fifteen thousand in the bag and do like I said."

"At least we know the twins are all right. Well, we hope they're . . ." Margaret wiped away a tear.

"Does he want fifteen thousand or twenty thousand, and where am I going to get that much cash?" Cole asked in a daze.

"Don't worry, sir. That's our job," said Agent Moyes, head of the FBI team assembled at the McBride home. Margaret had gasped when he had taken off his jacket and revealed the gun in its holster. "Sorry to startle you, ma'am," he had apologized. Now he turned to her. "I've handled dozens of missing children cases in New York, where I'm from, Mrs. McBride. We'll find your grandchildren."

Chapter Fifty-six

Bo opened the driver's window and looked down at the two young men on bikes who had stopped beside him. "Can we help you, sir? Are you looking for an address?" They wore bicycle helmets, dark slacks, white shirts, and ties. Heavy black backpacks were slung over their shoulders, and they had black name tags on their shirt pockets, with their names in white letters. Curiously, both fellows had the same first name, E-L-D-E-R.

"Oh, look, Bo! They're Mormon missionaries! Aren't they sweet? Such nice, polite young men. So clean-cut," said Jane, smiling at them.

"Where's the Mormon church?" Bo asked.

The two missionaries looked at each other, beaming.

"We could lead you there, if you'd like to follow us," the taller one said.

"Naw, I gotta go alone. Going to see the bishop. Just tell me where it is."

The missionaries gave directions. Then they watched Bo drive to the intersection two blocks down the street and turn the wrong way.

"Was that a golden contact, Elder?" the younger missionary asked.

"Beats me."

Bo didn't see a birthday present by the back door when he finally found the church, but the parking lot was full of cars. Bishop McBride probably didn't want to leave the package where so many people could see it and maybe pick it up and take it home. Little wooden stakes with streamers and flowers decorated the grass next to the sidewalk, all the way to the front door. A parked car was covered with shaving cream and balloons, a trail of tin cans was tied to the bumper, and a sign was taped to the hood. He hesitated for a moment. "Looks like a wedding for sure. Bishop's likely to be there. What the heck, I'll just go in and act like a wedding guest and pick up my present on the way out."

Bo wasn't prepared for the scene he found inside the church, though. In the lobby several young boys with slicked-back hair, bow ties, and matching vests chased each other up and down the halls, their shirt tails flapping as they ran. A little girl in a ruffled dress slept in an armchair, a basket of flowers in her lap.

A large room with a shiny wood floor and the painted lines of a basketball court had been transformed into a flower garden, complete with a white picket fence and a painted wooden lattice arch. Even the basketball standards and hoops were festooned with flowers and ribbons. Bo scrawled his name in the book where the pretty girl at the table told him to. Then he shook hands with a dozen young men in tuxedos, each politely introducing him to the next one in line.

Finally he met the bride's parents. "Brother . . . Rawlins, is it?" the father said. "Brother Rawlins, this is my daughter Marilyn and her new husband, Jake." Marilyn was a lovely girl, dressed in a beautiful, flowing white gown, and Jake was a good-looking, clean-cut young man, staring in awe at the gold band on his left hand.

"What, only one bride today?" Bo asked the couple.

The bride giggled and the groom flushed. "Uh, Dad," he said, turning to his father, "this is Brother Rawlins."

Bo took the groom's elbow. "Wait a minute, Jake, something I gotta ask. You don't know where the bishop is, do you?"

Jake laughed and turned again to his father, clapping him on the shoulder. "That would be my dad, Bishop Howell."

"Bishop who?" Bo asked. Maybe he should have his hearing checked.

The man wasn't dressed like the churchy people Bo had seen on TV, the ones who wore fancy black nightshirts with colorful ribbons over their shoulders, but maybe Mormon bishops were more modern than that. Bo took a step forward and muttered into the man's ear. "You got it?"

"I'm sorry?" The bishop's eyes watered. "What did you say?"

"The package. You know."

"The package? Oh, I'm sure your gift was delivered. The kids will be opening their gifts after they get home from their honeymoon. But thank you so much."

Bo was propelled quickly down the reception line. He hadn't been able to kiss the bride, and that was a disappointment. He shook hands with a dozen pretty young ladies in yellow frocks. Three of them wore wedding rings and were obviously pregnant behind their bouquets. Then he met the grandparents, sitting on love seats, wearing flowers on their dresses and lapels.

"Who are you?" he asked a tuxedo-clad man holding a video camera.

"I'm the bride's uncle. I'm videotaping everybody who comes through the line, so Marilyn and Jake will always remember their special day. Thanks for coming."

"Happy to oblige," said Bo with a wink at the camera.

A little girl with a basket of napkins and a frilly apron invited him to sit and have some refreshments. "Don't mind if I do," he said, as he had time to kill while he formulated another plan. This man, Bishop What's-His-Name, was a fake. He'd just have a bite of refreshments and call the real one again. He sat at a table covered with a glitter-sprinkled lacy cloth and framed pictures of charming little children, evidently the bride and groom as kids. The girl put a tiny napkin in front of him.

"Smile!" A woman sitting across from Bo picked up a little white camera from the table and snapped his picture. "Now would you take one of us?" She cuddled up to her husband and smiled. Bo took the camera and obliged. "What ward are you in?" she asked.

From the expression on her face, Bo knew this was something important, but it was something he didn't know. First of all, what was a ward, anyway? "What ward? Uh, well—"

"We're from the second ward. We've known Jake since he was in diapers."

"That long, huh?" Bo wiped the pineapple-lime sherbet foam off his lip and set his dainty glass cup on the oval-shaped glass plate. He could use some more of those little sandwiches and cookies and nuts, and the punch wasn't half bad either, though it tasted a little flat.

Bo pawed through the neatly stacked piles of gifts, looking for a package that might contain his cash.

"Excuse me," said a gray-haired lady with a corsage on her lapel. "Is there something we can do for you?"

"Uh, I'm just checking through the gifts. You know, to see if mine arrived. I, uh, I think I forgot to sign the card."

"We're keeping track of all the cards and taping them right on the gifts. So far we don't have any presents without cards."

"Oh," Bo said. Maybe the bishop hadn't put it in the pile yet. These women were surely organized. Maybe it was a Mormon thing.

"What's your name?" they asked. "We'll write it down and let you know if we find a present that doesn't have a card."

"Rawlins. Bo Rawlins."

"What ward do you live in, Brother Rawlins?"

"Well, you see, I'm just passing through," Bo exclaimed, giving her a broad grin. "Wouldn't 'a wanted to miss this for anything."

"And how do you know the bride and groom, Brother Rawlins?"

Brother Rawlins? Bo scratched his head. Everyone he met

here at the wedding party seemed to call him Brother Rawlins. Were all the folks in Salt Lake City related to each other? Oh, well, that was the case at home in Hawthorn Valley.

"Oh, the bishop and me, Sister, we go way back."

That seemed to satisfy the first woman, who gave a knowing nod.

"No," said her partner with the clipboard, "we don't have any gifts without cards, and all the cards are signed. Your name isn't on the list. You may want to check with the department store in the morning, to see if it was delivered."

"Yeah, I'll do that," said Bo. He swore under his breath as he turned away. Then, trying to appear natural, he stopped in front of a huge display of quilts, pillowcases, kitchen towels, and other handmade articles. "Must be planning on a big family with all them quilts." He saw a large stack of embroidered dish towels. "Holy cow, that's a lot of dishes to wash!" He shook his head and headed out the door, with one last look at the large pile of gifts.

All in all they were friendly folks, these Mormons. But he'd obviously not found his man. But when he did, he'd tell McBride some other fella was pretending to be the bishop. That would for sure get *his* knickers in a knot.

Chapter Fifty-seven

"Well, that's just it," Agent Moyes tried to explain to his supervisor, cell phone to his ear. "It's just that the guy's so . . . dumb, we haven't been able to stay on his tail. I can't believe I just said that. Anyway, we lost him. Yeah, we've followed his trail, starting with the flight to Las Vegas, McDonald's, Wal-Mart, the Dicey Casino, the Lucky Inn Motel, and the big payoff at the Last Chance Mini-Mart slot machine. I mean, there's a trail of eyewitnesses and even pictures of them, from Vegas to Salt Lake. We know where he's been and we know where he's headed. If he doesn't get lost again." He held the phone some distance from his ear, wincing. "Yes, sir. No more screw-ups. *No*, sir. I *don't* want to be transferred back to New York."

Bishop Howell, father of the groom, unlocked his office in the church, just down the hall from the festivities. He found his directory of other bishops in the stake, picked up his phone, and dialed Cole McBride's number. "Cole? Oh, Agent . . . Percy? Could I speak to Cole McBride? This is John Howell, and I have information—yes, I'll call him right back on his cell phone." He hung up and dialed Cole's cell phone. "Cole? John Howell here. Speakerphone? Sure. Sorry I called your home number—you're waiting to hear from the kidnapper? Well, that's what I'm calling about. I'm here at the church. Tonight's Jake's wedding reception.

"Listen, I saw the story about your missing grandchildren on the news last night. You must be frantic. That's why I'm calling. There was a man who came to the reception looking for the bishop, he said, and the more I think about it, I could swear he looked like the man in the picture, the suspect. Something a little different about his smile, though. Anyway, he said something about a package, and he seemed to think I had one for *him*. It may be a coincidence but . . . yes, I think he did say his name was Rawlins. He went right through the line and shook hands with everybody. But when I realized he might be the suspect, I looked everywhere. I don't think he's in the building. Of course, I'll tell the agents everything I know. Somebody probably took his picture, and I'll bet he's on the video, too. We're just praying that the children are safe and that you find them soon."

Bishop Howell sighed and locked his office door again. He checked his watch. The reception was nearly over, and he knew FBI agents would be dressed in suits. They would be polite and discrete and wouldn't disrupt the party at all. He was heartsick about Cole's missing grandchildren, stunned that the suspect might have been right here at Jake and Marilyn's wedding reception, and frustrated that he hadn't connected the man with the picture on the news sooner. He didn't feel very social anymore; his rented patent leather shoes were pinching his toes, and the starched shirt collar itched. "They should send a dozen agents. Heaven knows there's enough food," he muttered.

Moyes looked at his watch. "He'll call soon. He will. He can smell that ransom, and he wants to get his hands on it. And when he does, here's the plan: Mr. Martin and Mr. McBride, Agent Larsen will take you in an unmarked car to a safe location near the church. We'll wait for Moyes to give us the signal as soon as they've got Rawlins and his wife in custody and the site is secured. Then I'll take the two of you right to the church, so you can pick up the twins. We can minimize the trauma if they see you as soon as possible. Then you'll come back to this car and we'll go back to your place, Mr. McBride. Hopefully there will be no sirens or lights, and I pray to God there will be no gunfire."

"*Gunfire?*" Joshua asked. "I hadn't thought, I mean, I don't own a weapon, so I didn't even consider that possibility—do you think he's armed?"

Cole covered his face with his hands and shook his head. He whispered a prayer and then looked up at Moyes.

"We're prepared for any contingency," Moyes said. "Our profilers don't think Bo's looking for a fight."

"But he came after Andy with his rifle once . . ." Joshua said.

"Yes. We know. That was a few years ago and Bo was drunk. And he served time for that, so we hope the memory of jail time will be a deterrent. Today it's in his best interests to look like a regular neighbor taking a stroll, and not draw any attention to himself. He's made no threats to harm the children in any way. We've got witnesses coming out of the woodwork, testifying about his behavior at the casinos and motels, the stores, just about everywhere he's been since he left Kentucky with the twins. Even when he's been intoxicated and agitated, there's been no physical violence. We do have a report that he had a big bruise on his forehead, and we're not sure about that, but to our knowledge, he's only been . . . very verbal. He passed for a regular guest at the wedding reception this evening, too. His whole charade is that he's jolly old Uncle Bo, taking the twins to see Grandpa in Salt Lake City, and that's the way we think it will play out. But, as I said, we're prepared for any contingency."

Cole took a deep breath, looked at Joshua, and nodded.

"Of course, we'll do our best to keep the children from knowing anything is out of the ordinary," Larsen said. "The Agency will get after us because we don't have booster seats for the children, but we're only a few blocks away, and the important thing is to bring the Chatterboxes, I mean, the twins, safely to their grandfather's home."

Chapter Fifty-eight

Bo called Cole again from another phone booth. "Listen, here, McBride, I been to five different Mormon churches, and you wasn't in none of 'em! And there's some dude—a impostor, that's what he is, he was at one of them churches, he says *he's* the bishop. Thought you'd want to know some guy's pretending to be you."

"There are a lot of Mormon chapels around here," Cole said, his hands shaking. "And a lot of Mormon bishops. I'm glad you called back. The children—are they all right?"

"Sure." Bo glanced at the van, where Jane and the children were singing "The Eensy Weensy Spider" and making little motions with their hands, so the spider could crawl up the water spout. "Them twins, the Chatterboxes, they're having a lovely time. Just tell me how to get to the blasted church and I'll be more'n happy to unload 'em, graham crackers and all."

"All right." Cole glanced at the note Agent Moyes had scrawled and shoved in front of him. He took a deep breath and maintained a casual tone. "Listen. Tell me where you are, Bo, and I'll tell you how to find the right church." He looked up at Joshua, who put a steadying hand on his shoulder. "I'll—I'll be happy to take the Chatterboxes off your hands."

"Well, I'm by a big red brick school; it's got a big *H* on the front."

"Highland?"

"Uh, yeah. Probably."

"OK. Are you facing the front of the school now?"

"Yeah."

"Turn left, go straight for two blocks, and then turn right. It's a gray brick church with white trim. And Bo—"

Moyes shoved another note in front of Cole that said "stall him!"

Cole gulped and tried to keep his voice steady. "Uh, if you'll just tell me what your car looks like, I'll be there, watching for you."

"Silver minivan. Nevada plates. Graham cracker crumbs from one end to the other. Now, see here, fifteen minutes! I want that there birthday present in fifteen minutes!"

"I understand."

Bo hung up.

Agent Larsen pulled off his earphones and jumped to his feet. "Got it!" he said, pointing to the computer monitor. "Look at the coordinates on the screen. We know where he is!"

"Good work, Larsen. Mr. McBride, Mr. Martin, you'll please come with us. All right, men, let's move it! Operation Chatterbox is about to begin."

~

Bo finally found the gray and white steepled church Cole had described and then parked the van around the corner.

"All right, Troublemakers, I mean, kids, we're gonna meet your grandpappy in just a minute or two. He's gonna be real happy to see you."

"Yay! Grandpa Cole! Grandma Margaret! And then Mommy and Daddy!" the twins yelled, jumping up and down.

"Oh," Jane mourned, looking back at the children, "I'm going to miss you darlings so!"

"Yeah," Bo said. "Me, too," and he slammed the door.

⌒

"Good," Agent Larsen breathed. "The children won't see us take him down and cuff him. He's cooperating without knowing it."

"But what about his wife?" Joshua asked.

"We don't think she's in on any of this. We'll take her into custody after you've picked up the twins and they've said good-bye to her, so nothing will seem out of the ordinary for them."

Bo strolled casually up to the church, where a brightly wrapped package was propped against the front door. He grinned, rubbed his hands, and picked up the present. He would just open it quick and stuff the money in his pockets so Jane, safely out of sight, would never know about it. After all, he was old-fashioned; a man ought to have some money of his own.

Bo began to tear at the package, but the bow was tied tight and the wrapping paper was securely taped on all its edges. He began to swear under his breath.

"Can we help you, sir?"

Bo looked up. Durned if it wasn't two more missionaries with white shirts and ties, and durned if their name tags didn't both say E-L-D-E-R, too.

He clutched the package to his chest. "You guys are every-where! I seen some more of you this afternoon. Is there some kind of convention or something going on? Anyway, I was just here to see the bishop. We had us a . . . appointment." He looked down at the package and then at the missionaries. "It's my birthday," he beamed, "and he gave me a present."

The missionaries got off their bikes. "Yes, sir, we know all about the present."

Bo felt something hard against his ribcage. "Hey! That feels like a gun!"

"I'll just take that present, sir," one missionary said, and the other tackled Bo, wrestling him to the ground and cuffing his hands behind his back before he could say a word in protest.

Bo heard a quiet click. Then it began to rain.

"Bo Rawlins," said one of the missionaries, soaking wet, reading from a little card, "you're under arrest for the kidnapping of Lauren and Alex McBride. You have the right to remain silent . . ."

"*Wha*—?" Bo looked up just as a jet of water hit his face. He blinked the water away and saw that he was surrounded by more dripping men in white shirts, dark slacks, and ties, all wearing missionary name tags, who pulled him to his feet, patted him down rapidly from head to foot, and took the contents of his pockets, including his big soggy cashier's check. Another white-shirted man put his hand on Bo's head and hustled him into the back seat of a car.

Chapter Fifty-nine

Moyes sprinted around the corner and signaled to Larsen, who put the engine in gear and drove around the corner to the van. Cole and Joshua got out of the car and, as instructed, walked casually toward the van. The side door of the van was open, and the agent standing beside it greeted them with a grin and a thumbs up sign. Then he reconsidered and gave two thumbs up.

Cole motioned to Joshua, who climbed into the van.

"Grandpa Joshua!" Alex said. "We didn't know you were coming, too! We've been on a trip."

"Yes, my little man, I know." Joshua unbuckled Alex's seat belt, lifted him out of the van, and held him close. Above the boy's tousled red curls Joshua met Cole's eyes and smiled in relief. He stepped back and Cole climbed into the van.

"Grandpa Cole!" Lauren squealed, holding out her arms. "I'm four years old now! And I'm five minutes older than Alex."

Jane watched with her hand over her heart as the grandfathers took the children away. "Bye, Aunt Jane, dear!" Lauren called from Cole's arms, waving at the stricken woman in the van.

"Yeah," Alex said, his arm around Joshua's neck. "Tell Uncle Bo he's a real crack-up!"

The grandfathers and the children climbed into two cars. Two other men slid into the drivers' seats, slammed the doors, and quickly drove away.

～

A very wet missionary with plastered-down hair approached the van. "Good evening, ma'am," he said.

"Good evening," Jane said. "My goodness, is it raining? You're soaking wet."

"No, ma'am," Olsen said, "Just a computerized sprinkling system with bad timing." He flashed his FBI badge at Jane. "Please step out of the vehicle, ma'am, with your hands up."

Jane jumped out of the van, her hands high in the air, her eyes filled with terror. "Where's Bo? Where's my husband? There's been a mistake, a terrible mistake!" she cried.

"Yes, ma'am, we know. We know all about it. Mr. Rawlins is just around the corner. He's fine. We've come to assist you."

"Assist me?"

"Yes, ma'am," Olsen said. "Now, we're just going to take you in for questioning."

"Questioning? I beg your pardon! I must insist that you take your hands off me!" Jane shrieked as a soaking wet female agent quickly patted her down, finding nothing other than her linen hankie and a roll of hundred dollar bills where Bo hadn't thought to look for it, and secured her wrists in handcuffs.

"Where's my husband?" Jane shrieked.

"He just went for a little ride downtown." Moyes took her by the arm and gently urged her forward a few steps toward another unmarked car.

Olsen opened the door. "Watch your head, ma'am." With a whimper Jane pitched forward into his arms.

"Well, now, I'd call that a complete surrender," grunted Olsen, grabbing Jane by the waist. "Larsen, Nielsen, give me a hand here. She's out cold."

～

"Nice touch, Olsen," said Moyes, as cameras flashed, documenting the crime scene.

"What, the sprinkling system?" Moyes dodged another stream from a powerful Rain Bird sprinkler.

"Well, that definitely added some excitement. But I was talking about the fake missionaries. Very clever."

"They weren't all fake, Moyes," Olsen told his supervisor, tugging at his dripping necktie.

"What do you mean?"

"Jensen and Nielsen here, they used to be real Mormon missionaries."

"Yeah. Right!"

Jensen grinned and extended his hand. "Hi, I'm Elder Jensen. Served in Toronto, Canada."

"And I'm Elder Nielsen," his FBI companion said. "Hamburg, Germany. *Guten Abend. Es freut mich, Sie kennenzulehrnen.*"

"These tags are real, sir." Jensen said. "We wore them for two years on our missions. They came in handy today."

For once in his life, Moyes, soggy but normally glib and quick with a comeback, was speechless.

He looked from one to the other. "Well, I'll be—"

Chapter Sixty

Margaret opened the door to flashing cameras, pulled her son and daughter-in-law inside her home, and quickly closed the door again. "The children are fine, just fine, see for yourselves." She hurried them into the family room. There, side-by-side in reclining chairs, Cole and Joshua dozed, each with a sleeping child in his arms.

"You'll never see two finer men," Margaret said.

Louisa was by her father's side, touching his arm. He opened his eyes and smiled at her "Louisa. It's all over. He's sound asleep. He's fine." He pulled her down for a kiss, and she stroked Alex's hair with a trembling hand.

"Dad—" Andy choked.

Cole woke up. "I've got a mighty precious bundle here, son. Thank goodness they're both all right." Andy bent and kissed Lauren's plump cheek.

A "ding" sounded from the kitchen. "Dinner's ready," Margaret announced. She shrugged at their startled looks. "I know, it's nearly midnight. But when I'm anxious I cook." She dabbed at her eyes with the edge of her apron and hurried into the kitchen.

"The paramedics checked them over, and they said the twins

are just fine." Cole assured his son over their late dinner, while the children slept on the sofa, wrapped in afghans. "Evidently the kids really thought Bo was their uncle and that he was bringing them here to see us, so they weren't surprised at all when Joshua and I showed up and took them out of the van."

"We've told them never to talk to strangers, or get in a stranger's car . . ."

"That's just it. Bo told them he was their uncle, and he said you'd asked him to deliver them here, to Cole's. And he used a puppy to lure them out of the yard. The oldest trick in the book, we were told, the puppy."

"When life has calmed down, we'll be giving them more specific instructions about safety and strangers and strange cars. And we'll role play every possible scenario: puppy, fake uncle, and all," Andy said, his face grim.

"And we won't be letting them out of our sight until they're twenty-one," Louisa added.

Cole glanced at the sleeping twins. "The agents will be back in the morning. They told us not to ask the children many questions now. Over time, they'll tell us everything; children's memories are remarkable. We do know they're healthy, and they weren't harmed in any way. In fact, they think they've been on a grand adventure. They never saw Bo or Jane get arrested, or the flashing lights, or even the helicopters overhead, thank heavens. The van was around the corner from all the action."

"And the wife?" Andy asked.

"Duped. Completely," Joshua said. "Jane truly believed Bo was their uncle. Apparently she was very attentive to the twins. She even took three rolls of pictures. The FBI had them developed. The twins look happy as can be in all of them. There's one of a messed up motel room we're not sure about, though."

Margaret nodded. "It looks like a hurricane blew right through it. Anyway, as far as we can tell, the children had a wonderful time. Until they fell asleep, all they could talk about was Aunt Jane and Uncle Bo, riding on the airplane, and going to McDonald's and Wal-Mart and the park."

"Thank goodness Jane was there to take care of them," Andy said. "Bo can be downright mean when he's drunk."

"They think he was still courting Jane and her money," Joshua told him. "She hadn't put his name on her bank account yet, so he was evidently on his best behavior."

"Uh, Joshua, you should tell them about the . . . new words the twins learned," Cole said, rolling his eyes.

"New words?" Louisa asked.

"Well," Joshua cleared his throat, "Alex kept telling me I was a 'crack-up,' and Lauren calls everyone 'dear' and 'darling.' "

Cole tried to suppress a grin. "They've learned a bawdy song about a drunken sailor."

Joshua's eyes twinkled. "And I'm afraid they've both learned to swear like sailors, too."

Chapter Sixty-one

Mabel had flown all night to be at the side of her dear sister Jane at the hospital. It wasn't Jane's first nervous breakdown and, bless her heart, it wouldn't be her last.

The family lawyer, John Stephens, was taking care of everything, starting with the annulment. John was such a dear. As soon as Jane's nerves allowed them to fly they'd hurry home, in time for the next Garden Club meeting, and nobody would even guess she'd been away. Though her picture had been on the television, heaven knew there were thousands of middle-aged women with rhinestone-monogrammed glasses, flowered dresses, and upswept hairdos. Why, Mabel herself had been wearing hers that way for years.

Jane was grateful, she said, that she'd confided in only one person about her blossoming romance and her wedding. That was her sister Mabel, who was such a dear, who would take charge and get her home safely. One blessing, Jane had also admitted to Mabel with a deep blush, was that though she'd been married to Bo four days and three nights, her virtue had not been . . . compromised.

Mabel had slipped out into the hallway and taken a healthy swig from a small flask in her handbag.

She returned a few minutes later, calm and cheerful, fussed with her sister's blankets, and gave her a little smile. Then she told Jane to rest, and she would make their airline reservations. She saw the morning paper on the night stand and snatched it, hurrying out into the hallway again. On the front page of *The Salt Lake Tribune* was a picture of Jane with Bo, which had been posted on the Last Chance Mini-Mart's Sinners and Winners Wall of Fame. Both held large teddy bears in their arms. Bo appeared to be overjoyed, flashing a big smile. Jane, as usual, looked slightly confused.

Chapter Sixty-two

"Whoever thought I'd be breaking bread at my own table with a polygamist?" Cole chuckled at breakfast the next morning.

"Whoever thought I'd be waking up in the home of a Gentile?" Joshua countered. "Where I come from, anyway, you'd be called a Gentile. Margaret, your pecan rolls are delicious. My wives would love the recipe."

"Of course." Then, caught off guard for a moment at the mention of "wives," Margaret said, "I—I'll make two copies."

Joshua smiled at his plate and took a bite of scrambled eggs.

"Joshua, I'd be honored to drive you home to Gabriel's Landing tomorrow, after Andy and Louisa leave for Kentucky," Cole offered.

"Thank you kindly."

"Andy was right," Cole said.

"How so?"

"A woman like Louisa had to be raised by fine parents. Who could blame him for falling for your beautiful daughter?"

"It was hard to see her go," Joshua confessed, "but she didn't belong in Gabriel's Landing; we both knew that, and I knew her heart was always with Andy. I figured he had to be a remarkable young man. I'm proud to call him my son-in-law."

Margaret put a hand on each of their shoulders. "Those little tykes have definitely got Louisa's auburn hair. Her mother was a redhead, too, wasn't she?"

Joshua nodded.

"I think Alex favors the McBrides, with that chin, though," Cole said.

"Maybe. But Lauren gets her sweet nature from her mother," Joshua countered.

"Are you suggesting Alex is a mite stubborn, like his grandfather?" Cole asked. They all burst into laughter.

Andy and Louisa emerged from their bedroom, where the children still slept.

"You two look much better this morning," Margaret said. "There's some color in your cheeks, Louisa."

"Her blood pressure is lower than it was yesterday morning. And she's hungry, Mom. That's a good sign. I think," Andy squeezed Louisa's shoulders, "we're going to be all right."

Nibbling on a pecan roll and watching their fathers sharing a friendly breakfast and conversation, Louisa smiled for the first time in four days. The bedroom door opened and two sleepy redheaded children emerged, heading straight for their parents' laps.

"What woke you up?" Louisa asked, cradling Lauren in her arms.

"Something smelled real good," Alex told her.

"Well," Margaret said, with a kiss on the cheek for each of them, "I can do something about that."

"Can we sing for Grandpa Cole and Grandma Margaret and Grandpa Joshua?" Lauren asked.

Andy rumpled Alex's hair and then glanced at his father. "Uh," he said to Alex, "what do you want to sing?"

Cole and Joshua exchanged glances. "Maybe you can sing for us later," Margaret suggested hastily.

"We want to sing the one you taught us, Daddy." Alex

cupped his hand and whispered into his father's ear. A broad grin appeared on Andy's face.

"Sure."

The twins stood side by side in their pajamas and sang with gusto:

> *Gather round, girls, and listen to my noise,*
> *Don't you marry the Mormon boys.*
> *If you do your fortune it will be,*
> *Johnnycake and babies is all you'll see.*

About the Author

Janet Kay Jensen is co-author of *The Book Lover's Cookbook*. Her work also appears in *Writing Secrets, Everton's Family History Magazine, ByLine, Meridian,* and *The Magic of Stories*. She holds degrees in speech-language pathology from Utah State University and Northwestern University and is an adult literacy tutor. She is a member of Author's Guild and has won numerous awards from the League of Utah Writers. She and her husband are the parents of three college age sons.

To learn more about the author, you can visit her website at www.janetjensen.com.

Photo by Donna Barry,
Utah State University Photo Studio